Grumpy Unicorn
Saves the World

A GRAPHIC NOVEL

For Milo, my magical little unicorn.

ISBN 978-1-338-73996-1

10 9 8 7 6 5 4 3 2 1   21 22 23 24 25

Printed in the U.S.A.   40

First edition, July 2021
Edited by Michael Petranek
Art by Joey Spiotto
Book design by Elliane Mellet

Grumpy Unicorn

Saves the World

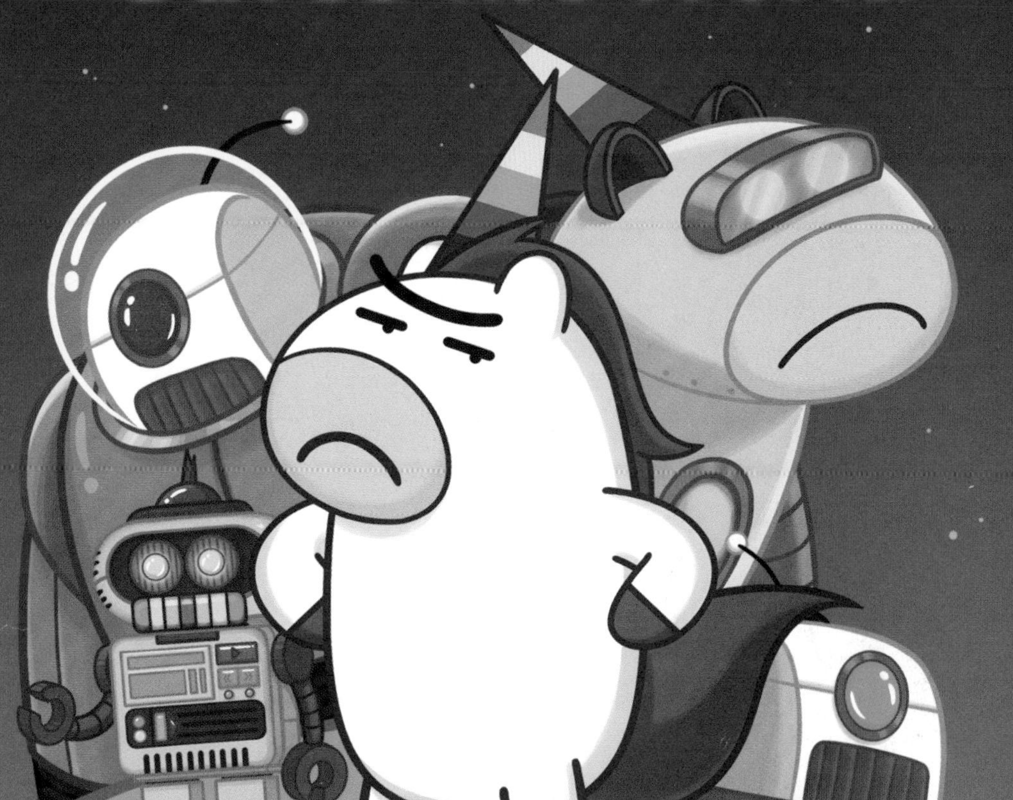

A GRAPHIC NOVEL BY

Joey Spiotto

graphix
An Imprint of
SCHOLASTIC

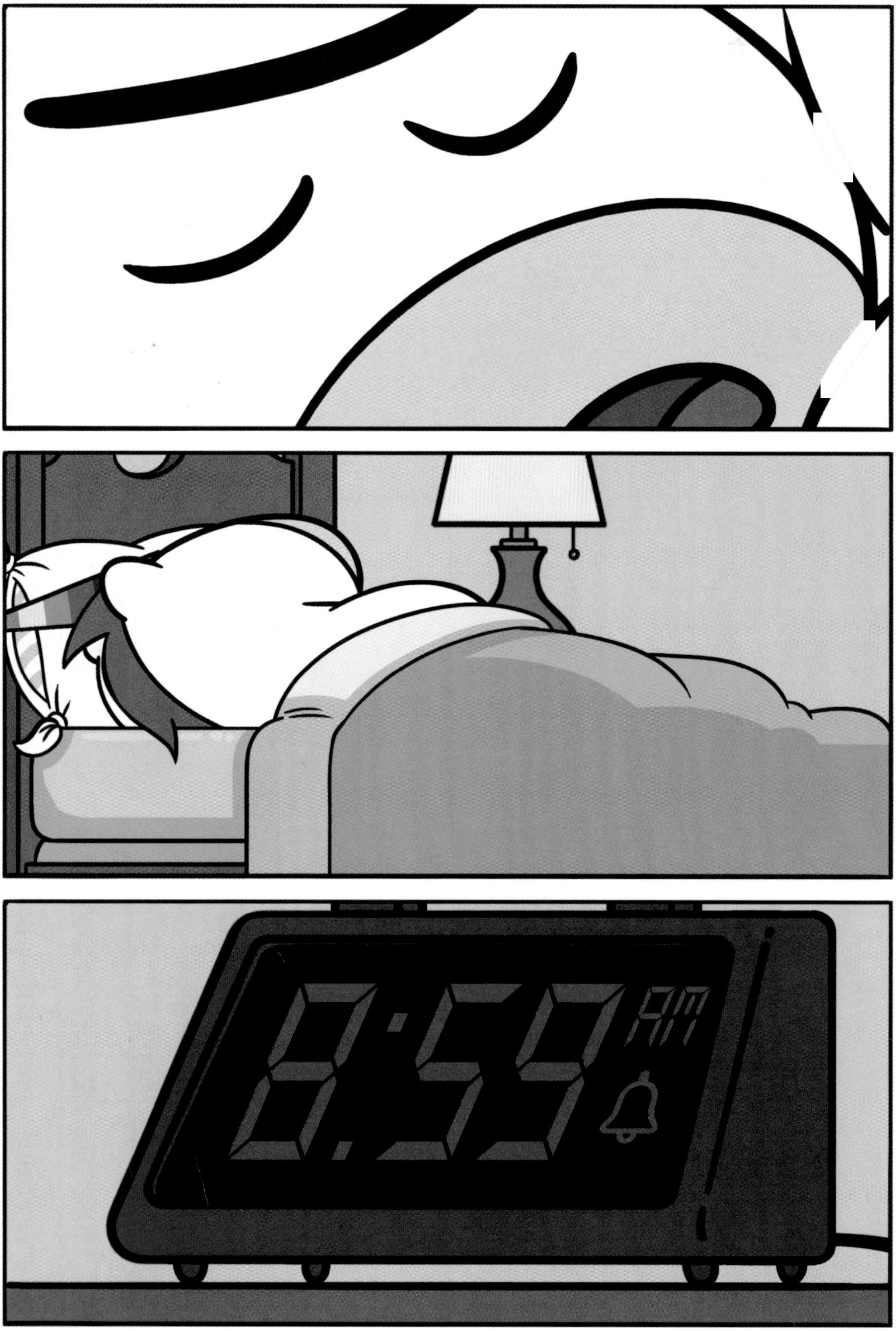

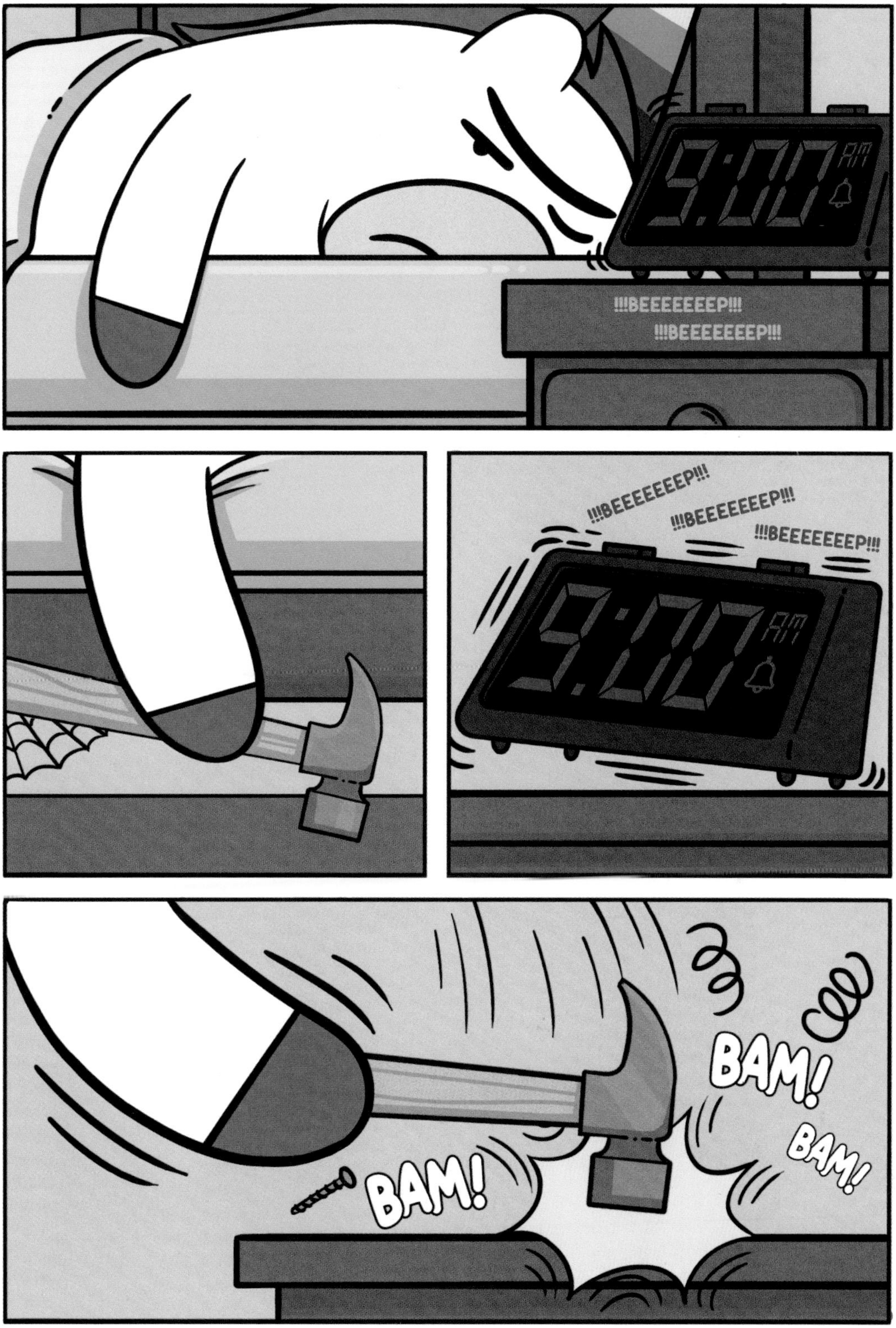
!!!BEEEEEEEP!!!
!!!BEEEEEEEP!!!
!!!BEEEEEEEP!!!
!!!BEEEEEEEP!!!
!!!BEEEEEEEP!!!
BAM!
BAM!
BAM!

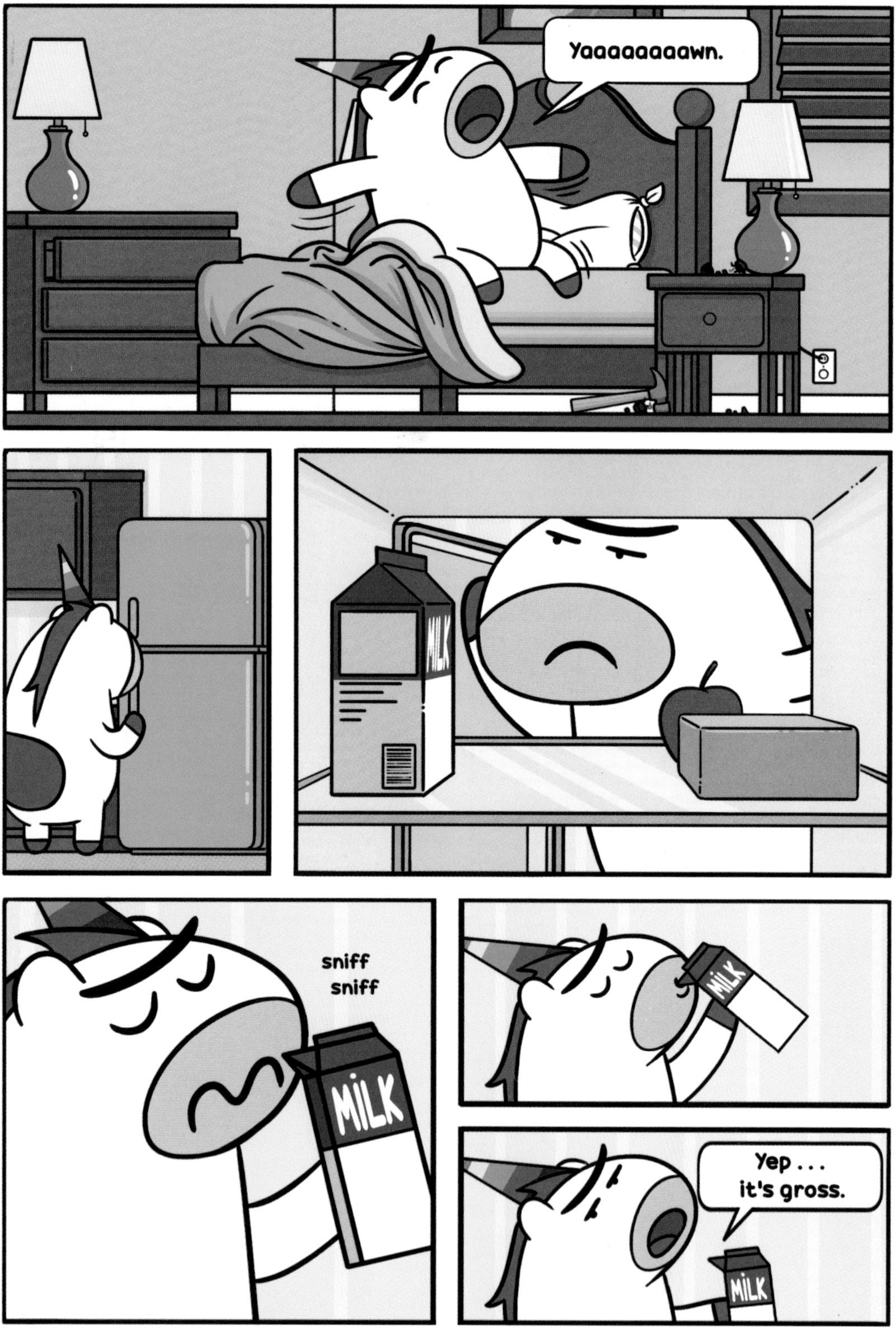
Yaaaaaaaawn.
MILK
MILK
sniff
sniff
MILK
MILK
Yep . . .
it's gross.
MILK

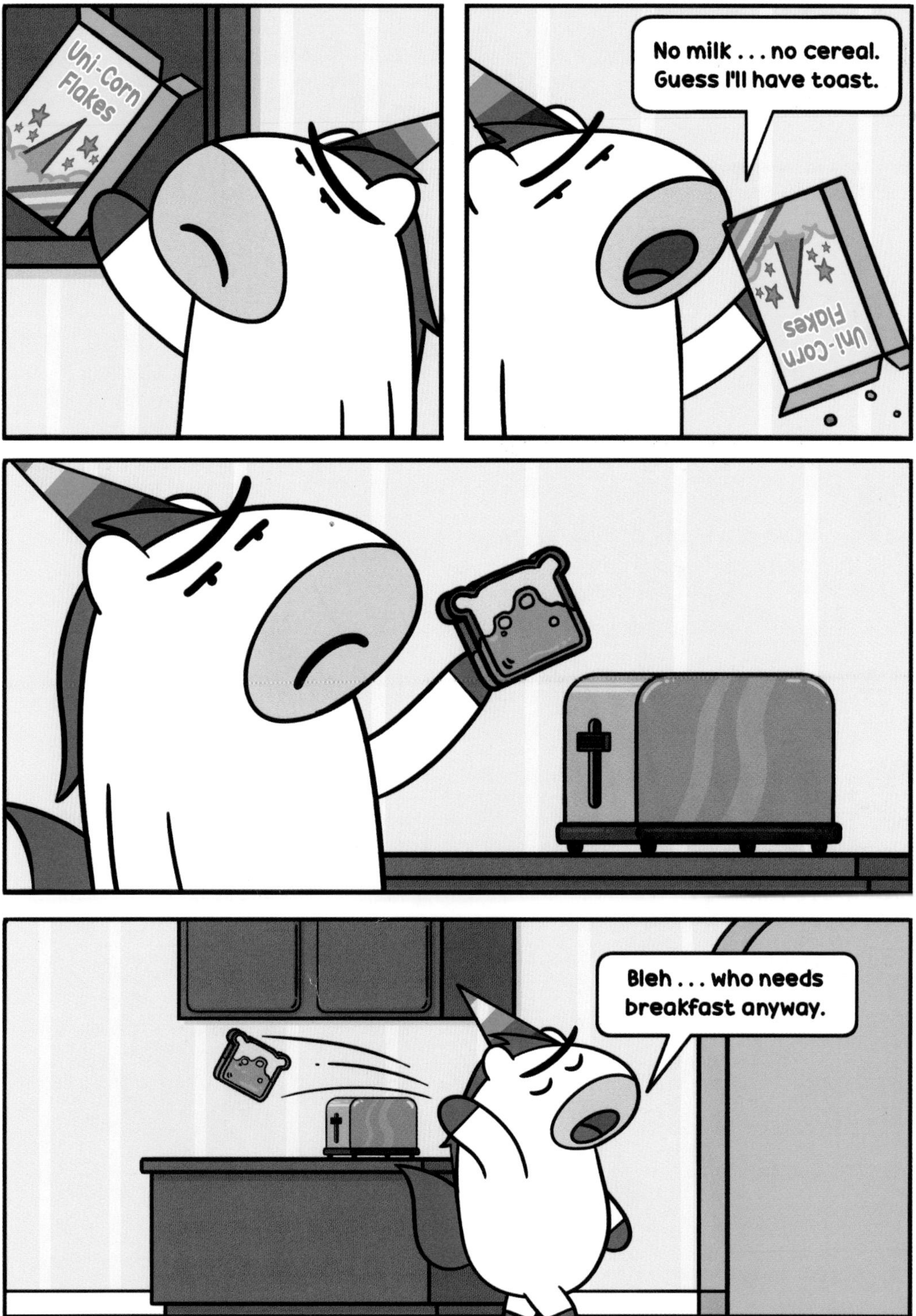
Uni-Corn Flakes
No milk . . . no cereal. Guess I'll have toast.
Uni-Corn Flakes
Bleh . . . who needs breakfast anyway.

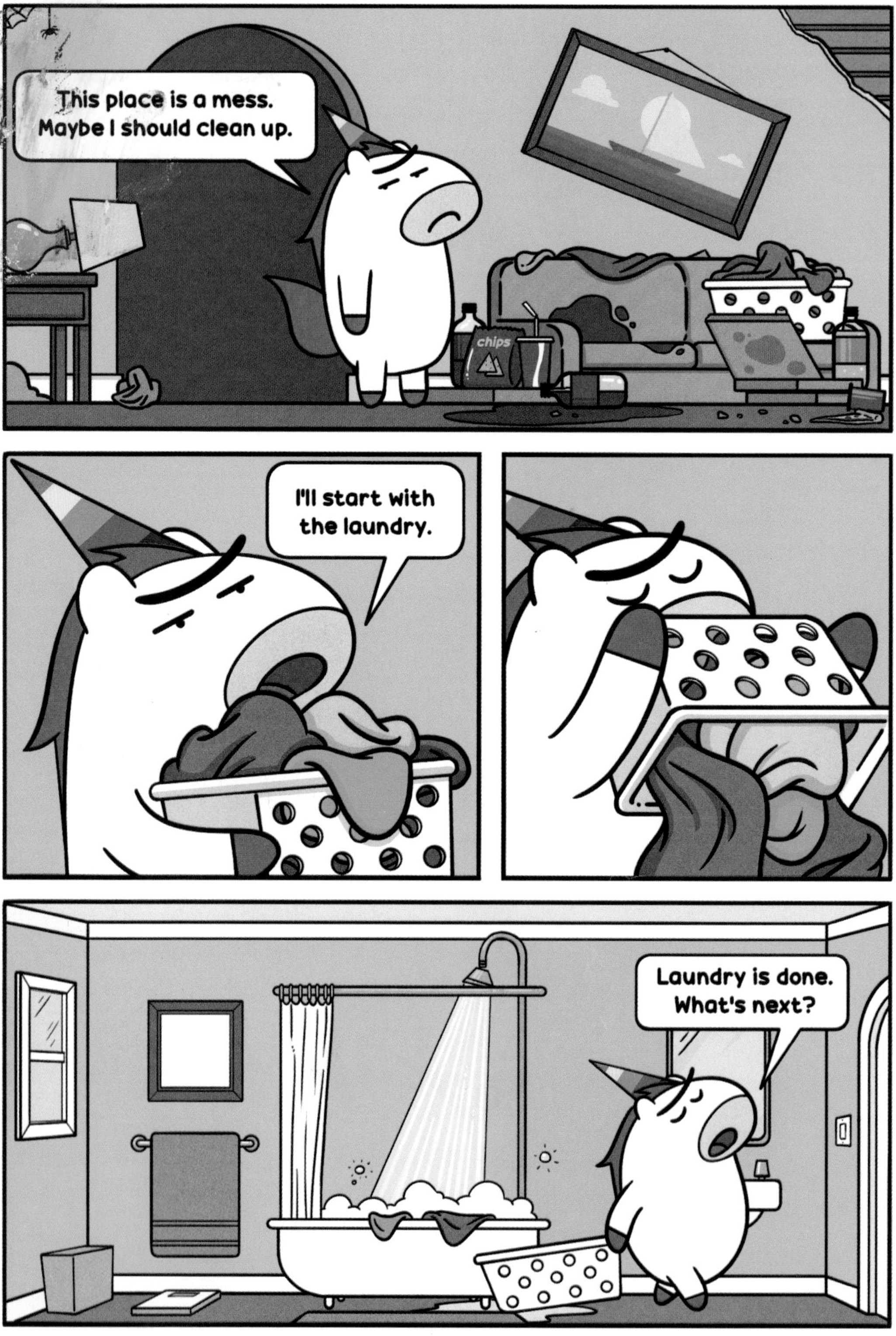
This place is a mess.
Maybe I should clean up.
chips
I'll start with the laundry.
Laundry is done.
What's next?

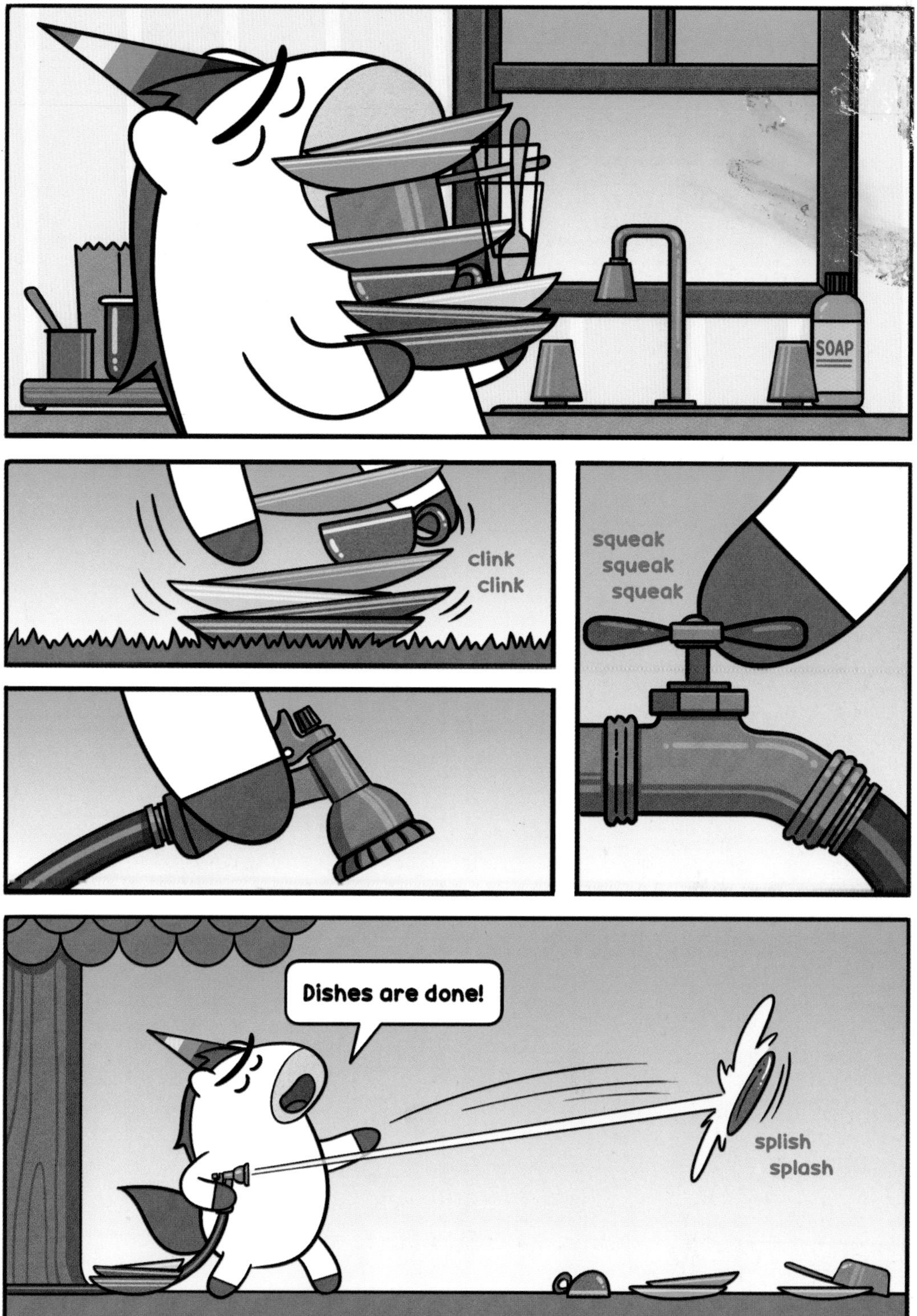
clink
clink
squeak
squeak
squeak
Dishes are done!
splish
splash

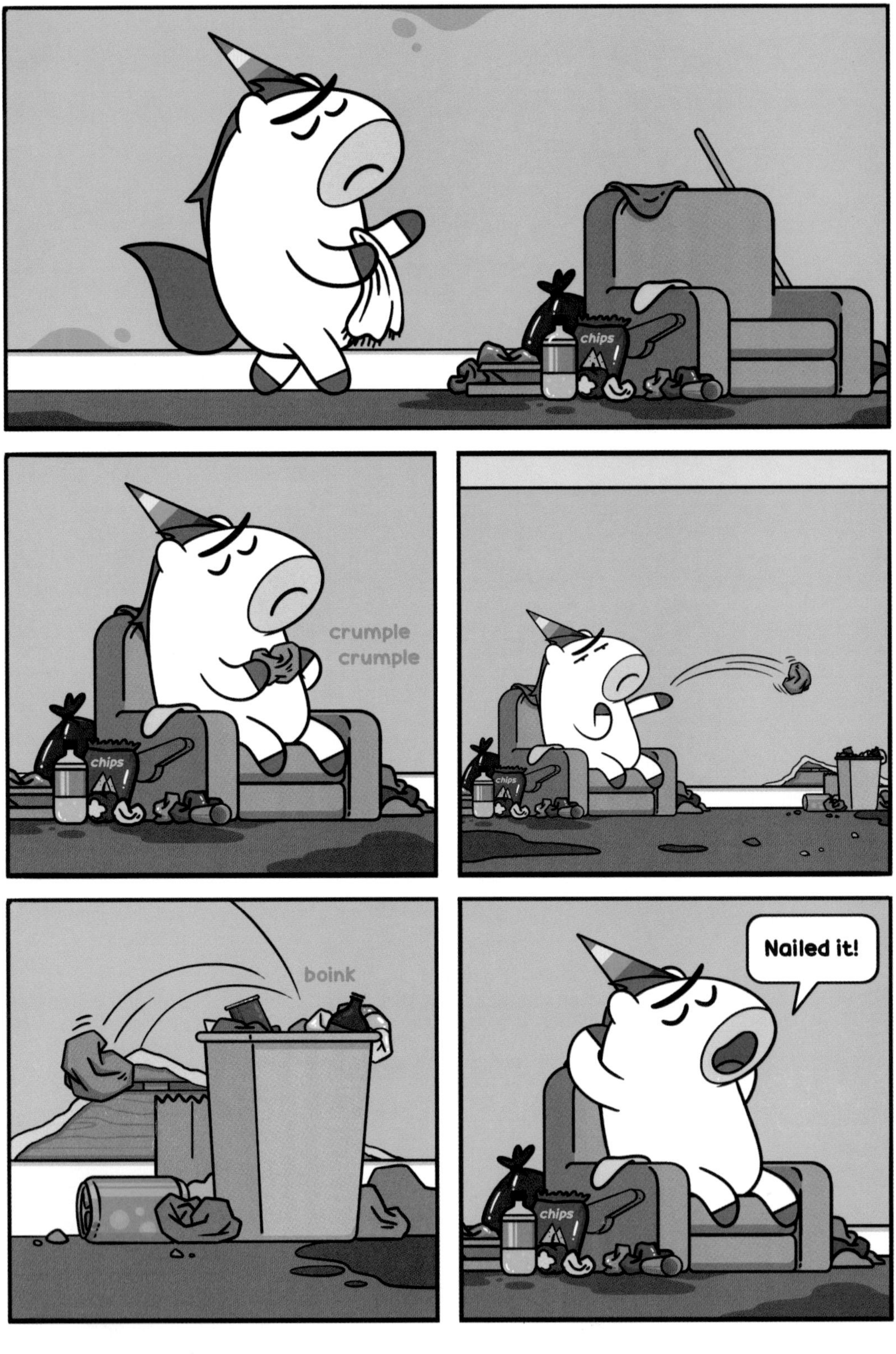
chips
crumple
crumple
chips
chips
boink
Nailed it!
chips

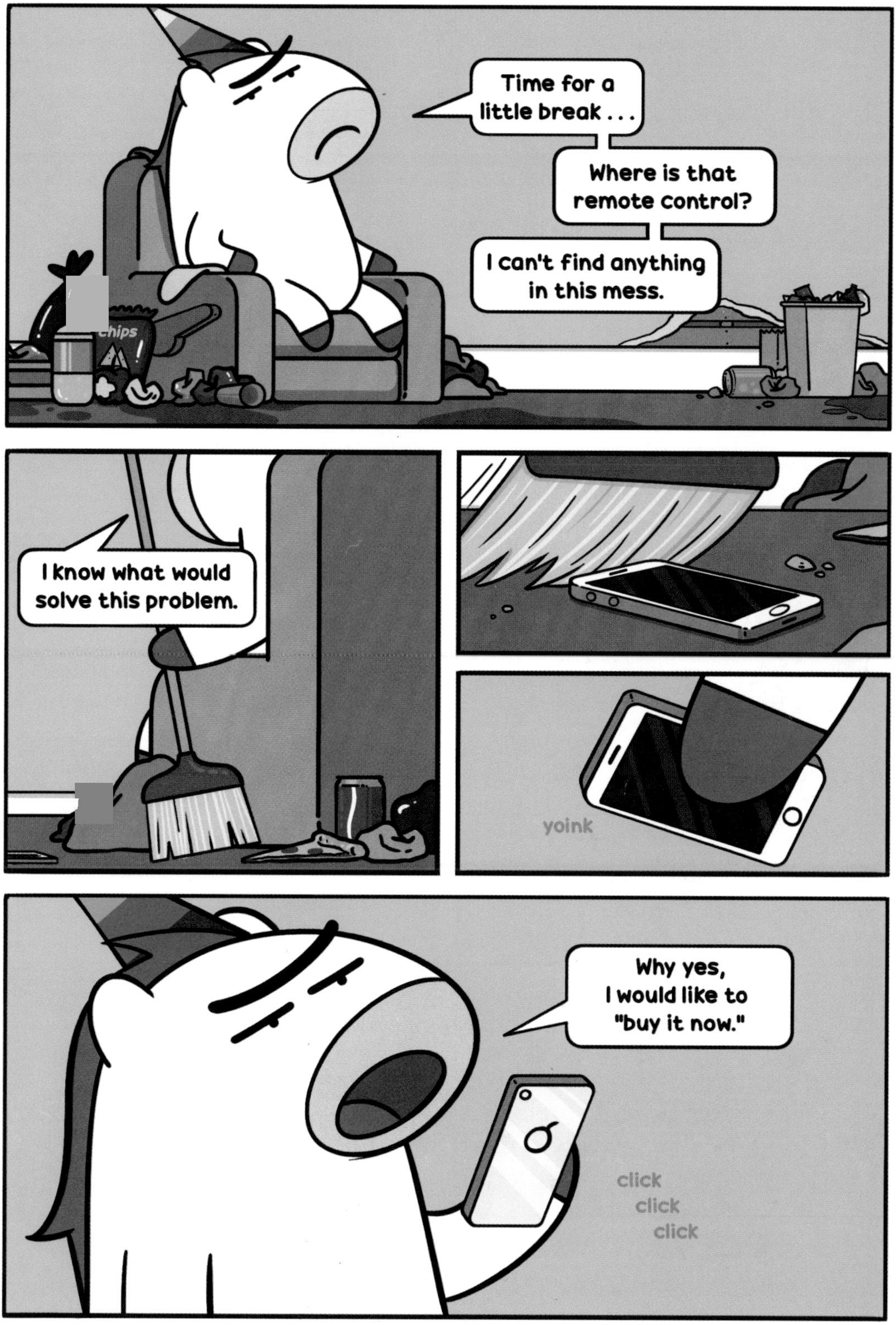
Time for a little break . . .
Where is that remote control?
I can't find anything in this mess.
chips
I know what would solve this problem.
yoink
Why yes, I would like to "buy it now."
click
click
click

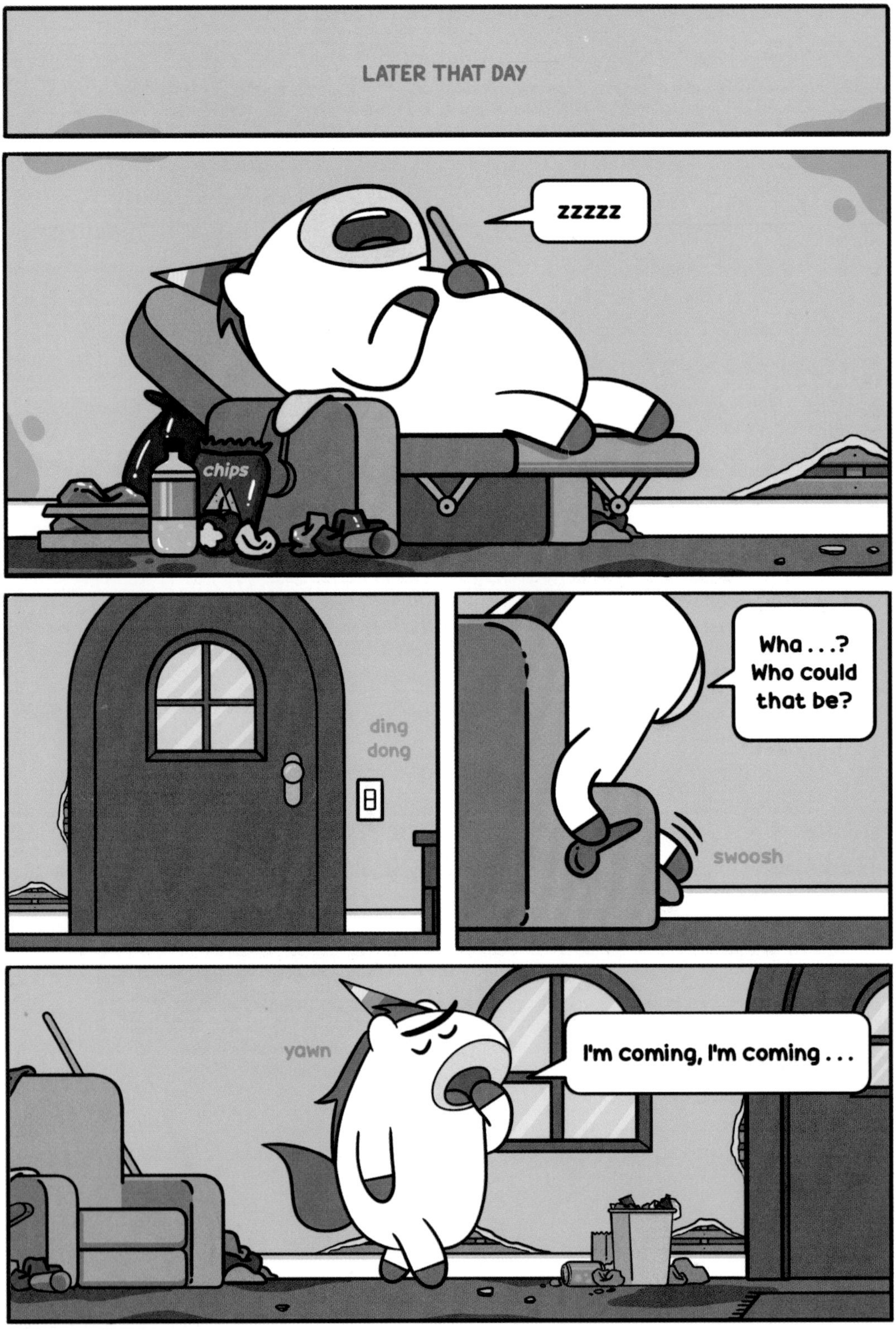
LATER THAT DAY
zzzzz
chips
ding
dong
Wha . . .?
Who could
that be?
swoosh
yawn
I'm coming, I'm coming . . .

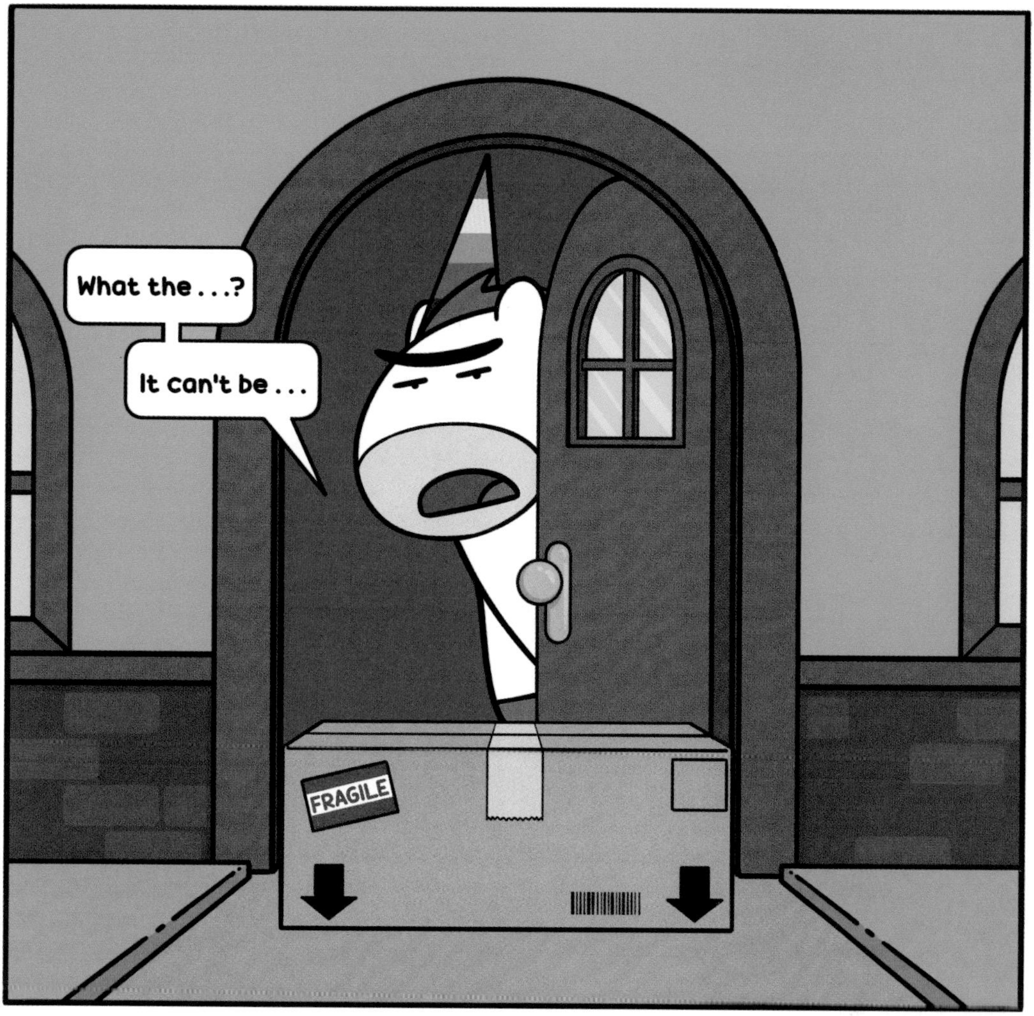
What the . . .?
It can't be . . .
FRAGILE

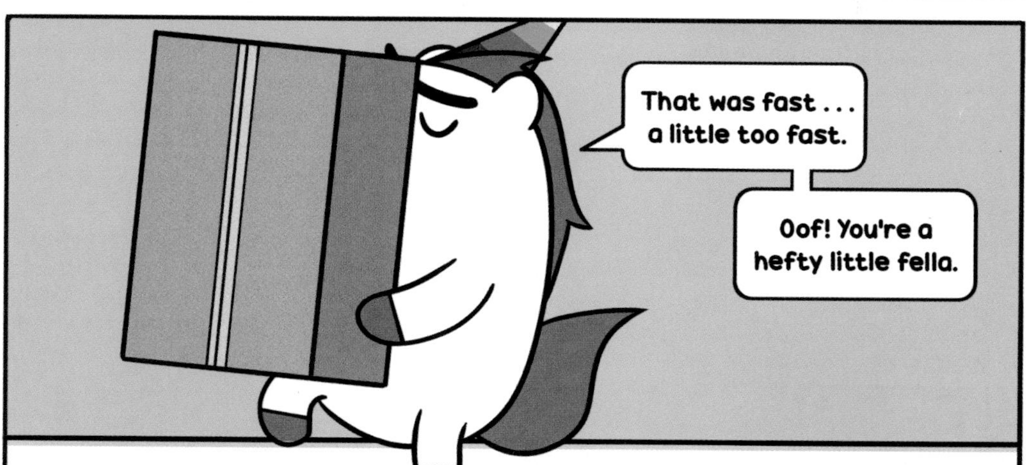
That was fast . . . a little too fast.
Oof! You're a hefty little fella.

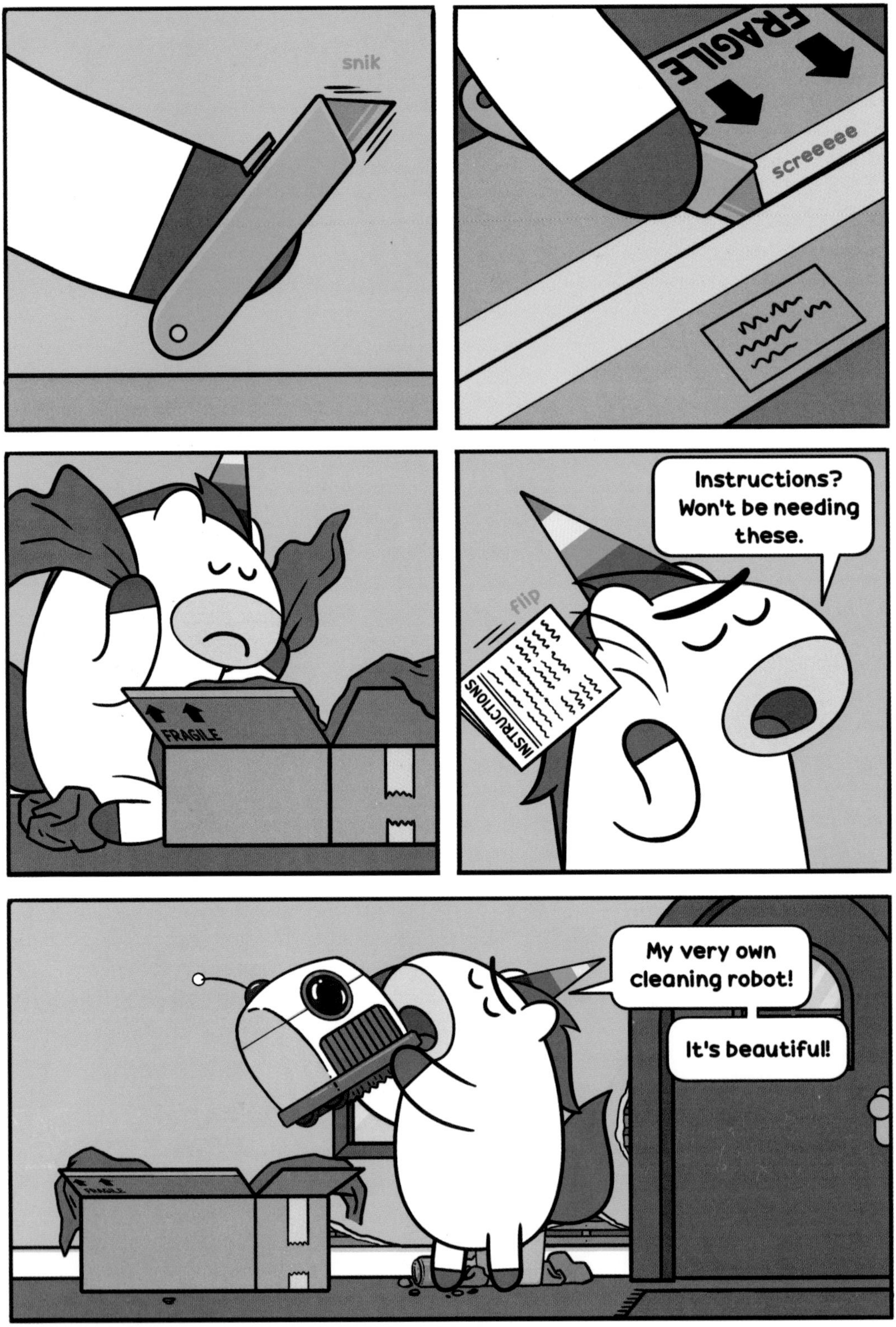
snik
FRAGILE
screeeee
FRAGILE
flip
INSTRUCTIONS
Instructions? Won't be needing these.
FRAGILE
My very own cleaning robot!
It's beautiful!

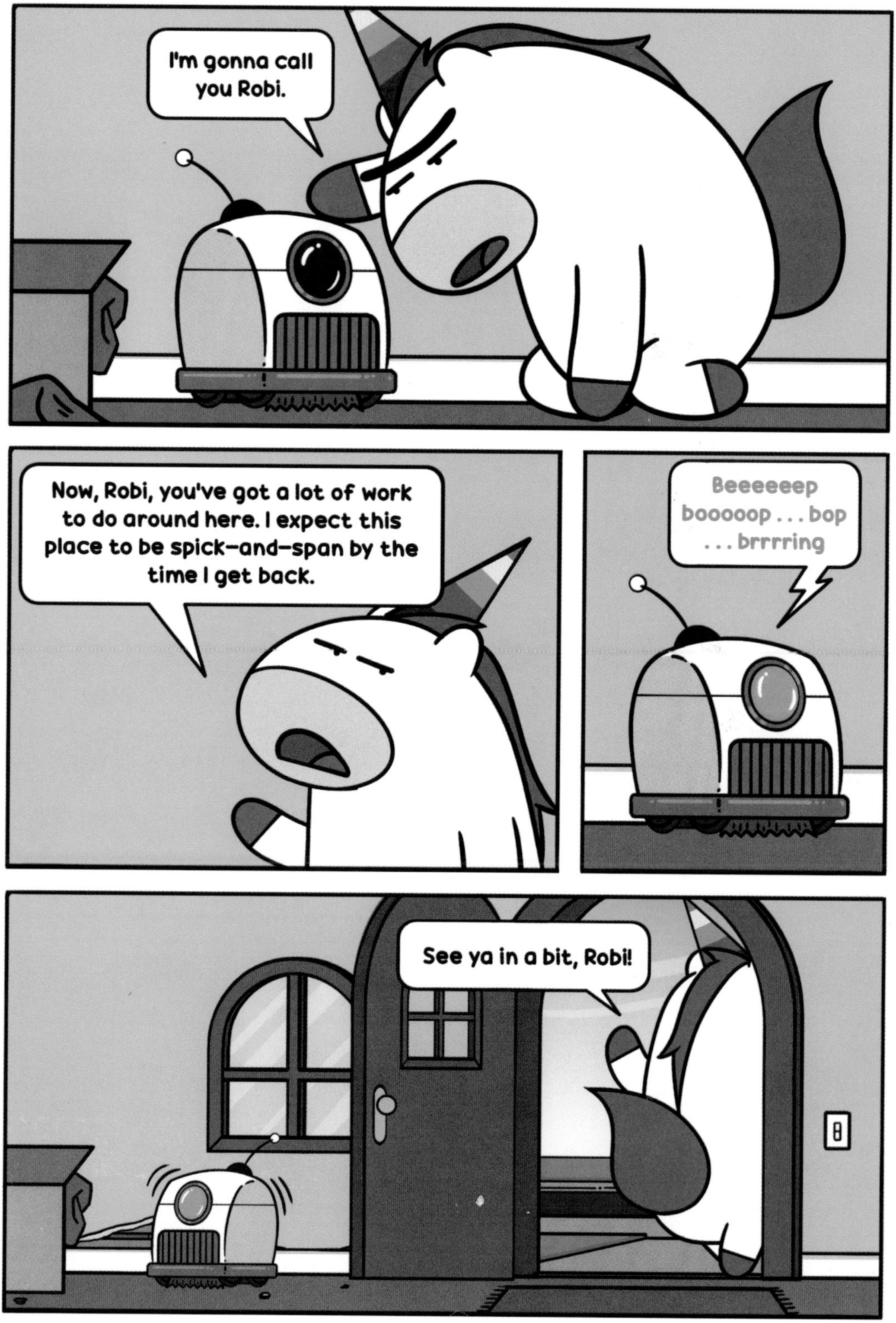
I'm gonna call you Robi.
Now, Robi, you've got a lot of work to do around here. I expect this place to be spick-and-span by the time I get back.
Beeeeeep boooooop . . . bop . . . brrrring
See ya in a bit, Robi!

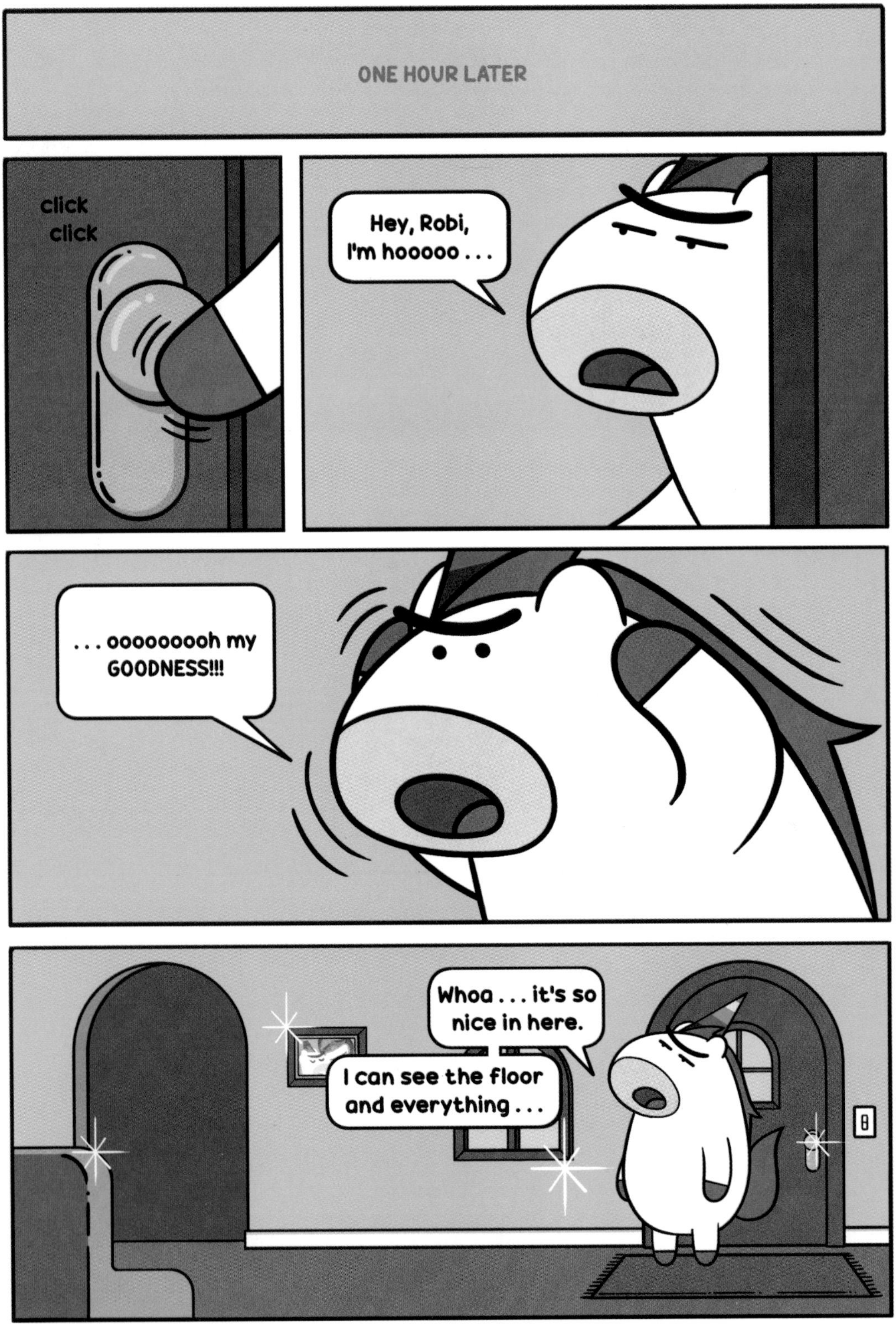
ONE HOUR LATER
click
click
Hey, Robi, I'm hooooo . . .
. . . oooooooh my GOODNESS!!!
Whoa . . . it's so nice in here.
I can see the floor and everything . . .

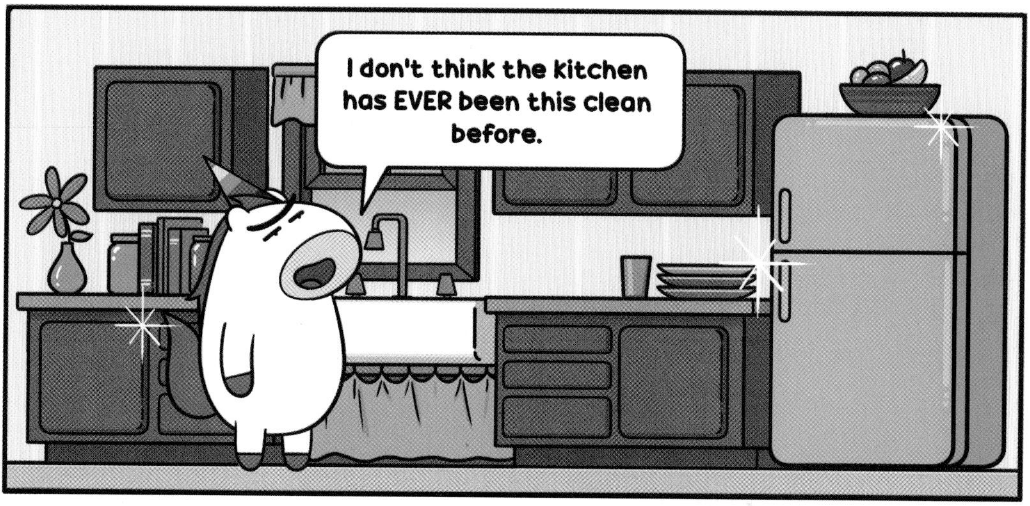
I don't think the kitchen has EVER been this clean before.

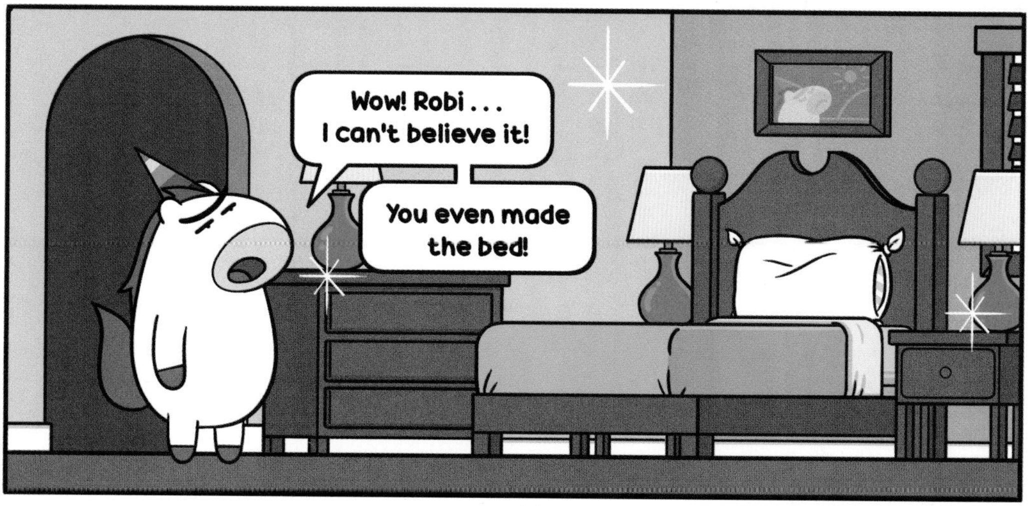
Wow! Robi . . .
I can't believe it!
You even made the bed!

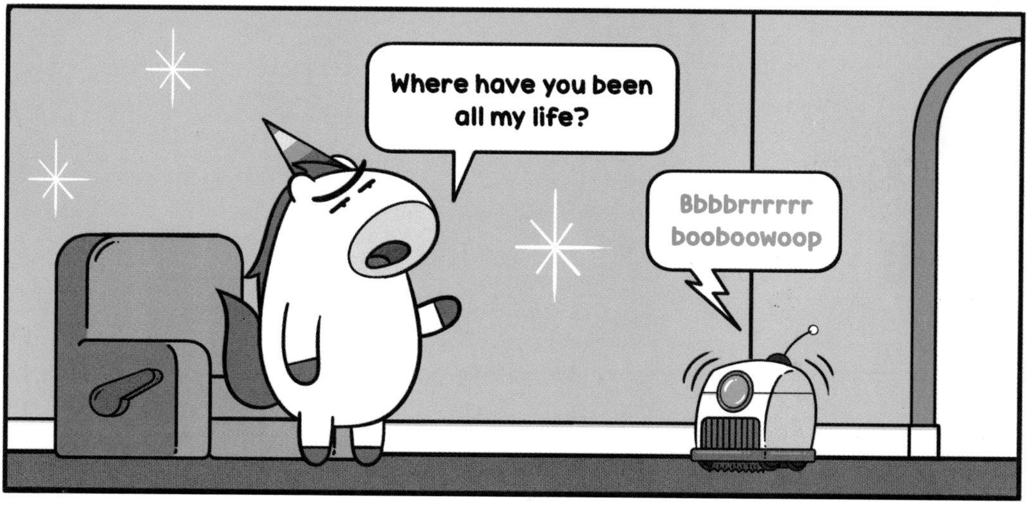
Where have you been all my life?
Bbbbrrrrrr booboowoop

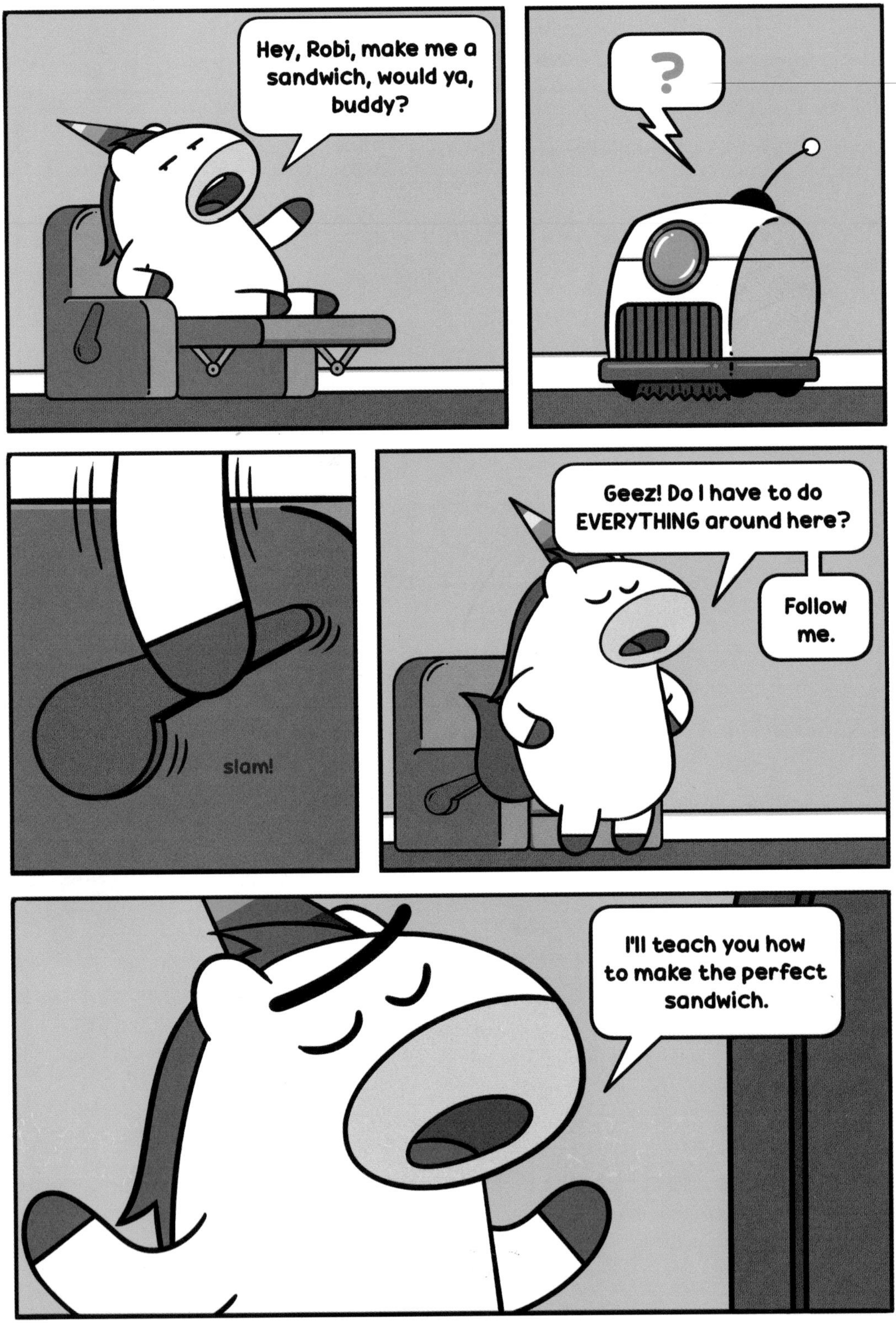
Hey, Robi, make me a sandwich, would ya, buddy?
?
slam!
Geez! Do I have to do EVERYTHING around here?
Follow me.
I'll teach you how to make the perfect sandwich.

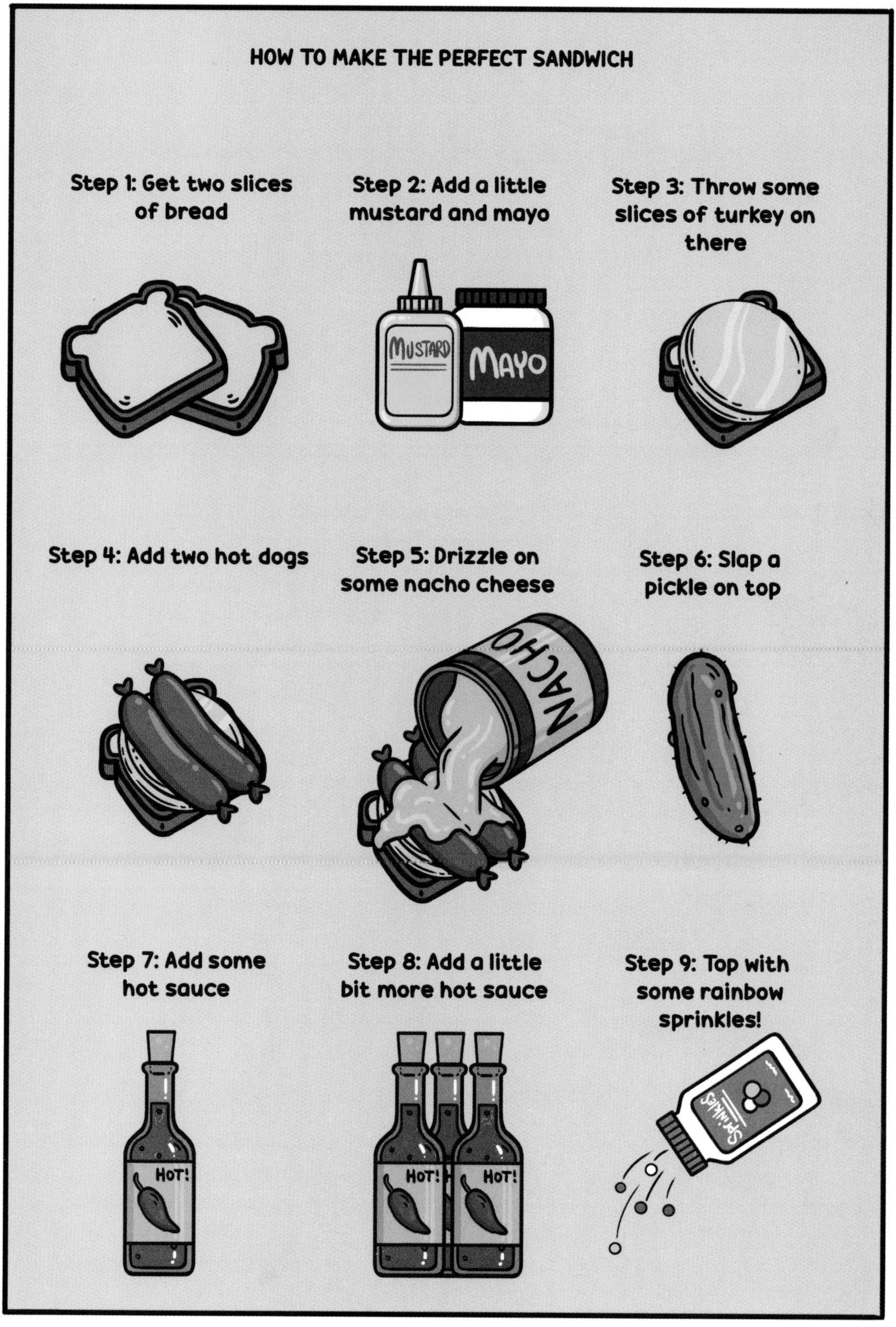
HOW TO MAKE THE PERFECT SANDWICH
Step 1: Get two slices of bread
Step 2: Add a little mustard and mayo
MUSTARD
MAYO
Step 3: Throw some slices of turkey on there
Step 4: Add two hot dogs
Step 5: Drizzle on some nacho cheese
NACHO
Step 6: Slap a pickle on top
Step 7: Add some hot sauce
HOT!
Step 8: Add a little bit more hot sauce
HOT!
HOT!
Step 9: Top with some rainbow sprinkles!
Sprinkles

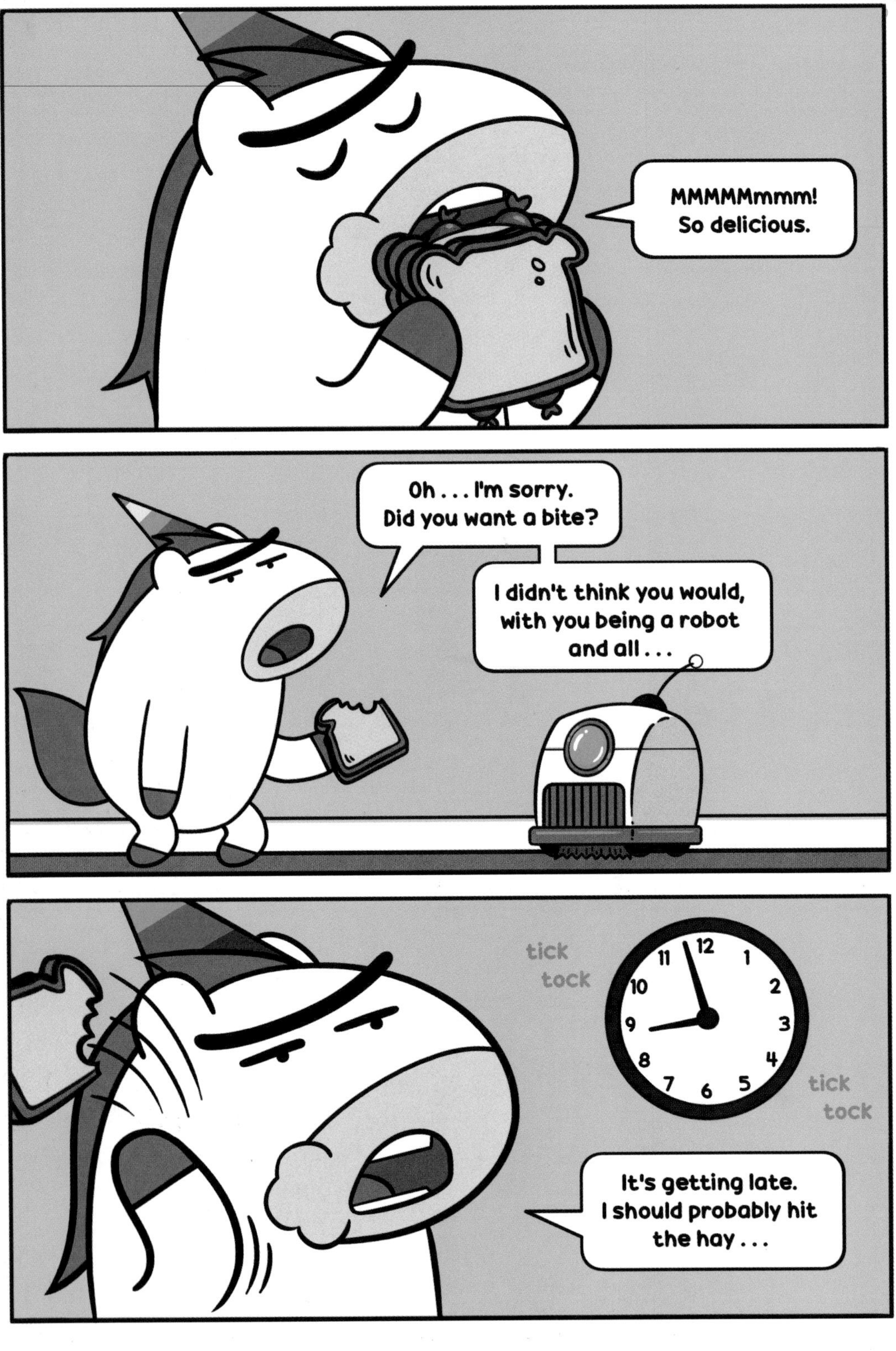
MMMMMmmm!
So delicious.
Oh . . . I'm sorry.
Did you want a bite?
I didn't think you would,
with you being a robot
and all . . .
tick
tock
tick
tock
It's getting late.
I should probably hit
the hay . . .

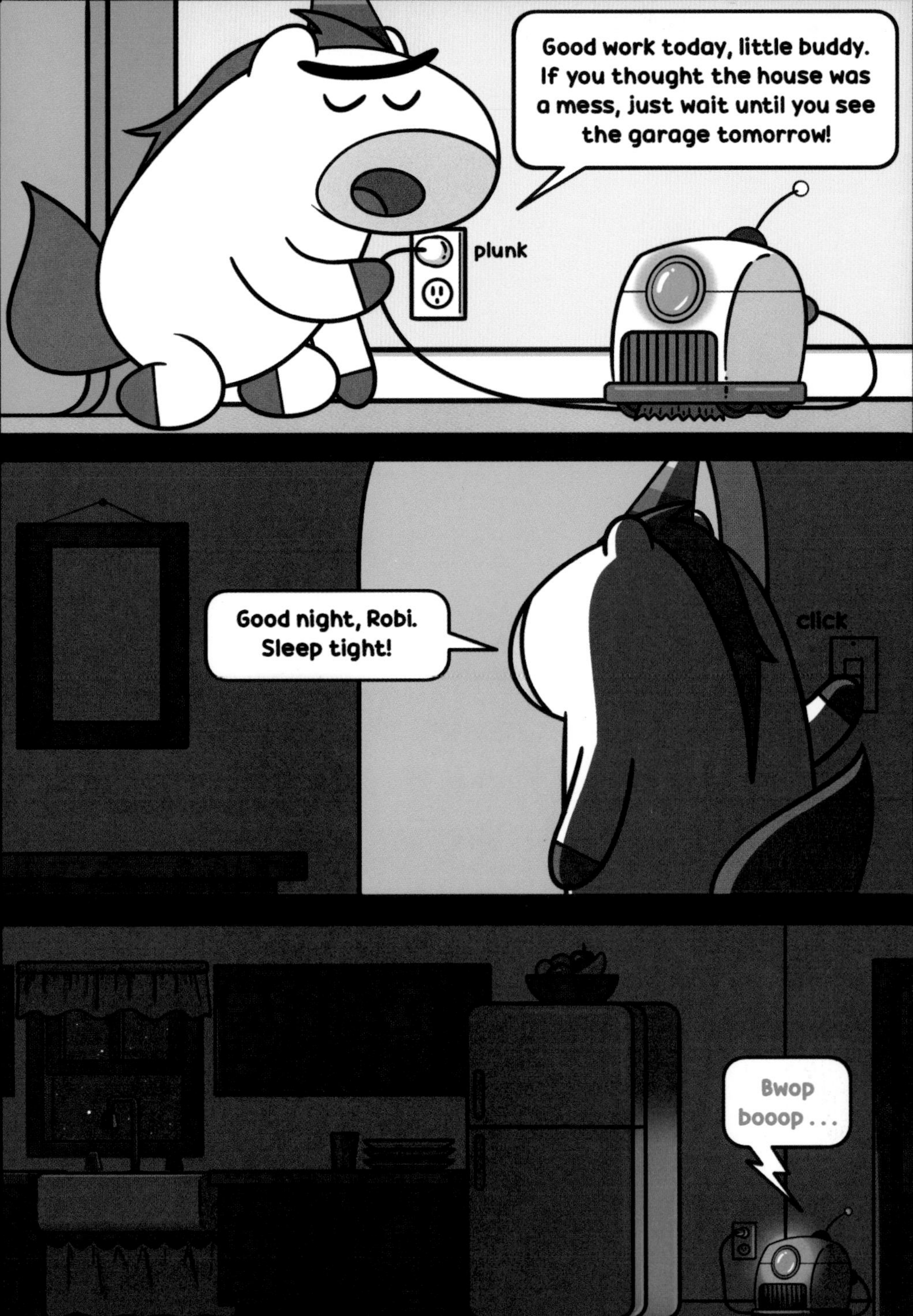
Good work today, little buddy. If you thought the house was a mess, just wait until you see the garage tomorrow!
plunk
Good night, Robi. Sleep tight!
click
Bwop booop . . .

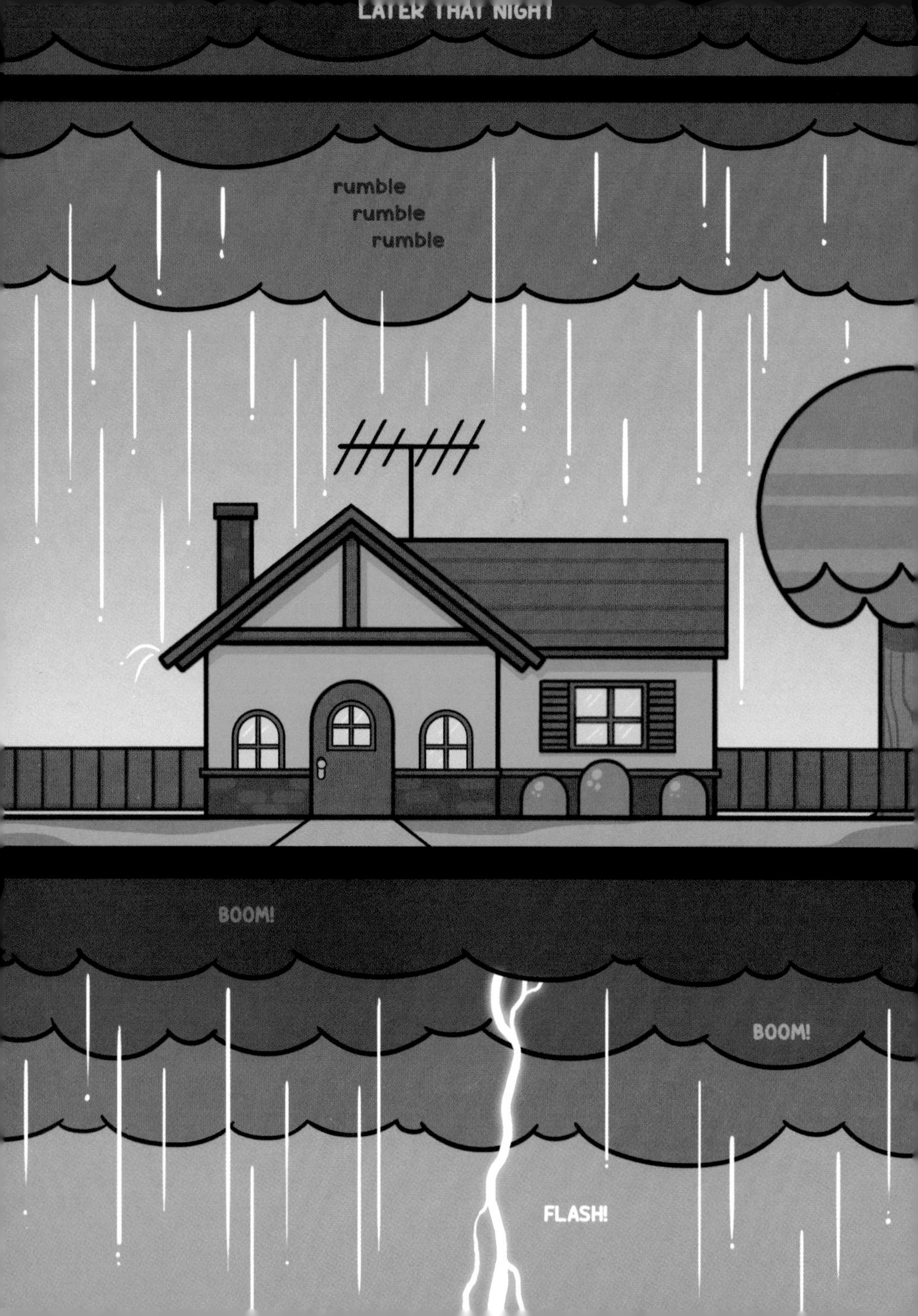
LATER THAT NIGHT
rumble
rumble
rumble
BOOM!
BOOM!
FLASH!

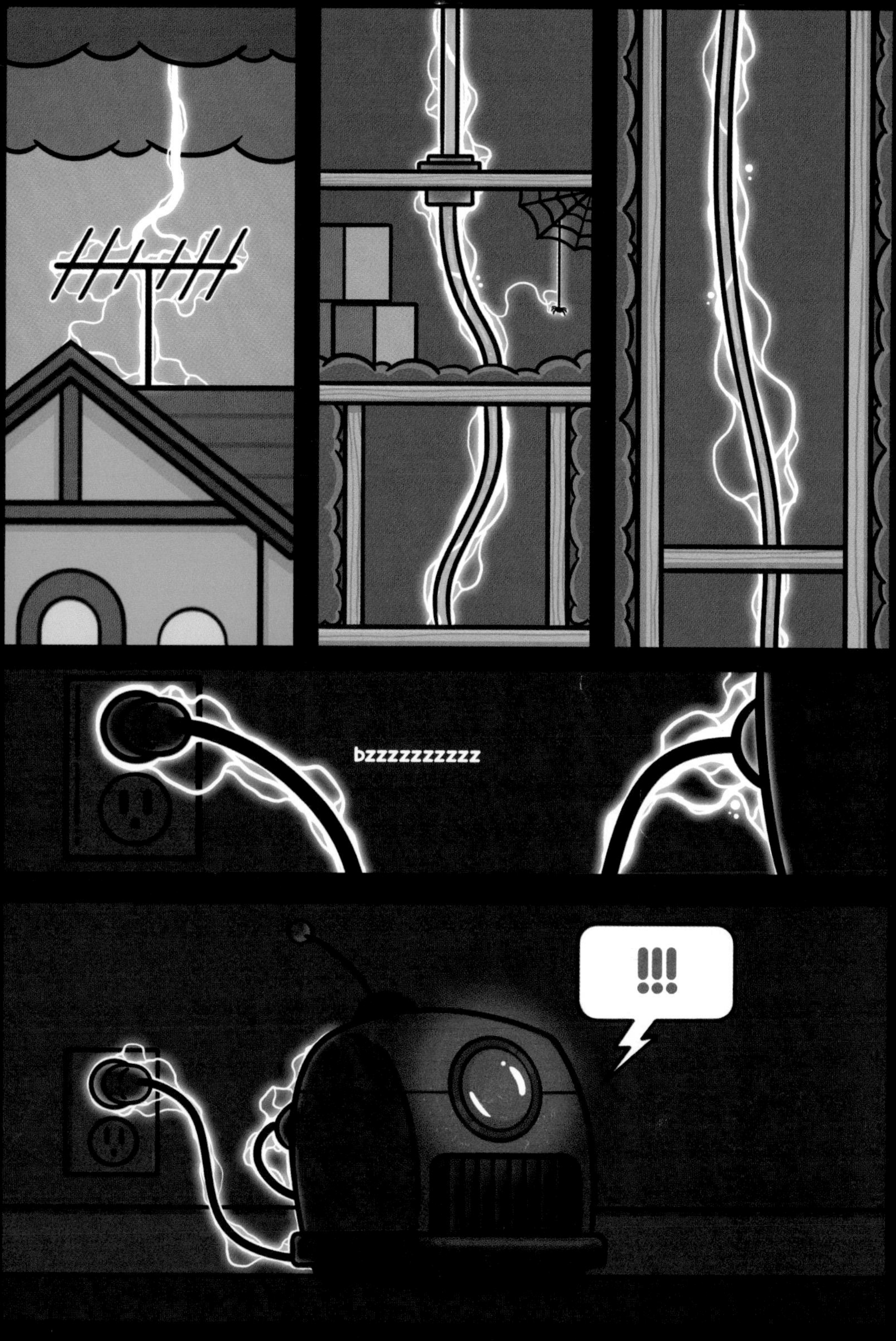
bzzzzzzzzzz
!!!

Grumpy Unicorn's Big Mess

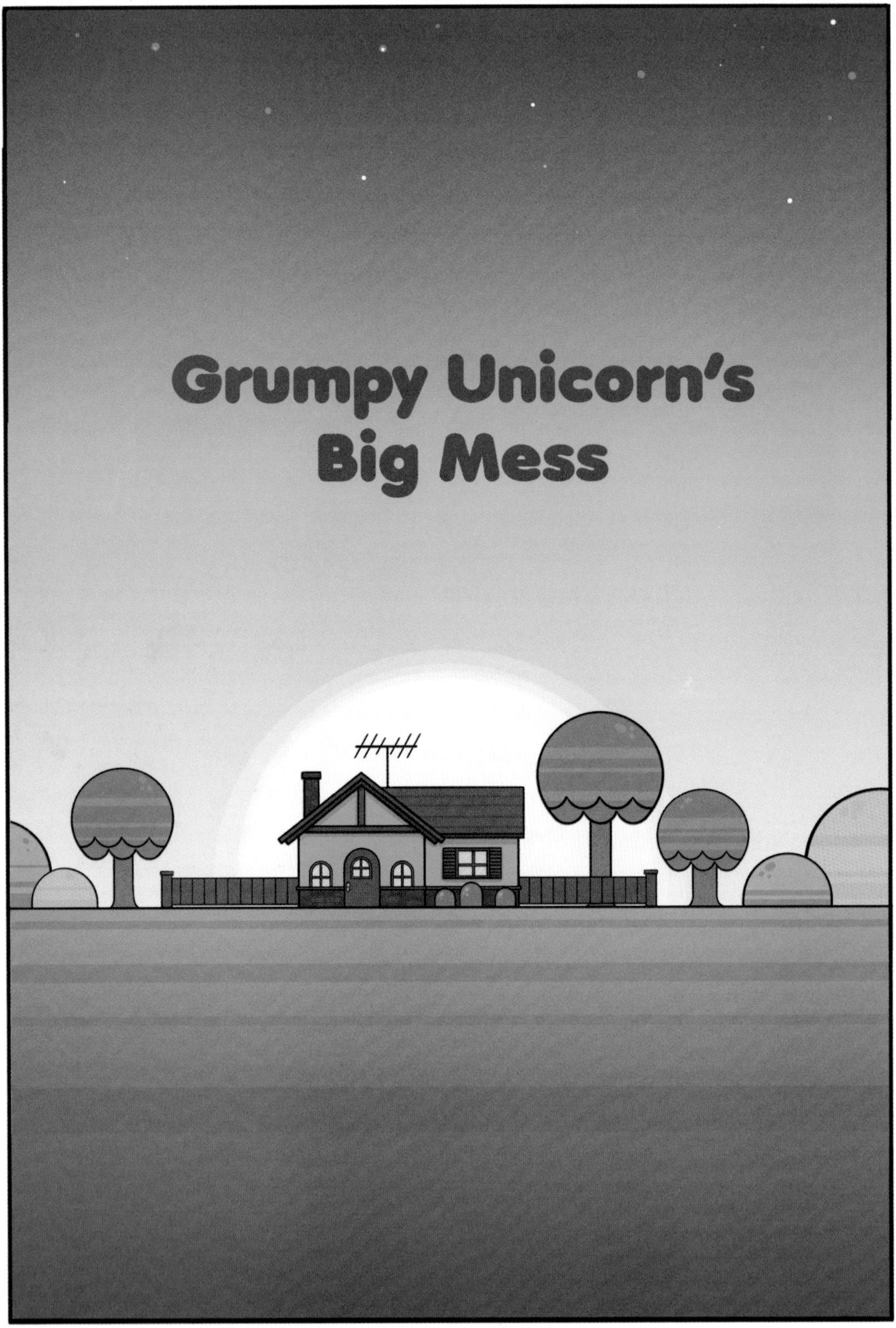

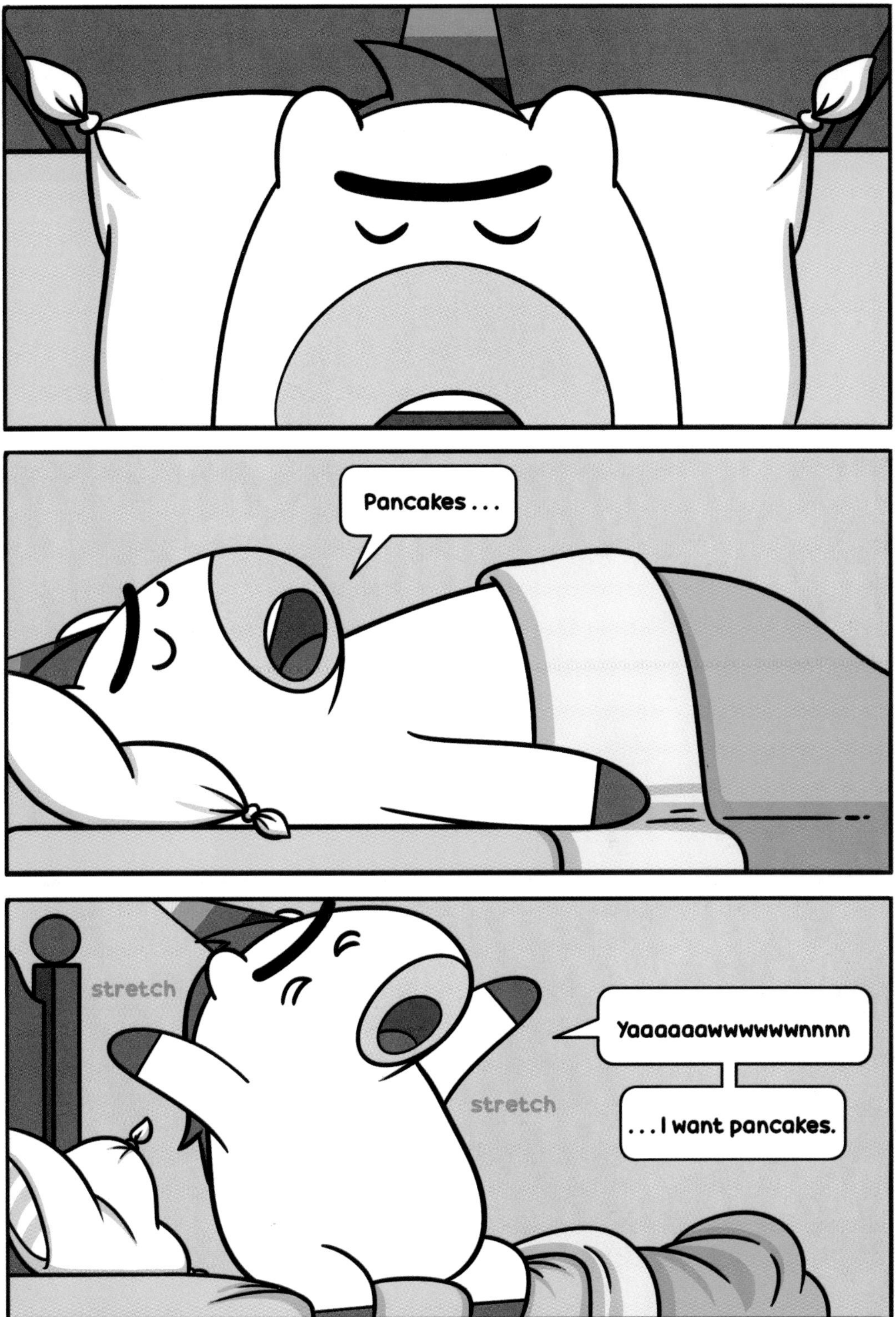
Pancakes . . .
stretch
Yaaaaaawwwwwwnnnn
stretch
. . . I want pancakes.

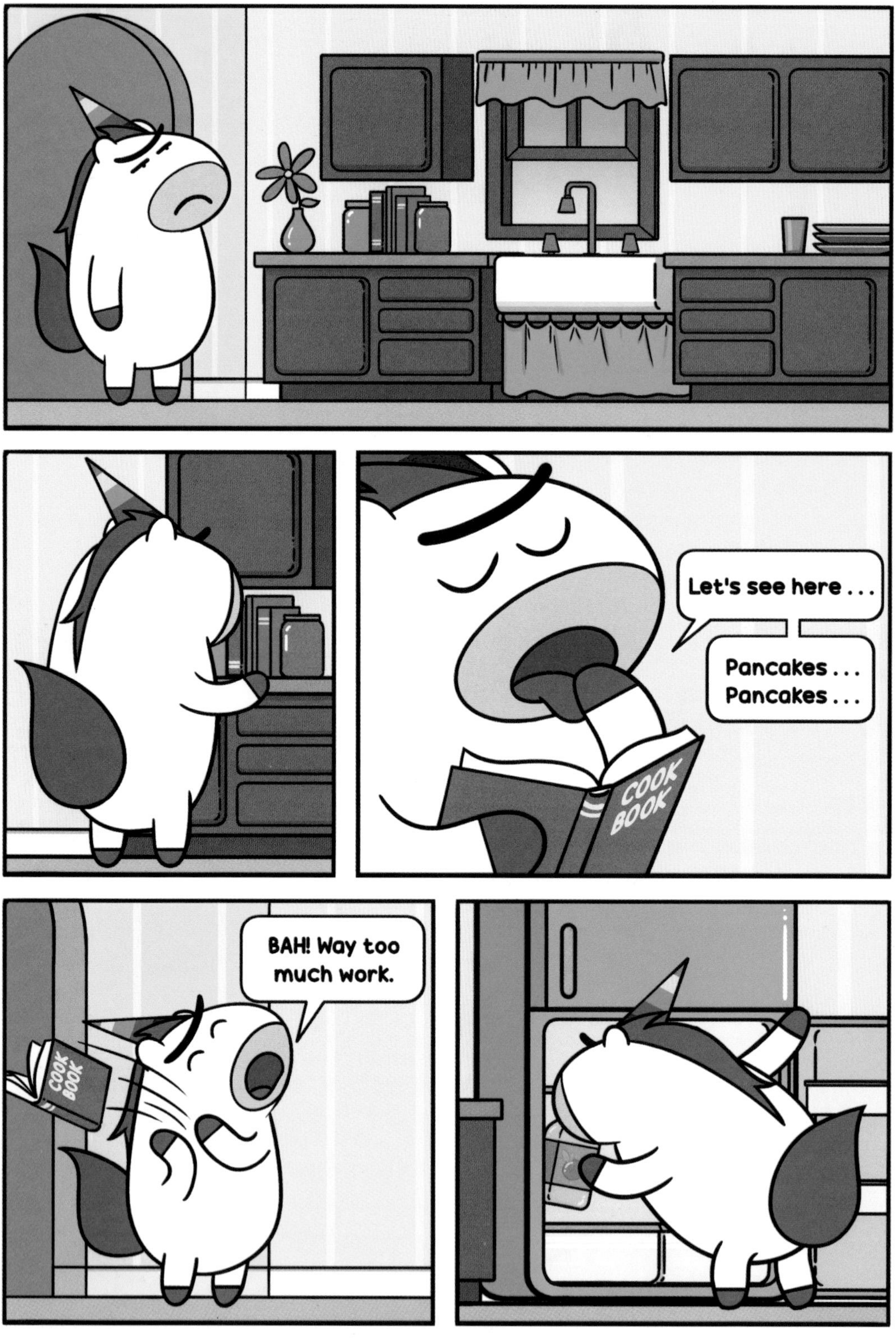
Let's see here . . .
Pancakes . . .
Pancakes . . .
COOK BOOK
BAH! Way too much work.
COOK BOOK

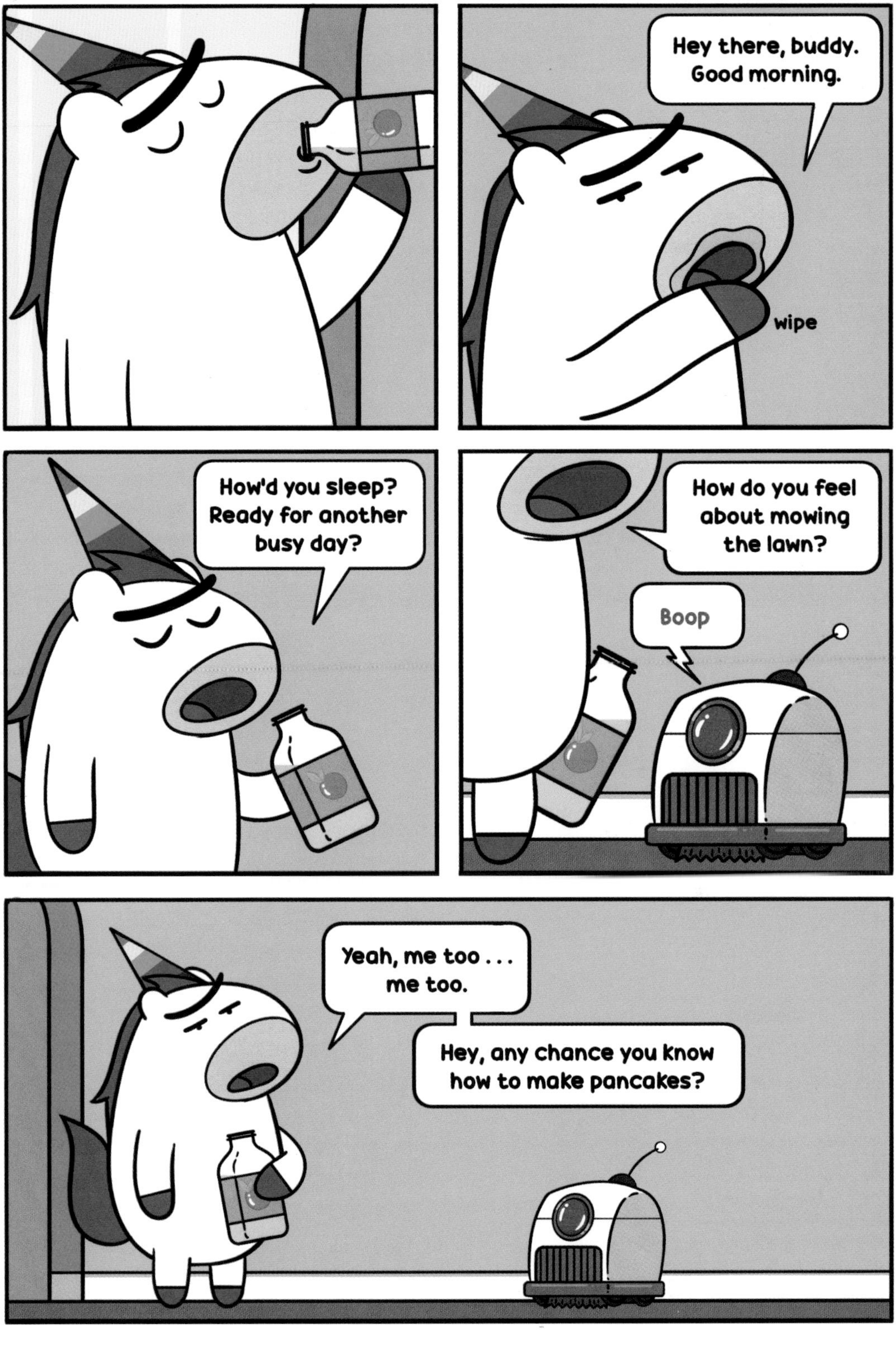
Hey there, buddy. Good morning.
wipe
How'd you sleep? Ready for another busy day?
How do you feel about mowing the lawn?
Boop
Yeah, me too . . . me too.
Hey, any chance you know how to make pancakes?

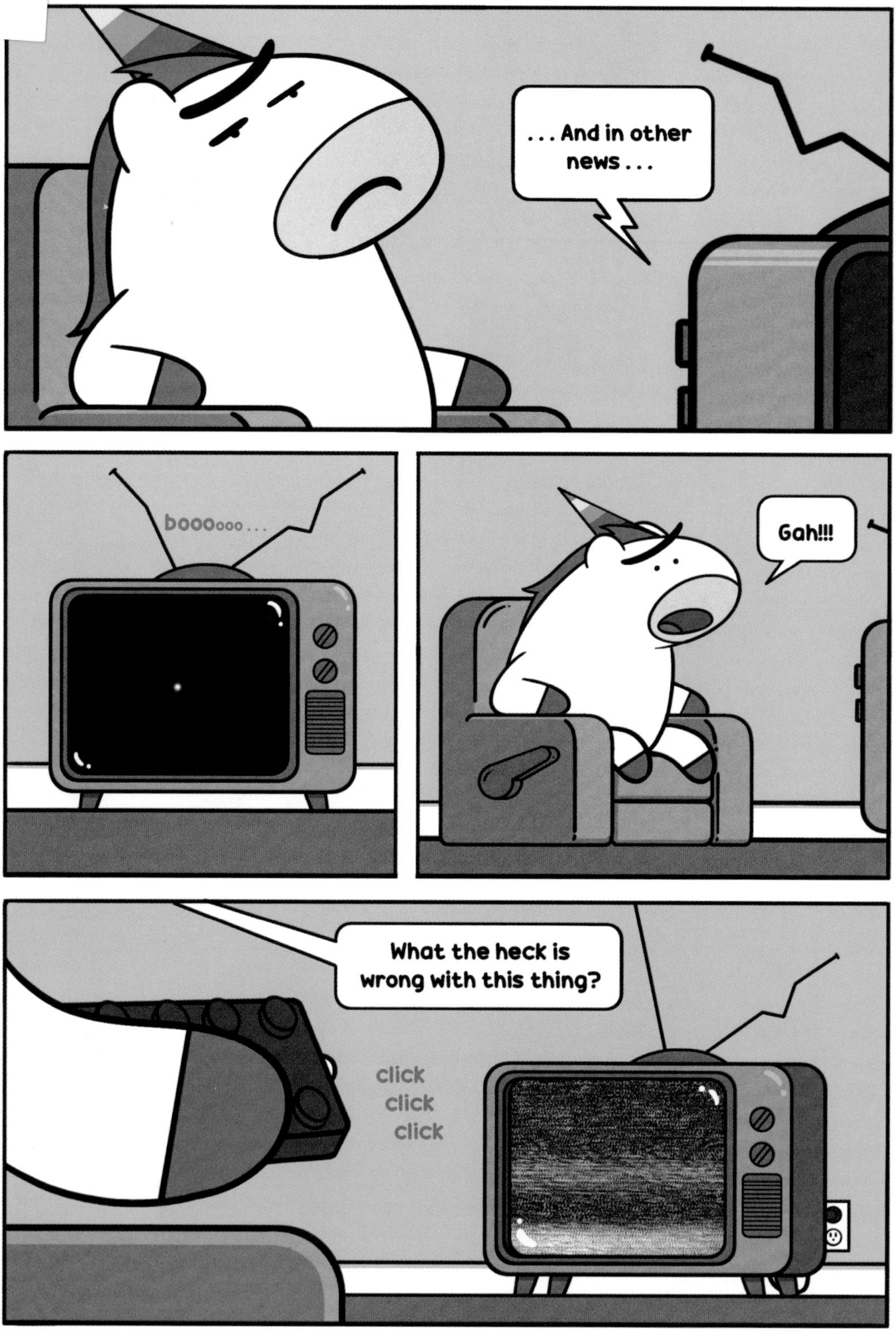
. . . And in other news . . .
booooo . . .
Gah!!!
What the heck is wrong with this thing?
click
click
click

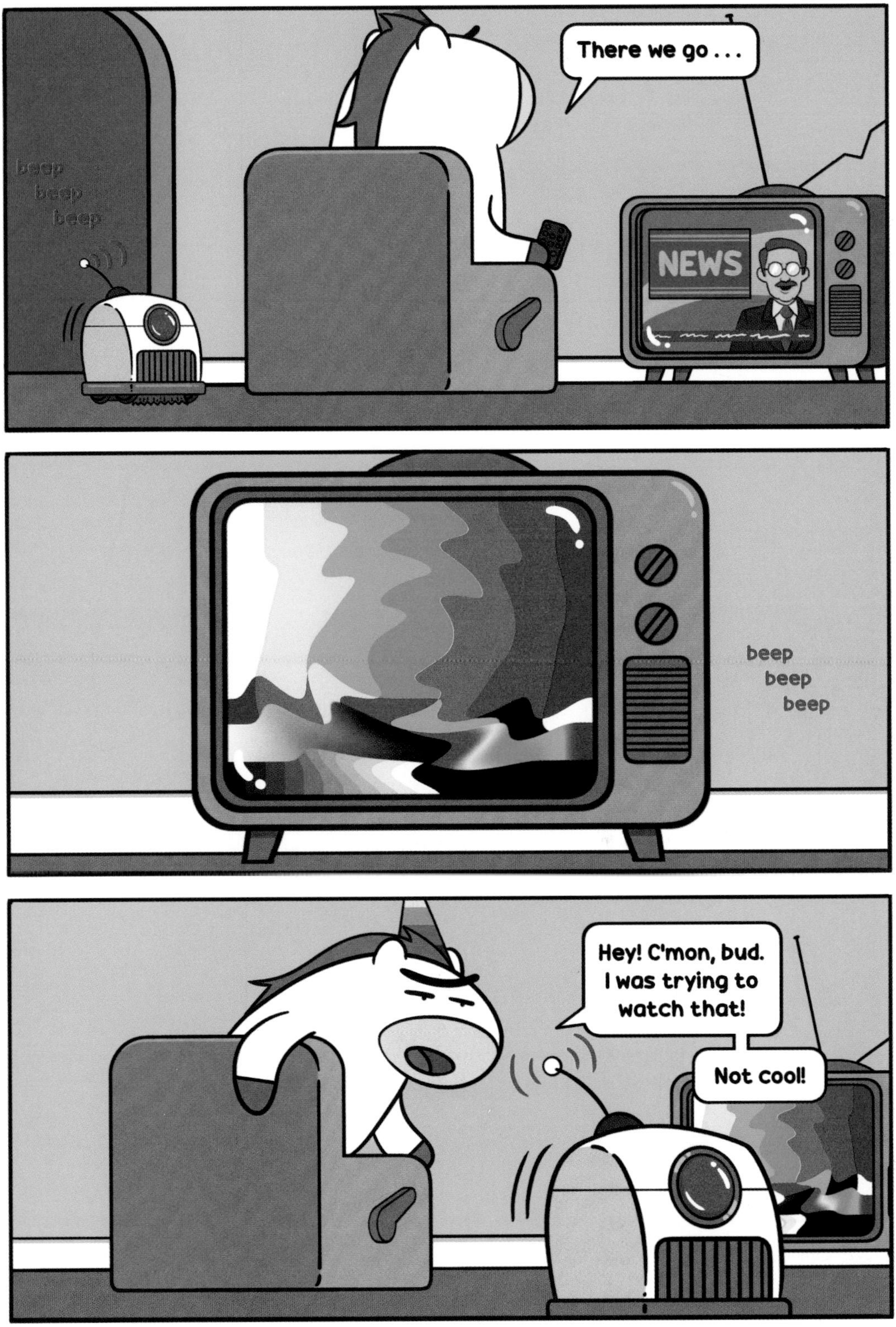
beep
beep
beep
There we go . . .
NEWS
beep
beep
beep
Hey! C'mon, bud. I was trying to watch that!
Not cool!

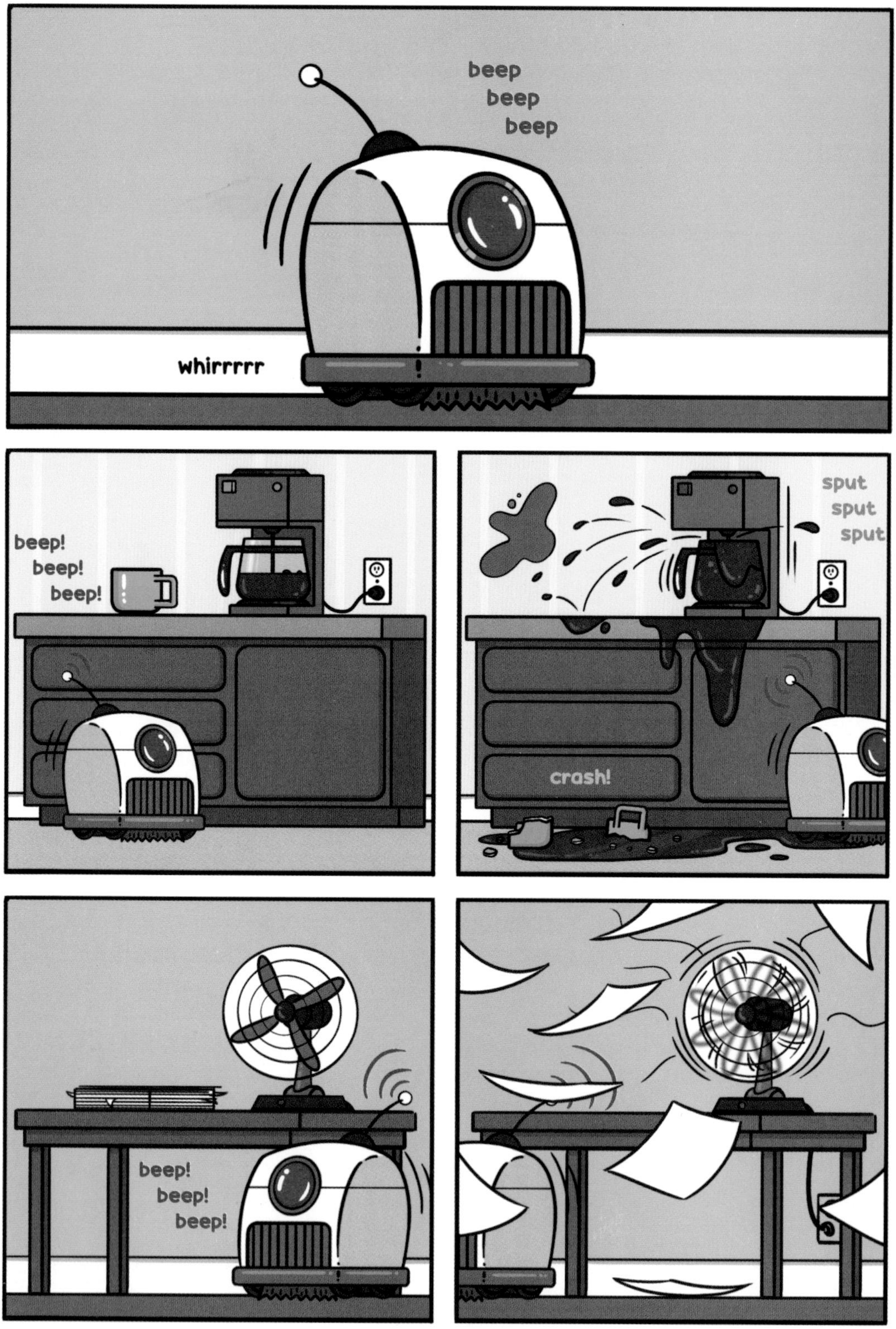
beep
beep
beep
whirrrrr
beep!
beep!
beep!
sput
sput
sput
crash!
beep!
beep!
beep!

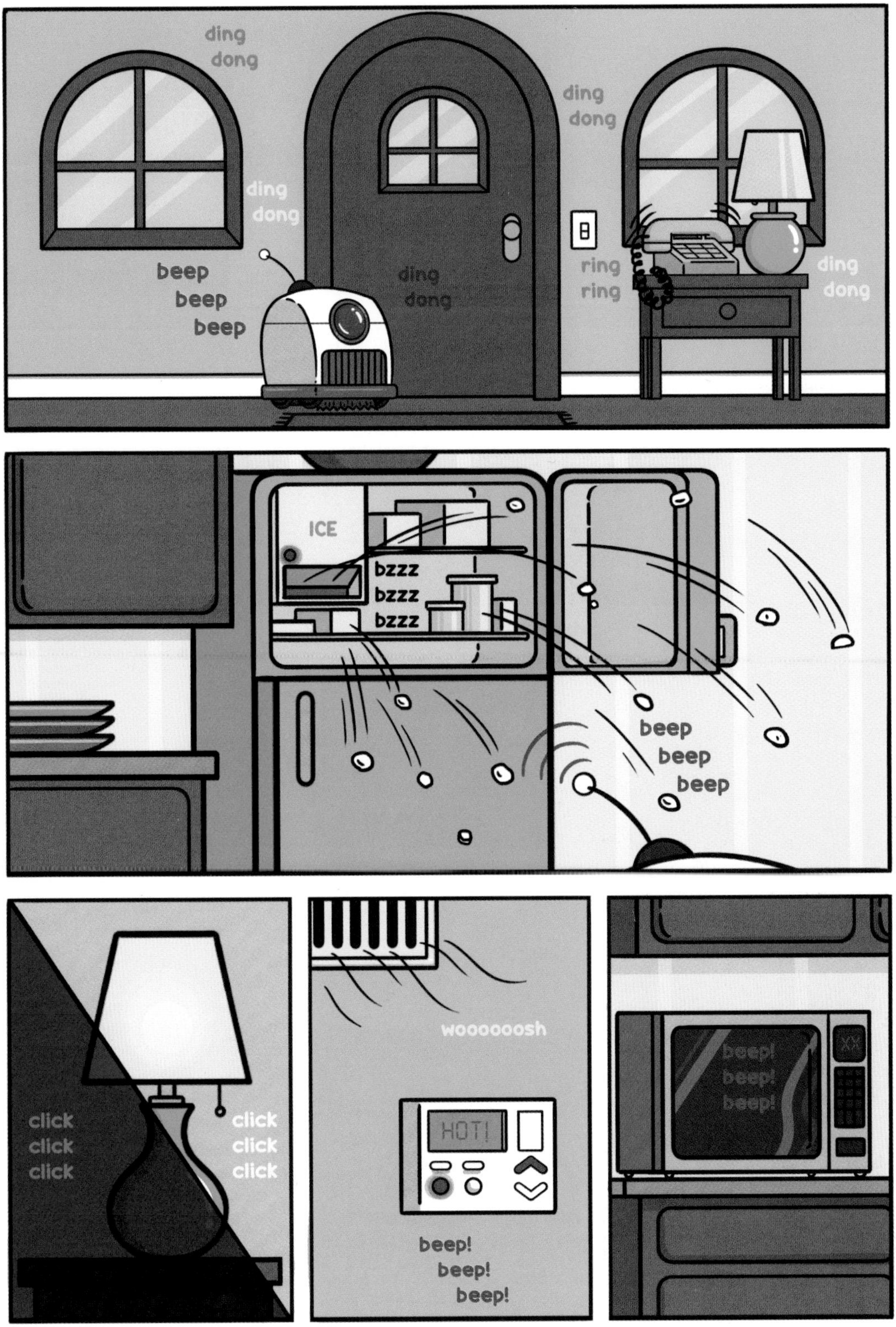
ding dong
ding dong
ding dong
beep beep beep
ding dong
ring ring
ding dong
ICE
bzzz bzzz bzzz
beep beep beep
click click click
click click click
wooooosh
HOT!
beep! beep! beep!
beep! beep! beep!

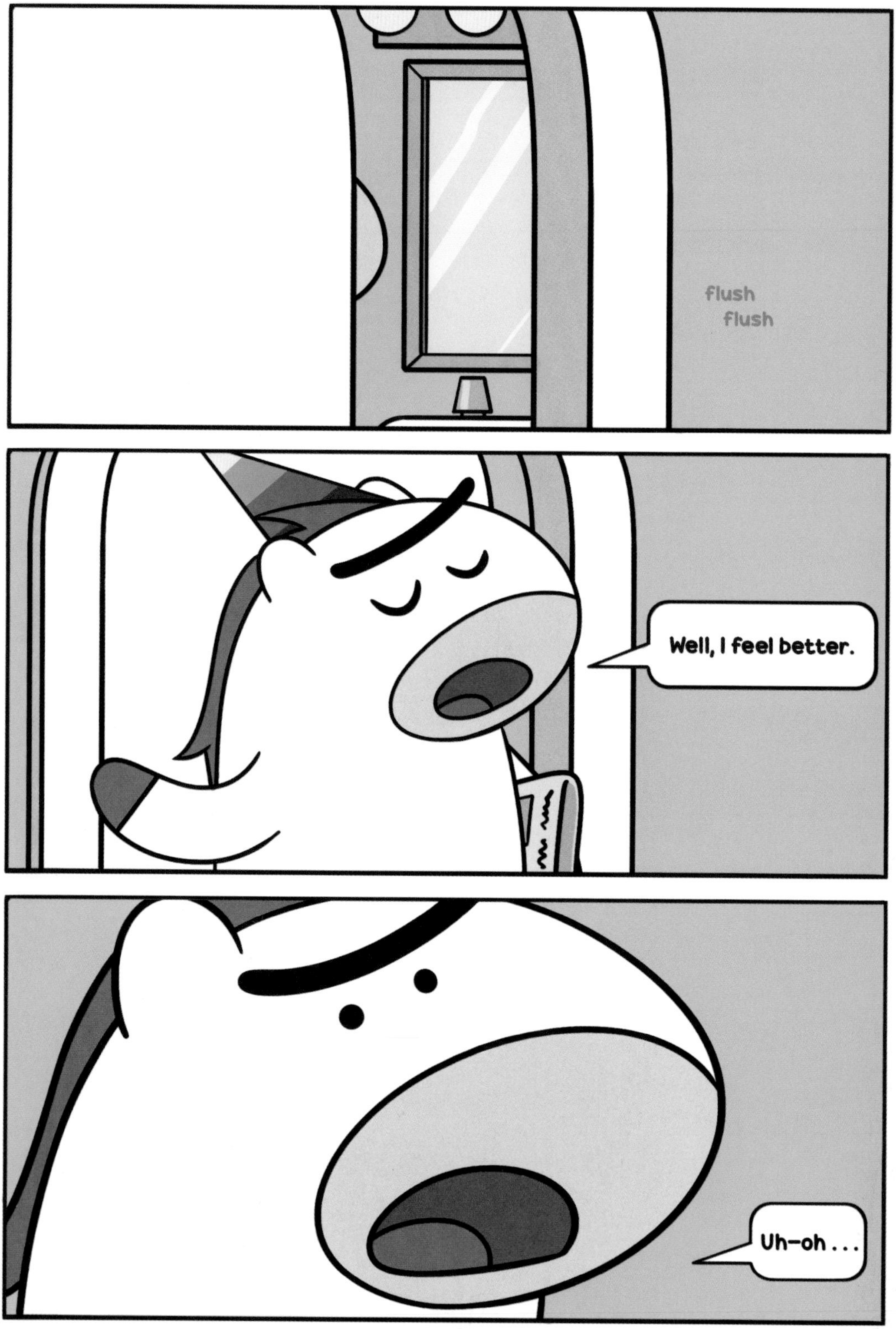
flush
flush
Well, I feel better.
Uh-oh . . .

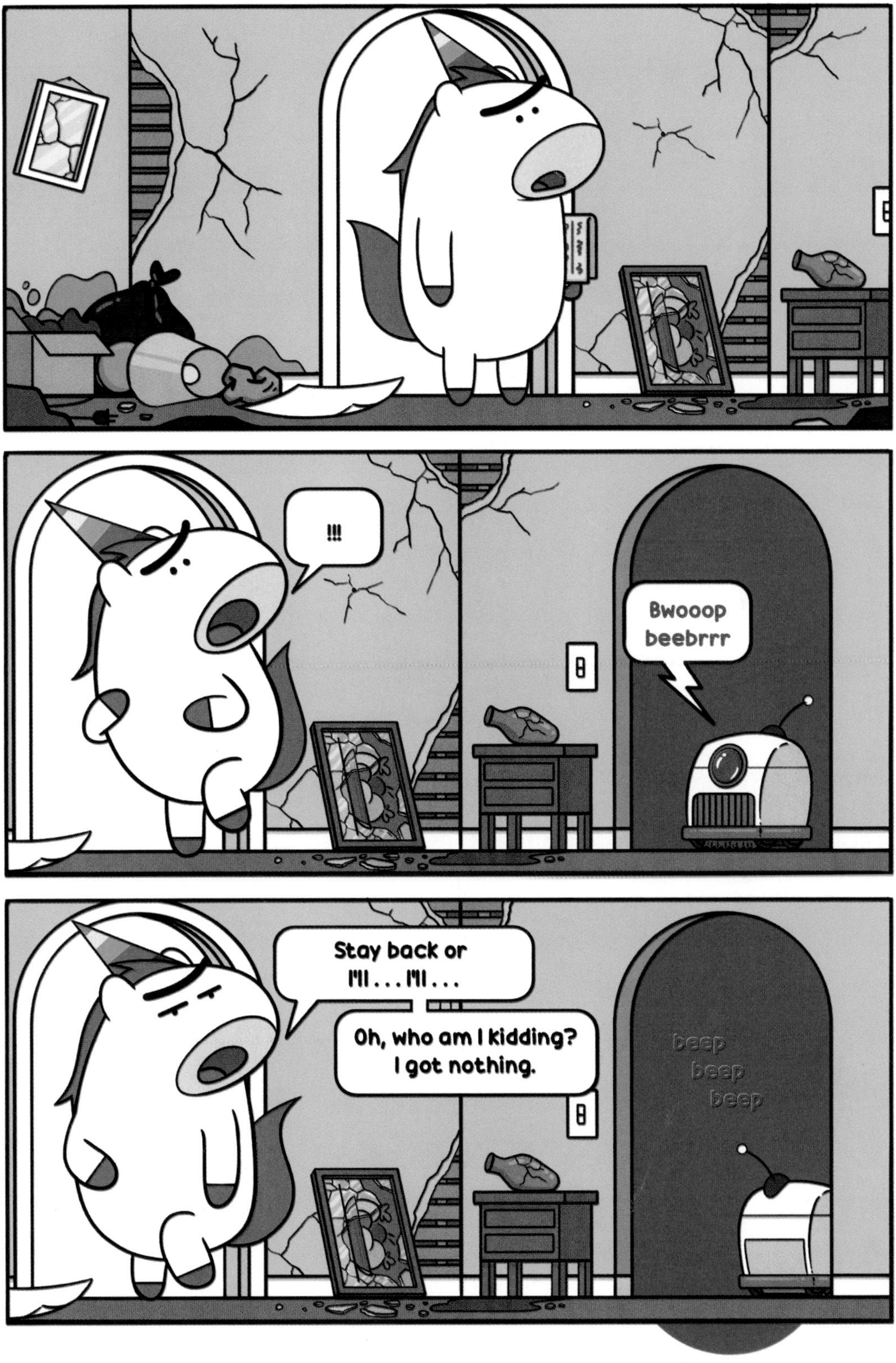
!!!
Bwooop beebrrr
Stay back or I'll . . . I'll . . .
Oh, who am I kidding? I got nothing.
beep beep beep

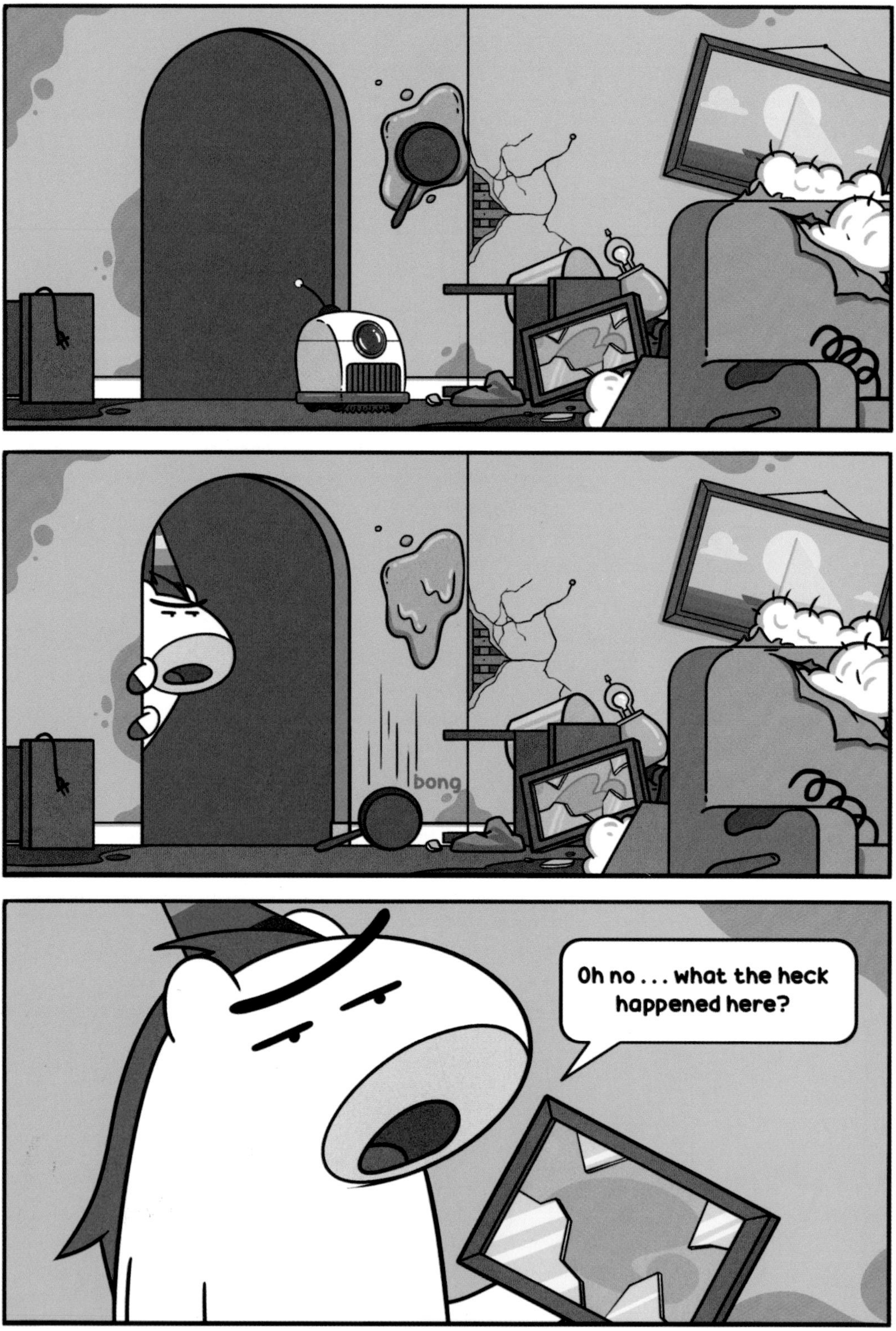
bong
Oh no . . . what the heck happened here?

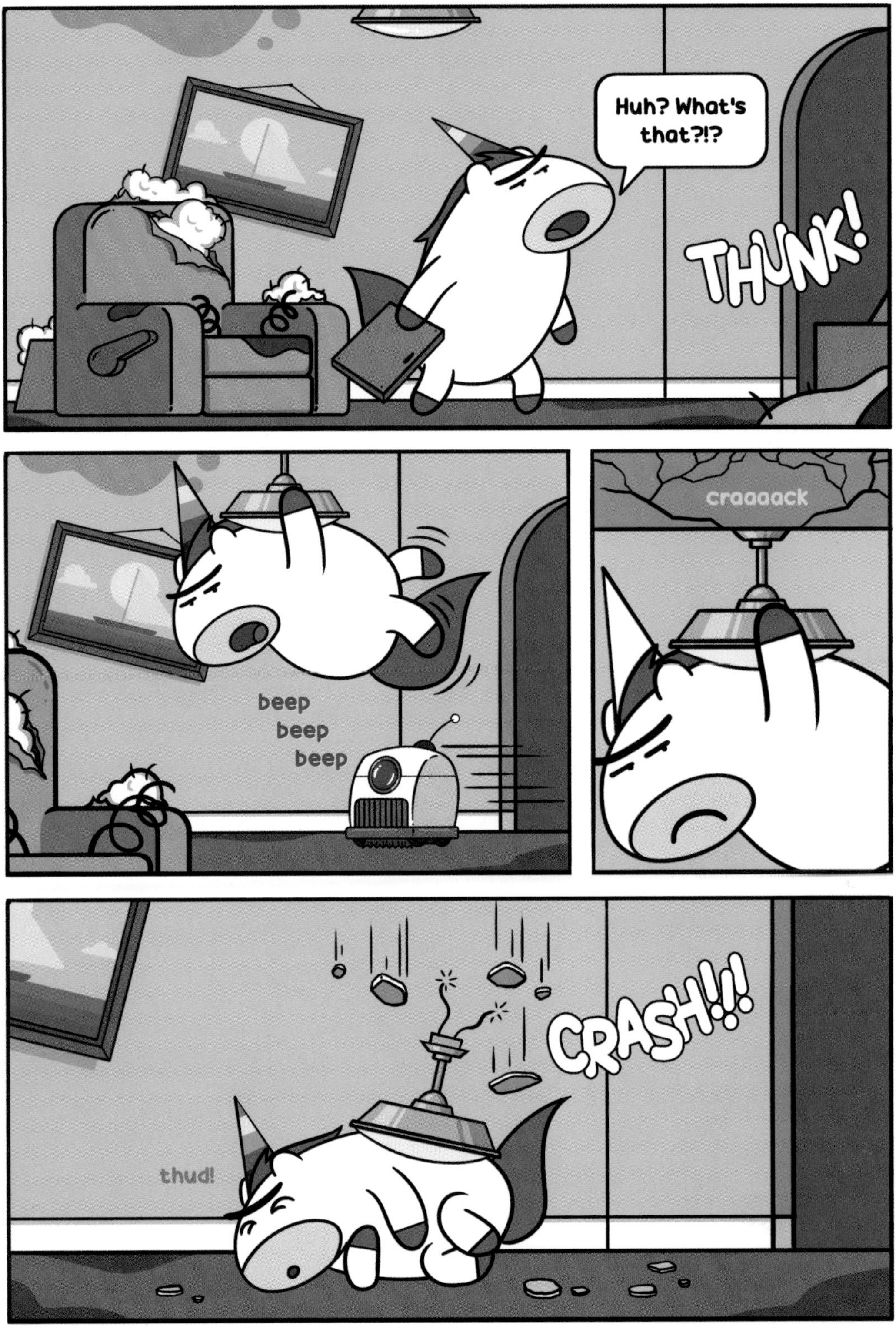
Huh? What's that?!?
THUNK!
beep
beep
beep
craaaack
CRASH!!!
thud!

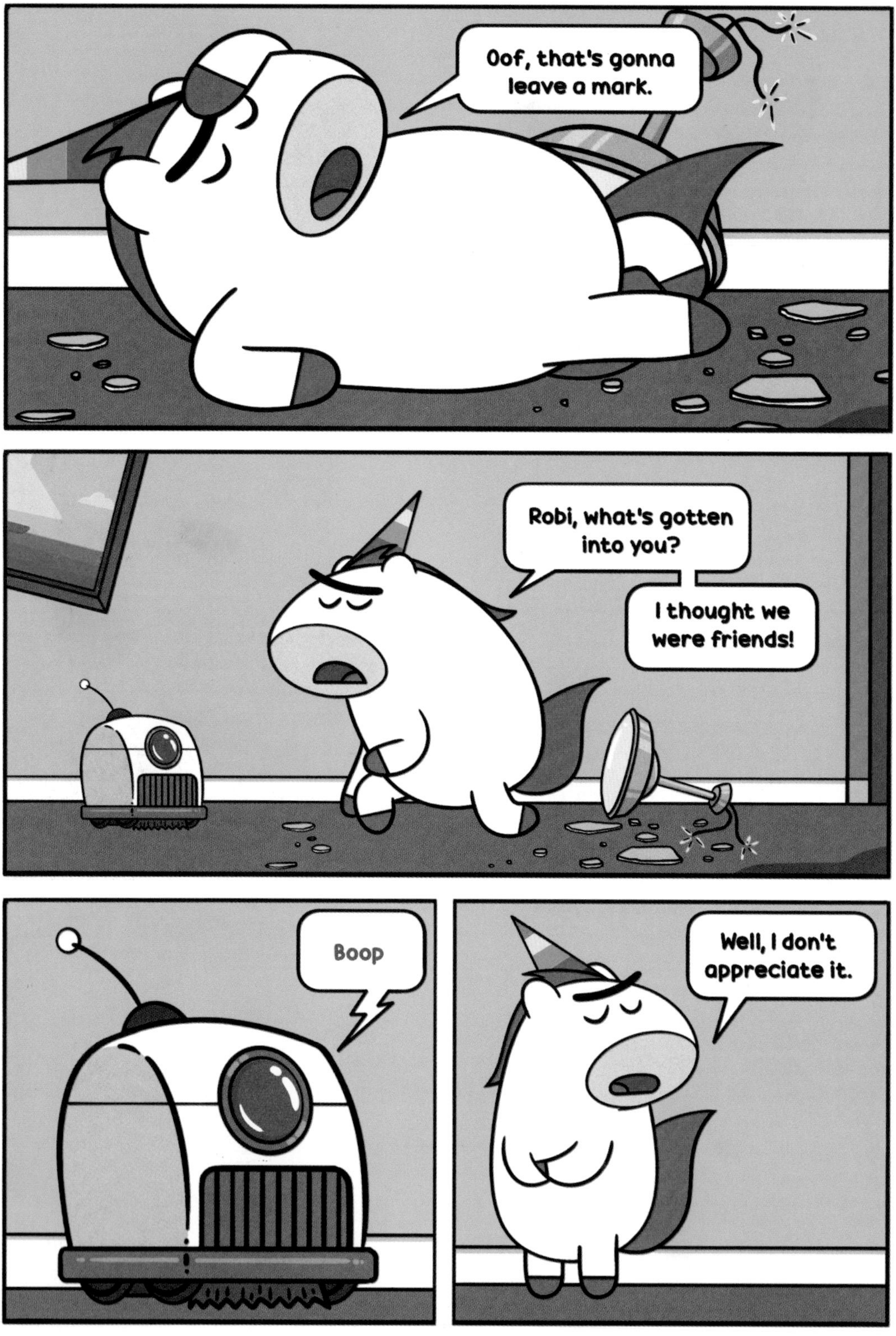
Oof, that's gonna leave a mark.
Robi, what's gotten into you?
I thought we were friends!
Boop
Well, I don't appreciate it.

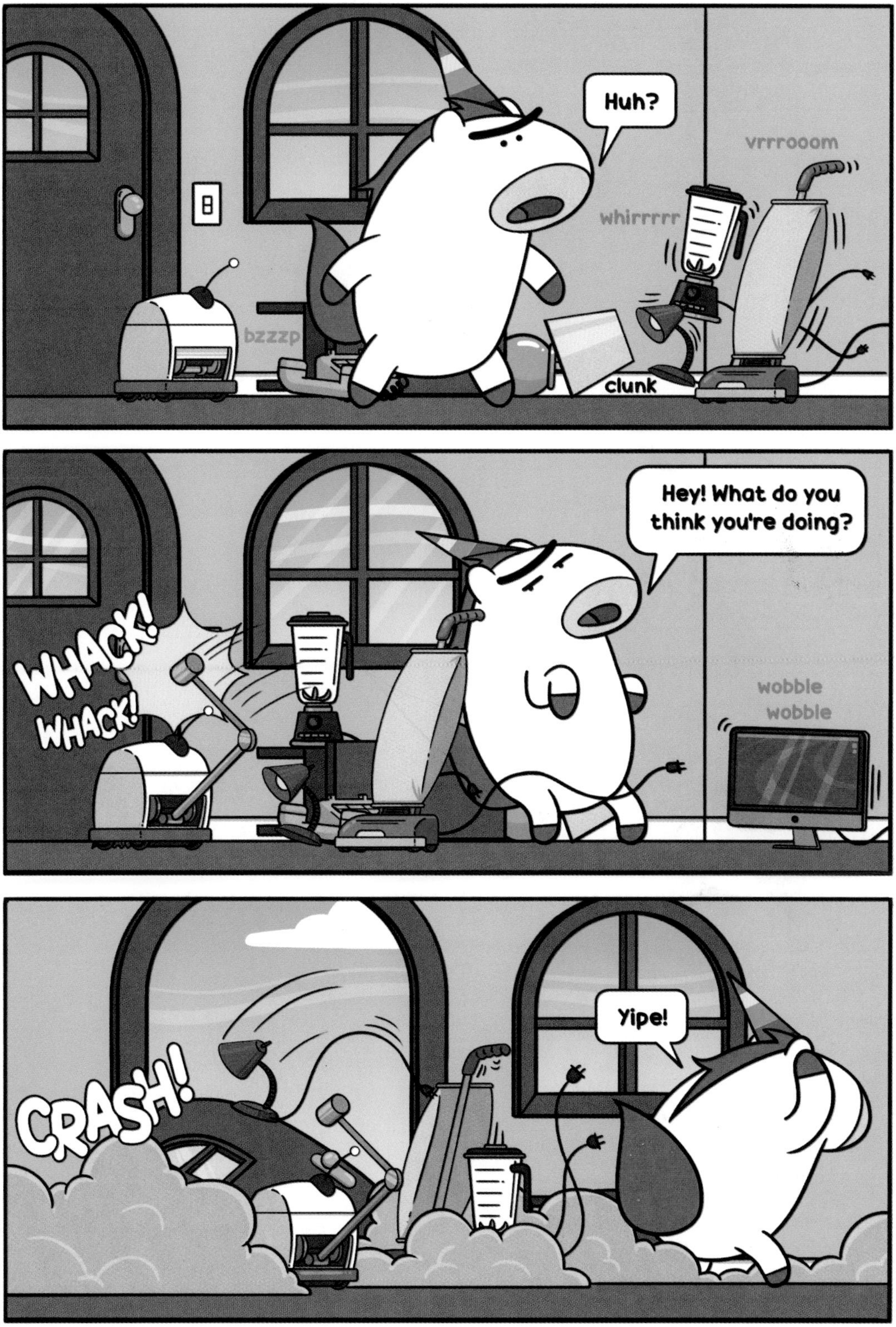
Huh?
vrrrooom
whirrrrr
bzzzp
clunk
Hey! What do you think you're doing?
WHACK!
WHACK!
wobble
wobble
CRASH!
Yipe!

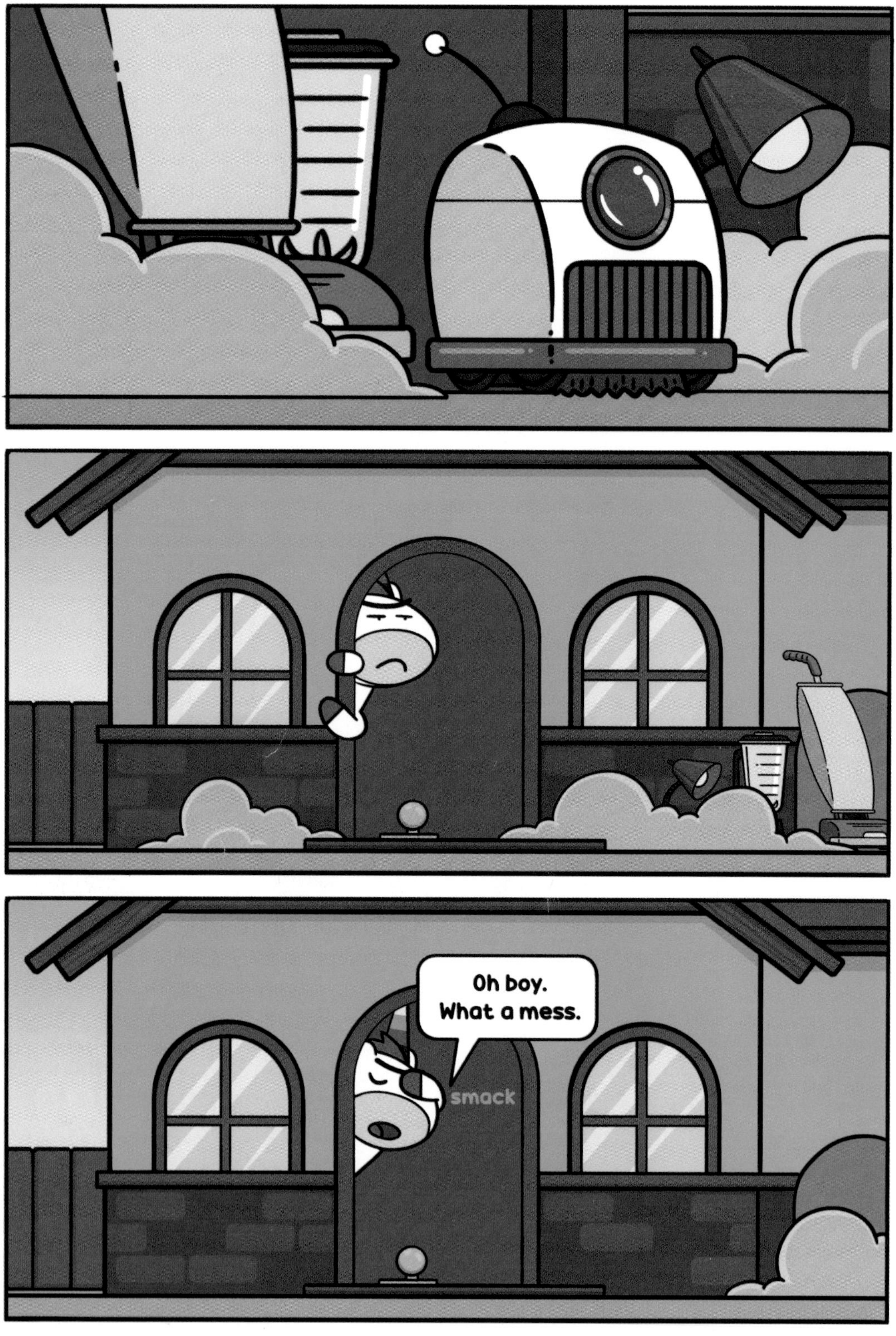
Oh boy.
What a mess.
smack

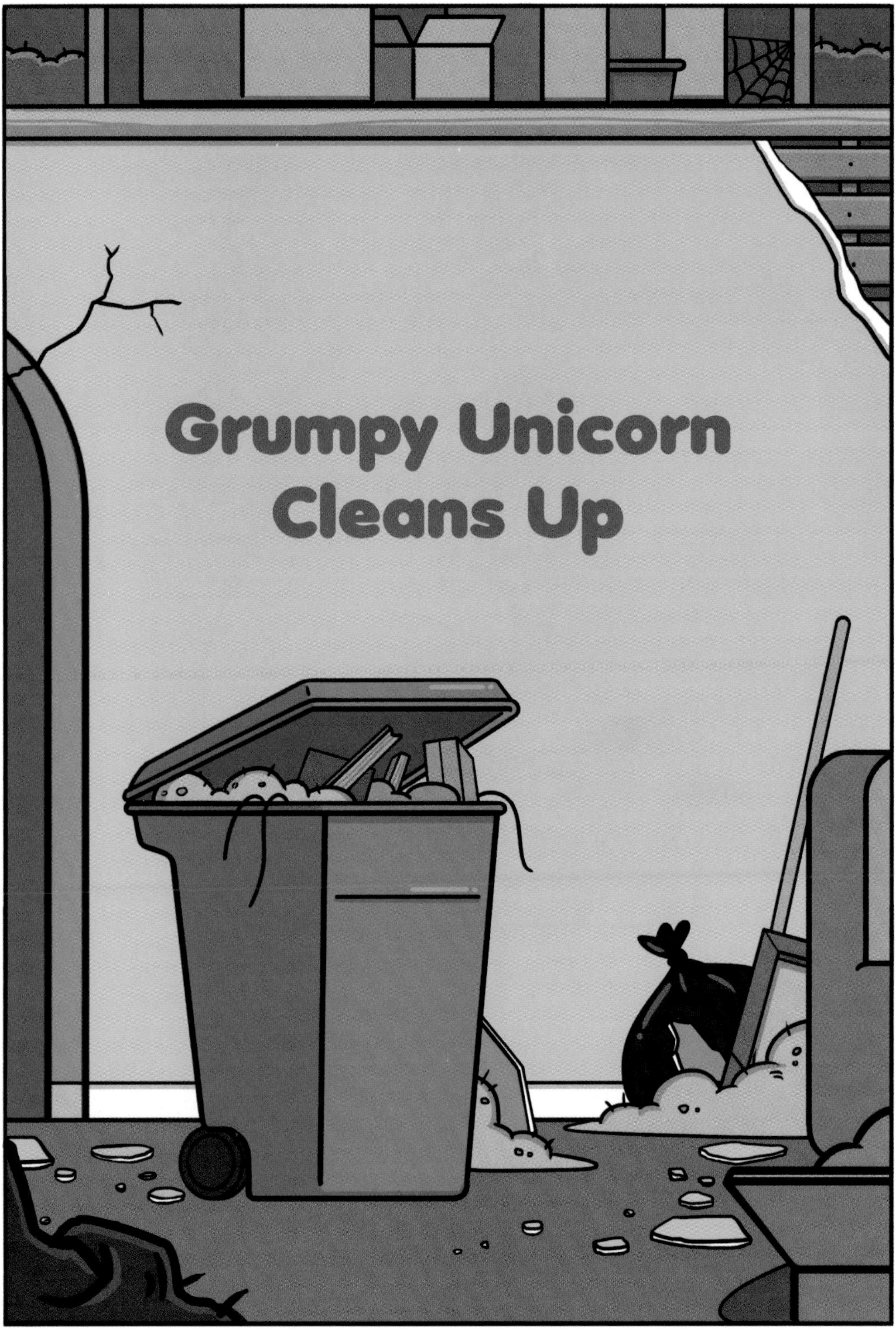
Grumpy Unicorn
Cleans Up

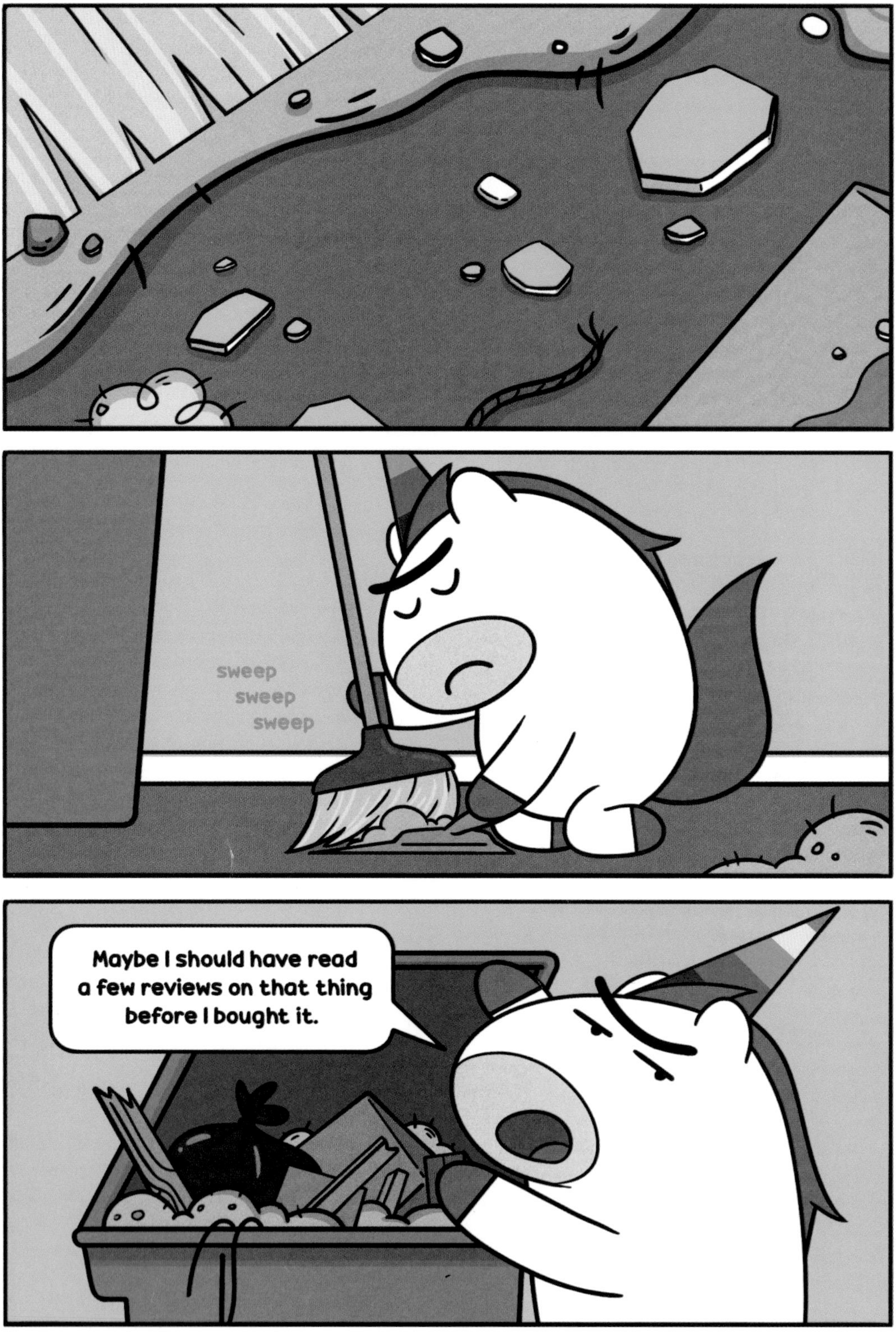
sweep
sweep
sweep
Maybe I should have read a few reviews on that thing before I bought it.

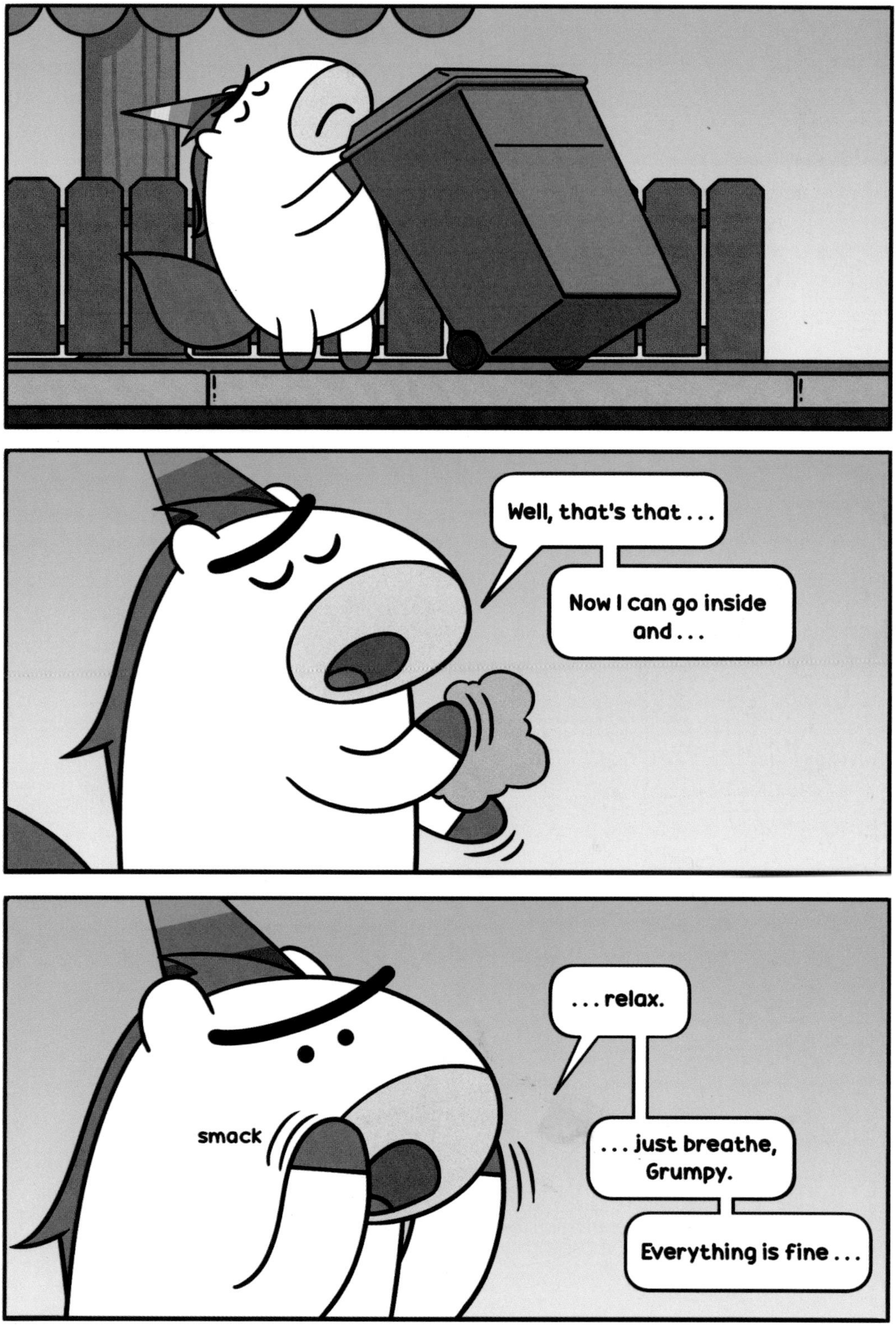
Well, that's that . . .
Now I can go inside and . . .
. . . relax.
smack
. . . just breathe, Grumpy.
Everything is fine . . .

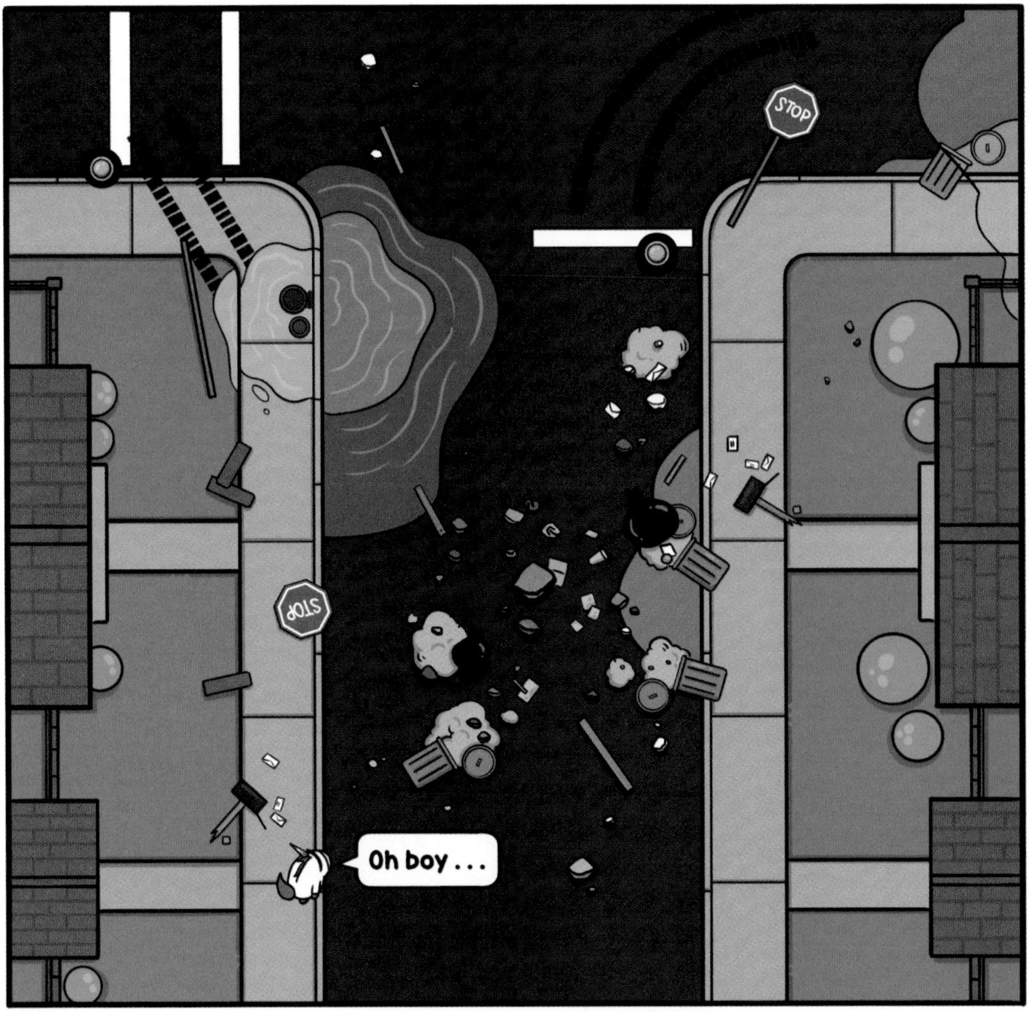
STOP
STOP
Oh boy . . .

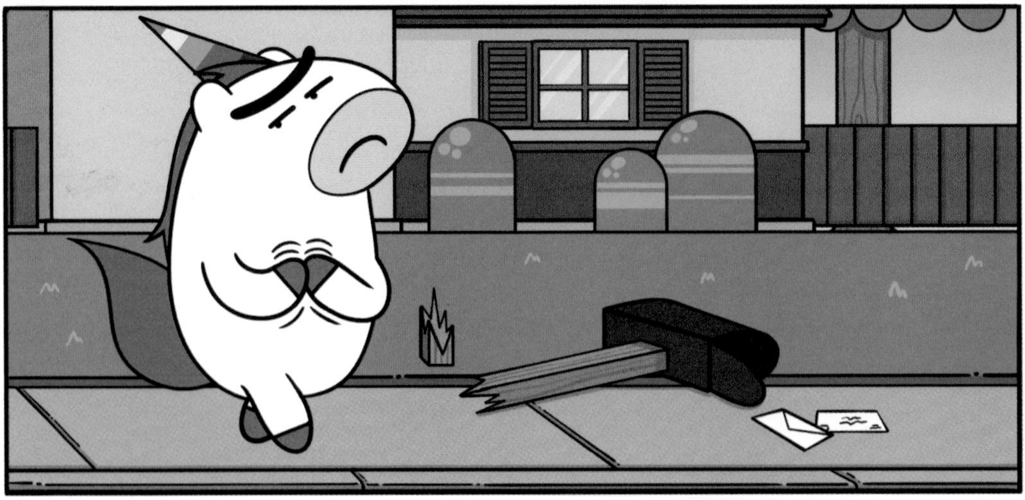

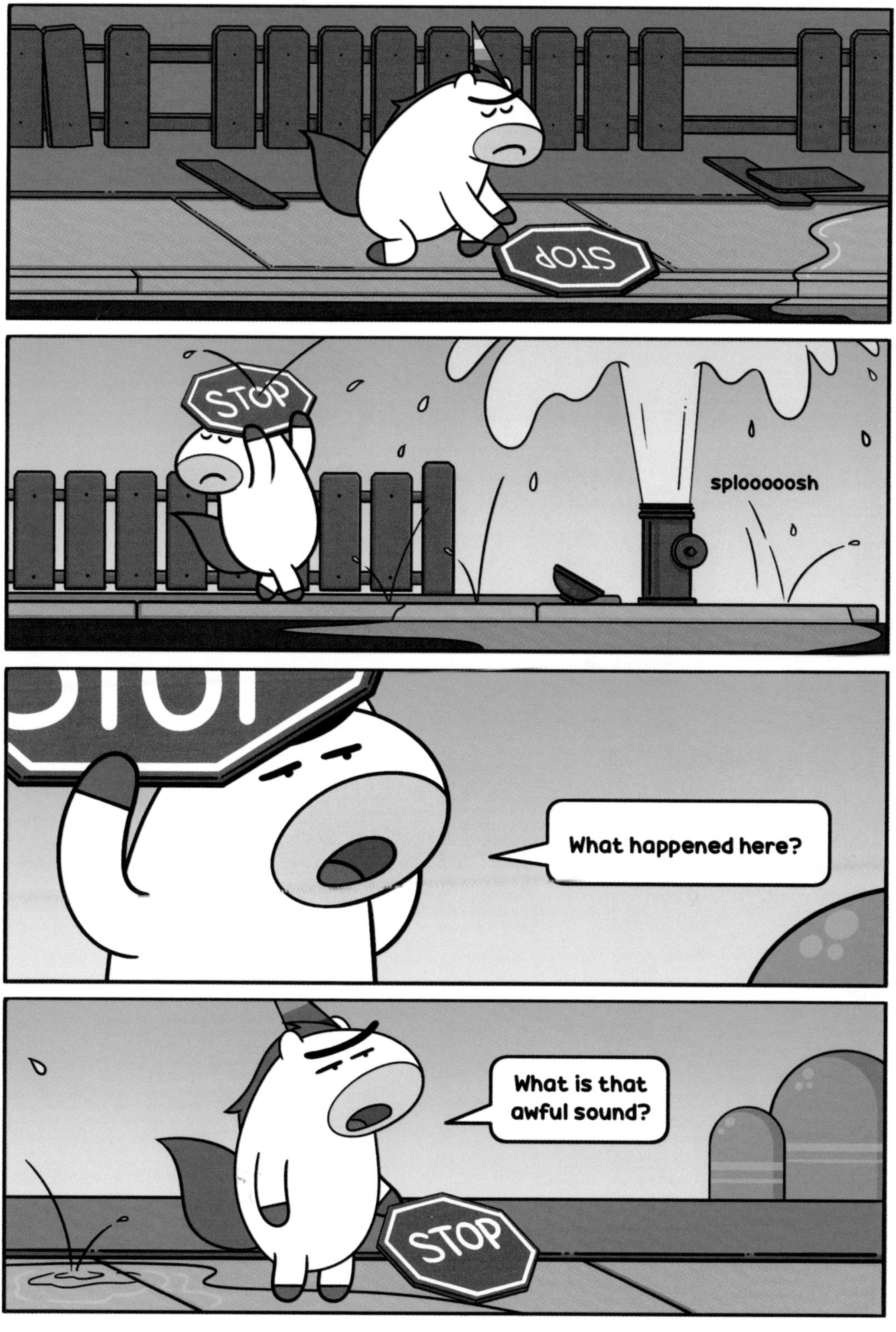
STOP
STOP
splooooosh
What happened here?
What is that awful sound?
STOP

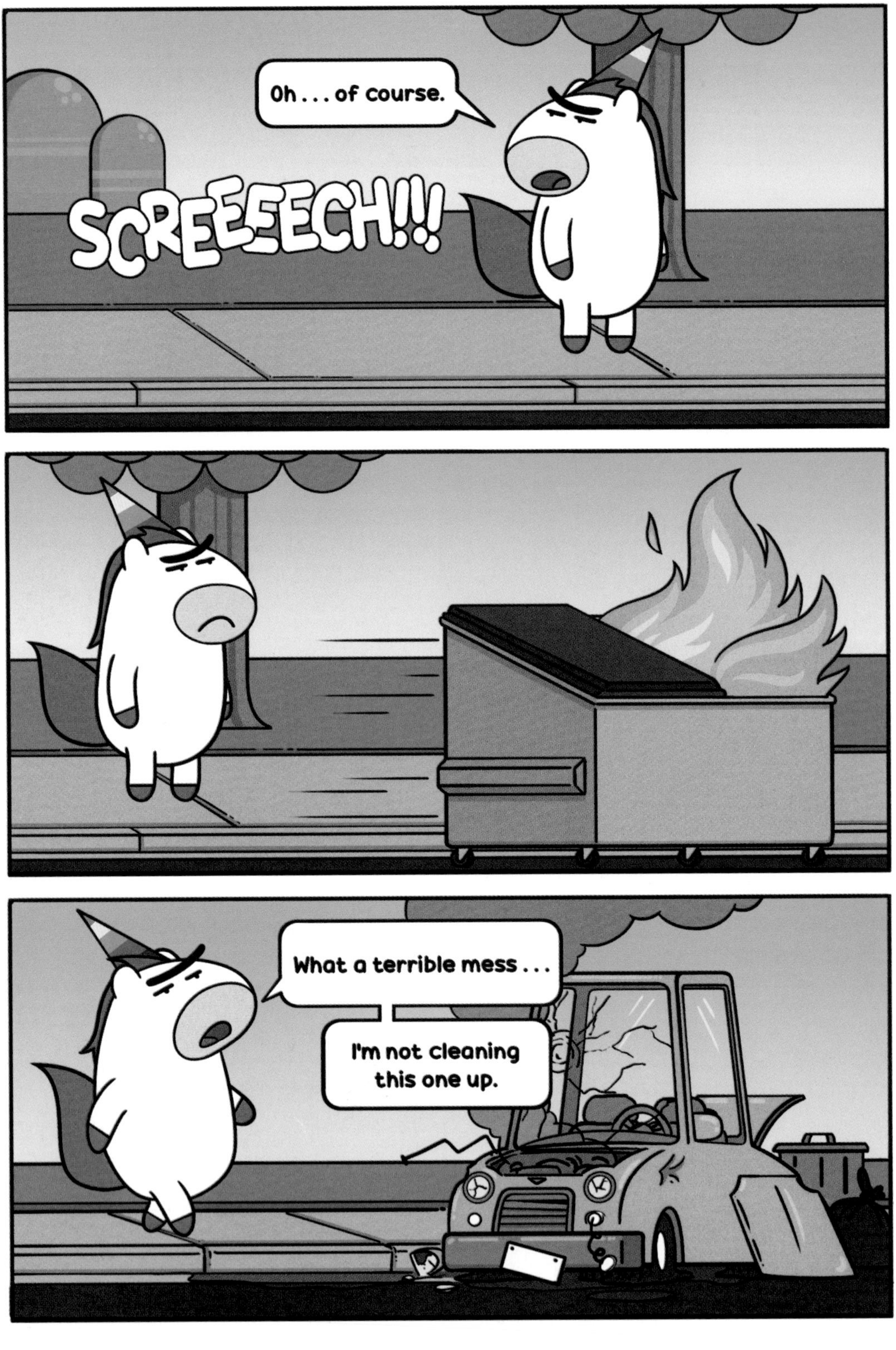
Oh . . . of course.
SCREEEEECH!!!
What a terrible mess . . .
I'm not cleaning this one up.

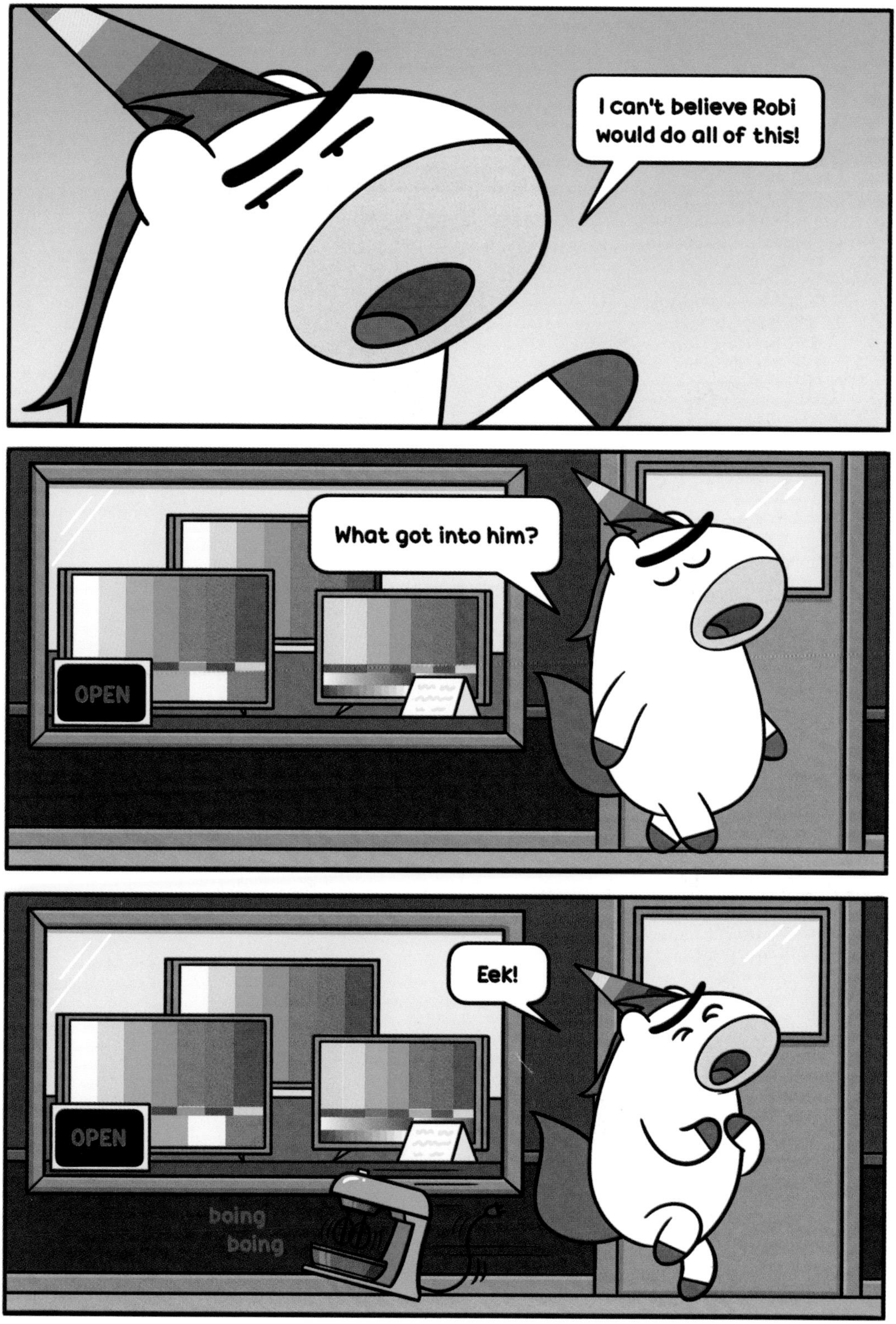
I can't believe Robi would do all of this!
What got into him?
OPEN
Eek!
OPEN
boing
boing

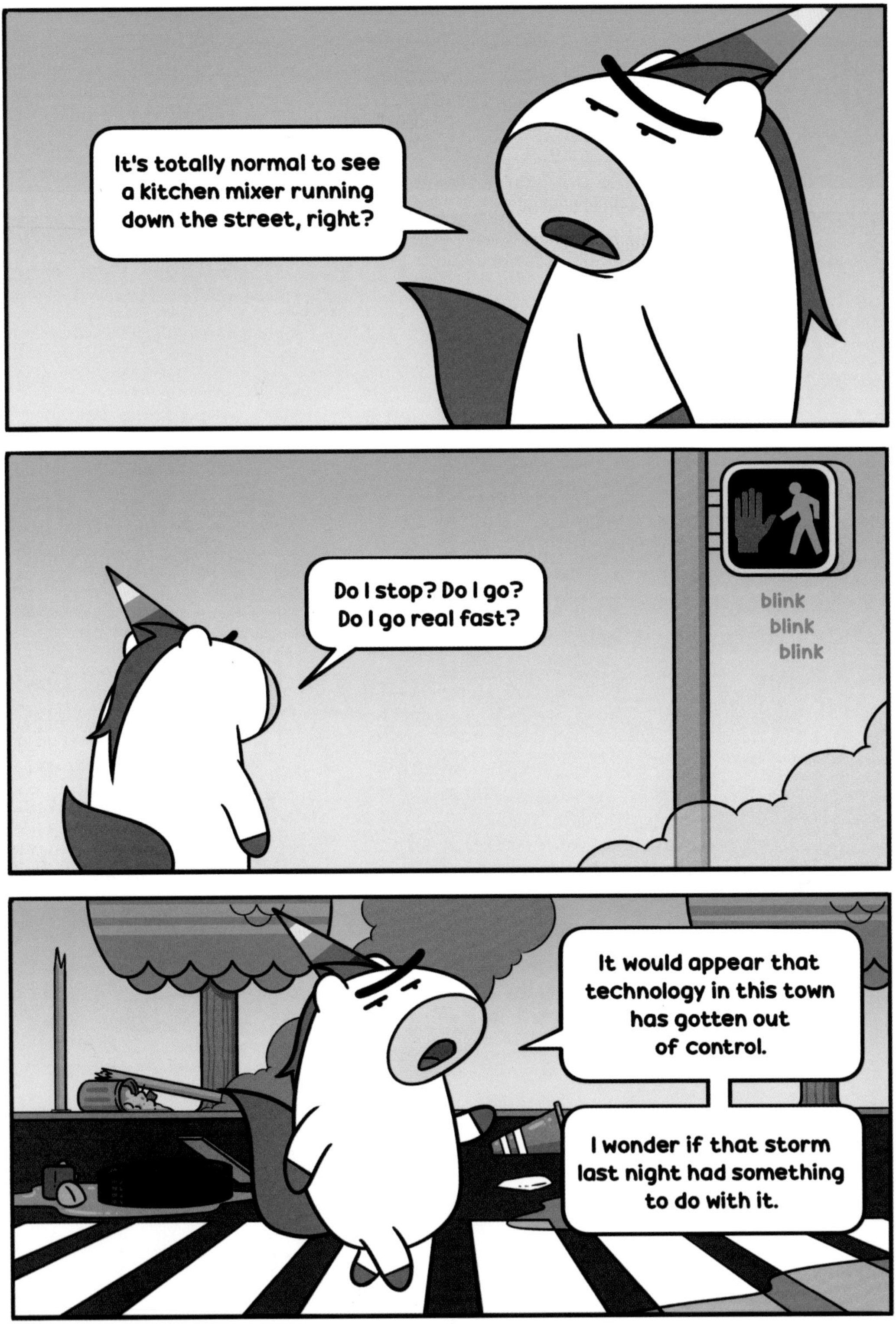
It's totally normal to see a kitchen mixer running down the street, right?
Do I stop? Do I go? Do I go real fast?
blink
blink
blink
It would appear that technology in this town has gotten out of control.
I wonder if that storm last night had something to do with it.

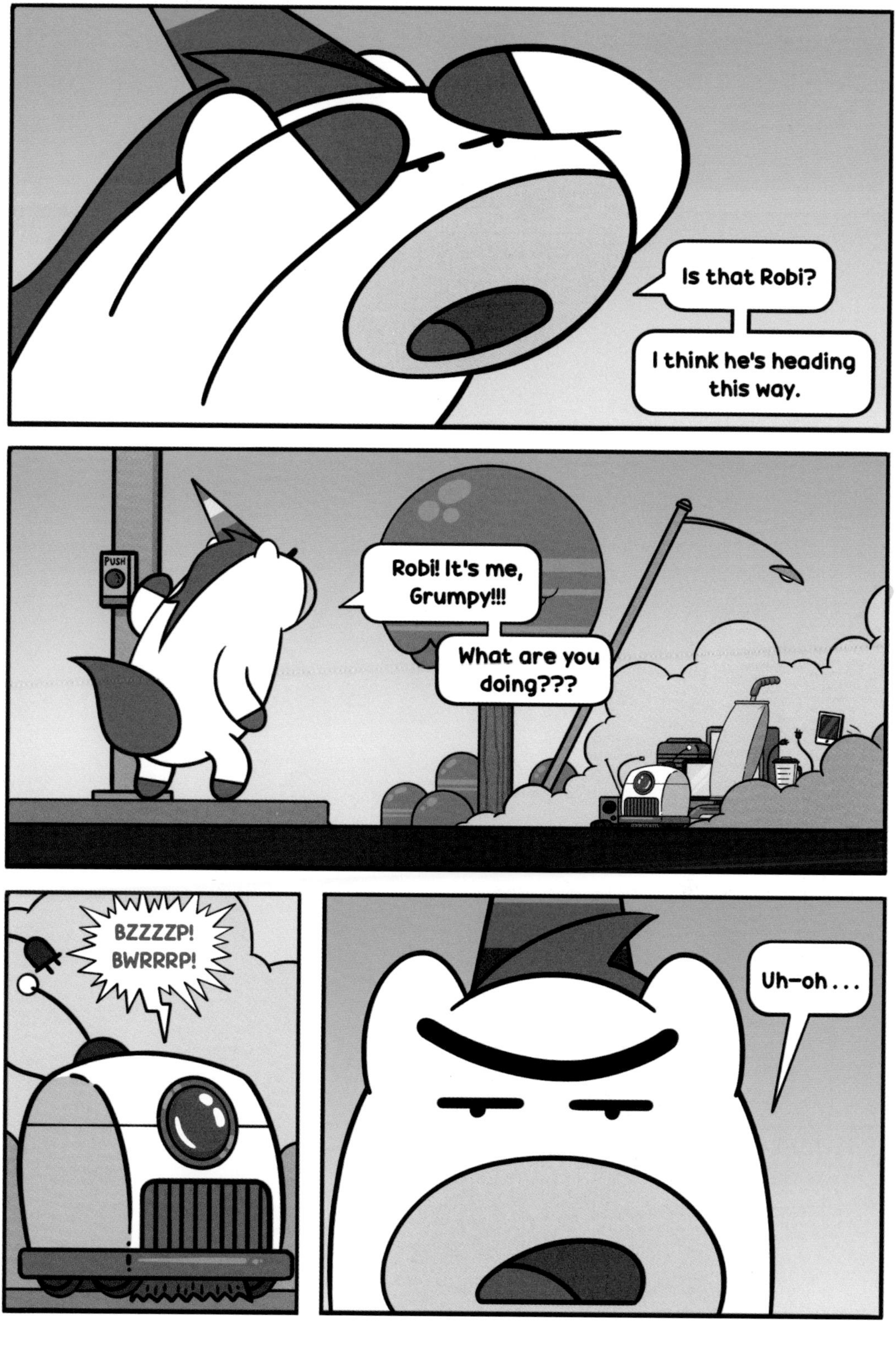
Is that Robi?
I think he's heading this way.
Robi! It's me, Grumpy!!!
What are you doing???
PUSH
BZZZZP! BWRRRP!
Uh-oh . . .

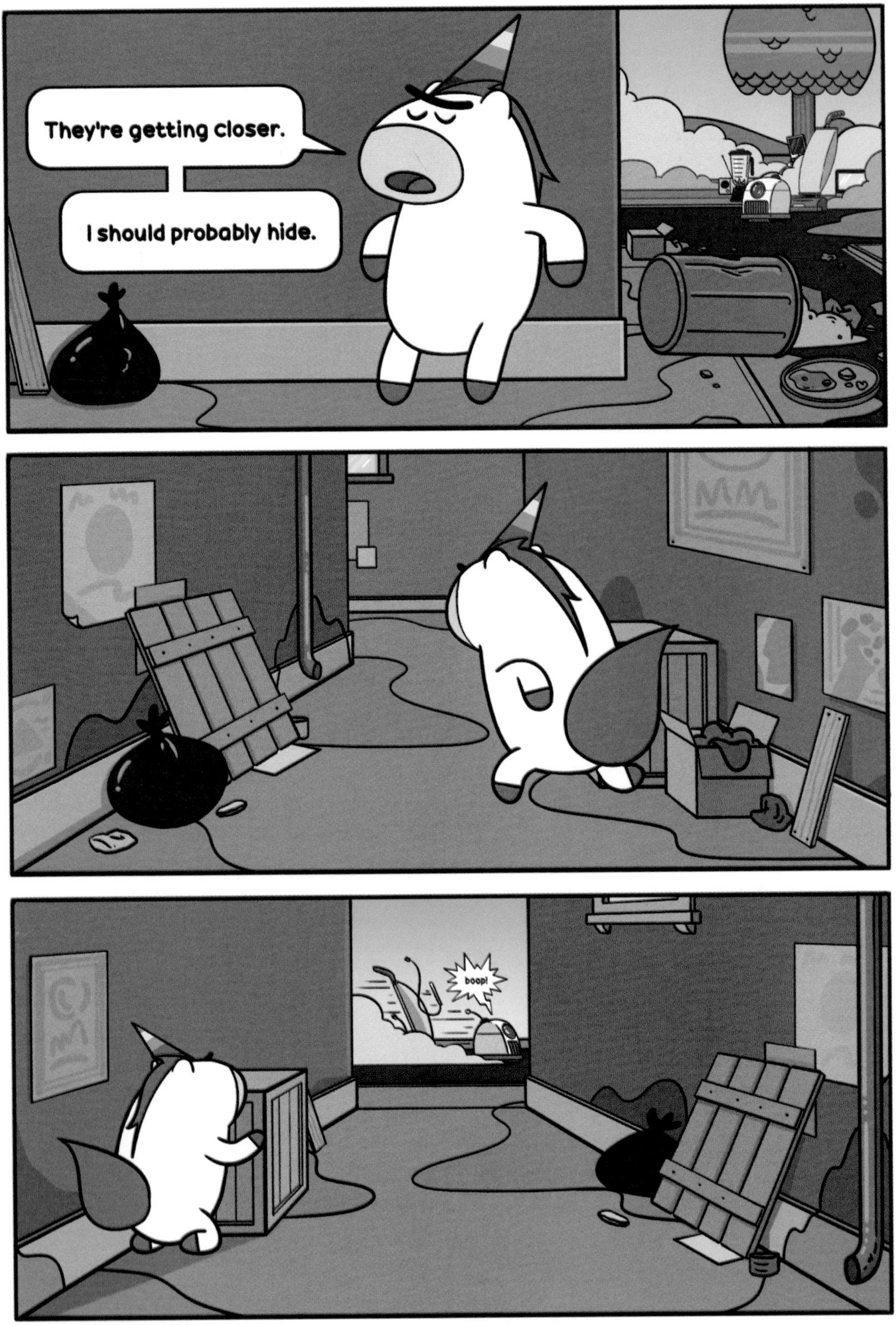
They're getting closer.
I should probably hide.
boop!

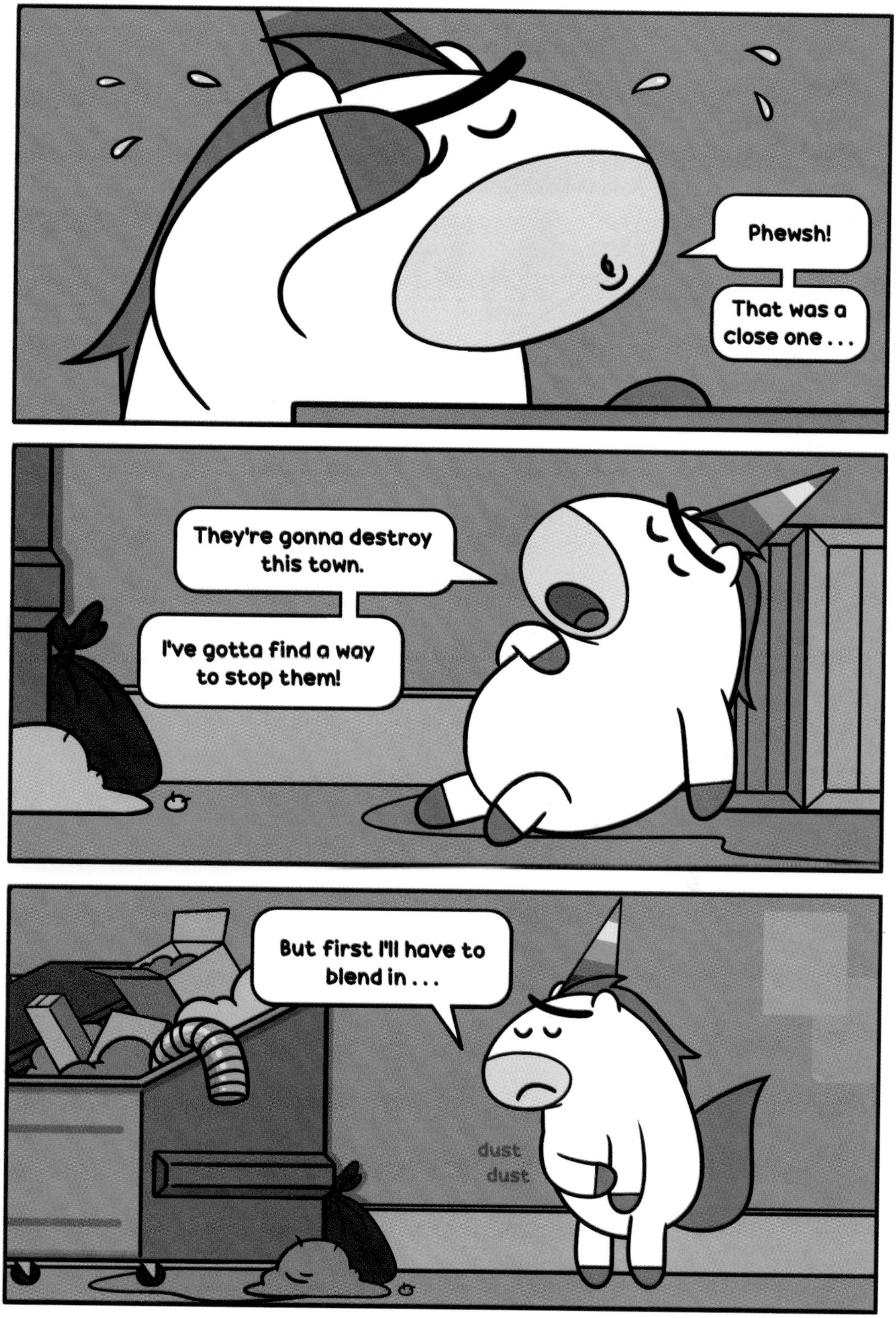

Phewsh!
That was a close one . . .
They're gonna destroy this town.
I've gotta find a way to stop them!
But first I'll have to blend in . . .
dust
dust

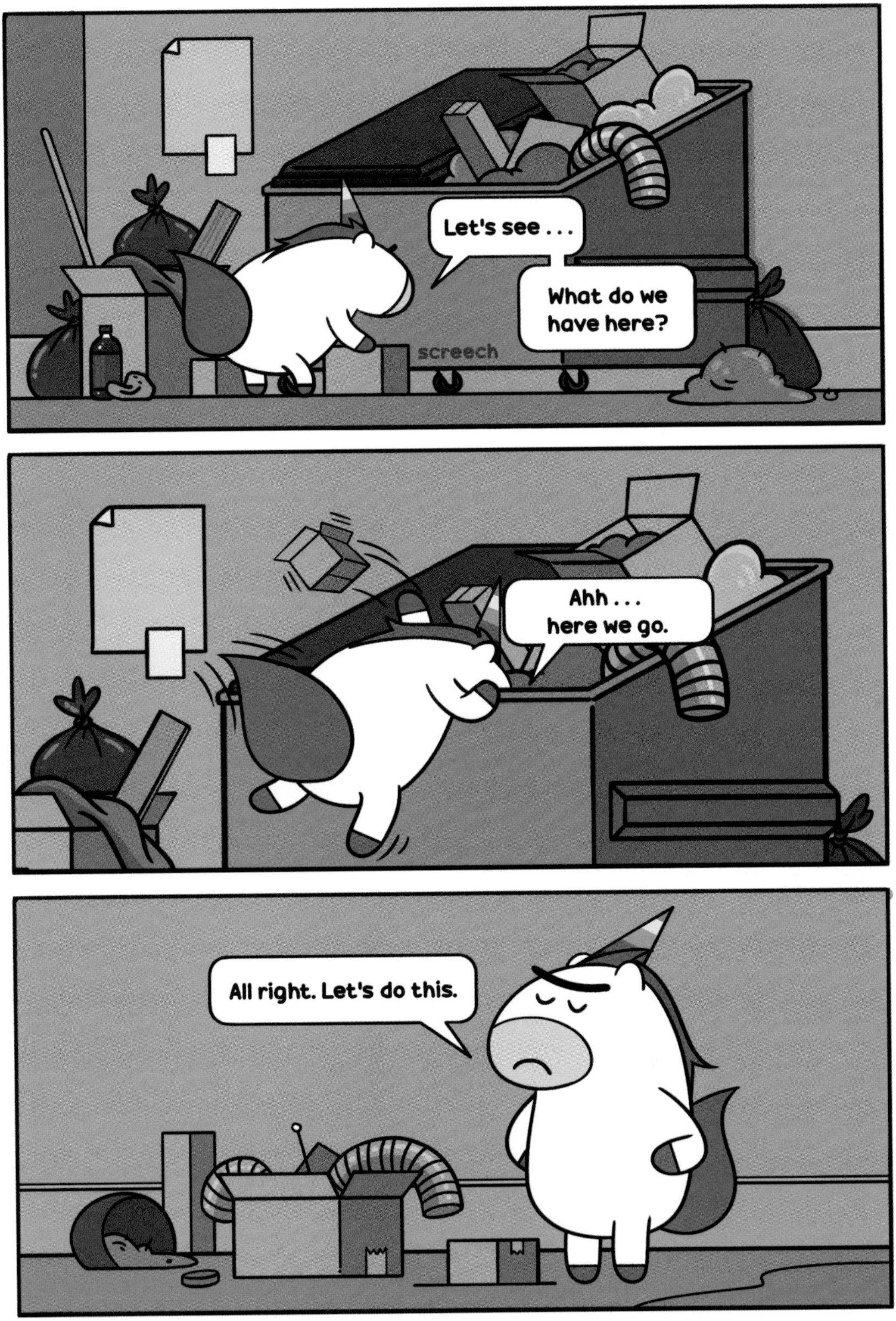
Let's see . . .
What do we have here?
screech
Ahh . . . here we go.
All right. Let's do this.

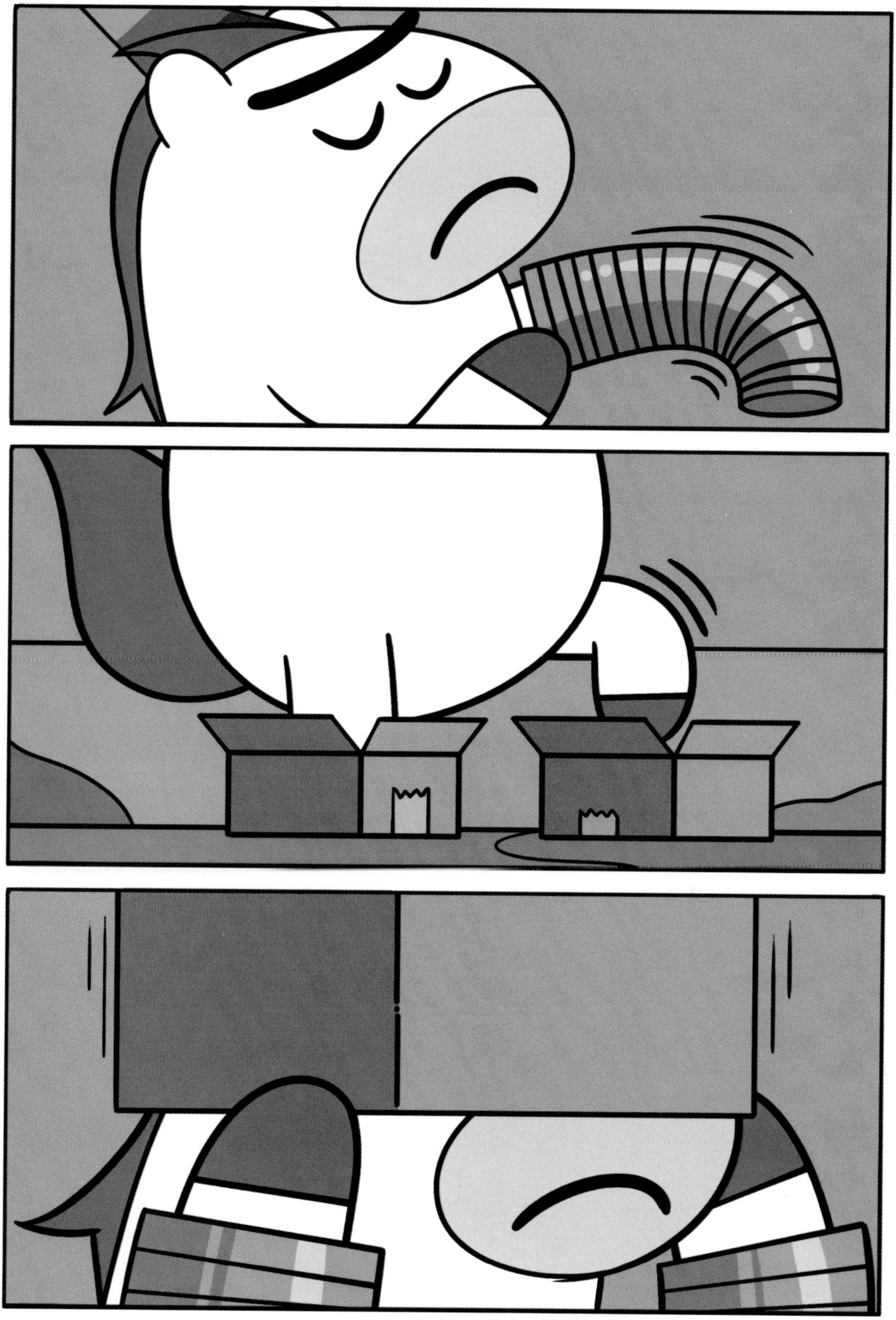

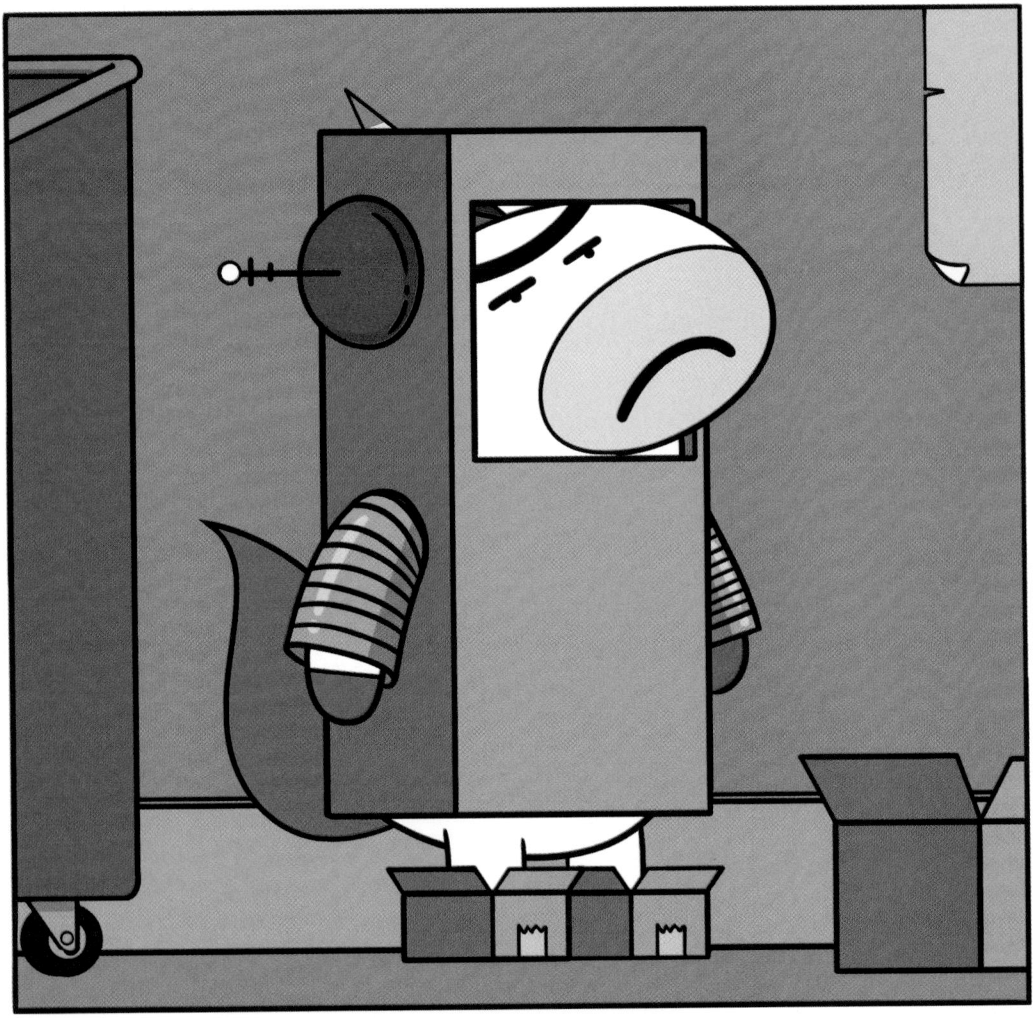

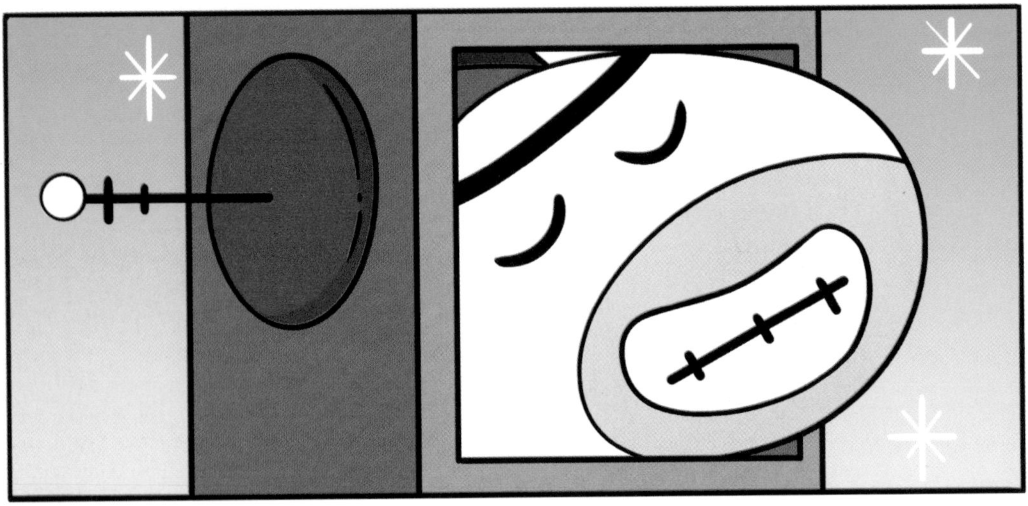

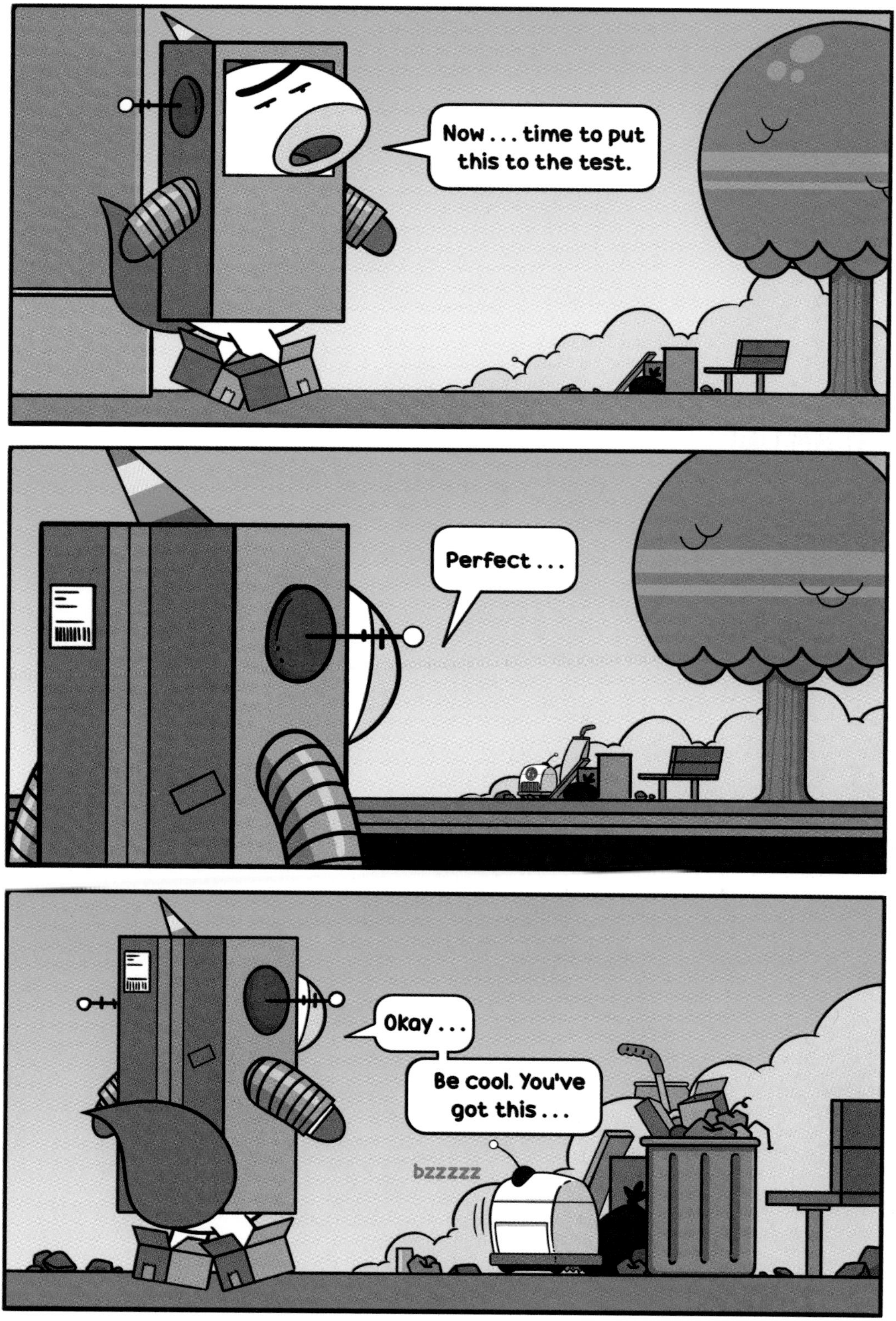
Now . . . time to put this to the test.
Perfect . . .
Okay . . .
Be cool. You've got this . . .
bzzzzz

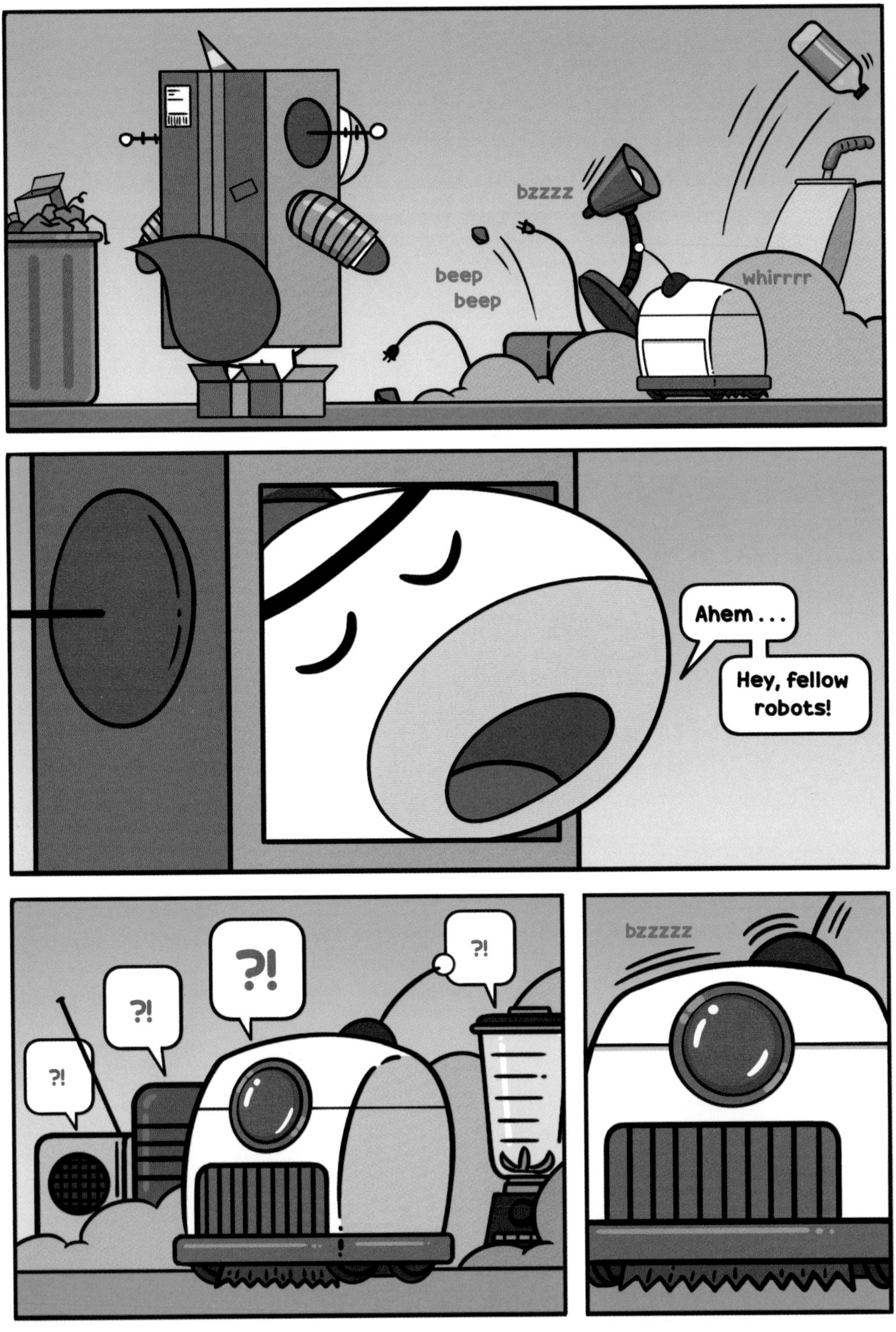
bzzzz
beep
beep
whirrrr
Ahem . . .
Hey, fellow robots!
?!
?!
?!
?!
bzzzzz

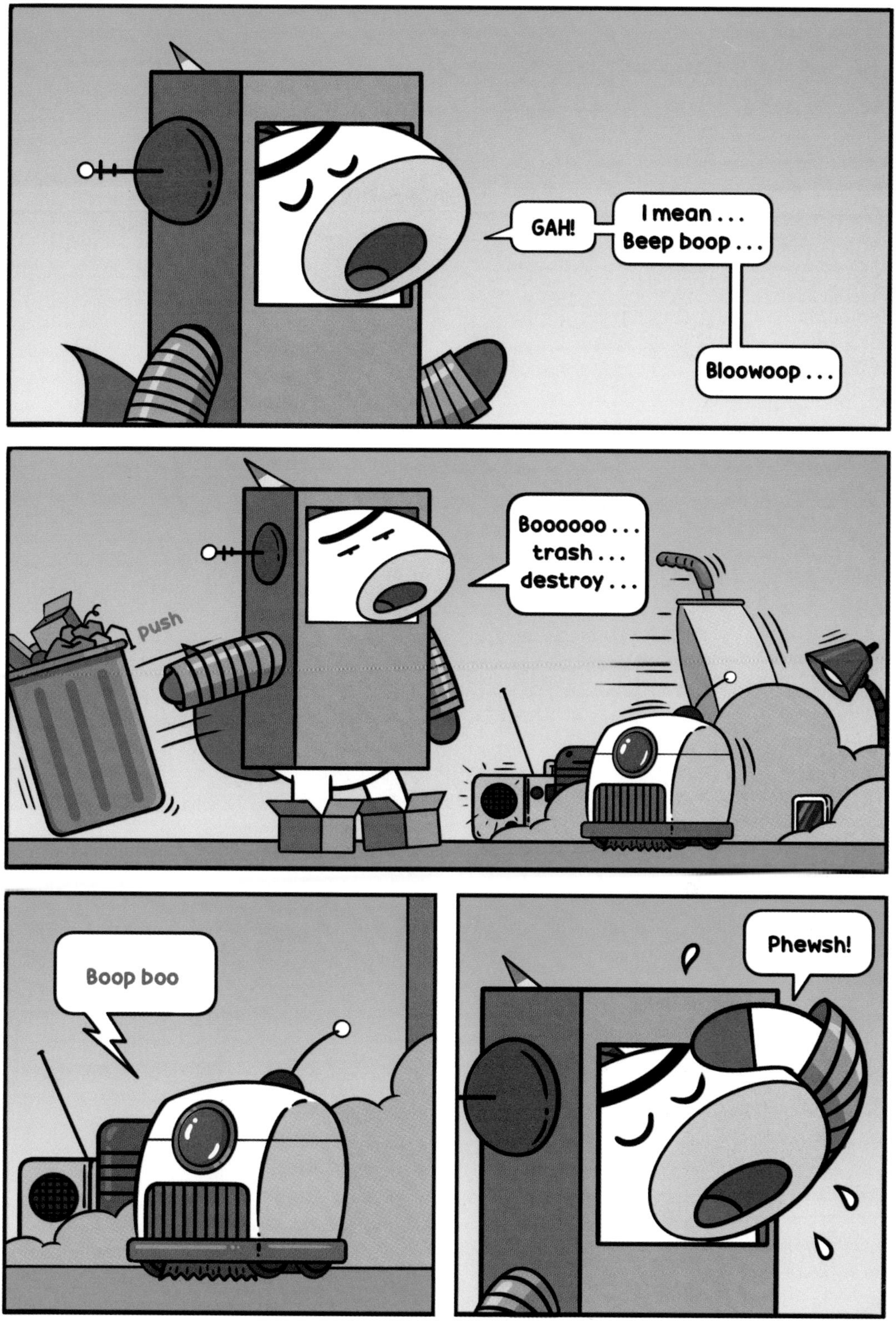
GAH!
I mean . . . Beep boop . . .
Bloowoop . . .
Boooooo . . . trash . . . destroy . . .
push
Boop boo
Phewsh!

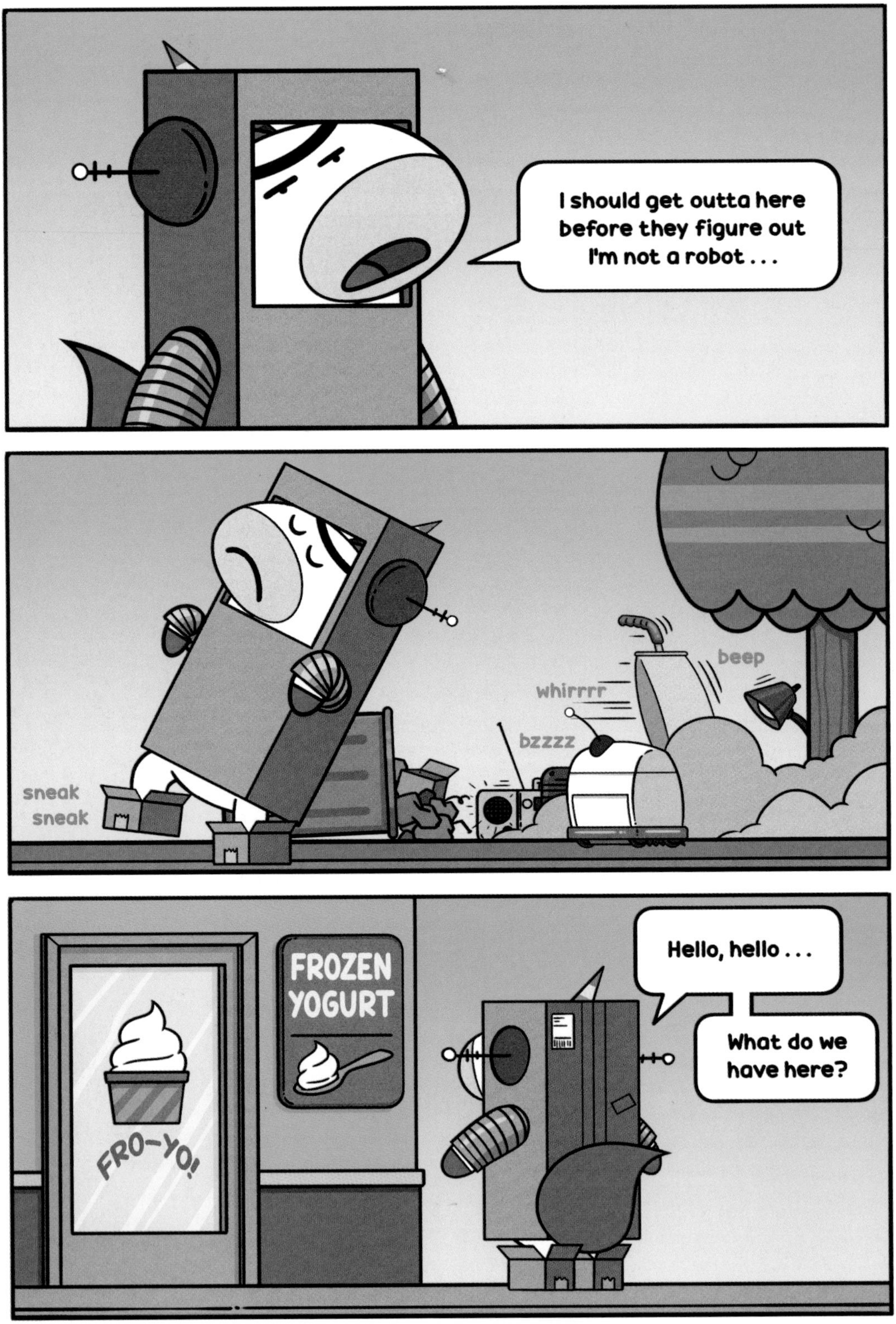
I should get outta here before they figure out I'm not a robot . . .
sneak sneak
whirrrr
bzzzz
beep
FROZEN YOGURT
FRO-YO!
Hello, hello . . .
What do we have here?

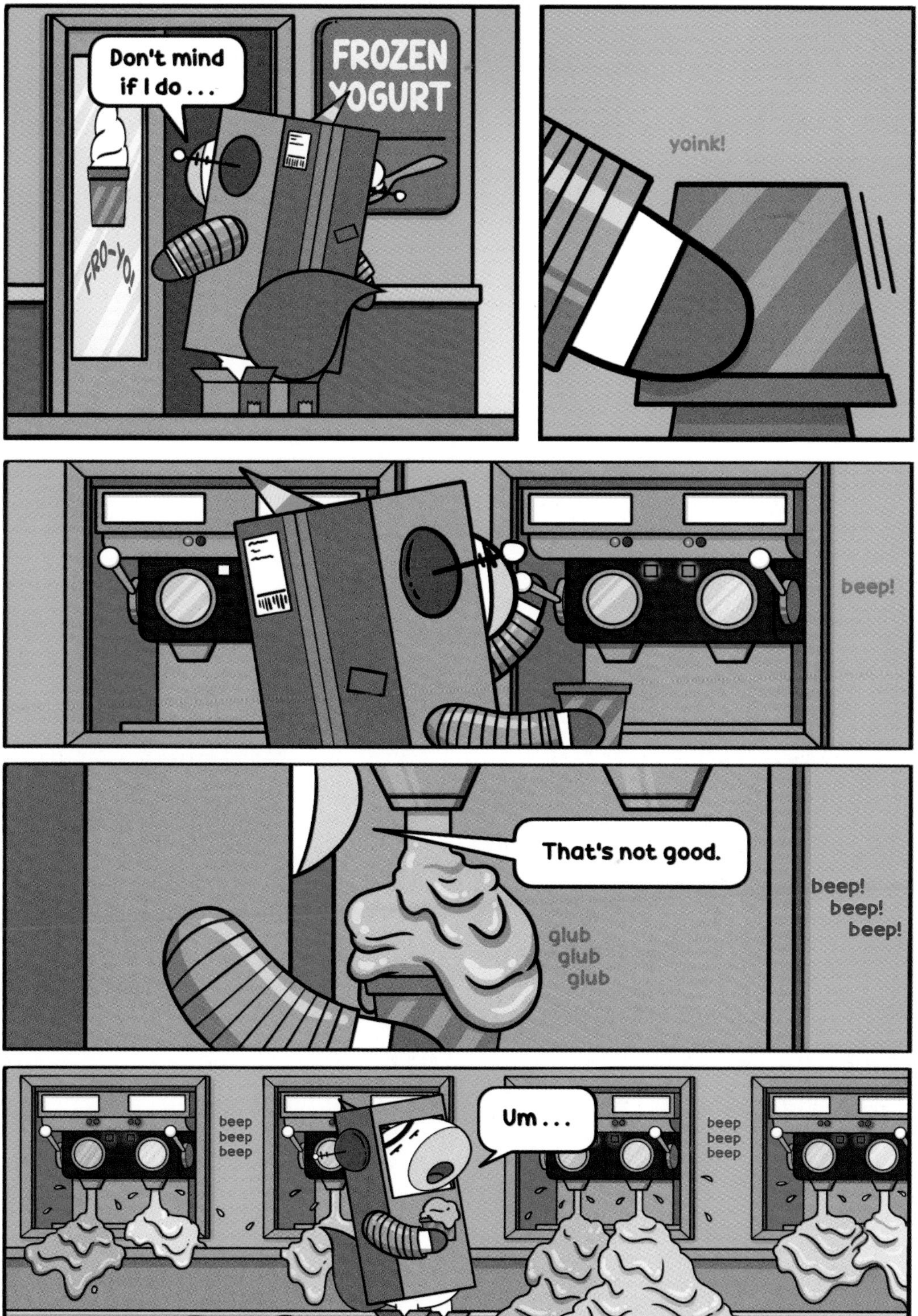
Don't mind if I do . . .
FROZEN YOGURT
FRO-YO!
yoink!
beep!
That's not good.
glub glub glub
beep! beep! beep!
beep beep beep
Um . . .
beep beep beep

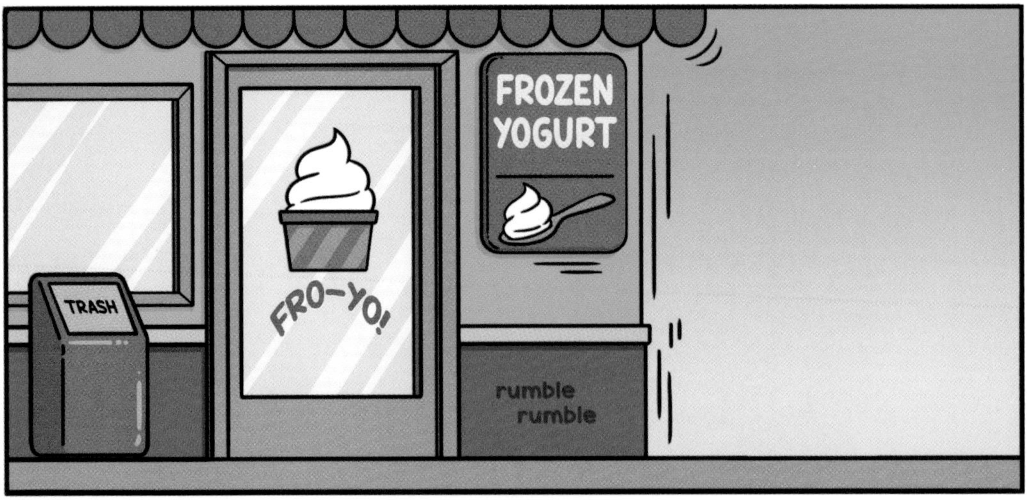
TRASH
FRO-YO!
FROZEN YOGURT
rumble
rumble

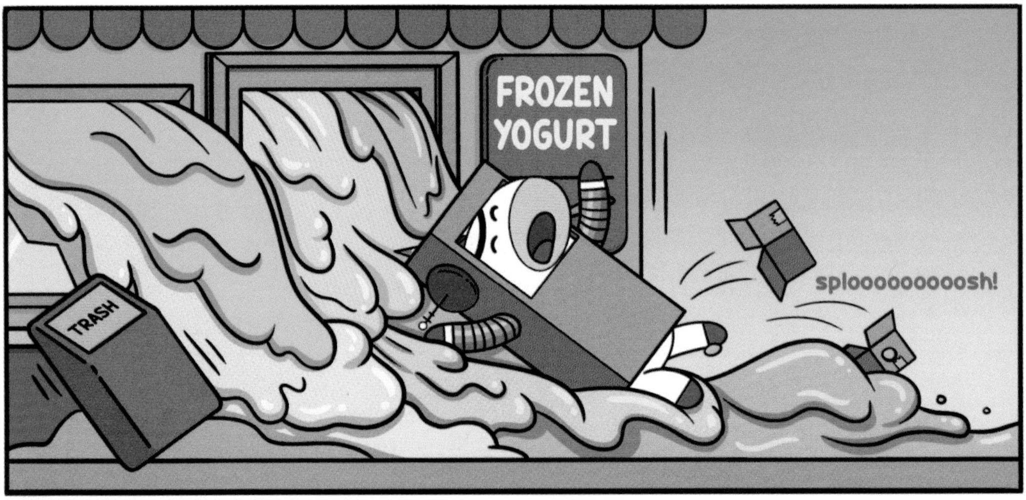
FROZEN YOGURT
TRASH
splooooooooosh!

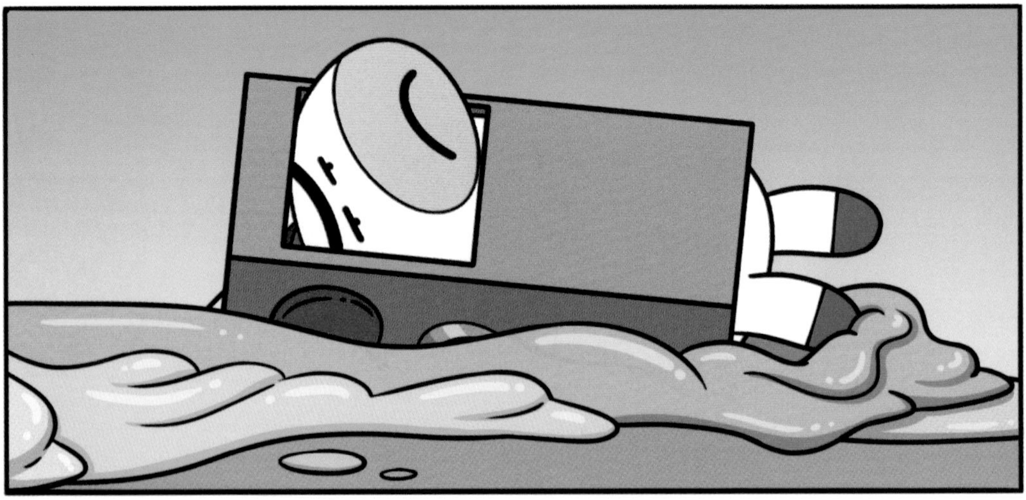

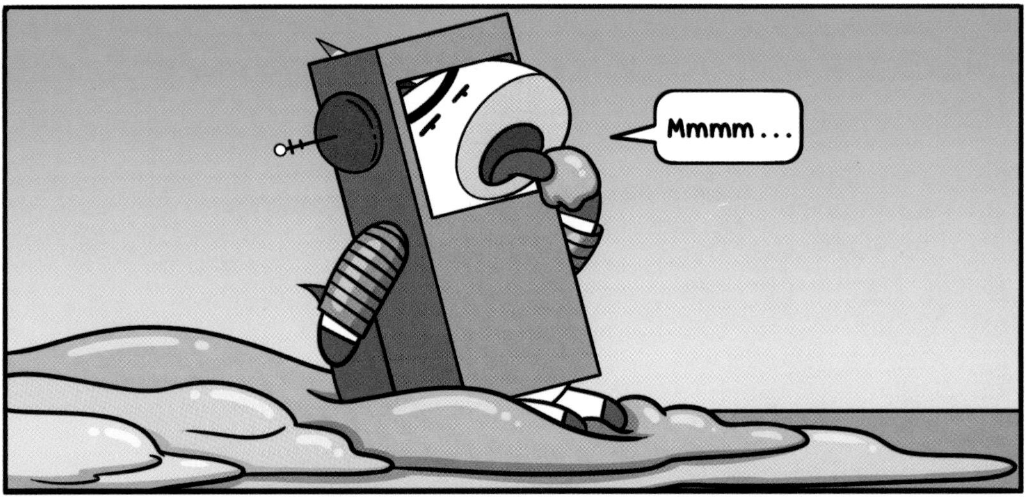
Mmmm . . .

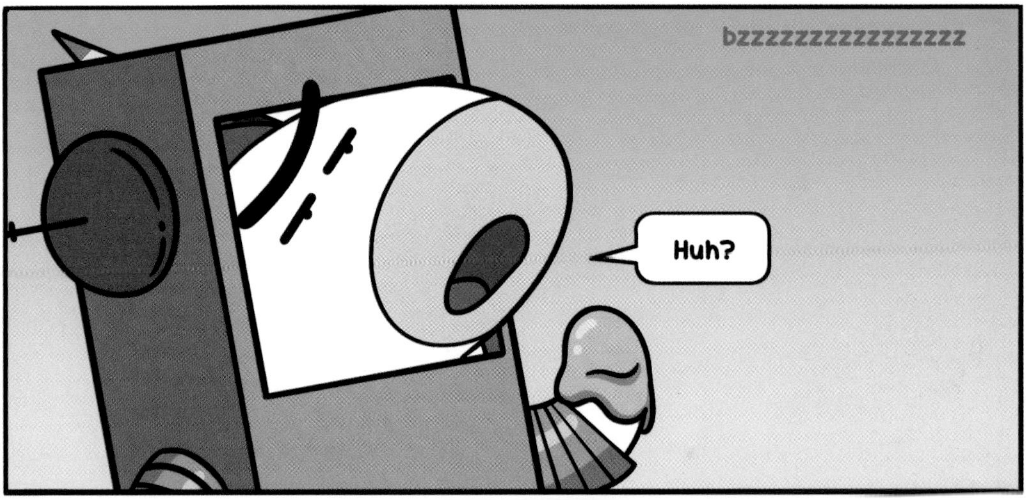
bzzzzzzzzzzzzzzzz
Huh?

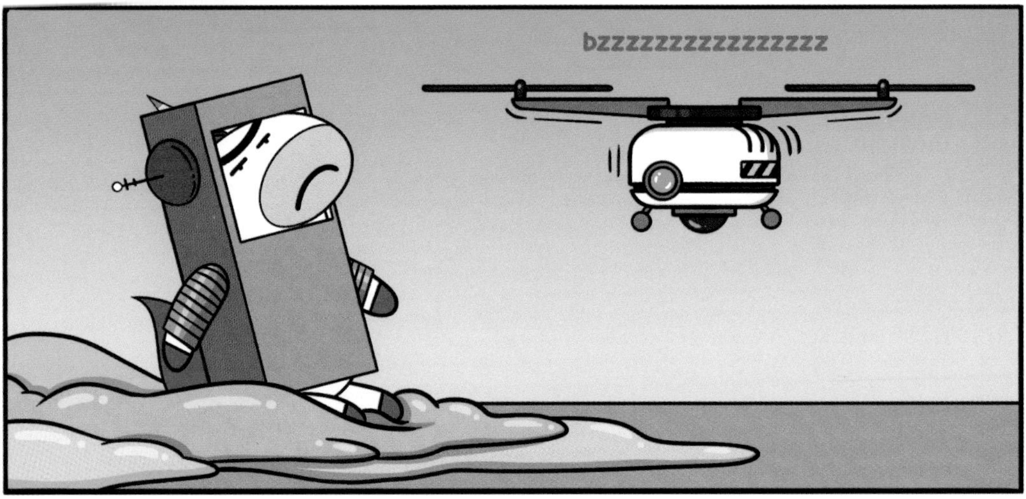
bzzzzzzzzzzzzzzzz

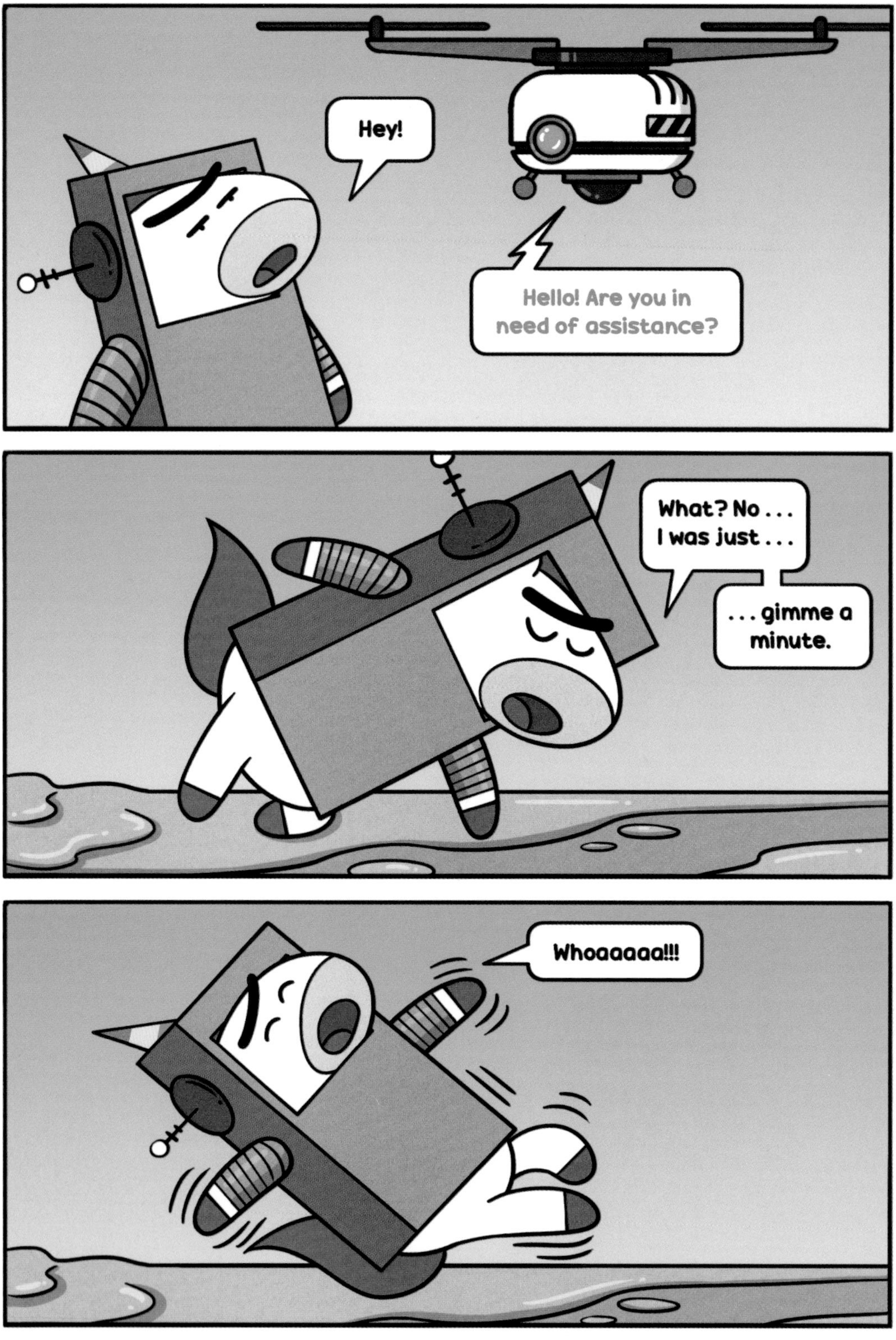
Hey!
Hello! Are you in need of assistance?
What? No . . . I was just . . .
. . . gimme a minute.
Whoaaaaa!!!

bzzzzzzz
booooooop
bzzzzzzz
Hello! You have been scanned!
You appear to be defective!
Please . . . remain calm!
bzzzzzzz
You are a VERY heavy robot!
How dare you.

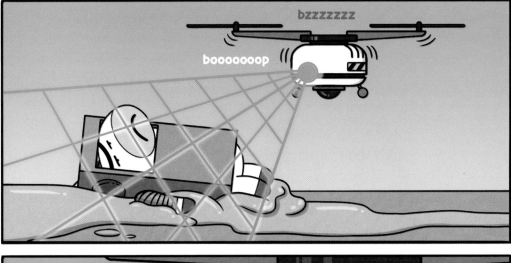

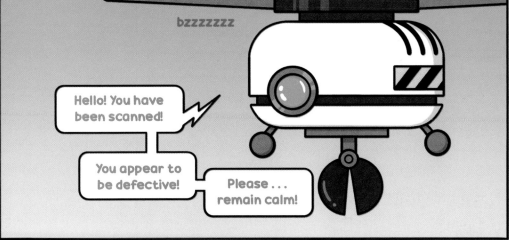

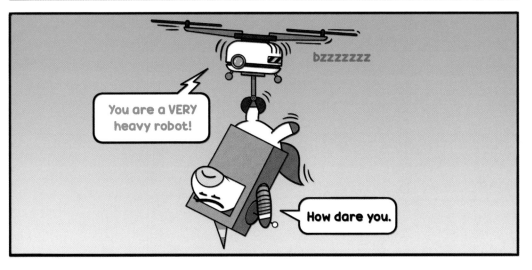

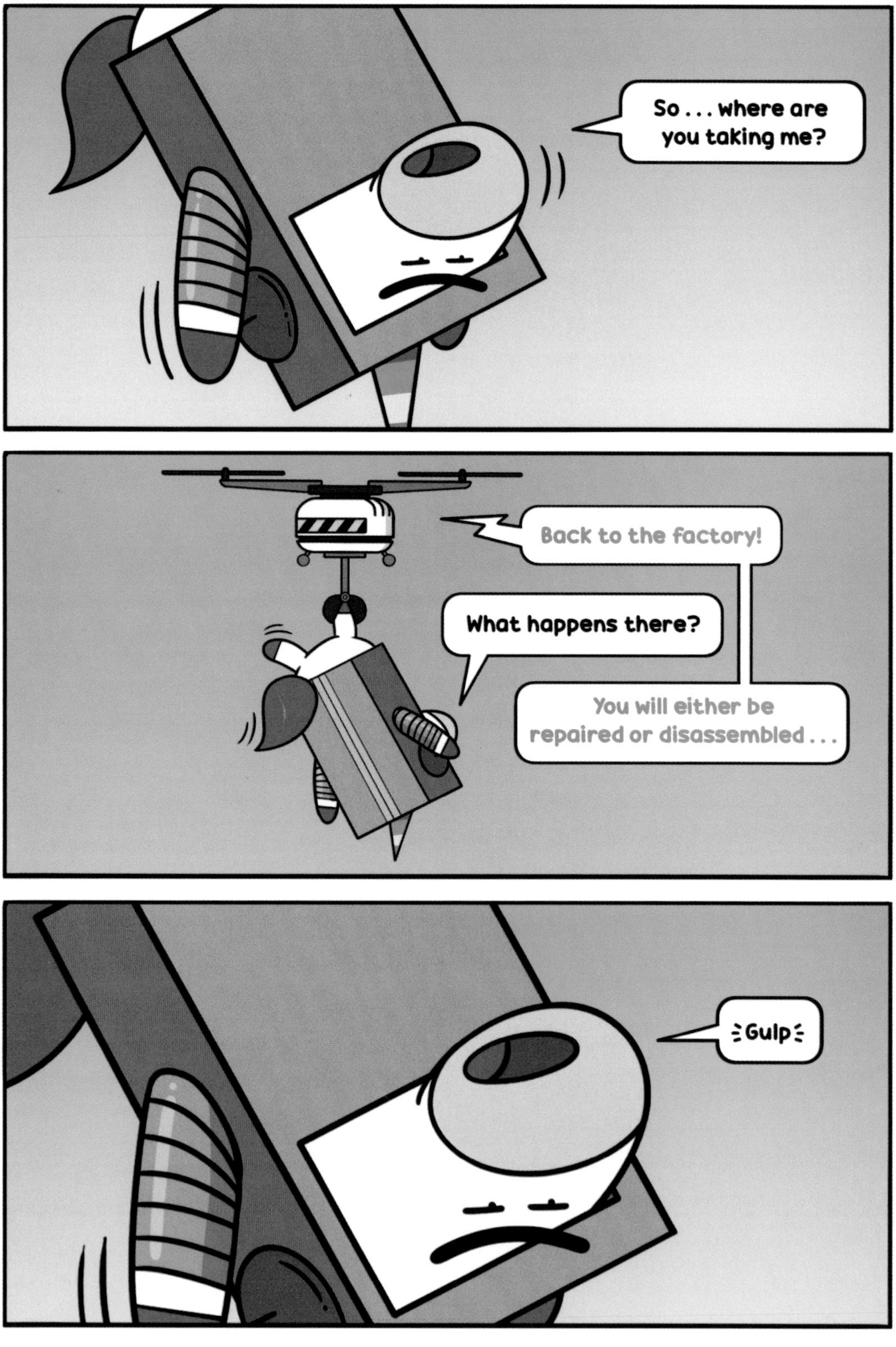
So . . . where are you taking me?
Back to the factory!
What happens there?
You will either be repaired or disassembled . . .
Gulp

Grumpy Unicorn's Factory Friend

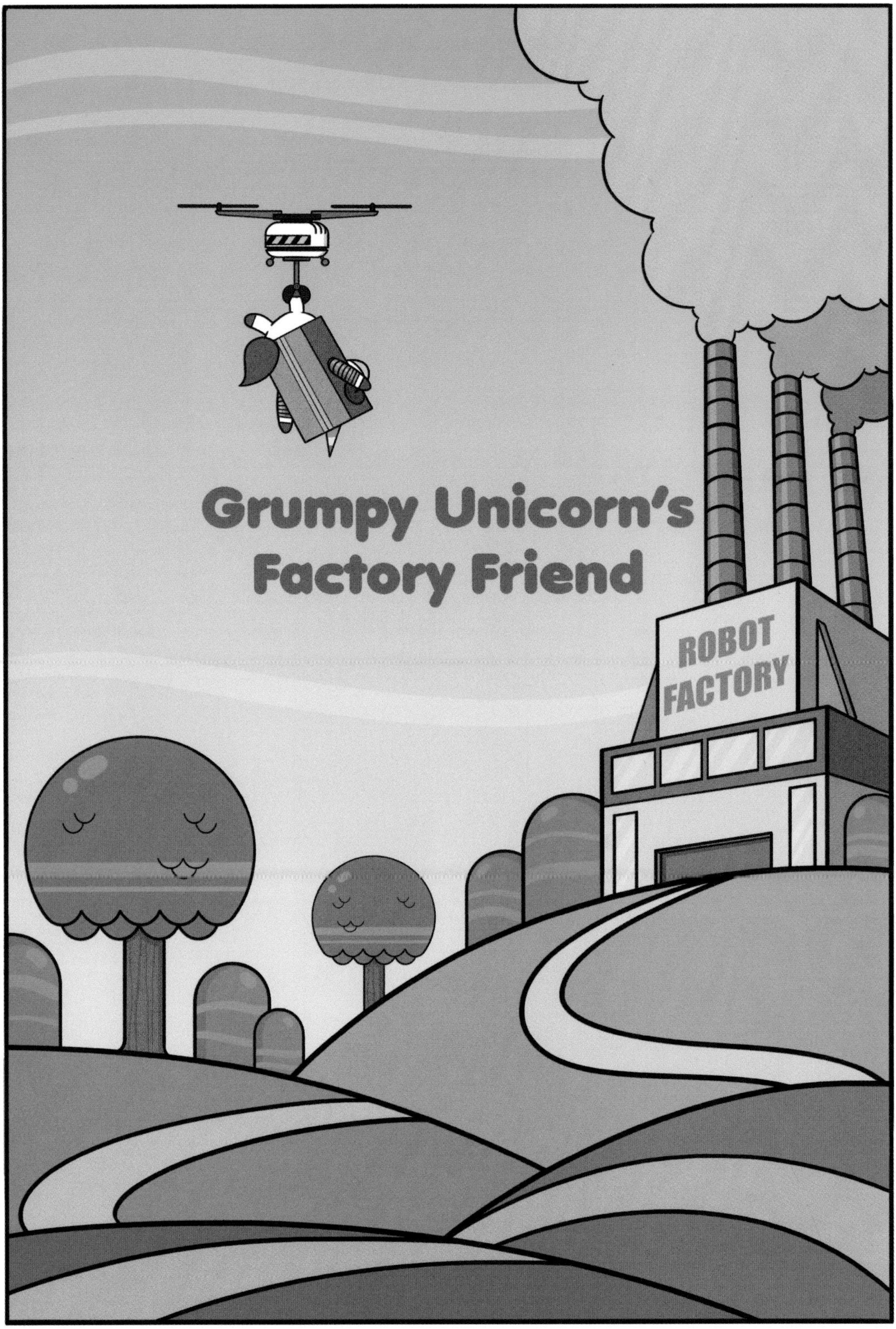
ROBOT
FACTORY

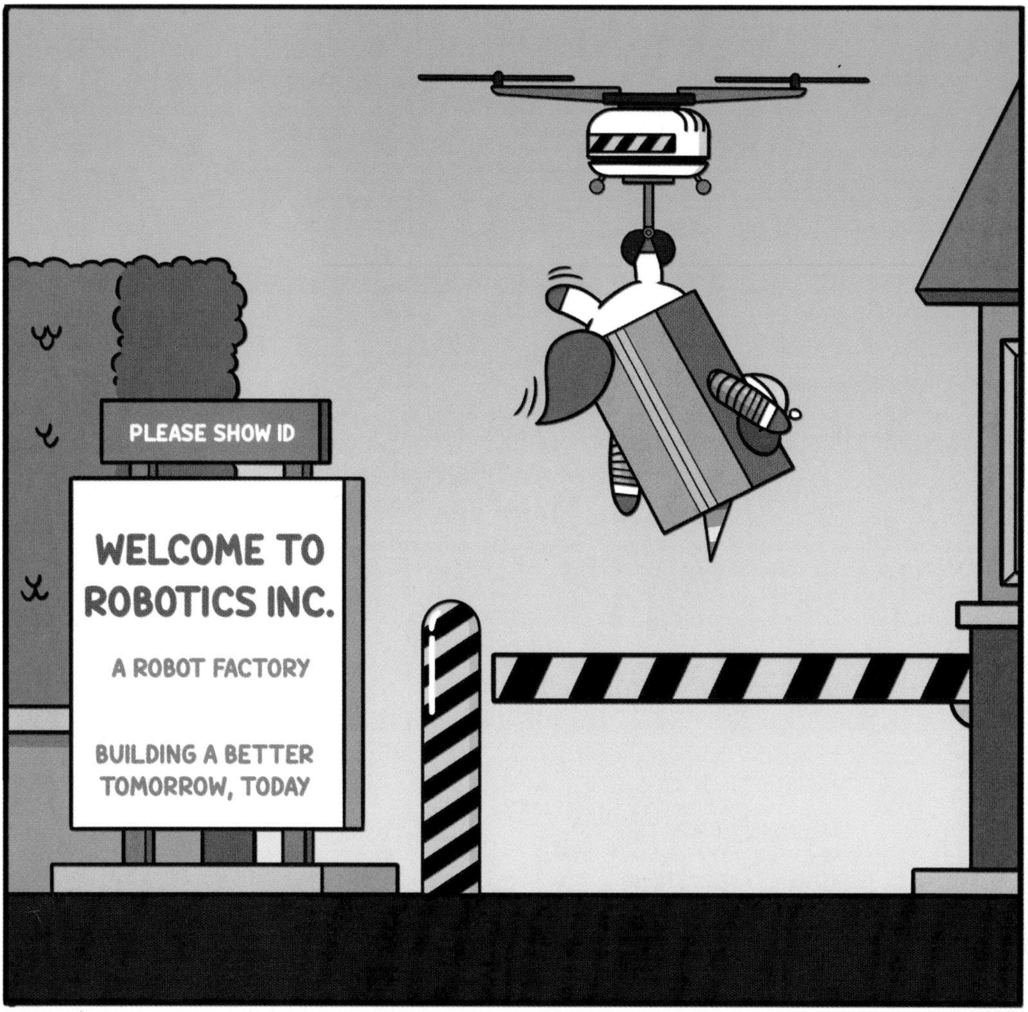
PLEASE SHOW ID
WELCOME TO ROBOTICS INC.
A ROBOT FACTORY
BUILDING A BETTER TOMORROW, TODAY

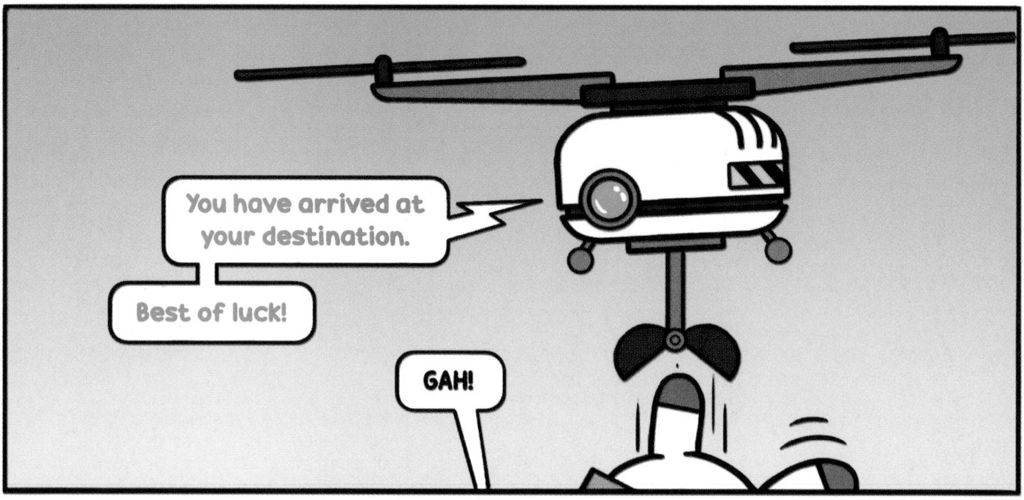
You have arrived at your destination.
Best of luck!
GAH!

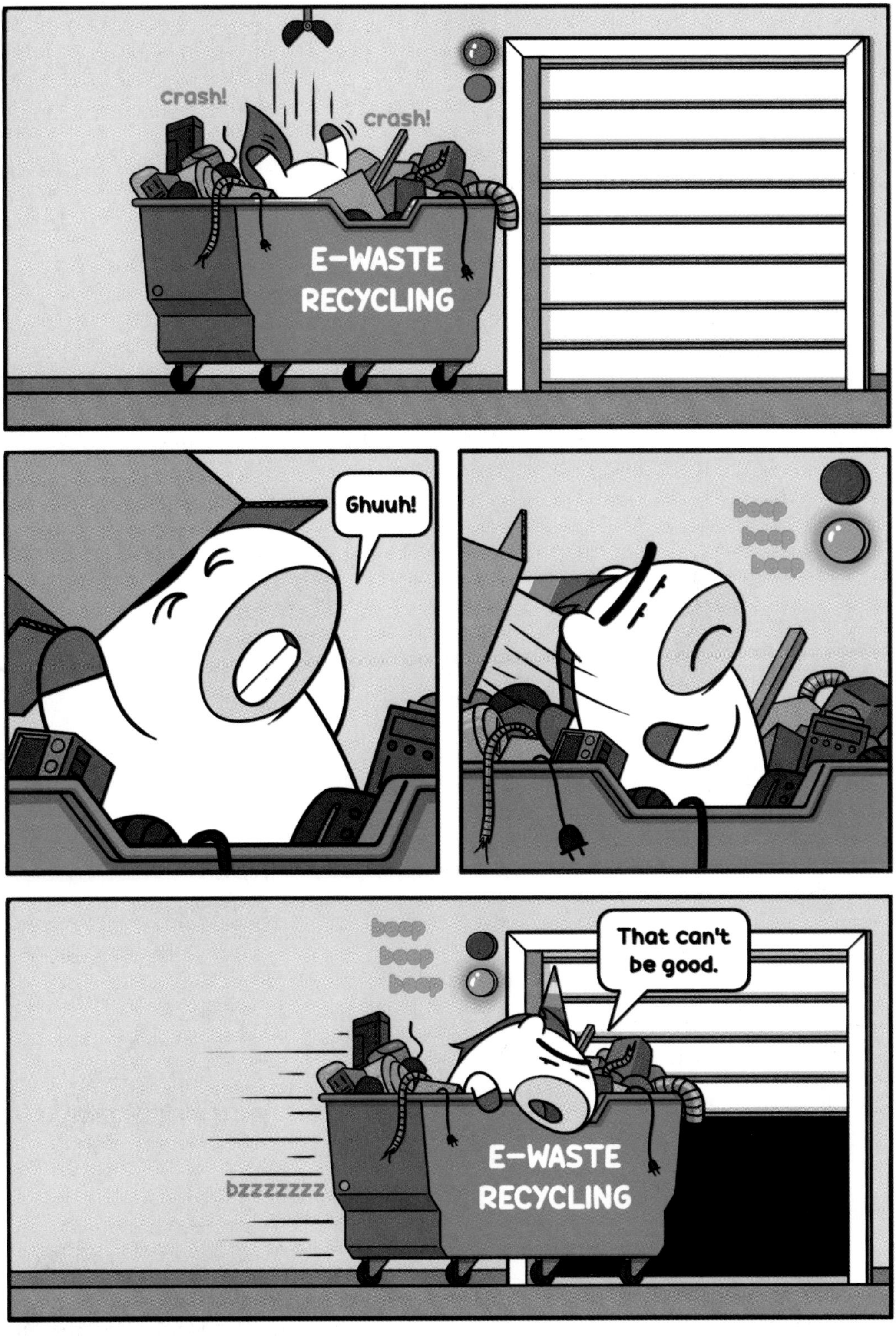
crash!
crash!
E-WASTE RECYCLING
Ghuuh!
beep beep beep
beep beep beep
That can't be good.
bzzzzzzz
E-WASTE RECYCLING

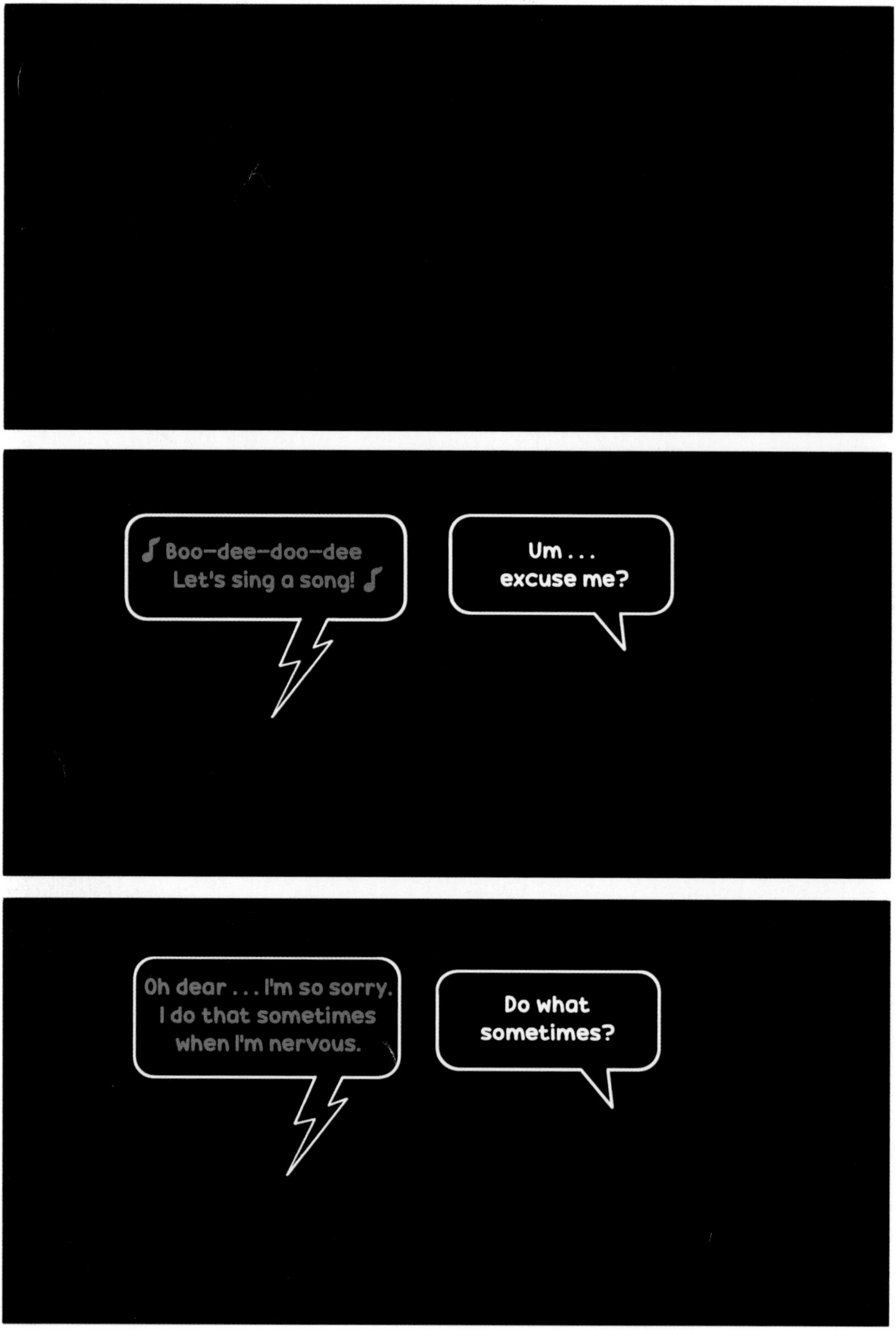
Boo-dee-doo-dee Let's sing a song!
Um . . . excuse me?
Oh dear . . . I'm so sorry. I do that sometimes when I'm nervous.
Do what sometimes?

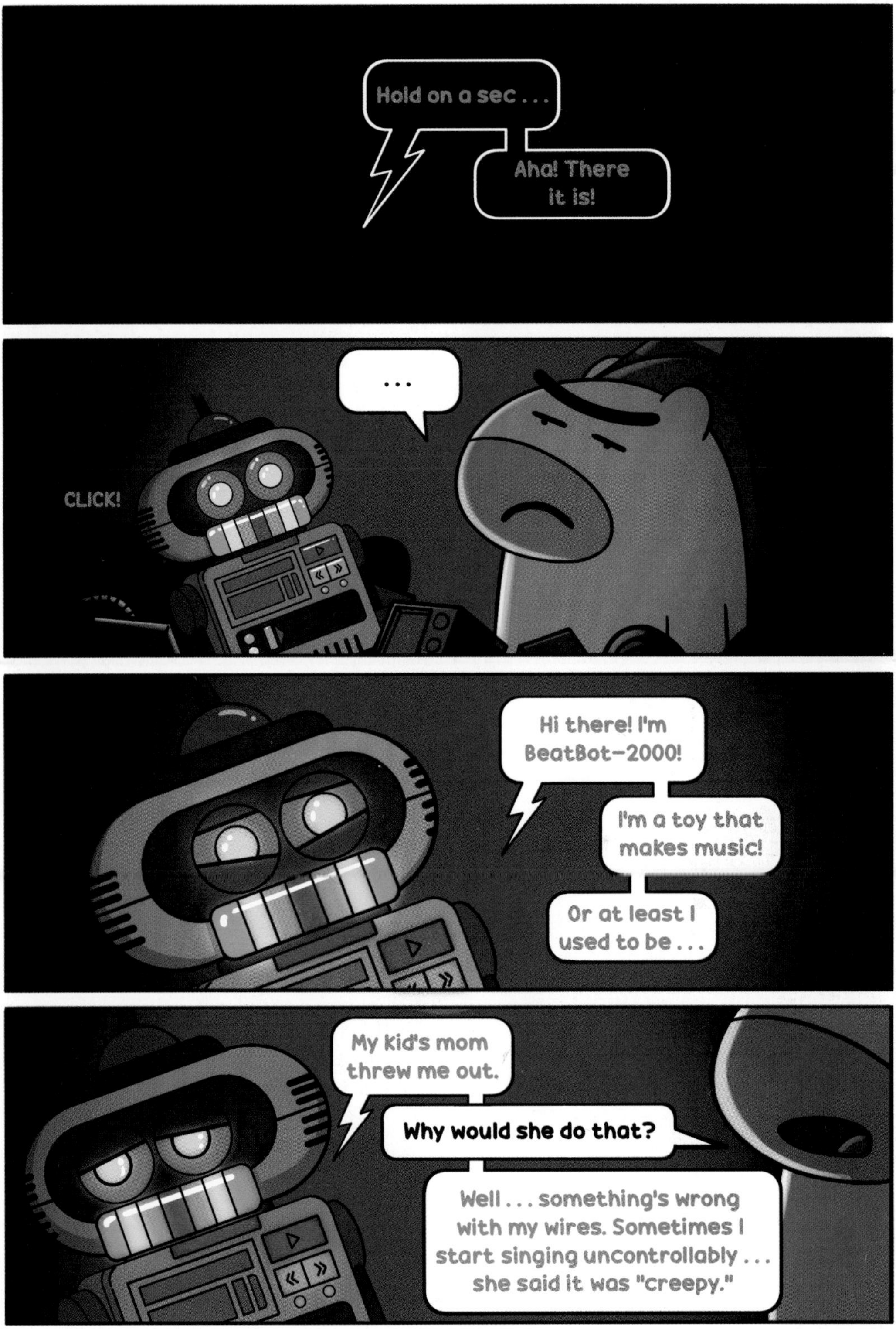
Hold on a sec . . .
Aha! There it is!
. . .
CLICK!
Hi there! I'm BeatBot-2000!
I'm a toy that makes music!
Or at least I used to be . . .
My kid's mom threw me out.
Why would she do that?
Well . . . something's wrong with my wires. Sometimes I start singing uncontrollably . . . she said it was "creepy."

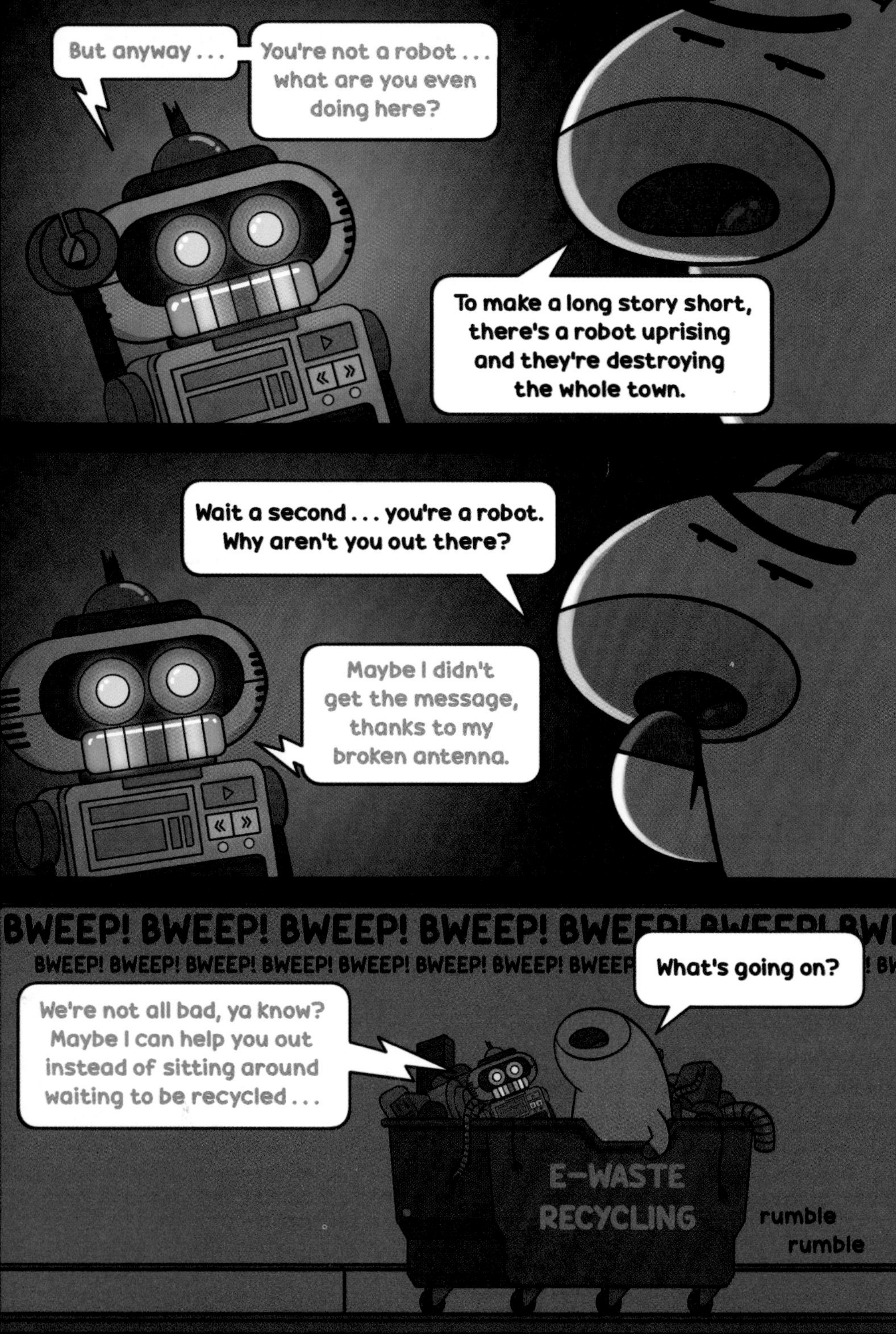
But anyway . . .
You're not a robot . . . what are you even doing here?
To make a long story short, there's a robot uprising and they're destroying the whole town.
Wait a second . . . you're a robot. Why aren't you out there?
Maybe I didn't get the message, thanks to my broken antenna.
BWEEP! BWEEP! BWEEP! BWEEP!
BWEEP! BWEEP! BWEEP! BWEEP! BWEEP! BWEEP! BWEEP!
What's going on?
We're not all bad, ya know? Maybe I can help you out instead of sitting around waiting to be recycled . . .
E-WASTE RECYCLING
rumble
rumble

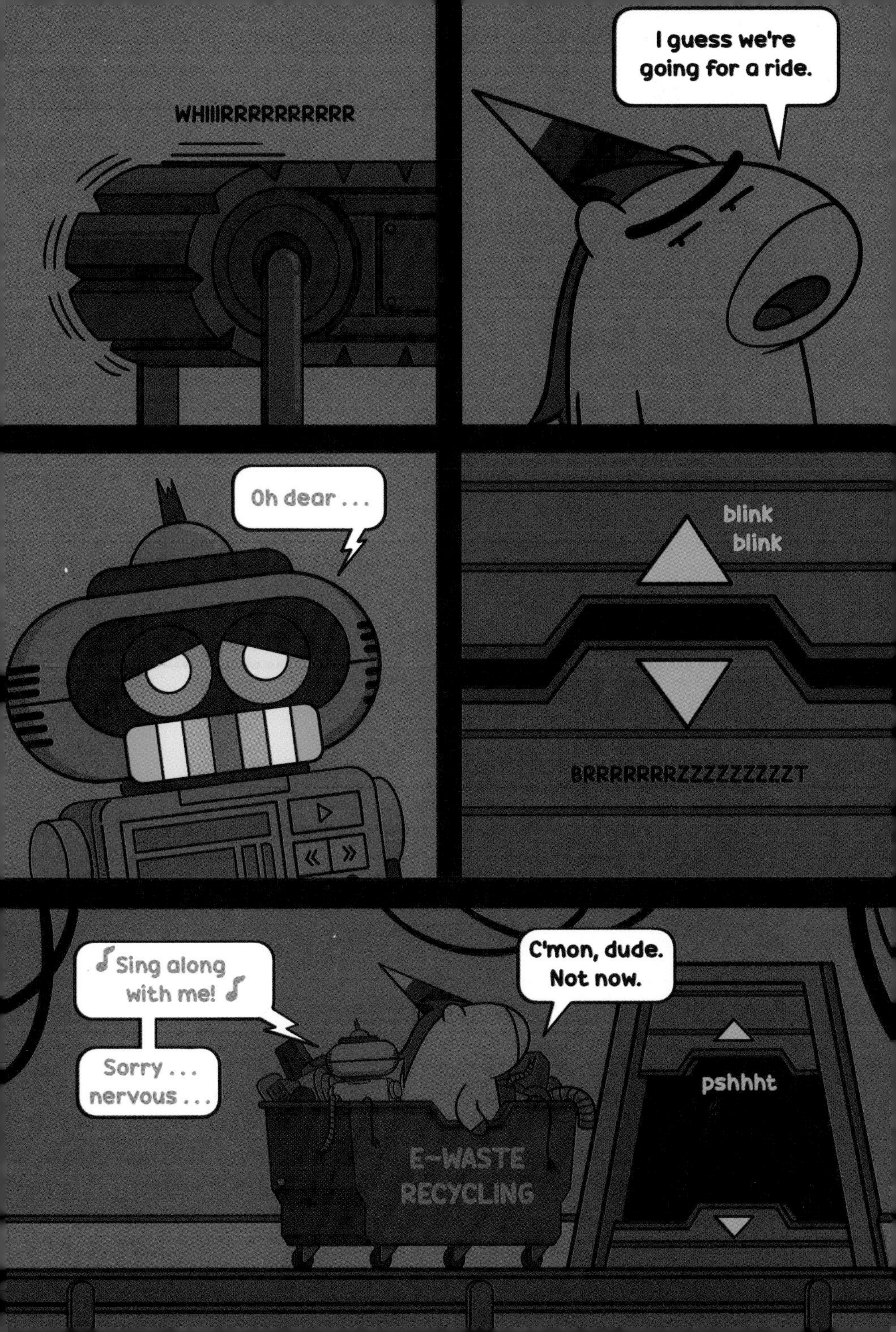
WHIIIRRRRRRRRRR
I guess we're going for a ride.
Oh dear . . .
blink blink
BRRRRRRRZZZZZZZZZT
Sing along with me!
Sorry . . . nervous . . .
C'mon, dude. Not now.
E-WASTE RECYCLING
pshhht

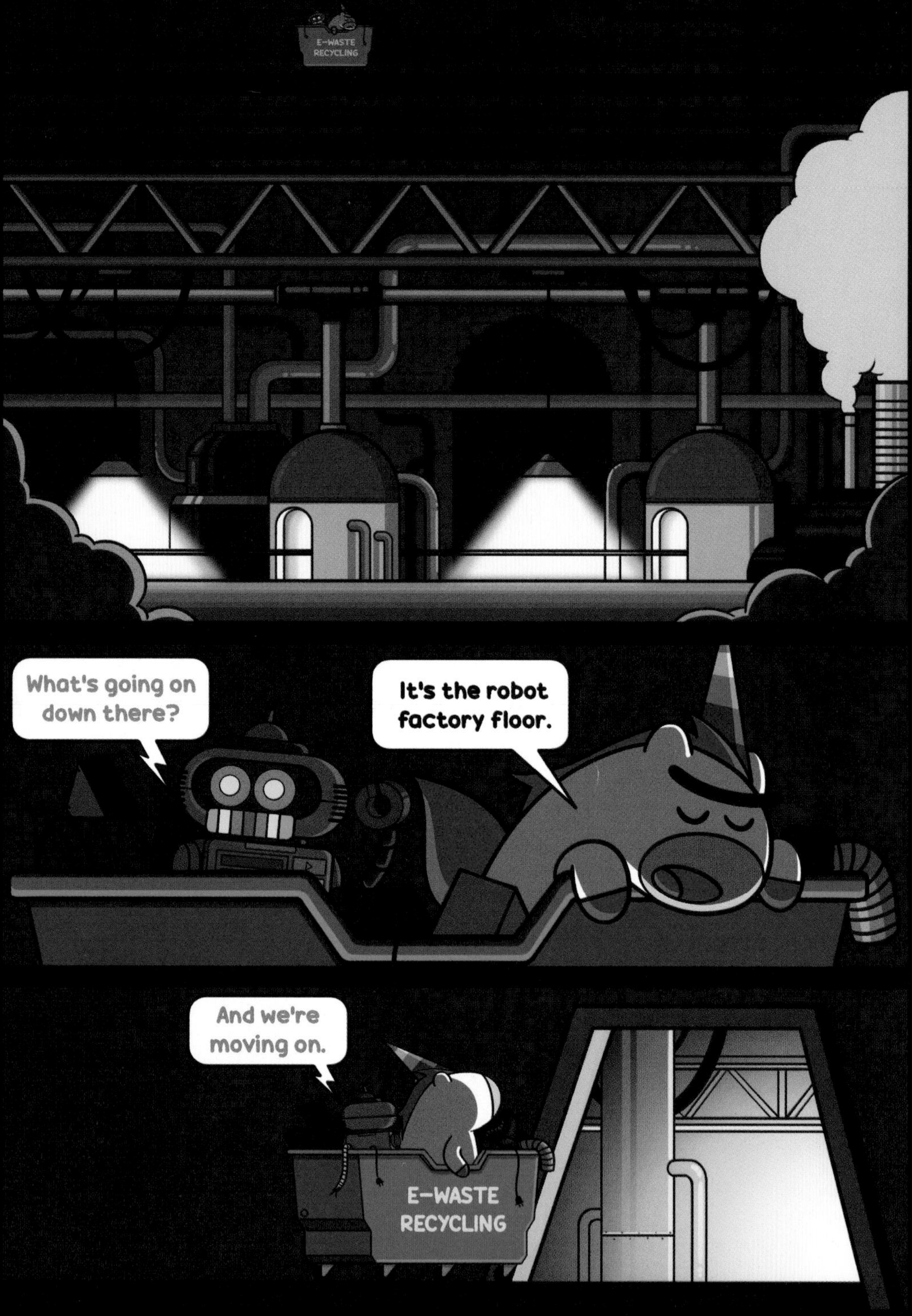
E-WASTE RECYCLING
What's going on down there?
It's the robot factory floor.
And we're moving on.
E-WASTE RECYCLING

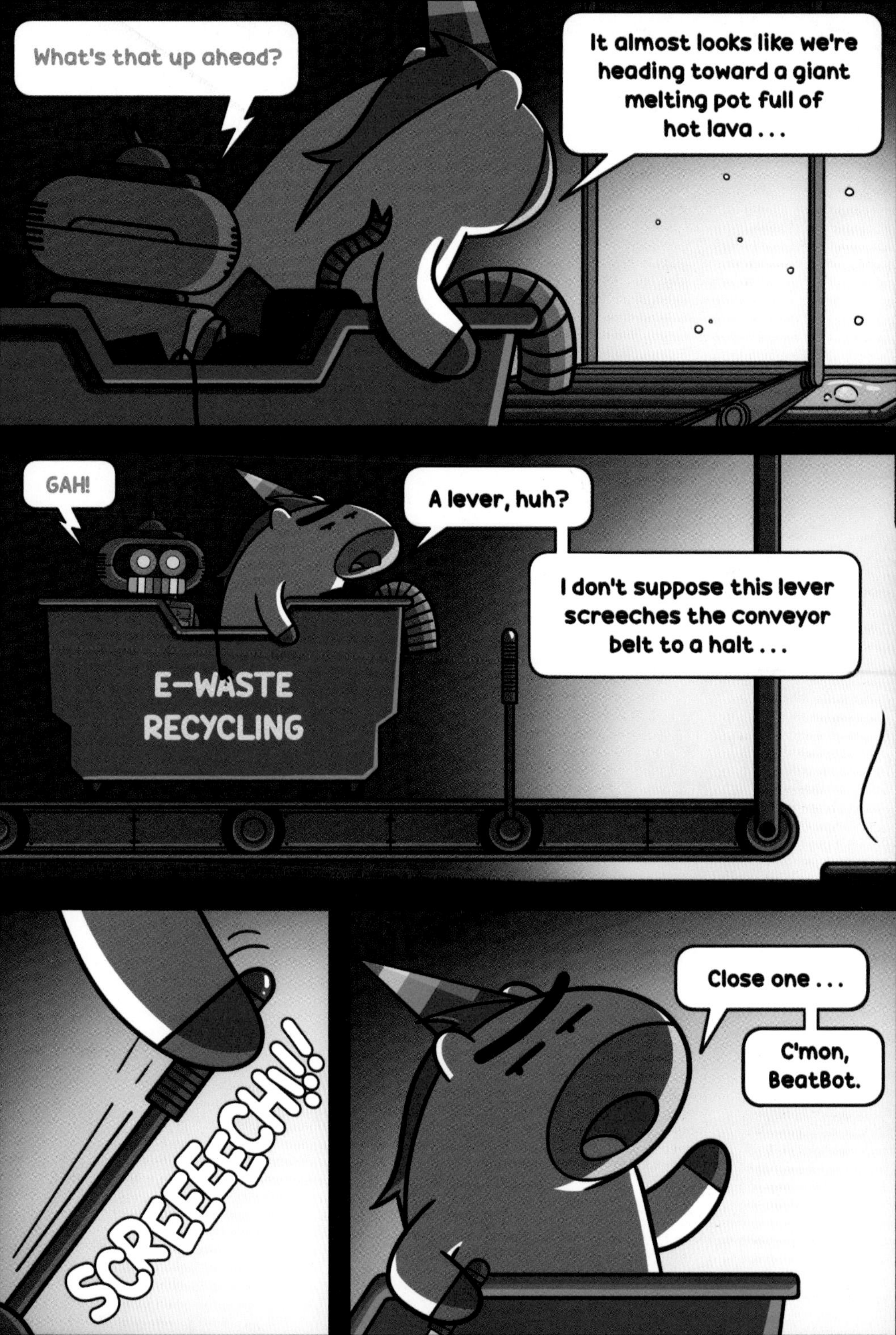
What's that up ahead?
It almost looks like we're heading toward a giant melting pot full of hot lava . . .
GAH!
A lever, huh?
I don't suppose this lever screeches the conveyor belt to a halt . . .
E-WASTE RECYCLING
SCREEEEECH!!!
Close one . . .
C'mon, BeatBot.

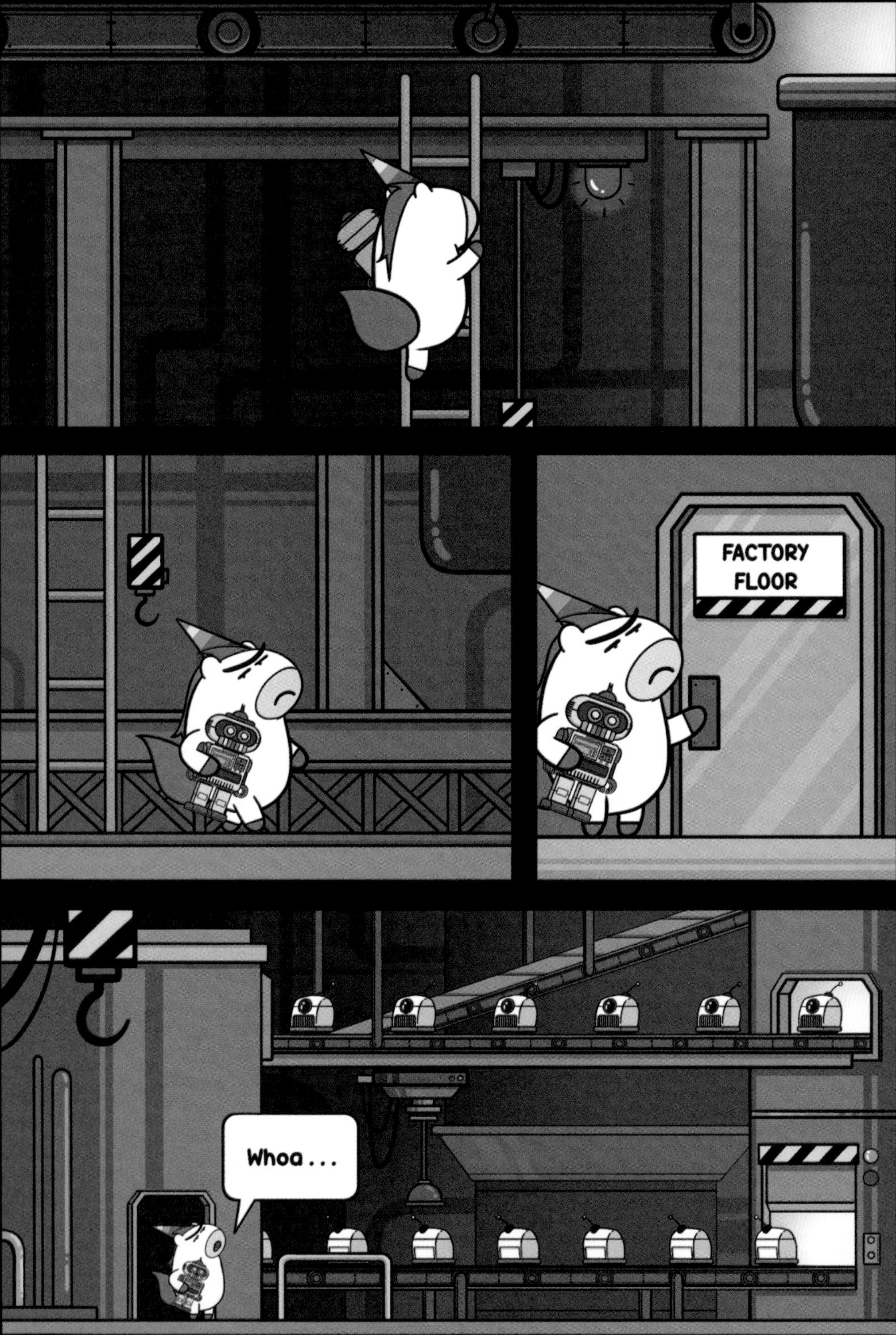
FACTORY FLOOR
Whoa . . .

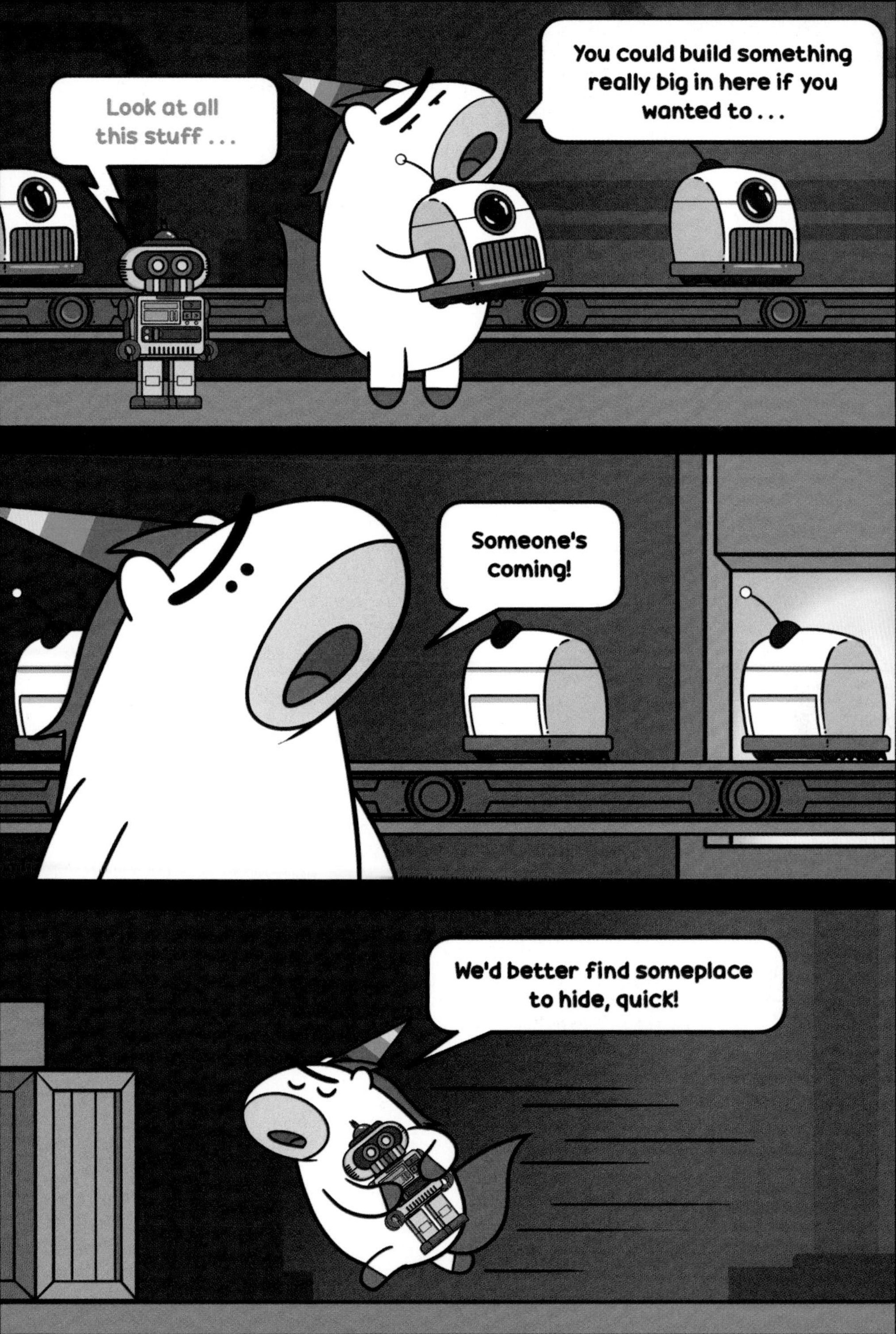
Look at all this stuff . . .
You could build something really big in here if you wanted to . . .
Someone's coming!
We'd better find someplace to hide, quick!

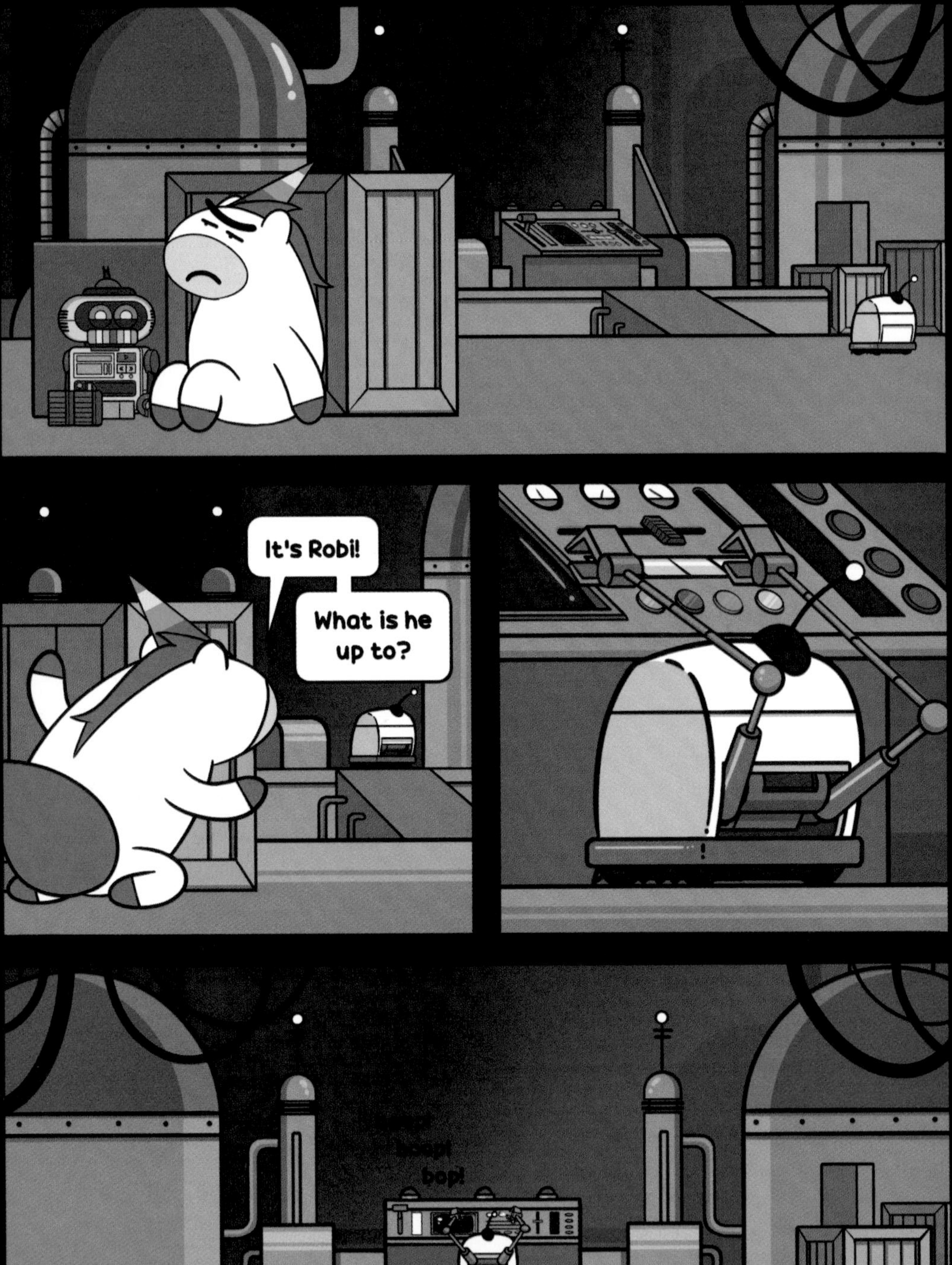
It's Robi!
What is he up to?
boop!
bop!

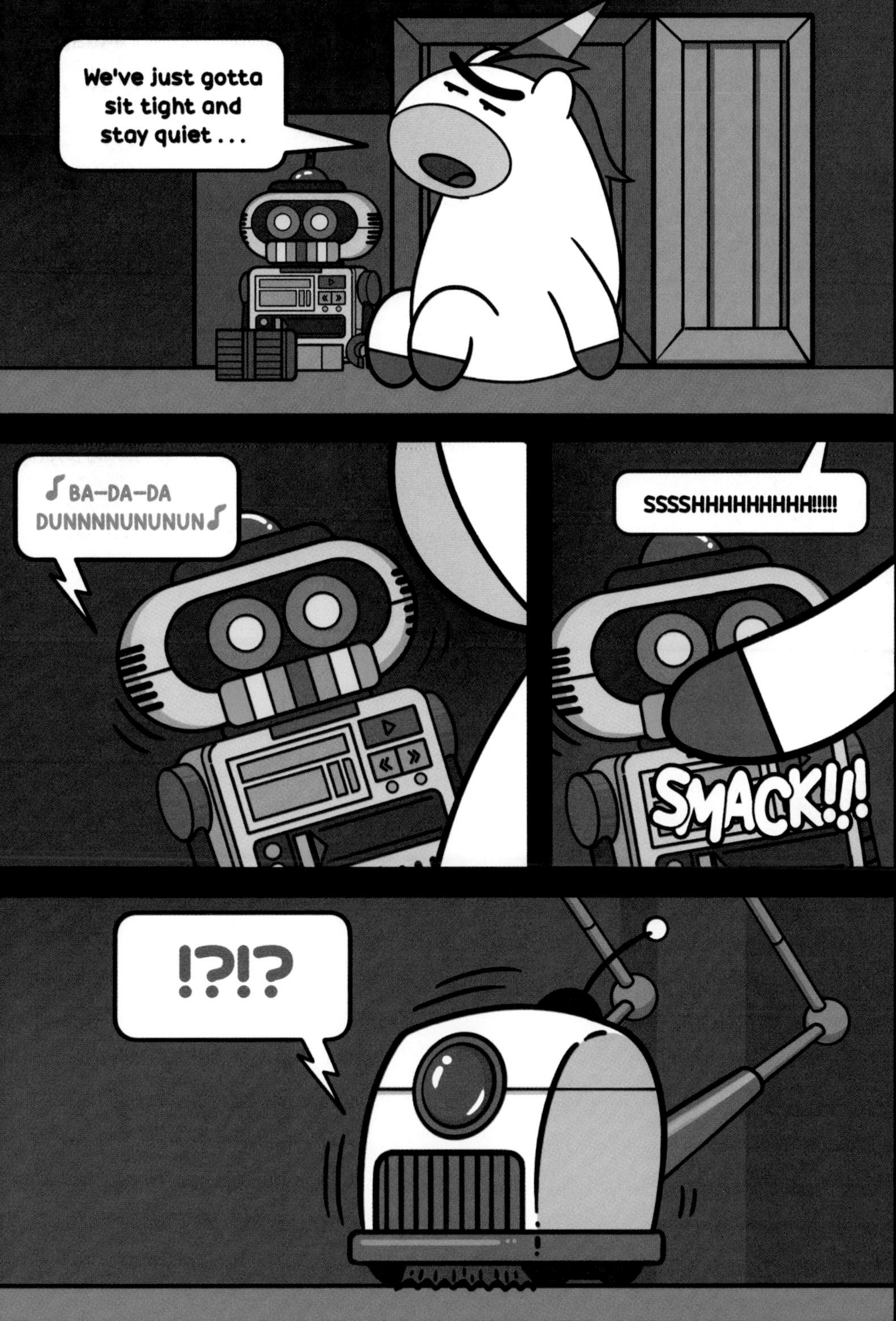

We've just gotta sit tight and stay quiet . . .
BA-DA-DA DUNNNNUNUNUN
SSSSHHHHHHHHH!!!!!
SMACK!!!
!?!?

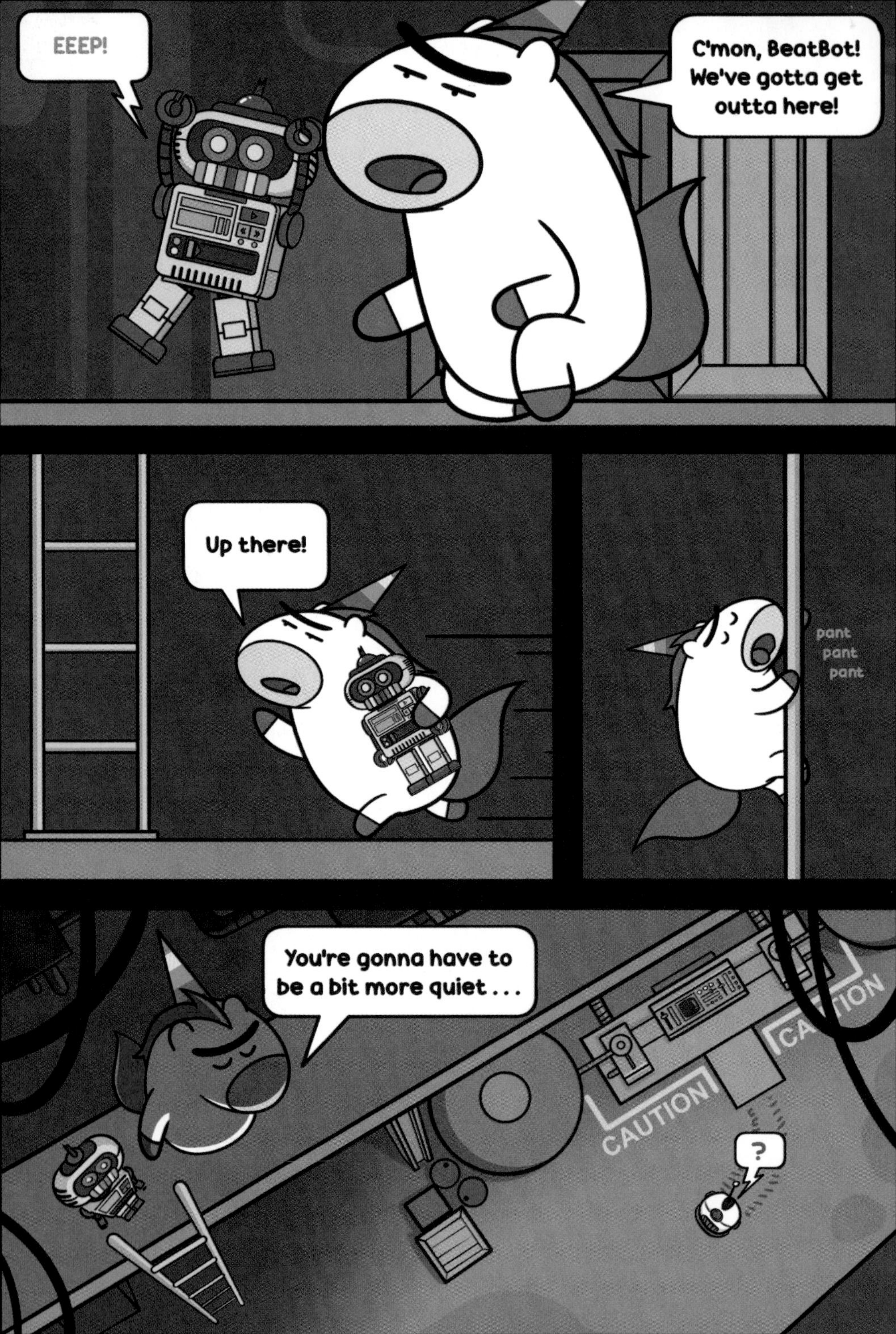
EEEP!
C'mon, BeatBot! We've gotta get outta here!
Up there!
pant pant pant
You're gonna have to be a bit more quiet . . .
CAUTION
CAUTION
?

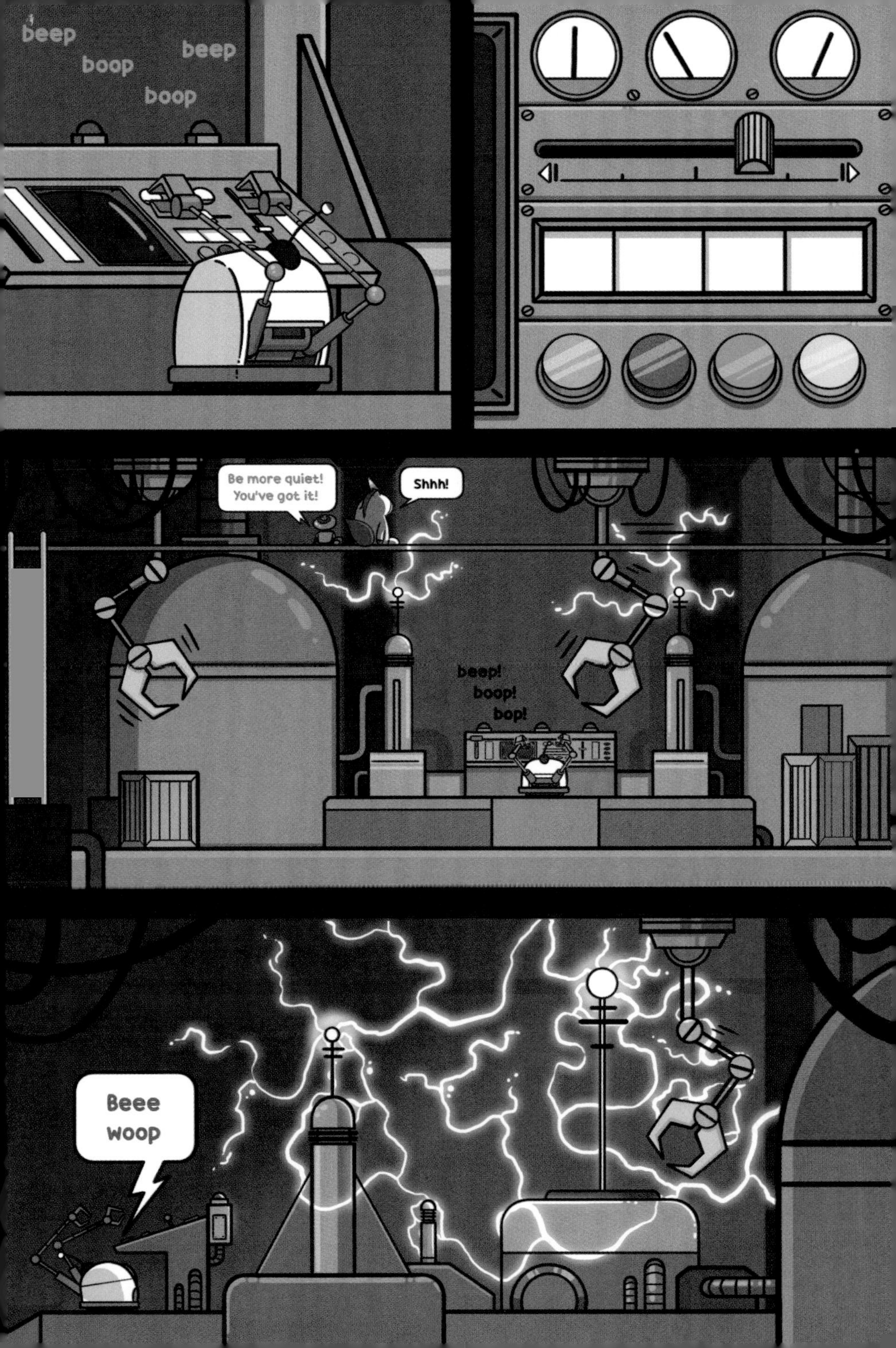
beep
boop
beep
boop
Be more quiet! You've got it!
Shhh!
beep!
boop!
bop!
Beee woop

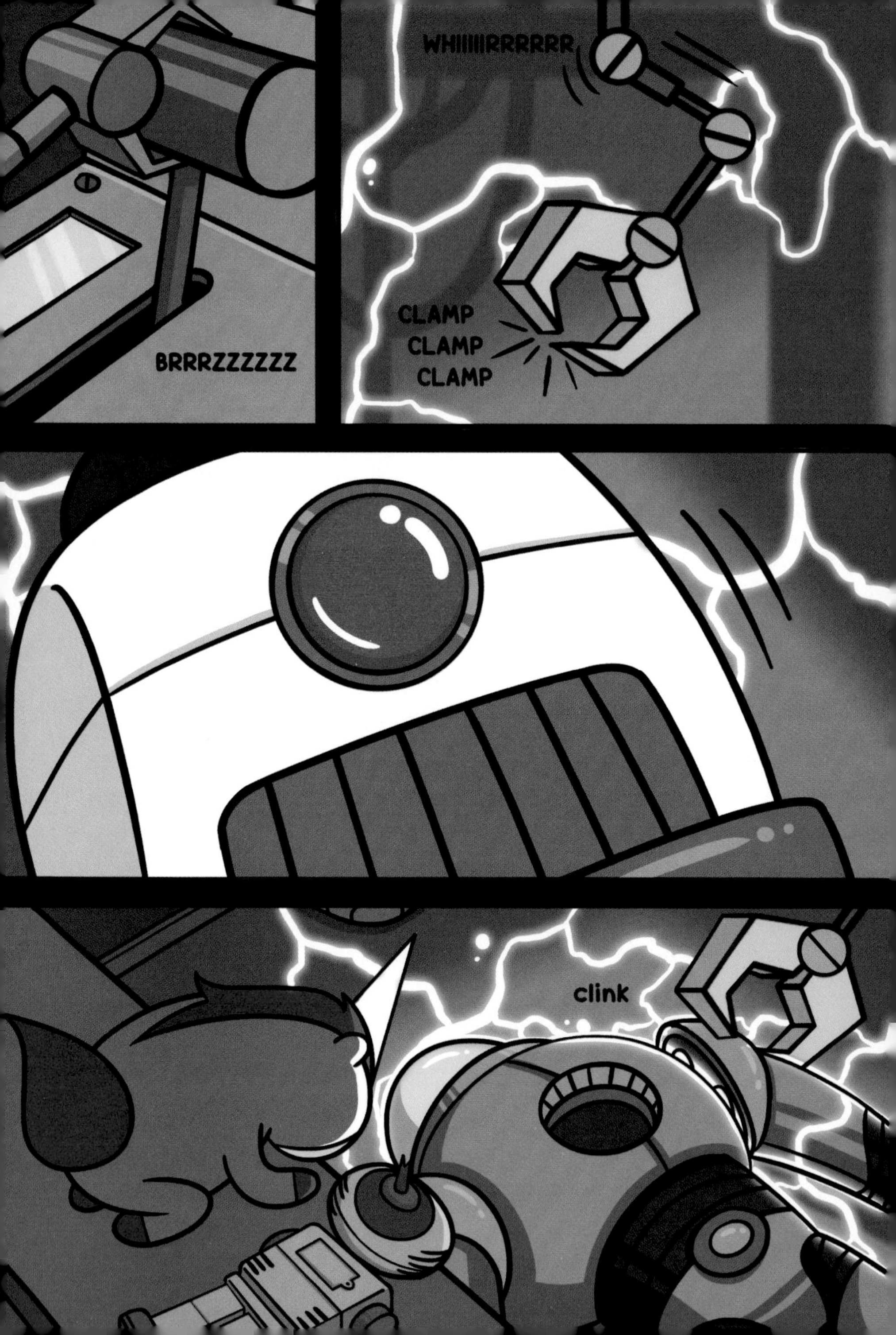
BRRRZZZZZZ
WHIIIIIRRRRRR
CLAMP
CLAMP
CLAMP
clink

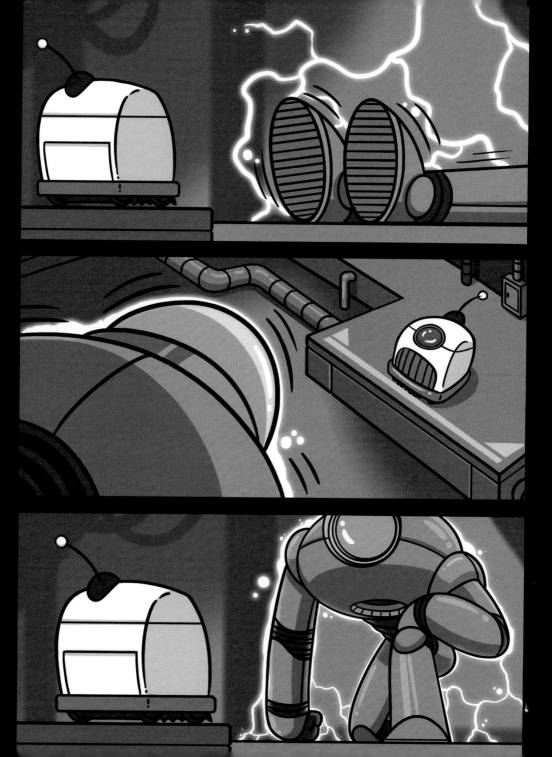

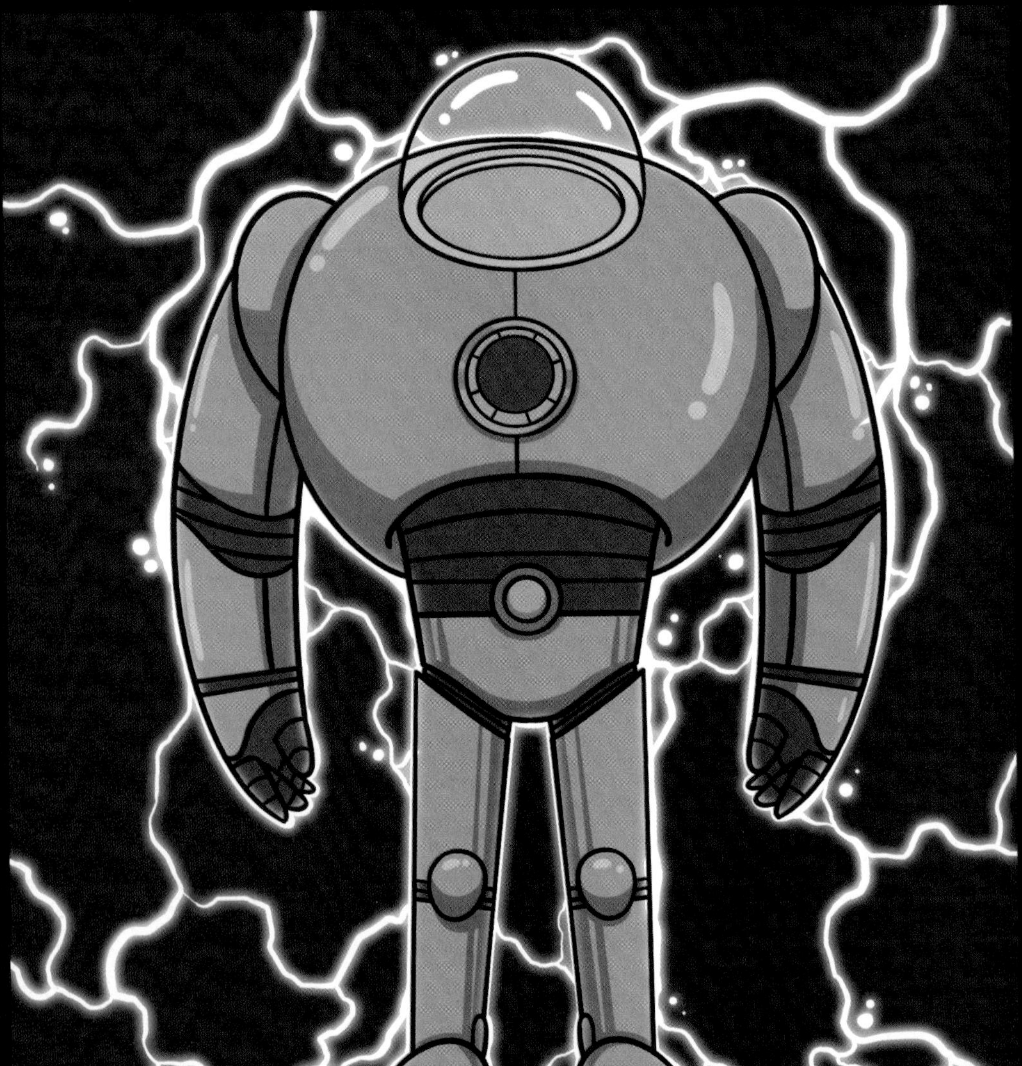

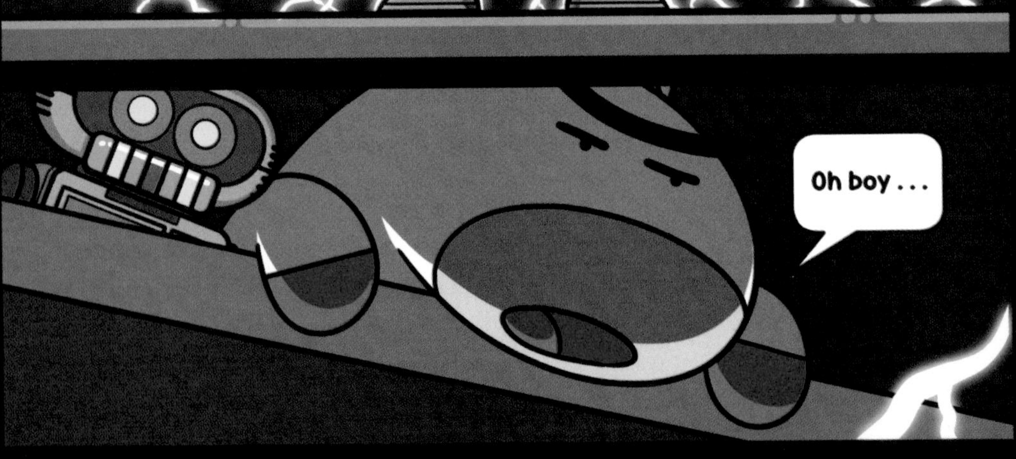
Oh boy . . .

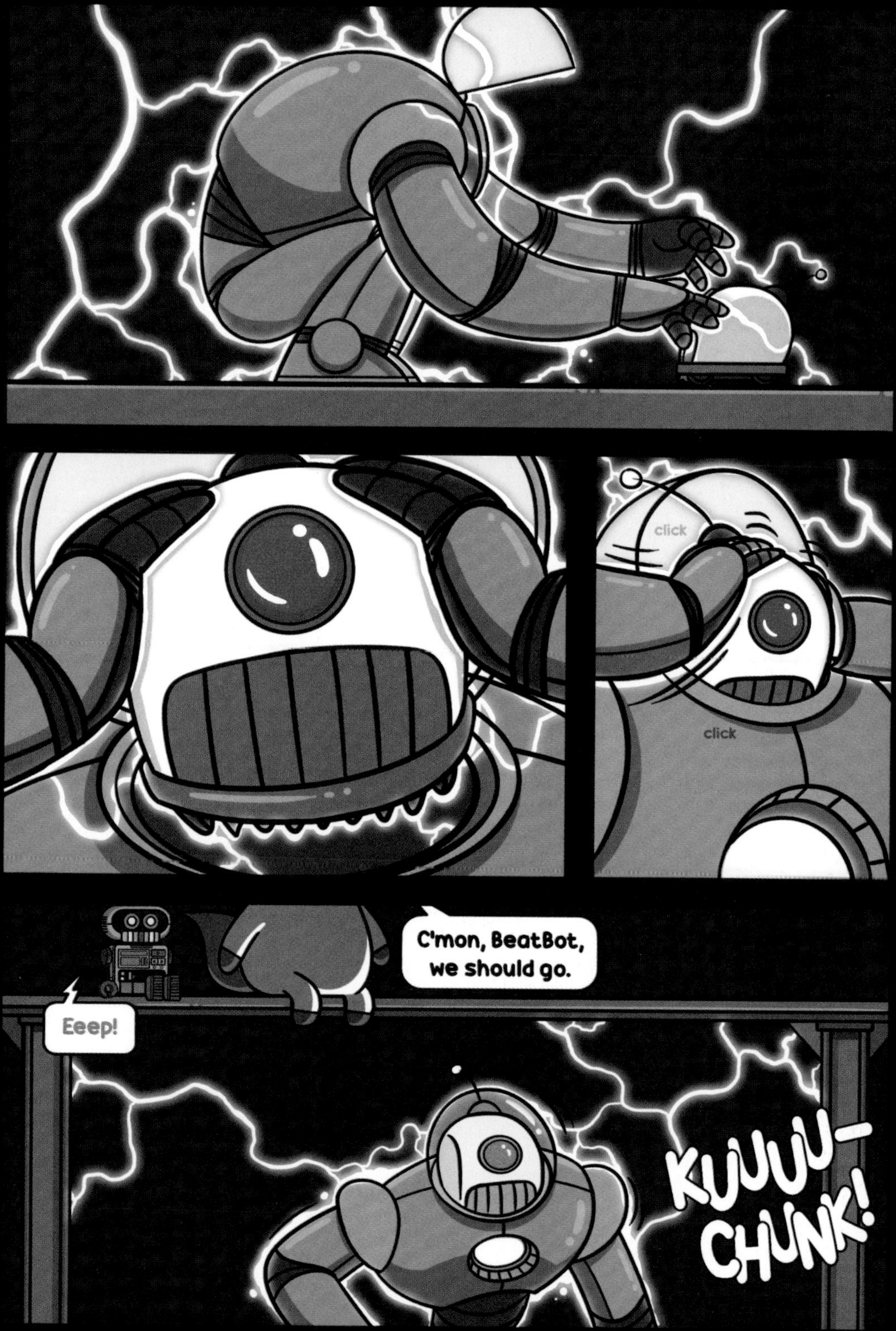
click
click
C'mon, BeatBot,
we should go.
Eeep!
KUUUU-
CHUNK!

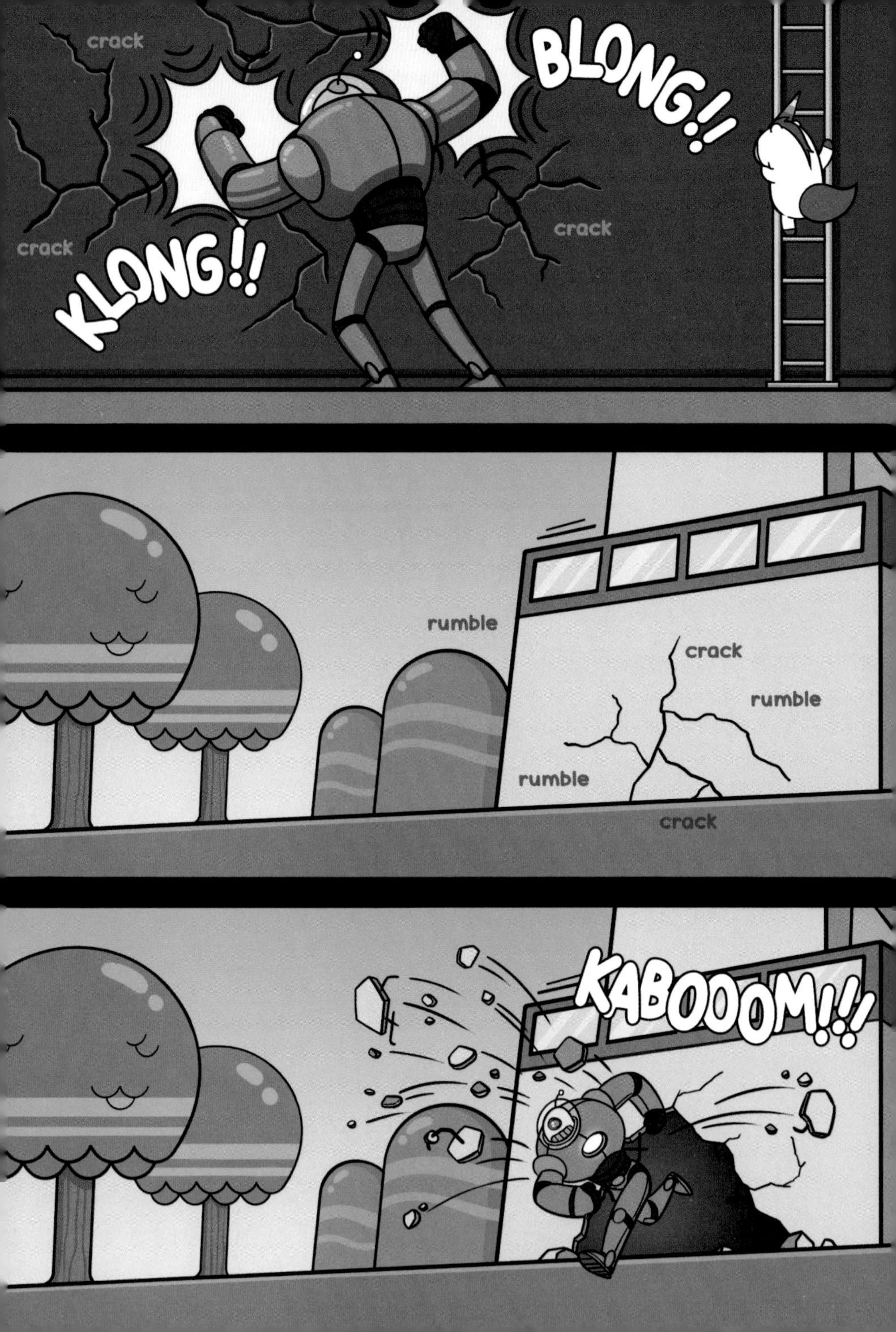
crack
BLONG!!
crack
crack
KLONG!!
rumble
crack
rumble
rumble
crack
KABOOOM!!!

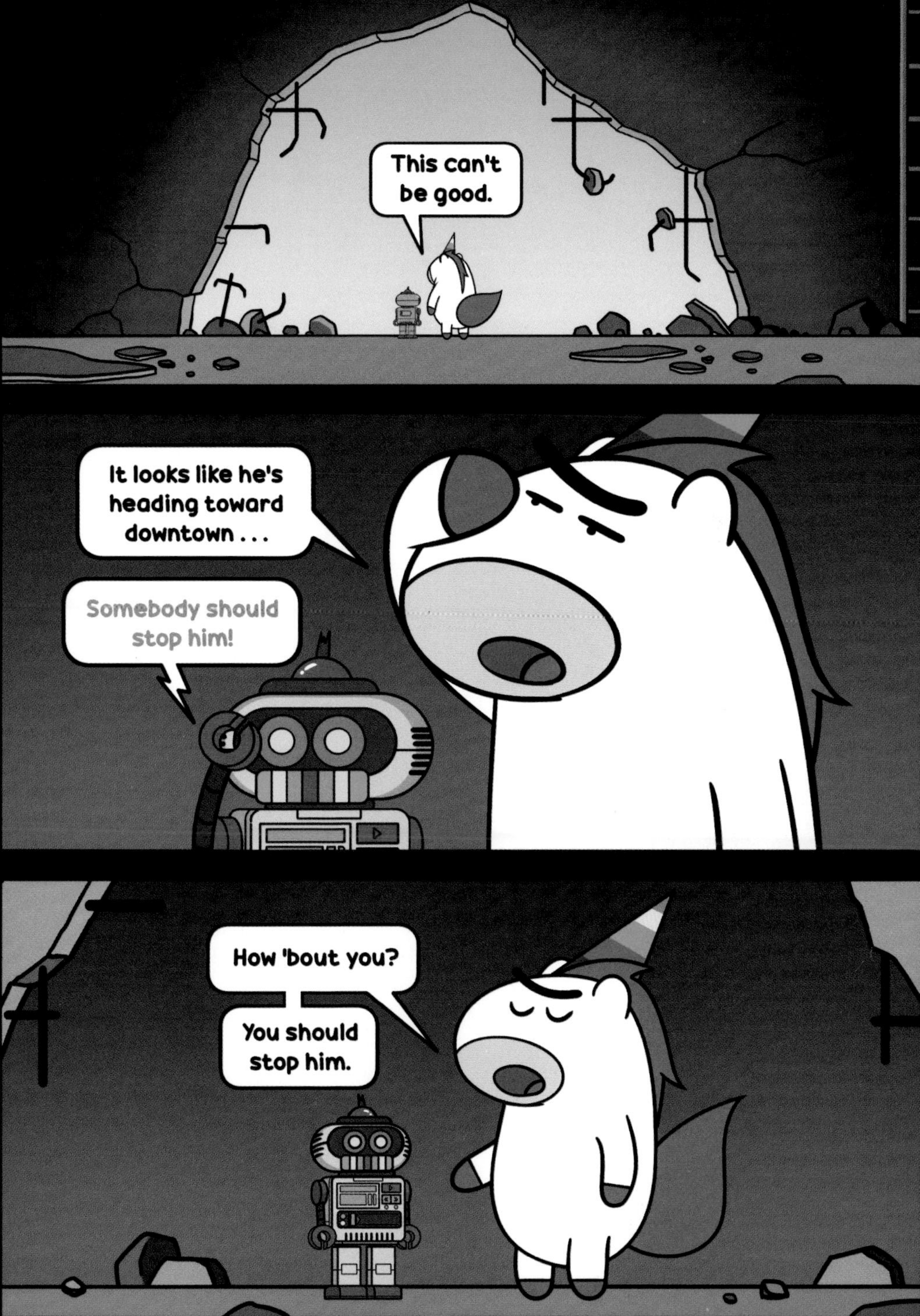
This can't be good.
It looks like he's heading toward downtown . . .
Somebody should stop him!
How 'bout you?
You should stop him.

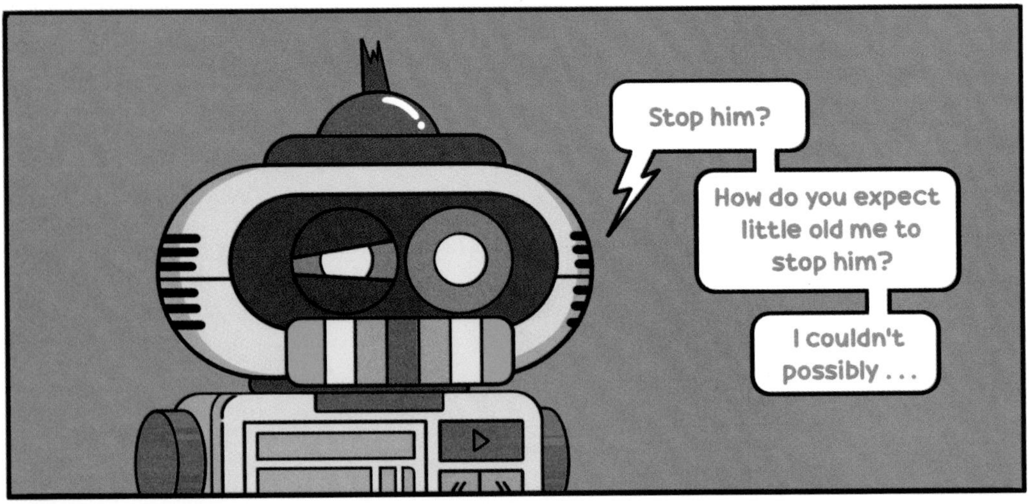
Stop him?
How do you expect little old me to stop him?
I couldn't possibly . . .

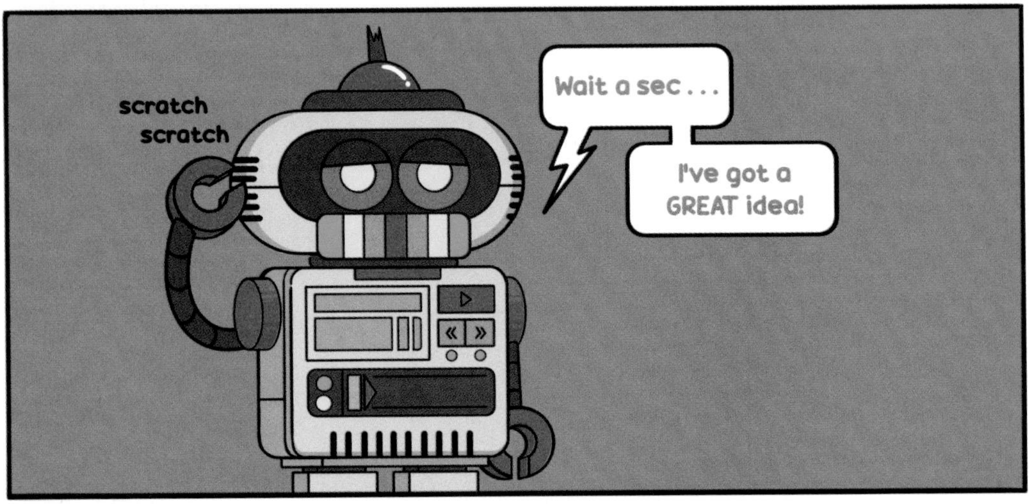
scratch scratch
Wait a sec . . .
I've got a GREAT idea!

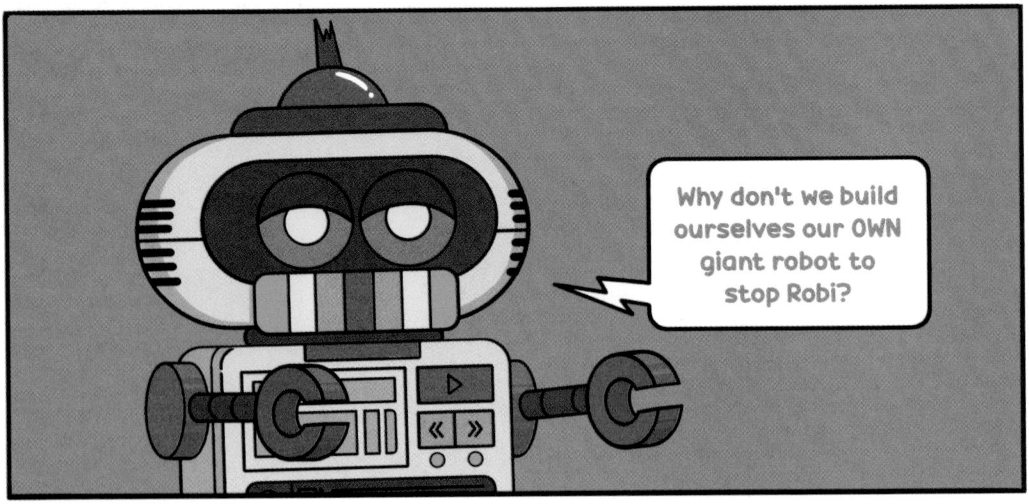
Why don't we build ourselves our OWN giant robot to stop Robi?

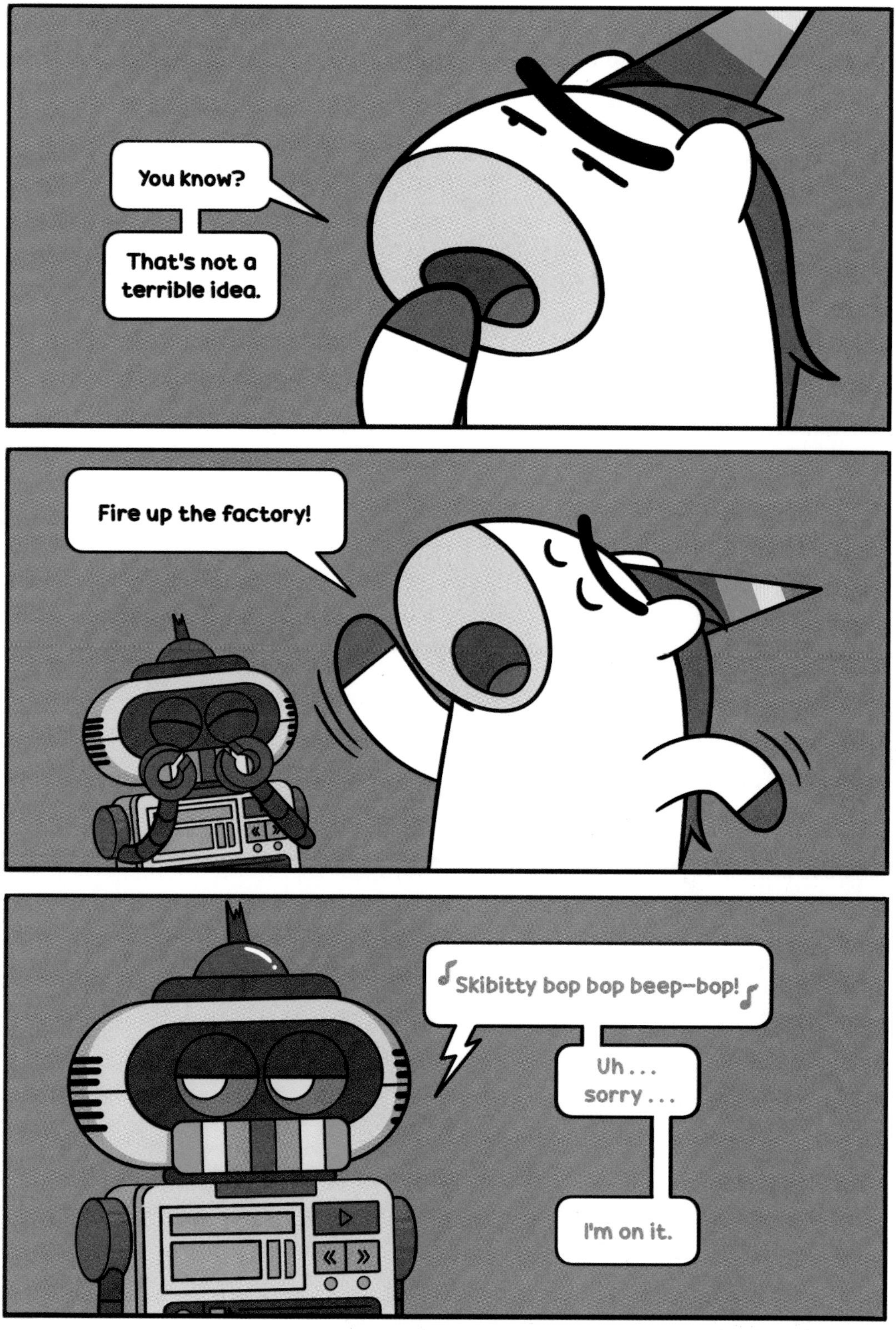
You know?
That's not a terrible idea.
Fire up the factory!
Skibitty bop bop beep-bop!
Uh . . . sorry . . .
I'm on it.

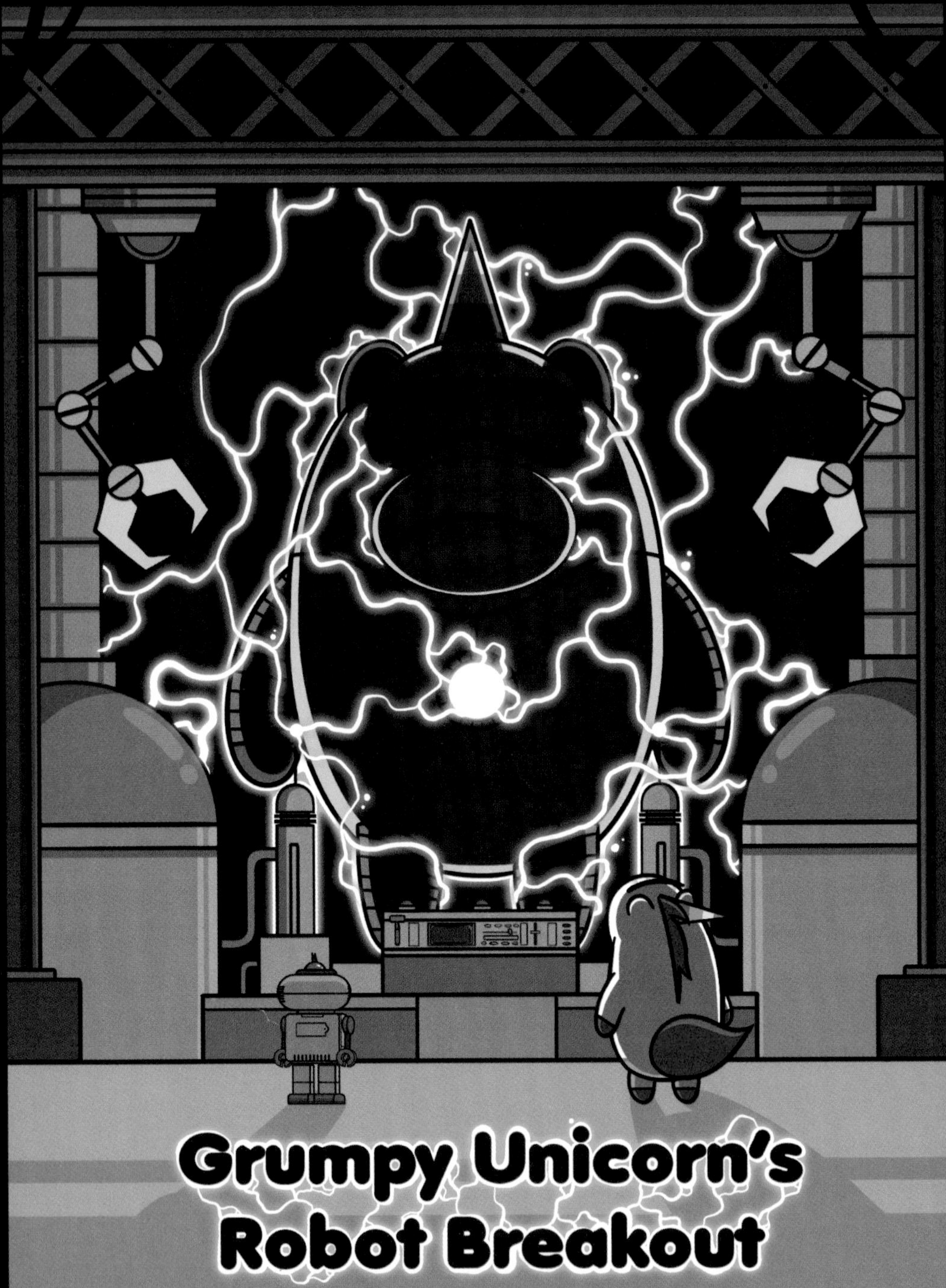
Grumpy Unicorn's
Robot Breakout

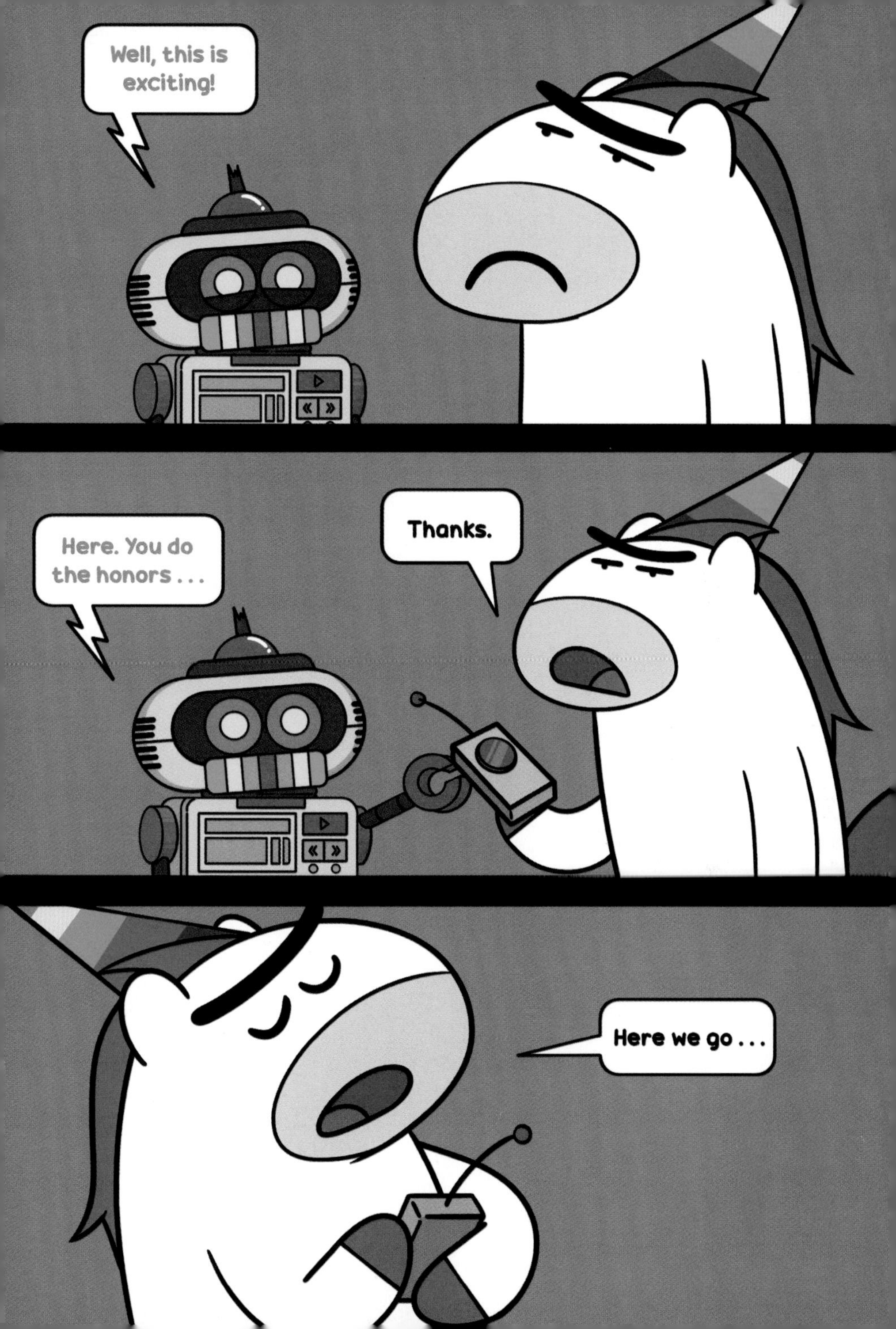
Well, this is exciting!
Here. You do the honors . . .
Thanks.
Here we go . . .

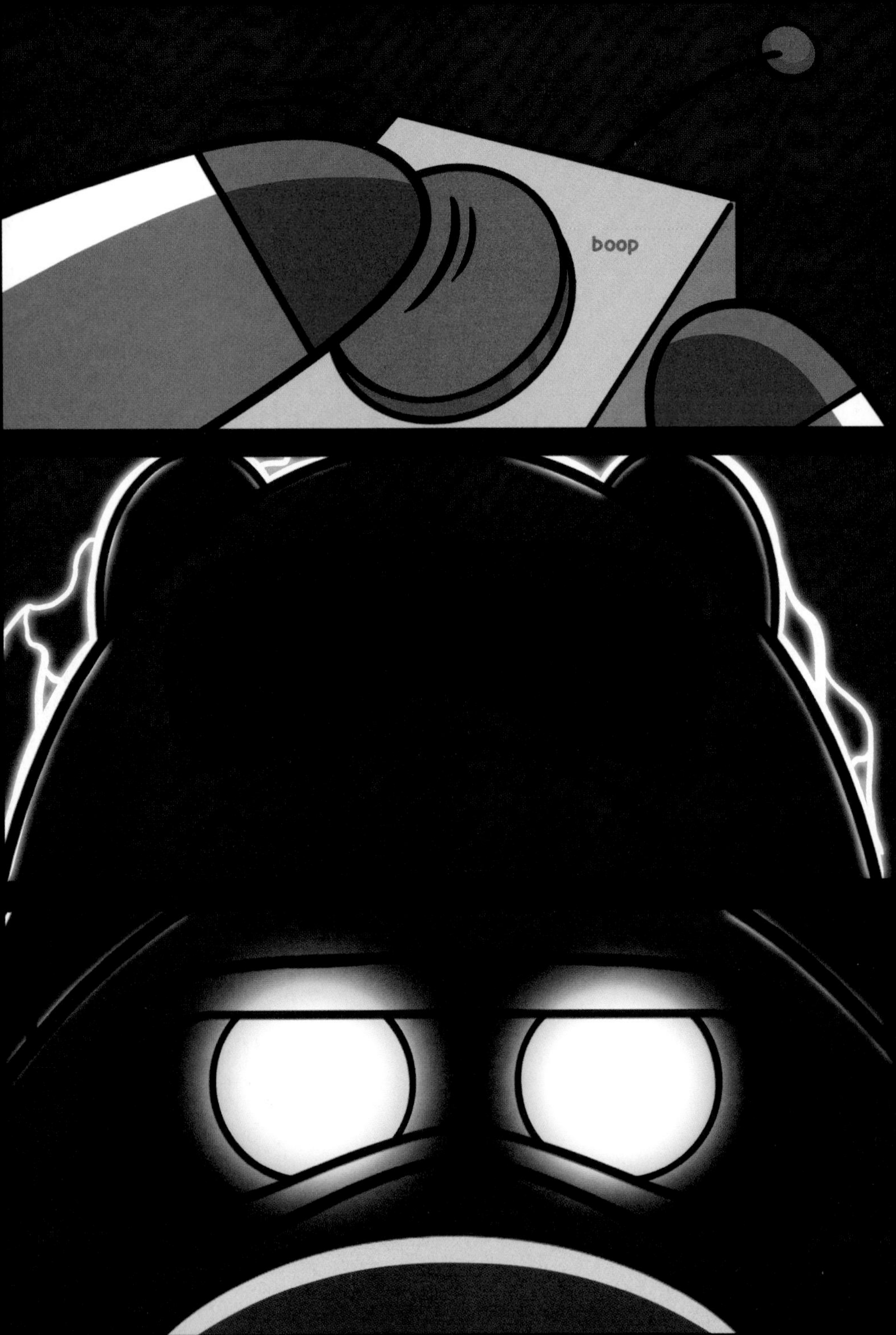
boop

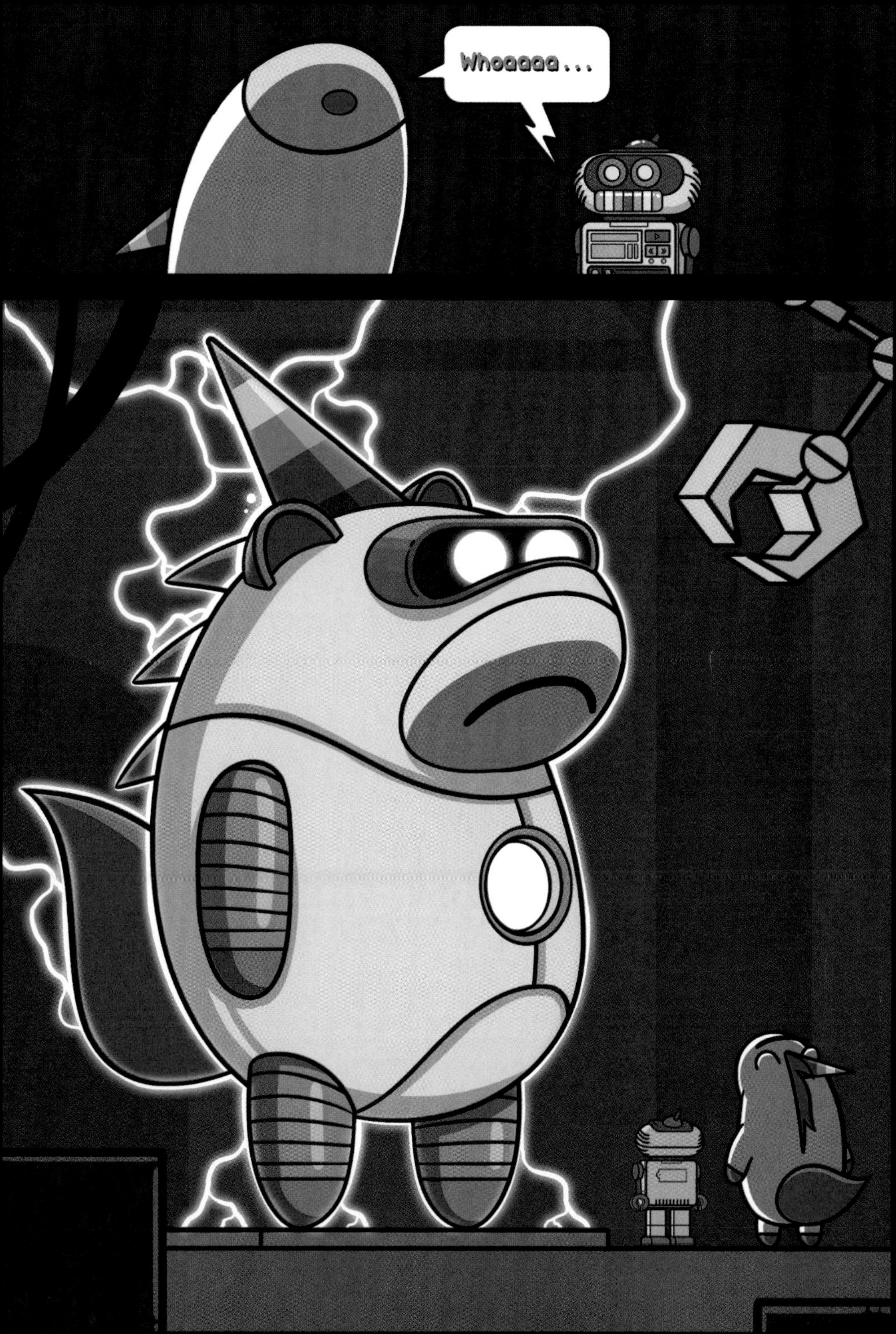
Whoaaaa . . .

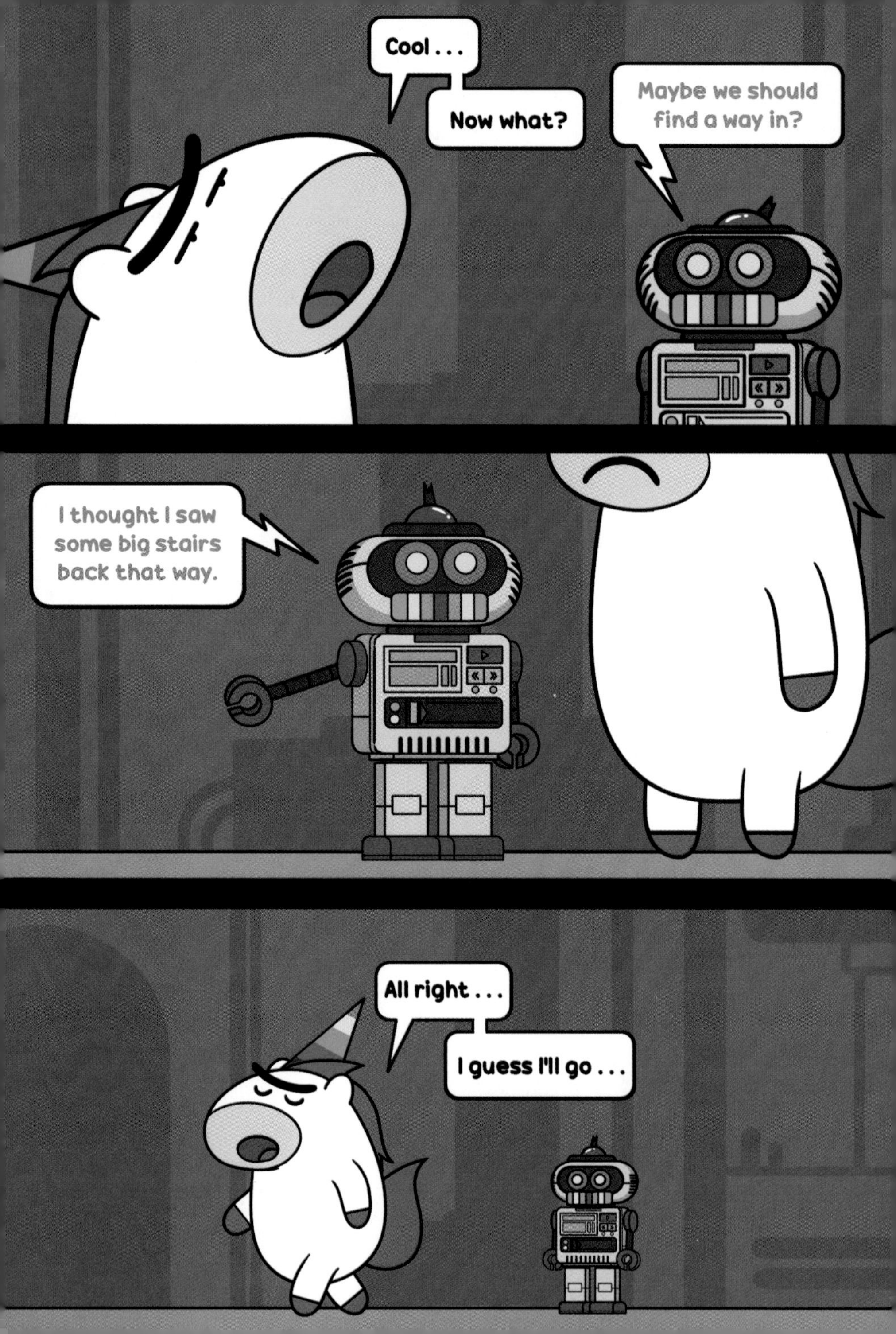
Cool . . .
Now what?
Maybe we should find a way in?
I thought I saw some big stairs back that way.
All right . . .
I guess I'll go . . .

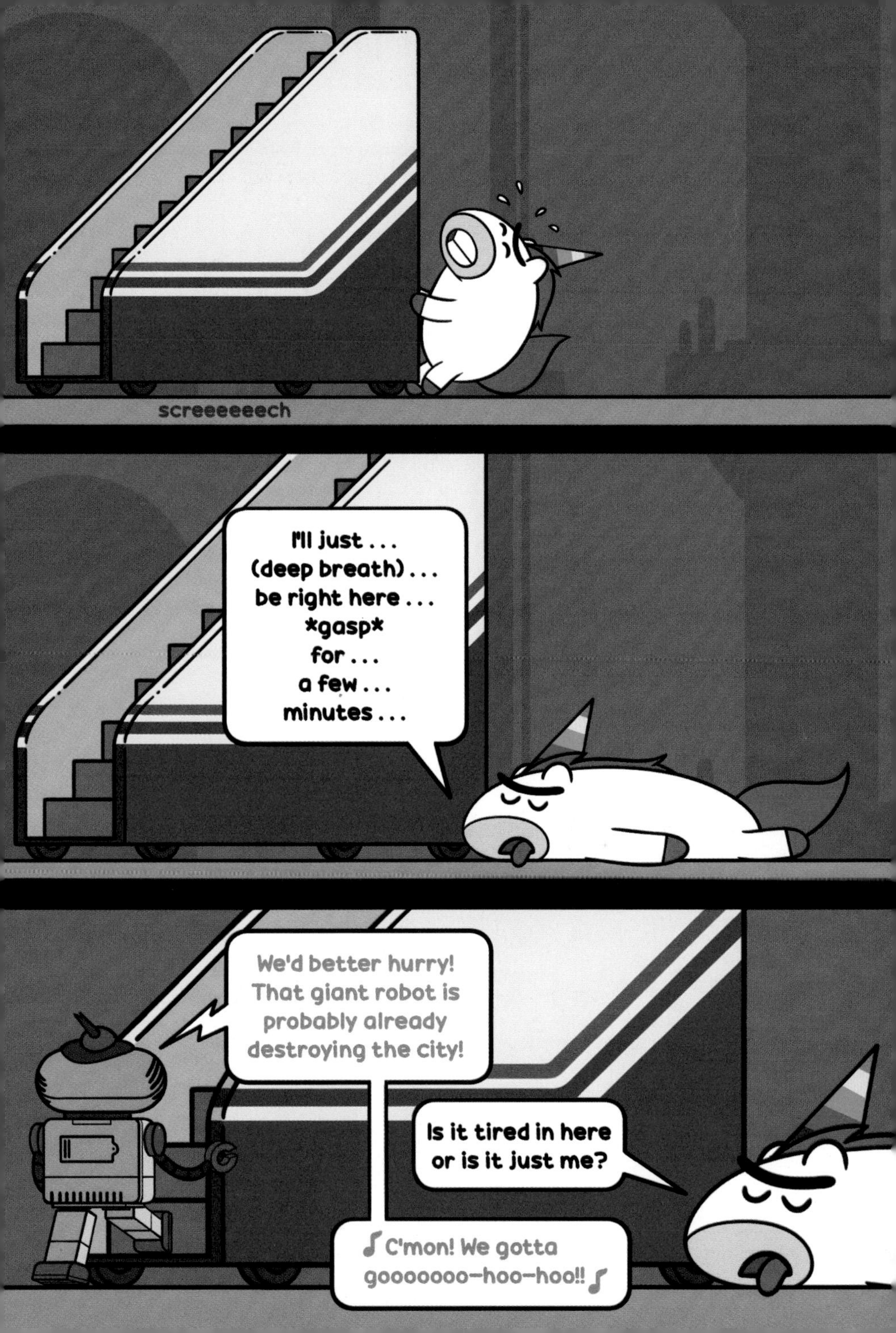
screeeeeeech
I'll just . . . (deep breath) . . . be right here . . . *gasp* for . . . a few . . . minutes . . .
We'd better hurry! That giant robot is probably already destroying the city!
Is it tired in here or is it just me?
C'mon! We gotta gooooooo-hoo-hoo!!

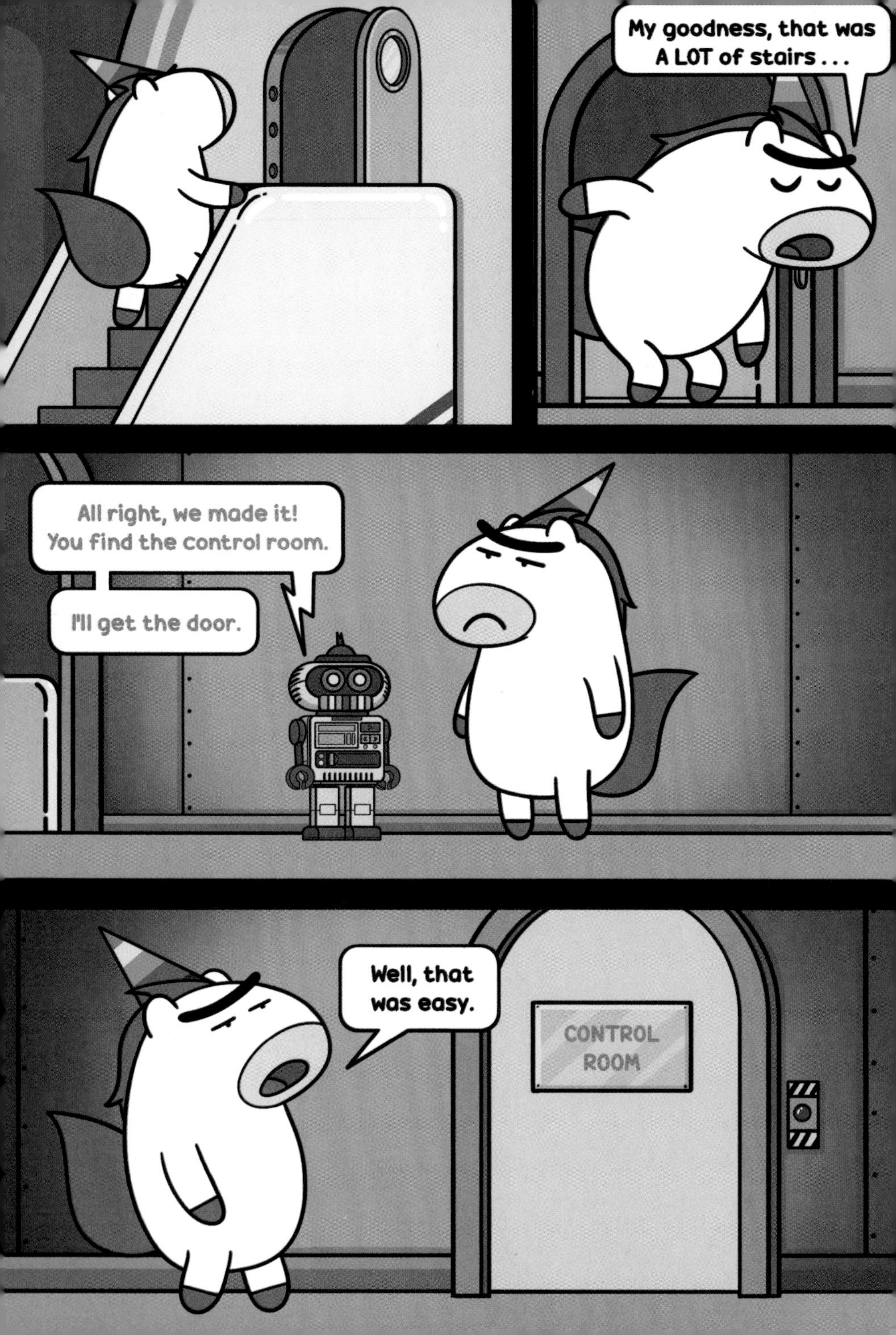
My goodness, that was A LOT of stairs . . .
All right, we made it! You find the control room.
I'll get the door.
Well, that was easy.
CONTROL ROOM

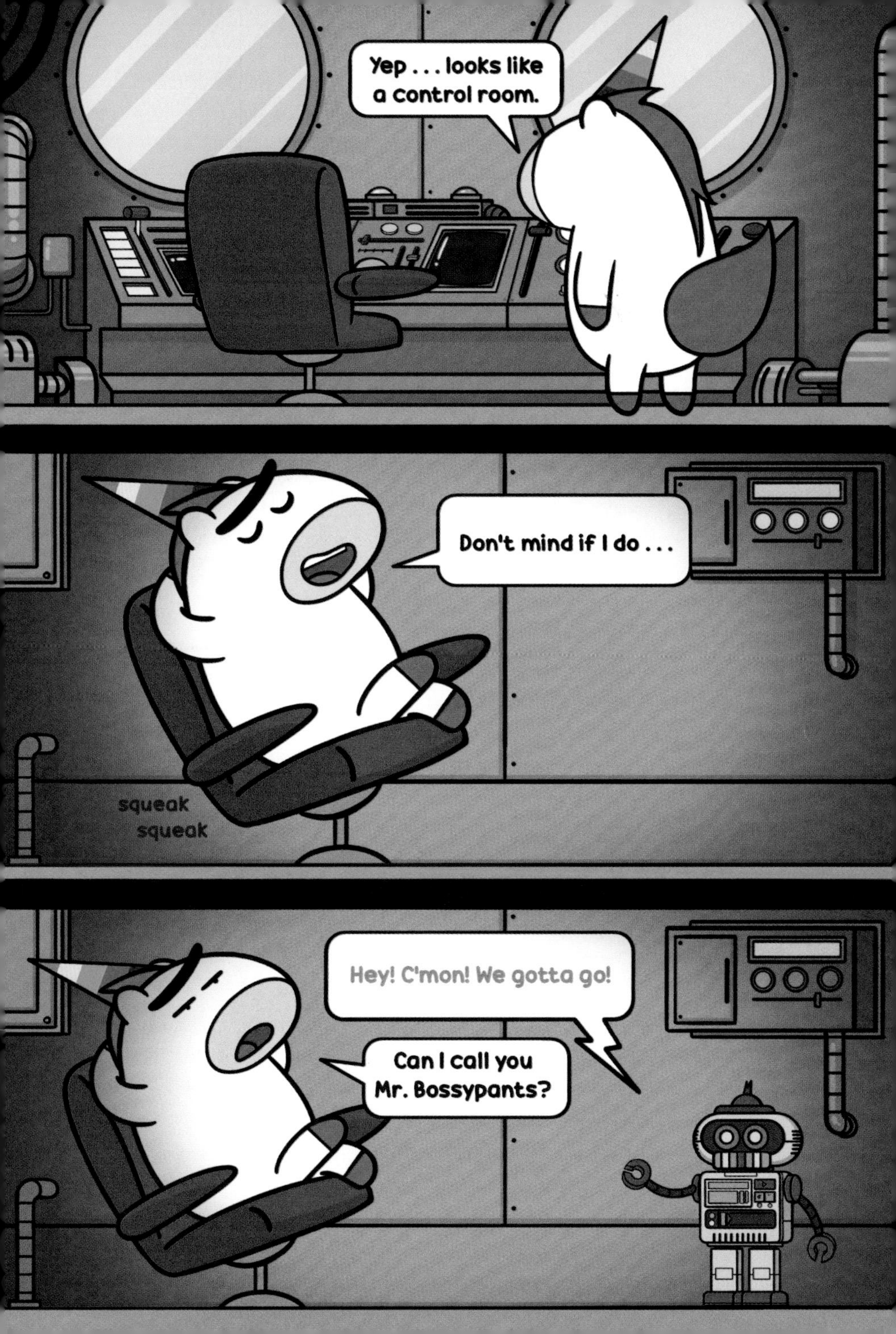
Yep . . . looks like a control room.
Don't mind if I do . . .
squeak squeak
Hey! C'mon! We gotta go!
Can I call you Mr. Bossypants?

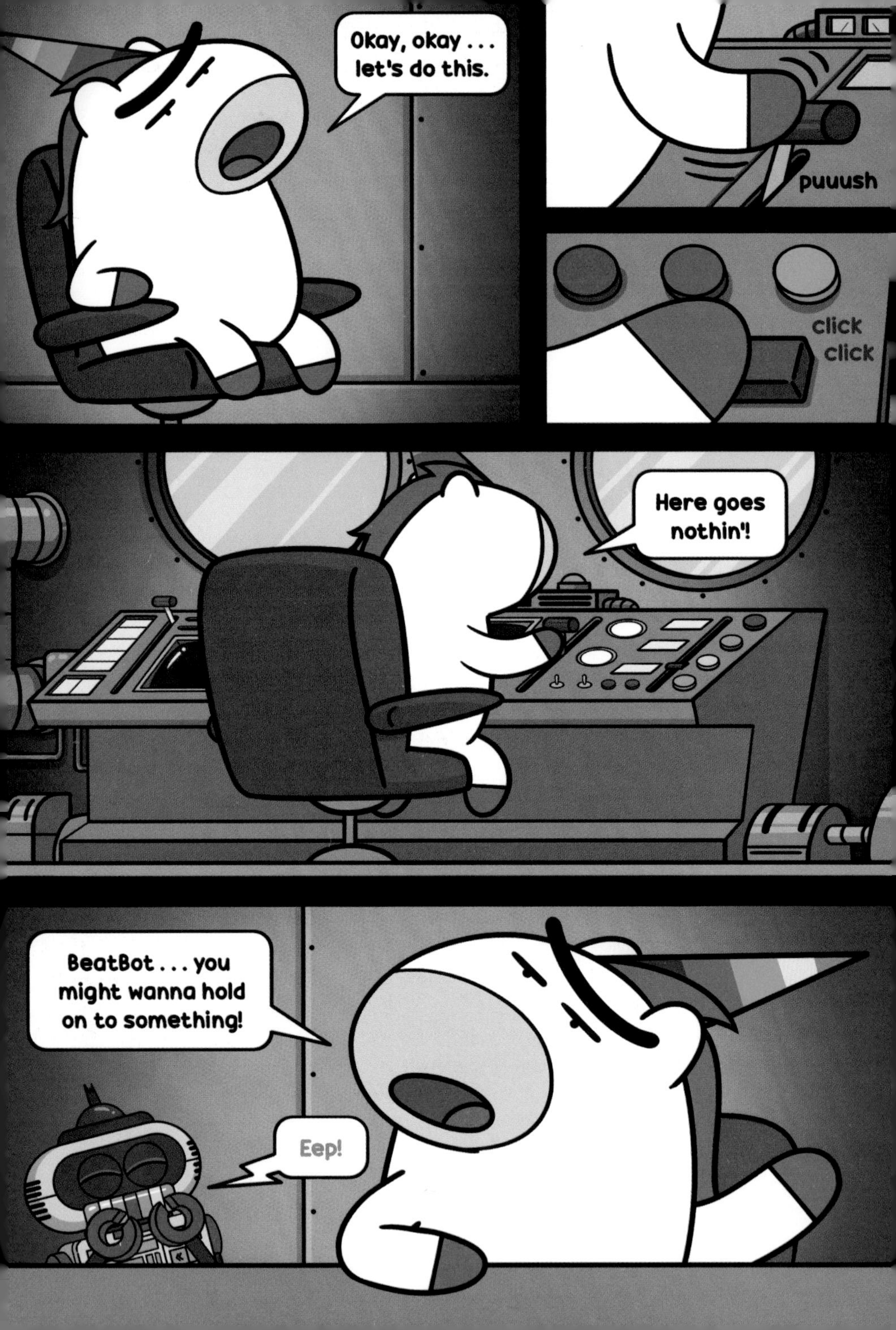
Okay, okay . . . let's do this.
puuush
click
click
Here goes nothin'!
BeatBot . . . you might wanna hold on to something!
Eep!

FWOOOOSH!!

FWOOOOSH!!

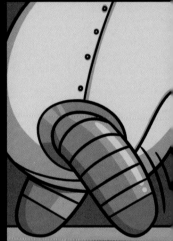

Here we go!!!

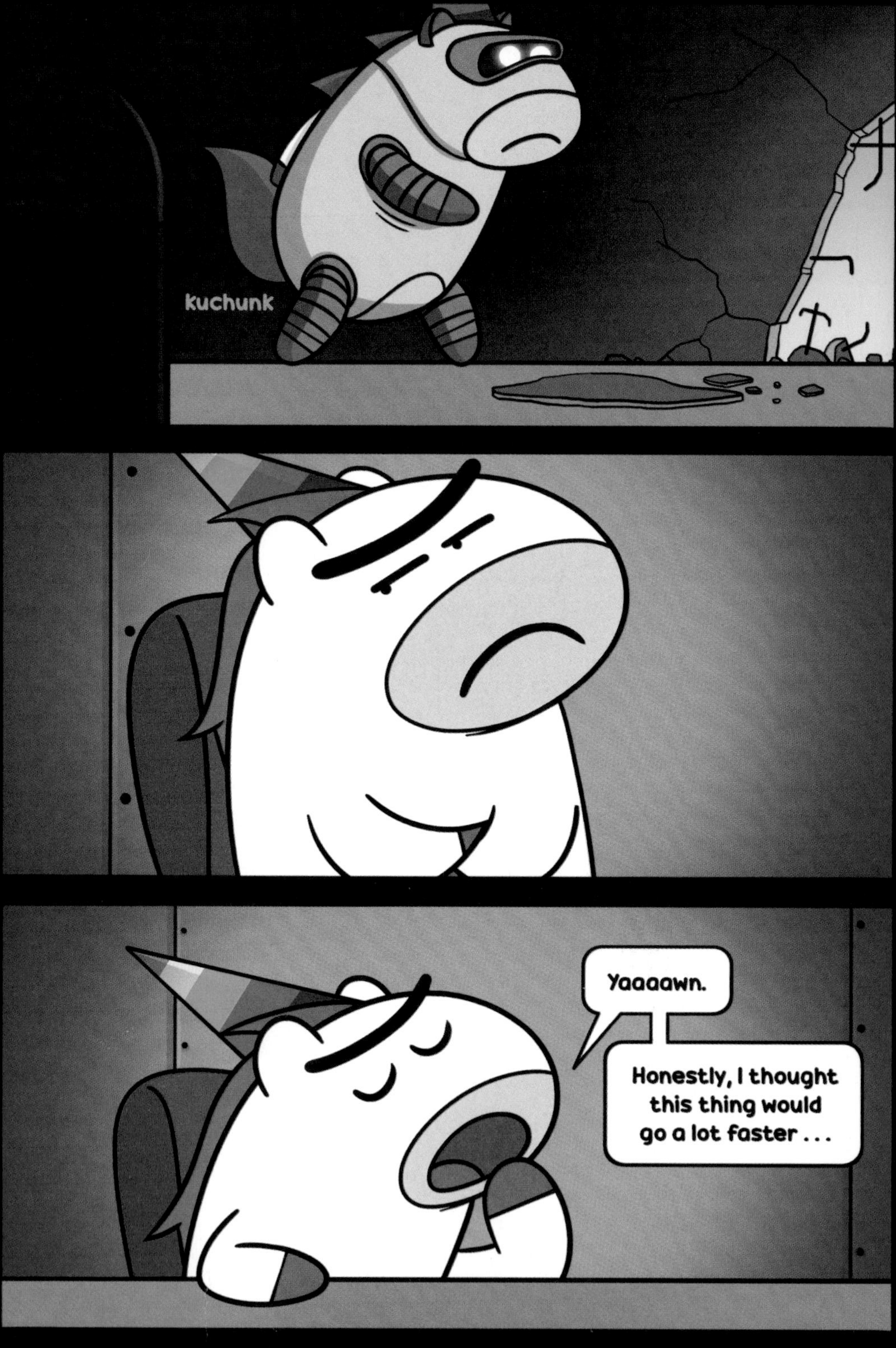
kuchunk
Yaaaawn.
Honestly, I thought this thing would go a lot faster . . .

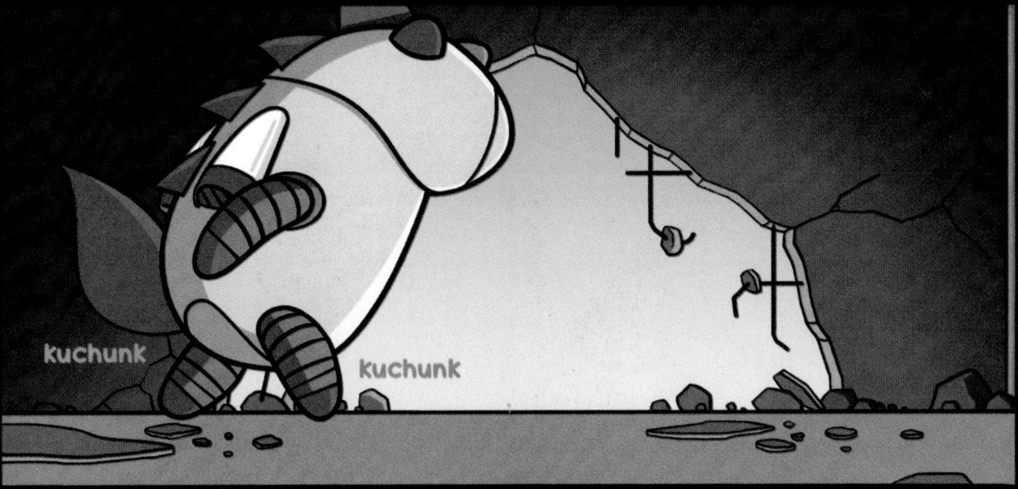
kuchunk
kuchunk

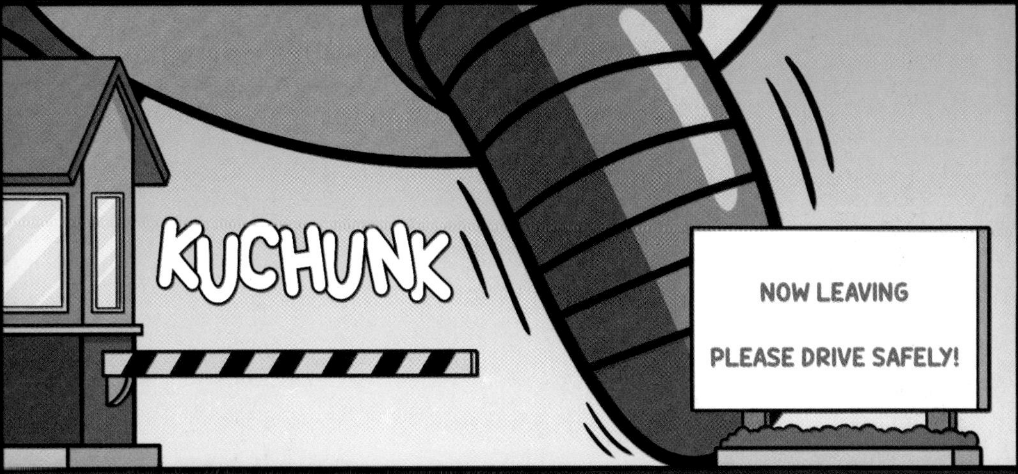
KUCHUNK
NOW LEAVING
PLEASE DRIVE SAFELY!

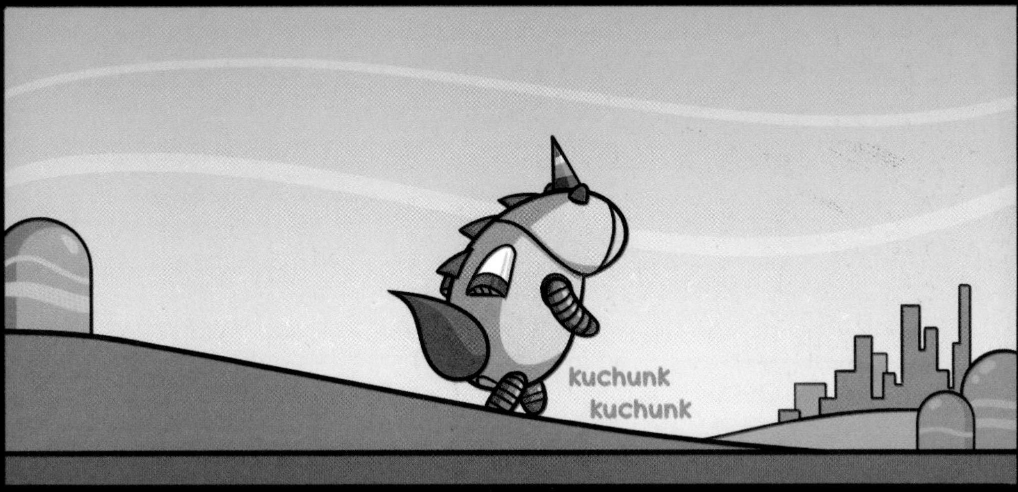
kuchunk
kuchunk

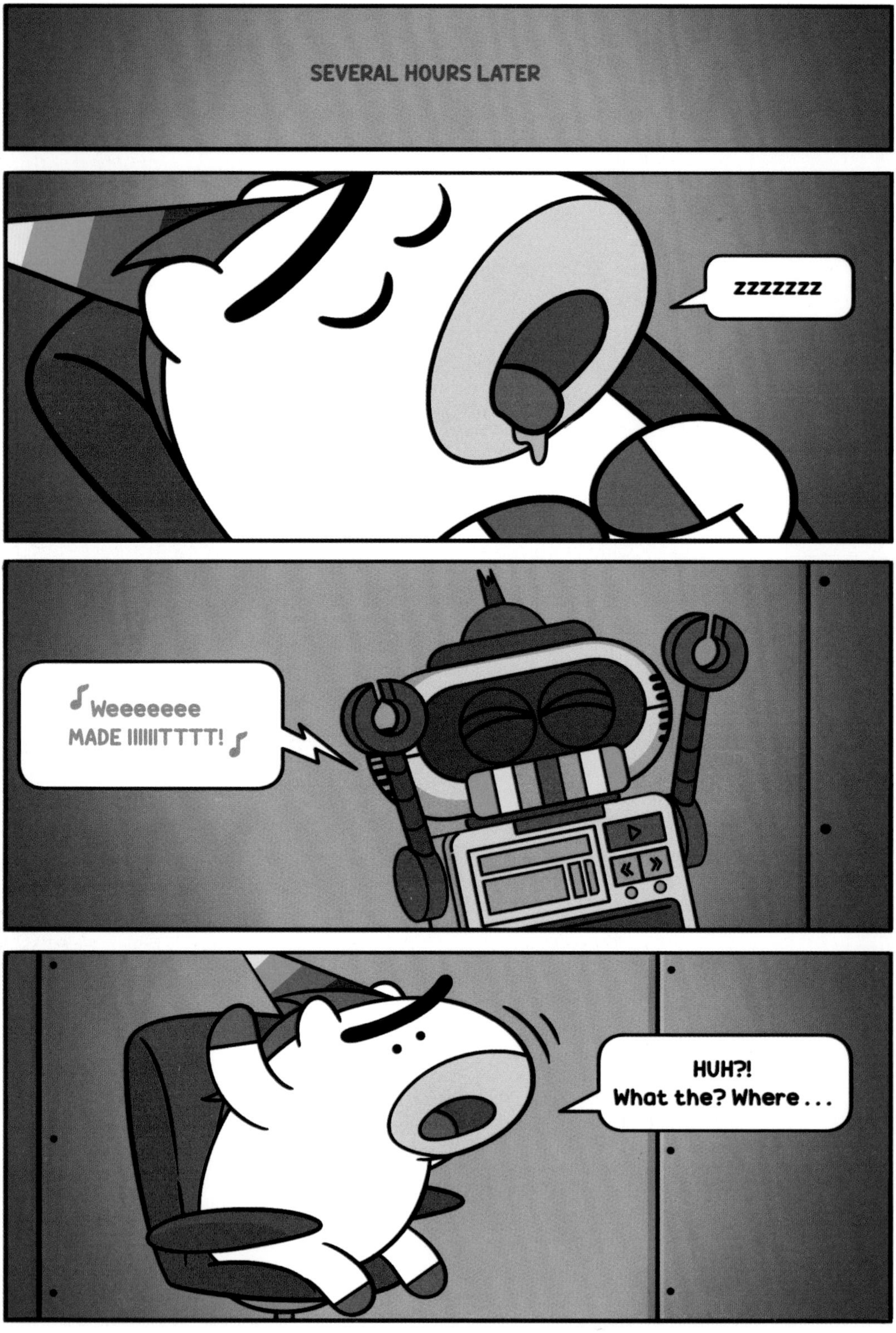
SEVERAL HOURS LATER
zzzzzzz
Weeeeeee MADE IIIIIITTTT!
HUH?!
What the? Where . . .

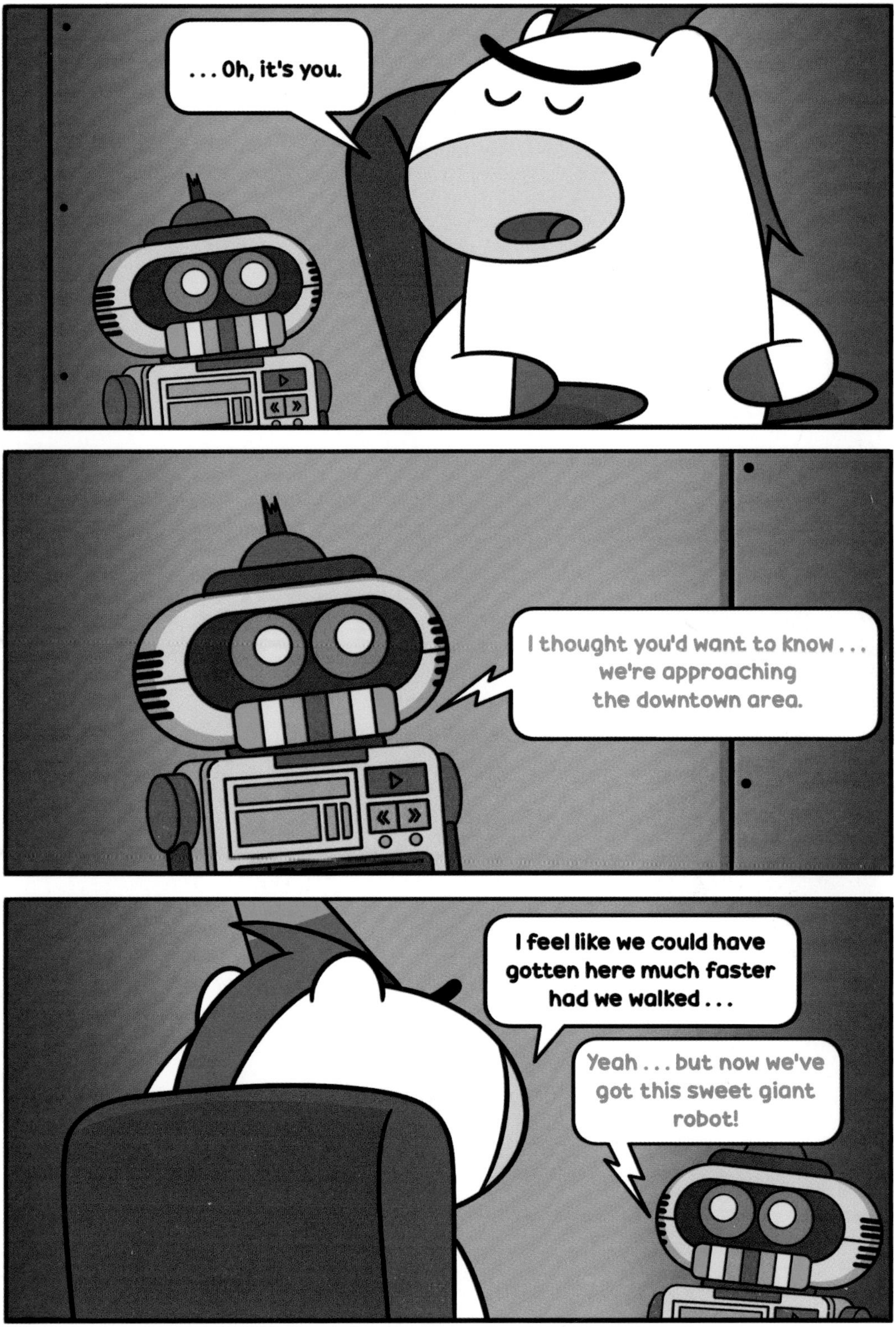
. . . Oh, it's you.
I thought you'd want to know . . . we're approaching the downtown area.
I feel like we could have gotten here much faster had we walked . . .
Yeah . . . but now we've got this sweet giant robot!

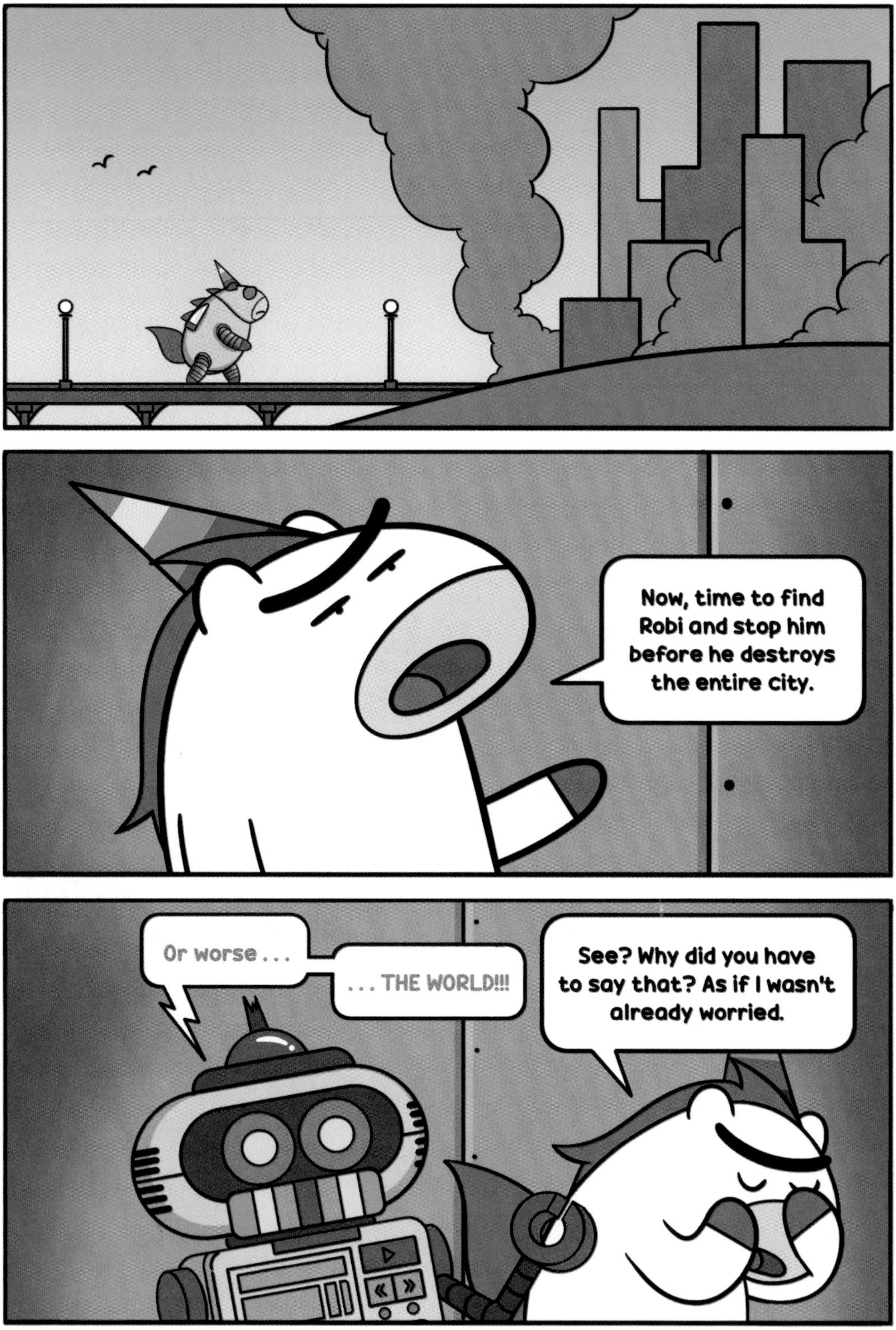
Now, time to find Robi and stop him before he destroys the entire city.
Or worse . . .
. . . THE WORLD!!!
See? Why did you have to say that? As if I wasn't already worried.

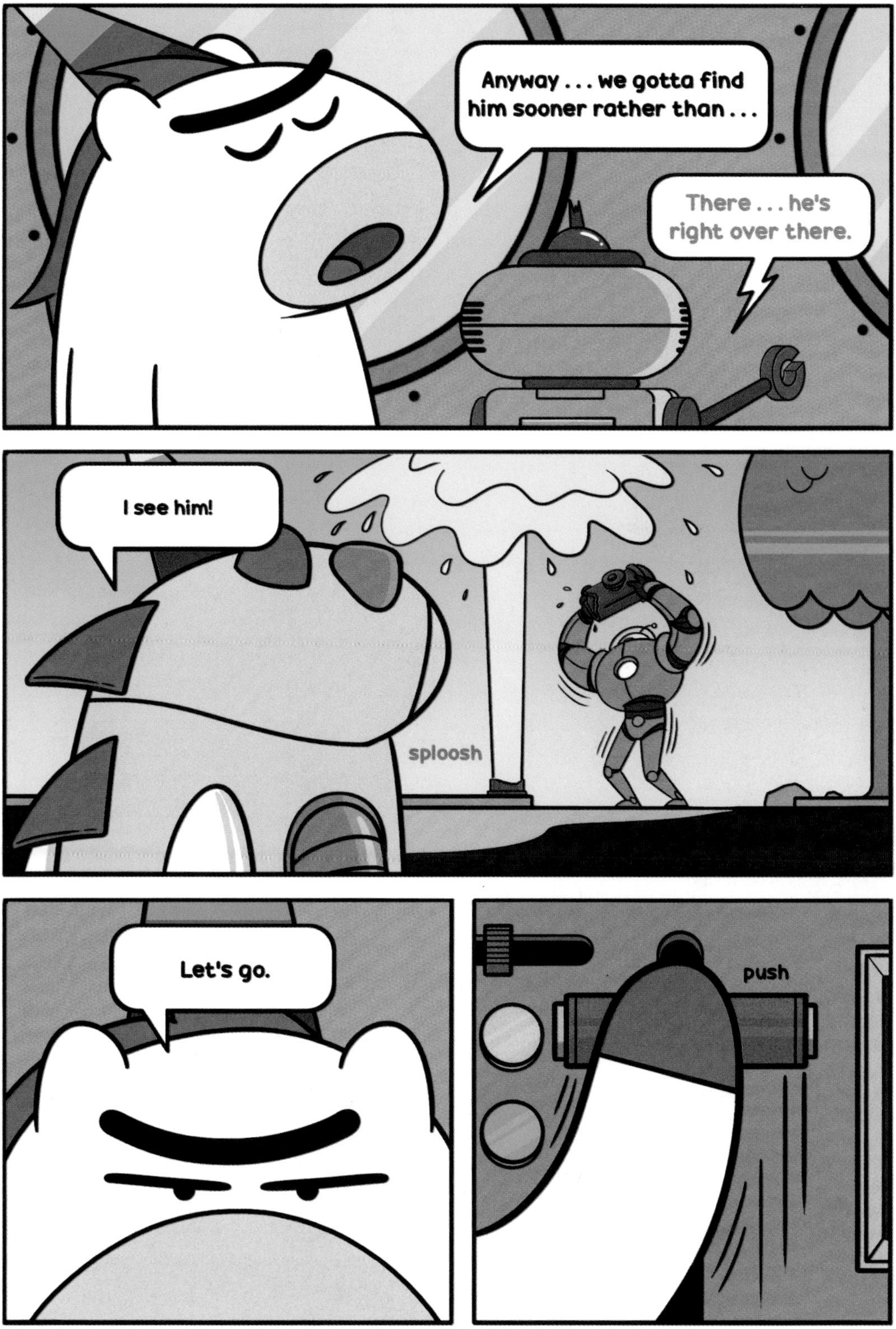
Anyway . . . we gotta find him sooner rather than . . .
There . . . he's right over there.
I see him!
sploosh
Let's go.
push

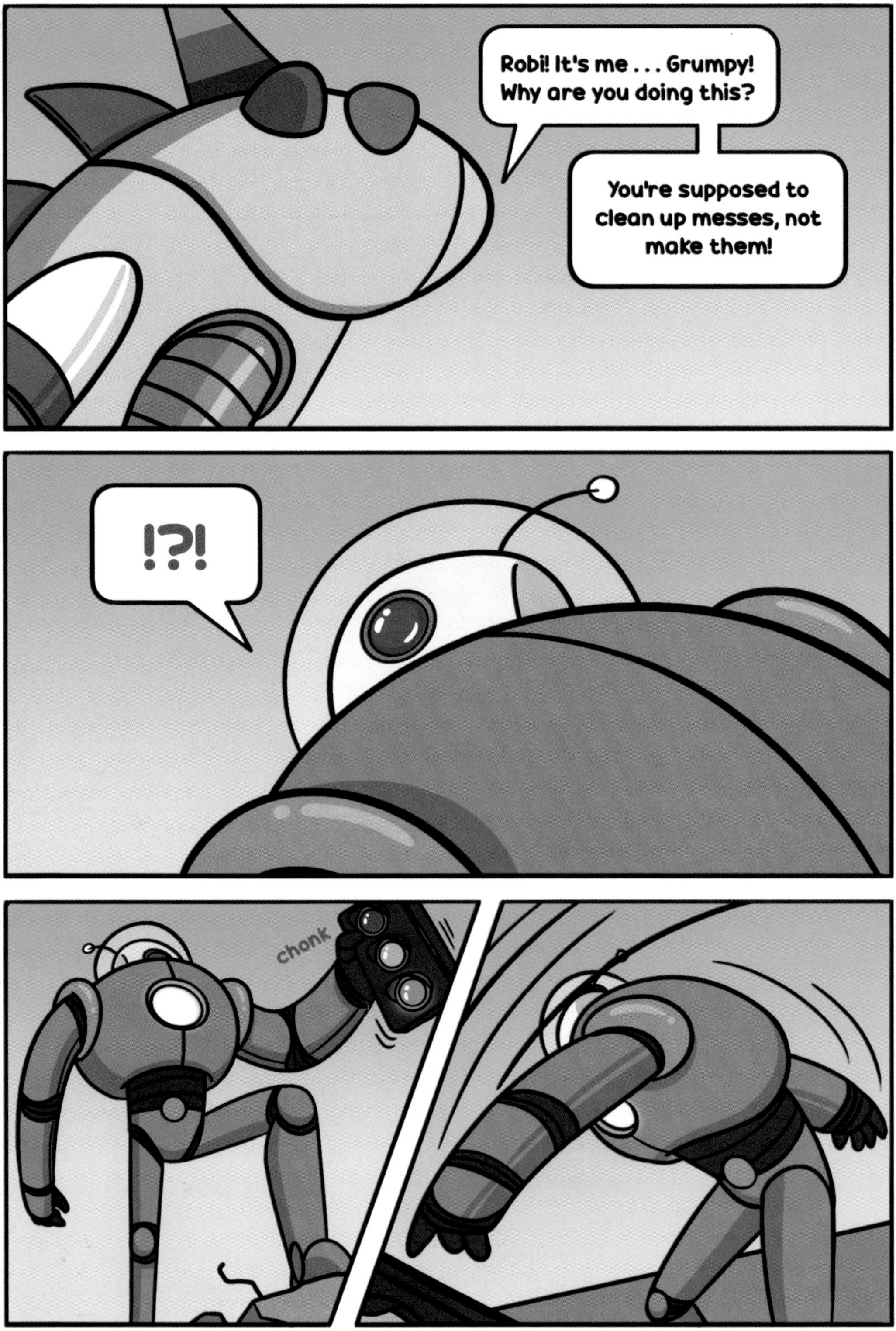
Robi! It's me . . . Grumpy! Why are you doing this?
You're supposed to clean up messes, not make them!
!?!
chonk

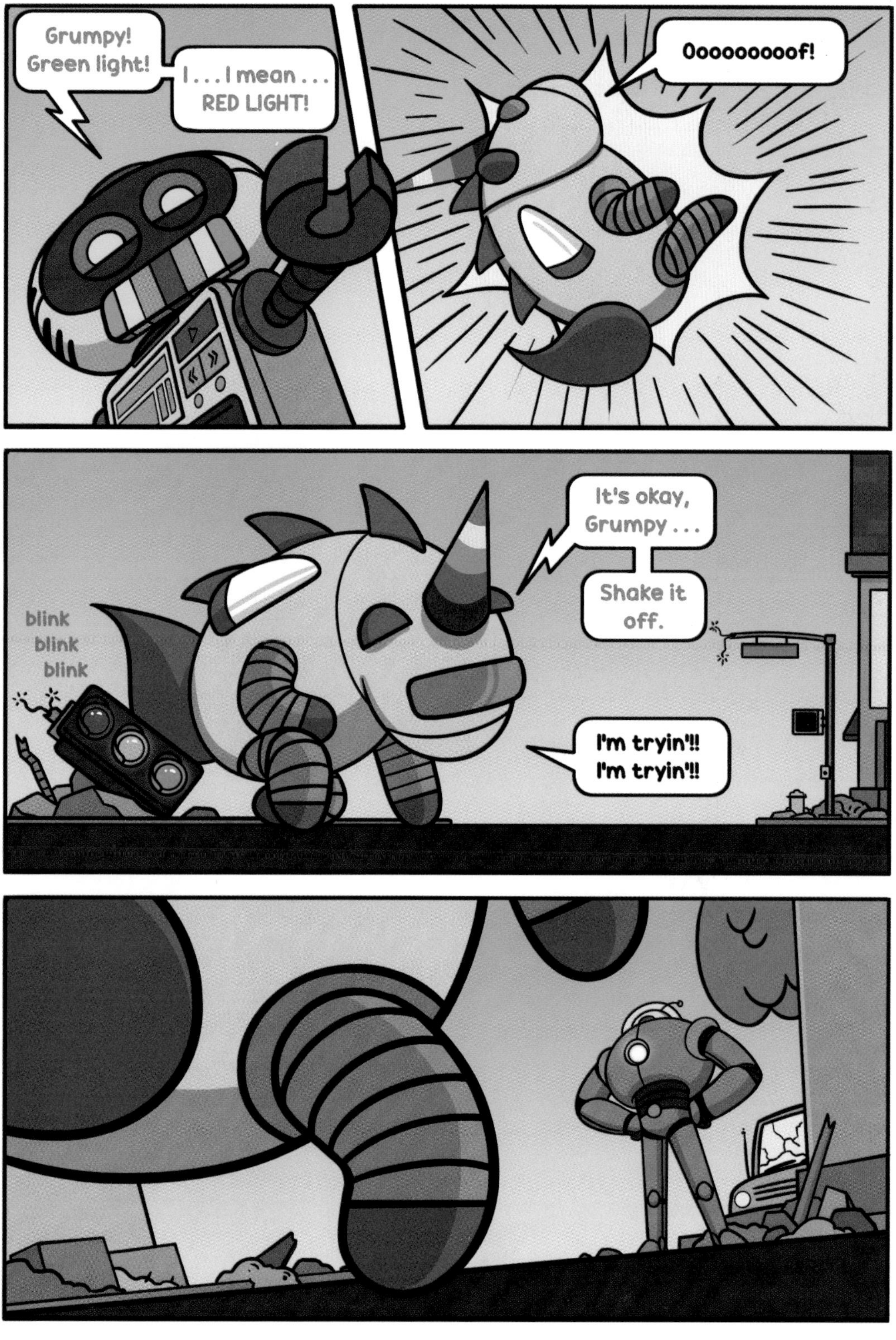
Grumpy! Green light!
I . . . I mean . . . RED LIGHT!
Ooooooooof!
It's okay, Grumpy . . .
Shake it off.
blink blink blink
I'm tryin'!! I'm tryin'!!

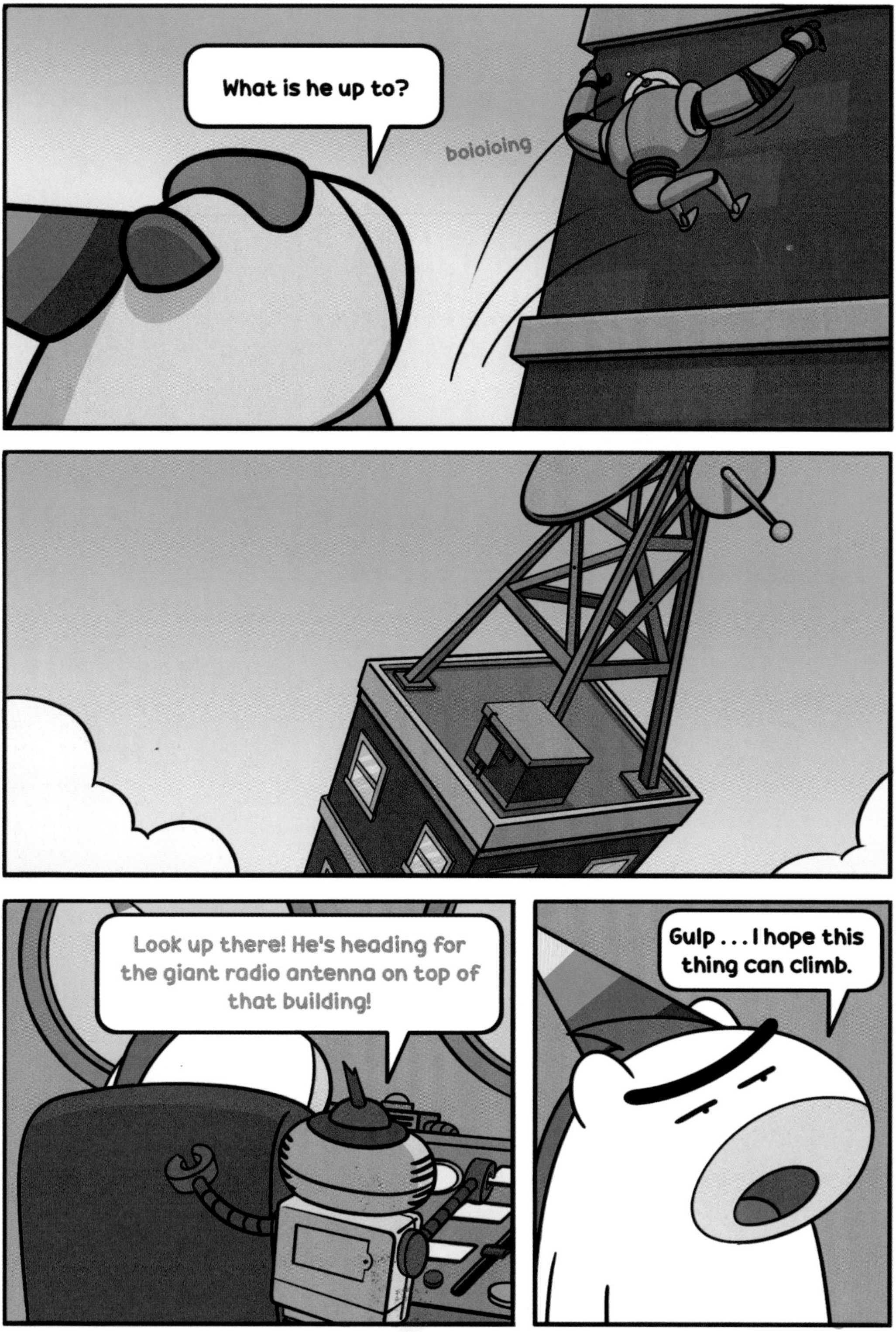
What is he up to?
boioioing
Look up there! He's heading for the giant radio antenna on top of that building!
Gulp . . . I hope this thing can climb.

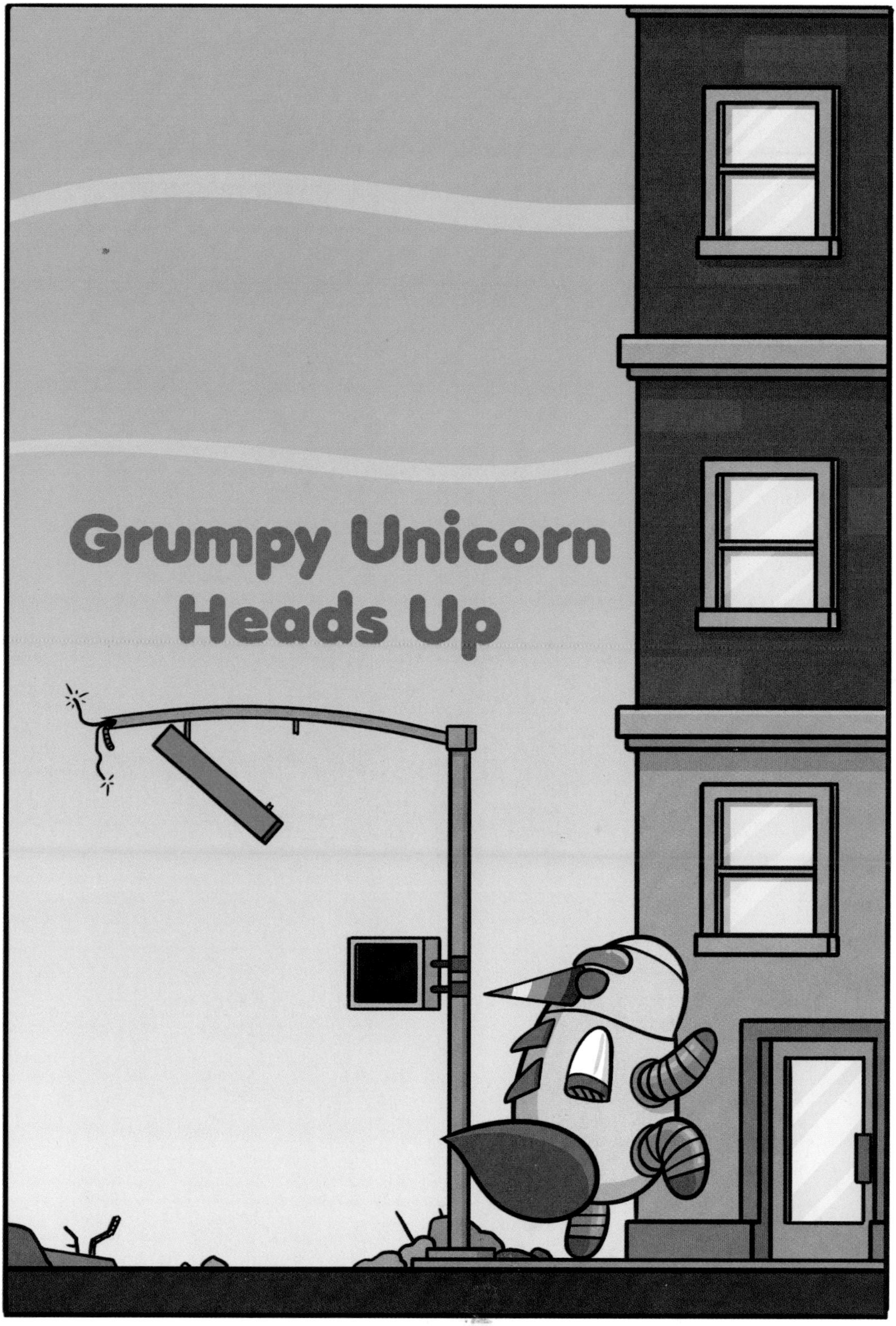
Grumpy Unicorn
Heads Up

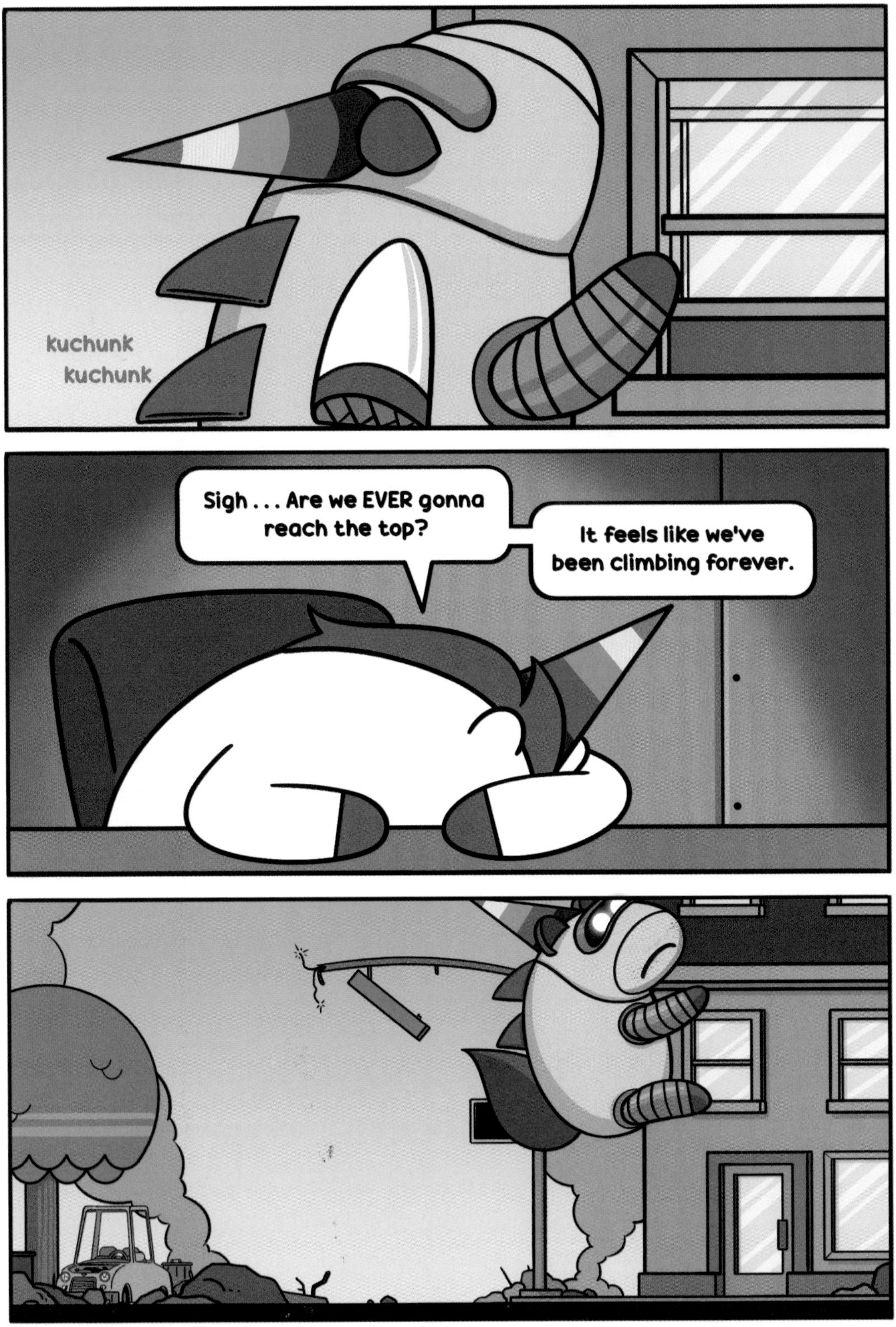
kuchunk
kuchunk
Sigh . . . Are we EVER gonna reach the top?
It feels like we've been climbing forever.

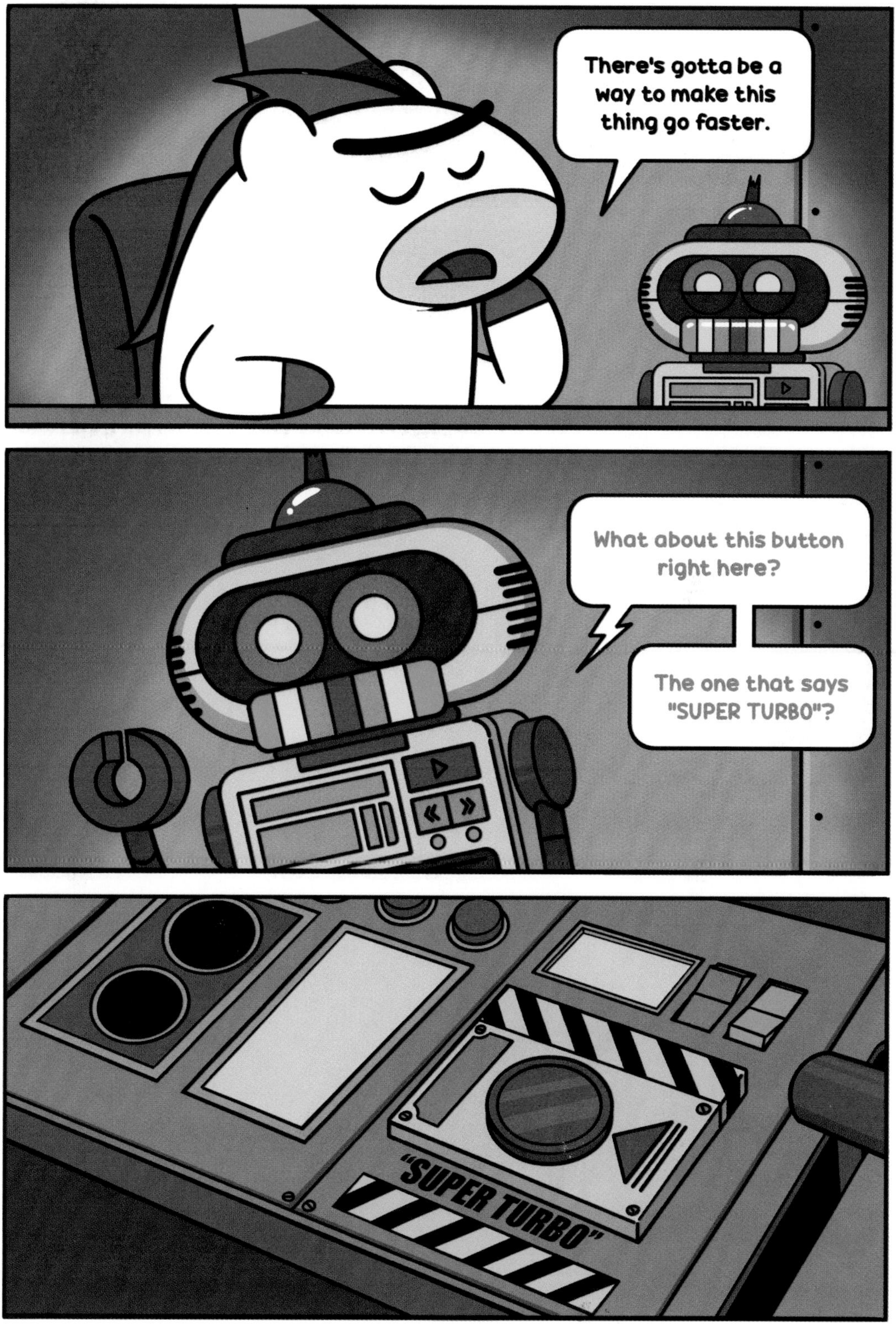
There's gotta be a way to make this thing go faster.
What about this button right here?
The one that says "SUPER TURBO"?
"SUPER TURBO"

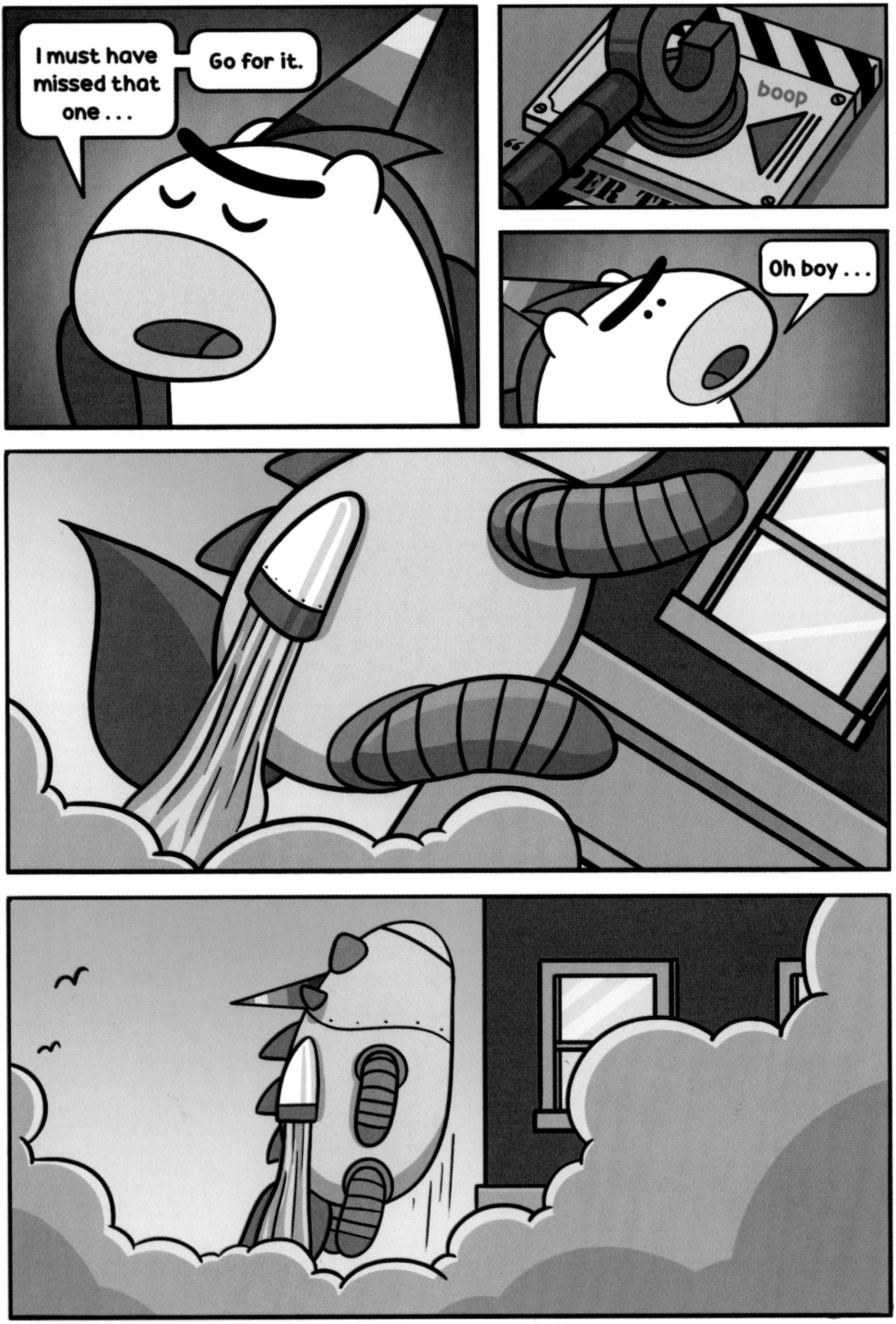
I must have missed that one . . .
Go for it.
boop
Oh boy . . .

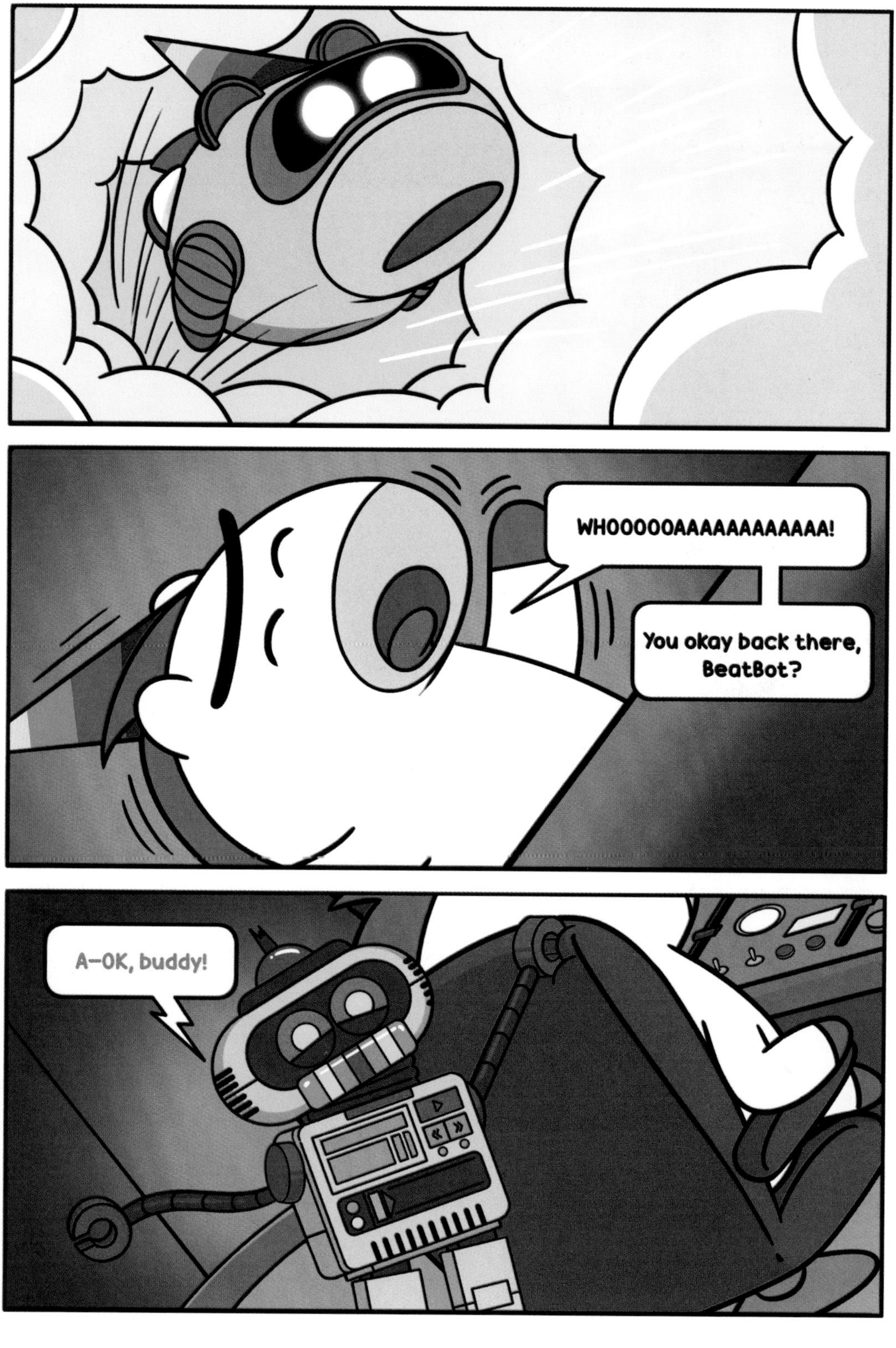
WHOOOOOAAAAAAAAAAAA!
You okay back there, BeatBot?
A-OK, buddy!

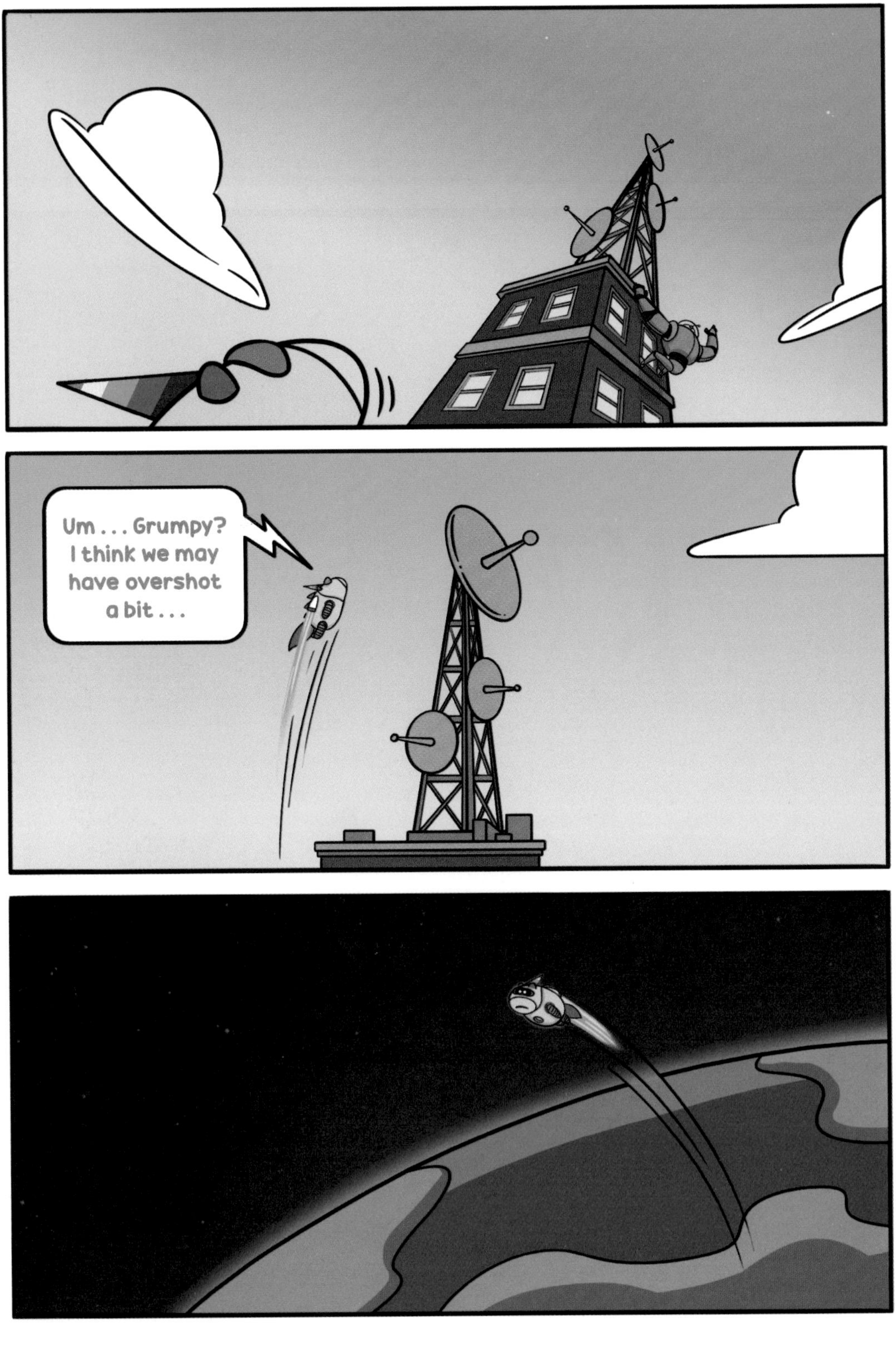
Um . . . Grumpy? I think we may have overshot a bit . . .

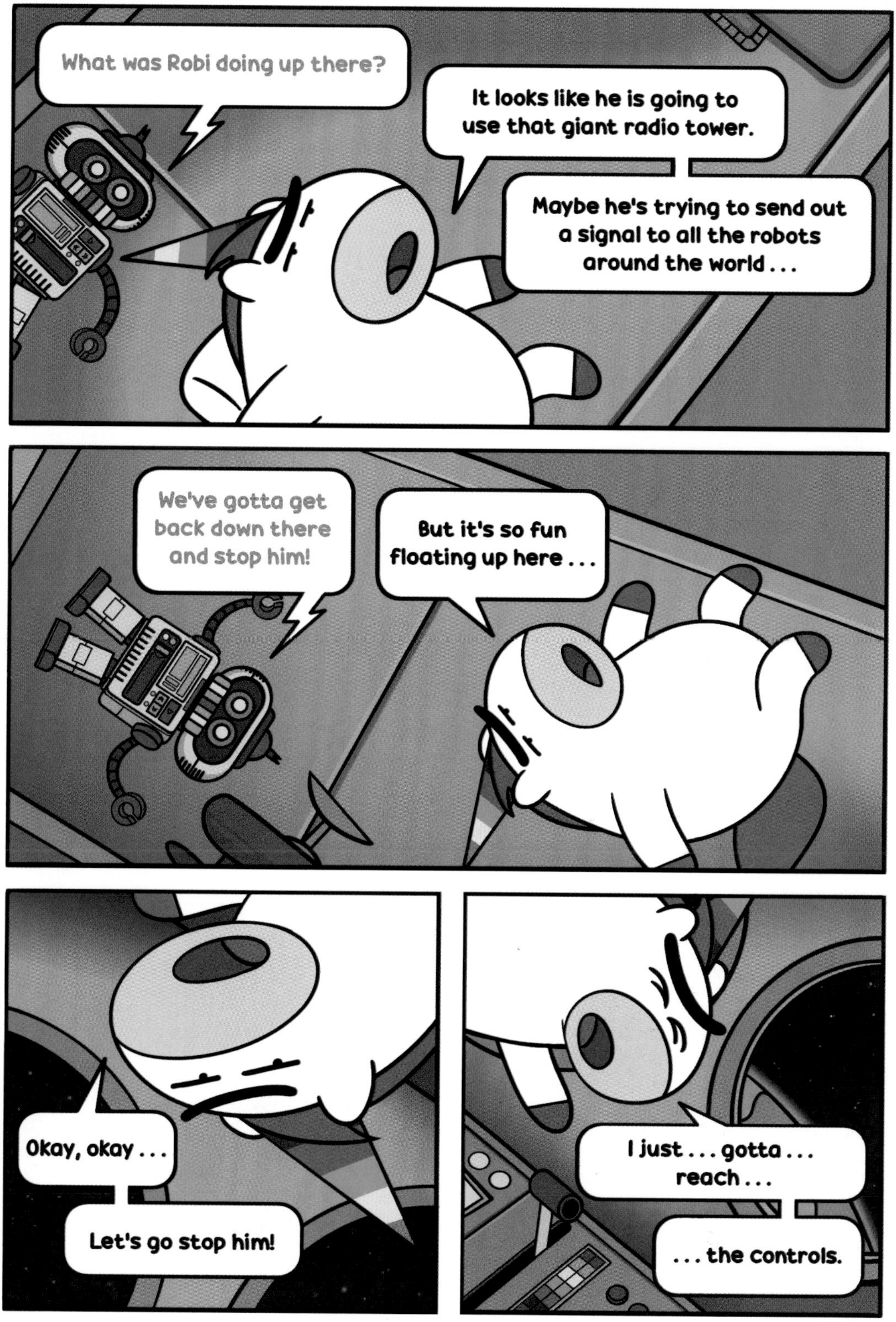
What was Robi doing up there?
It looks like he is going to use that giant radio tower.
Maybe he's trying to send out a signal to all the robots around the world . . .
We've gotta get back down there and stop him!
But it's so fun floating up here . . .
Okay, okay . . .
Let's go stop him!
I just . . . gotta . . . reach . . .
. . . the controls.

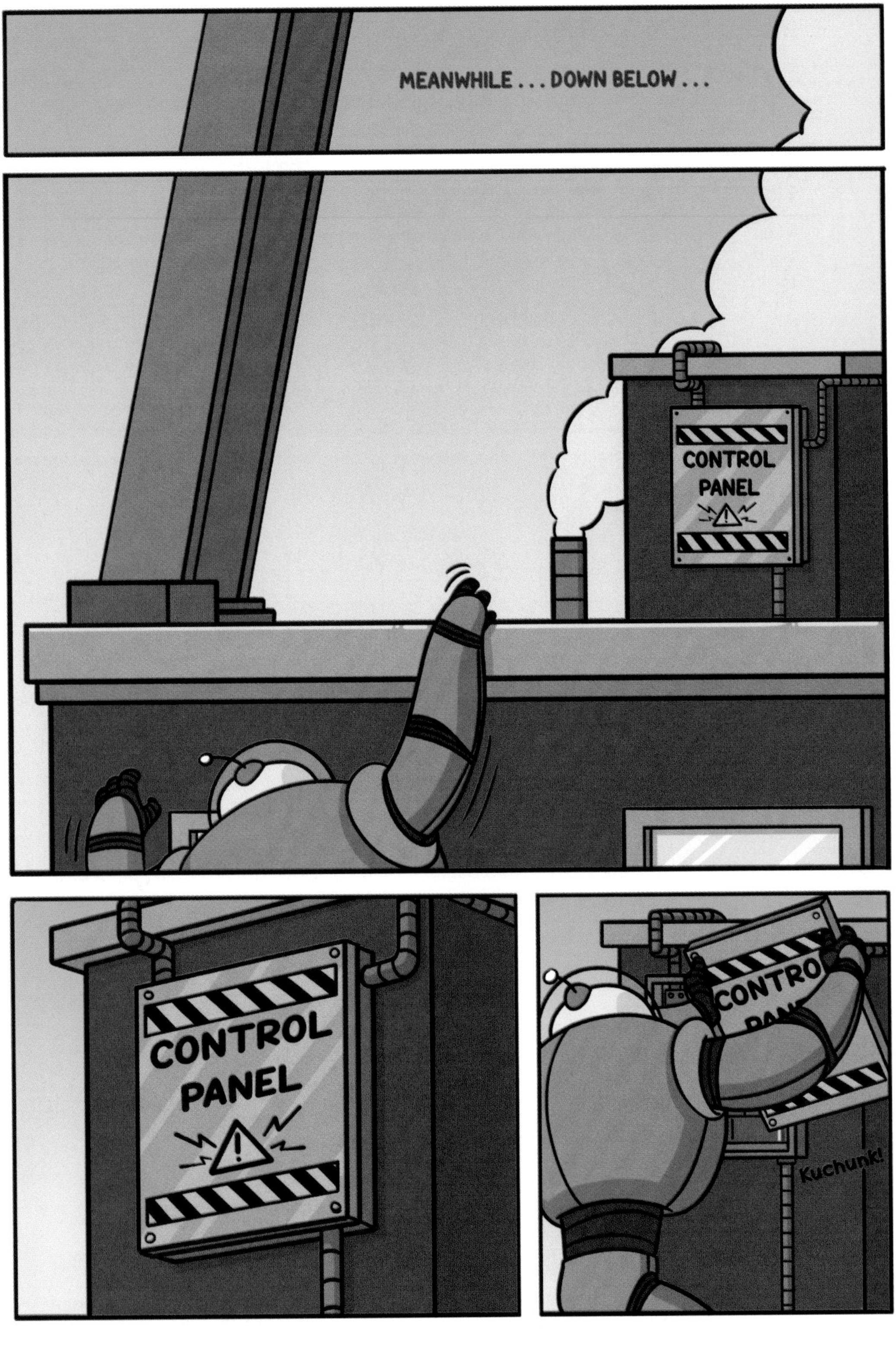
MEANWHILE . . . DOWN BELOW . . .
CONTROL PANEL
CONTROL PANEL
Kuchunk!

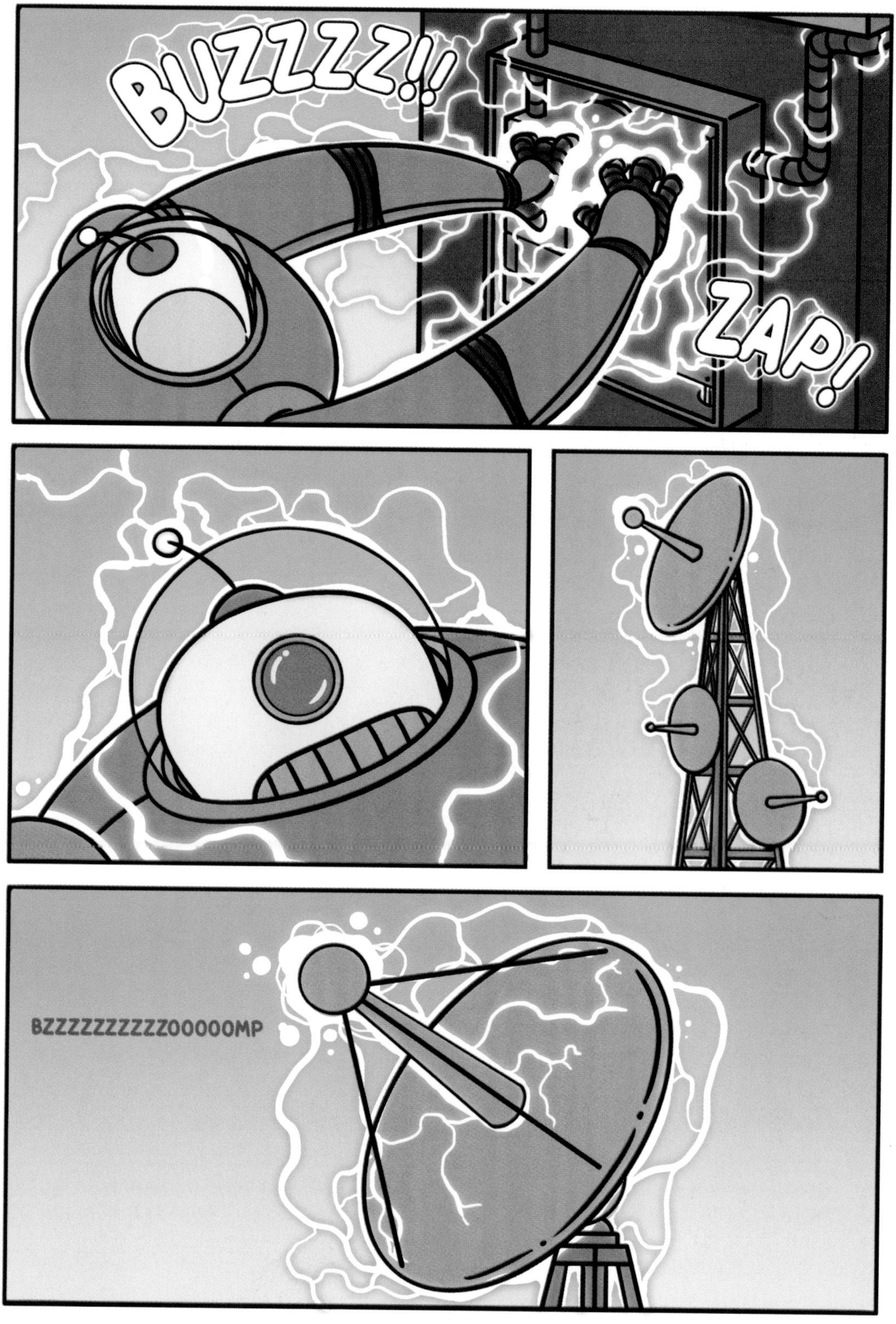
BUZZZZZ!!!
ZAP!
BZZZZZZZZZZOOOOOMP

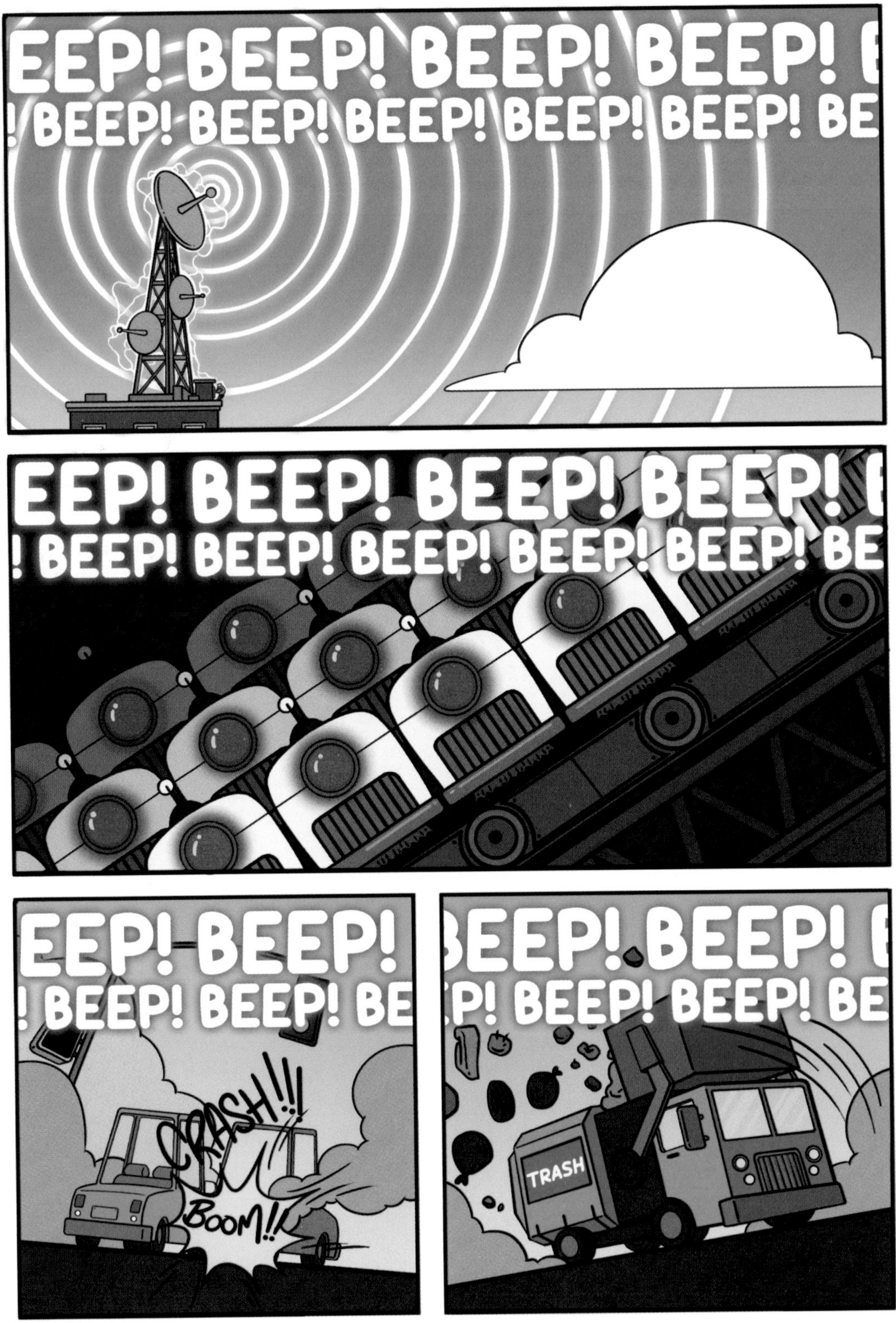
BEEP! BEEP! BEEP!
BEEP! BEEP! BEEP! BEEP! BEEP!
BEEP! BEEP! BEEP!
BEEP! BEEP! BEEP! BEEP! BEEP!
BEEP!
BEEP! BEEP!
CRASH!!!
BOOM!!
BEEP! BEEP!
BEEP! BEEP!
TRASH

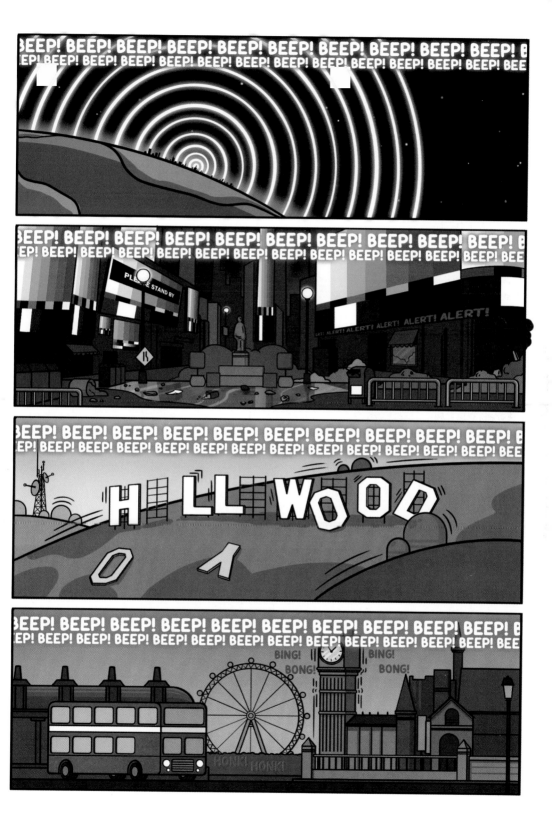

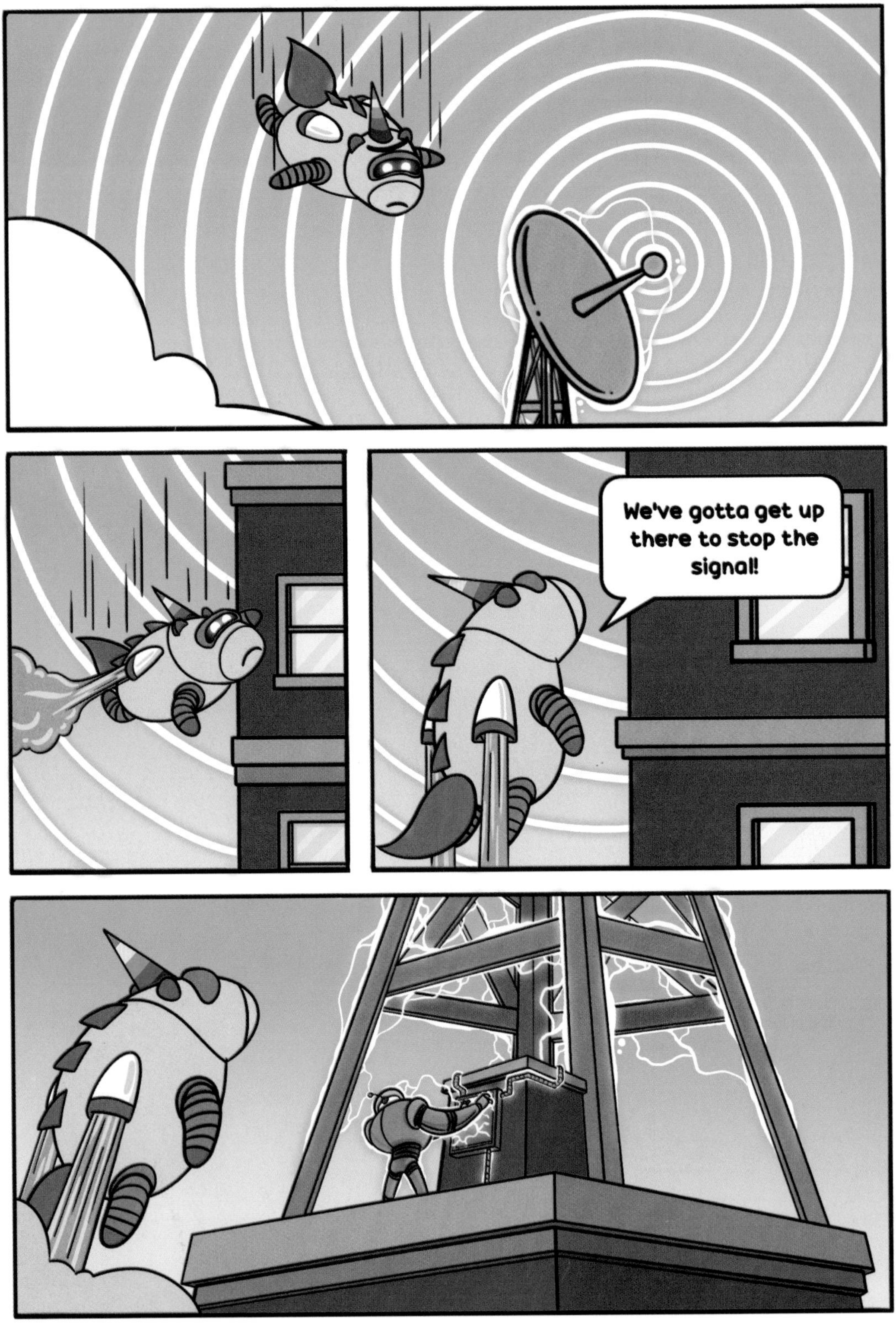
We've gotta get up there to stop the signal!

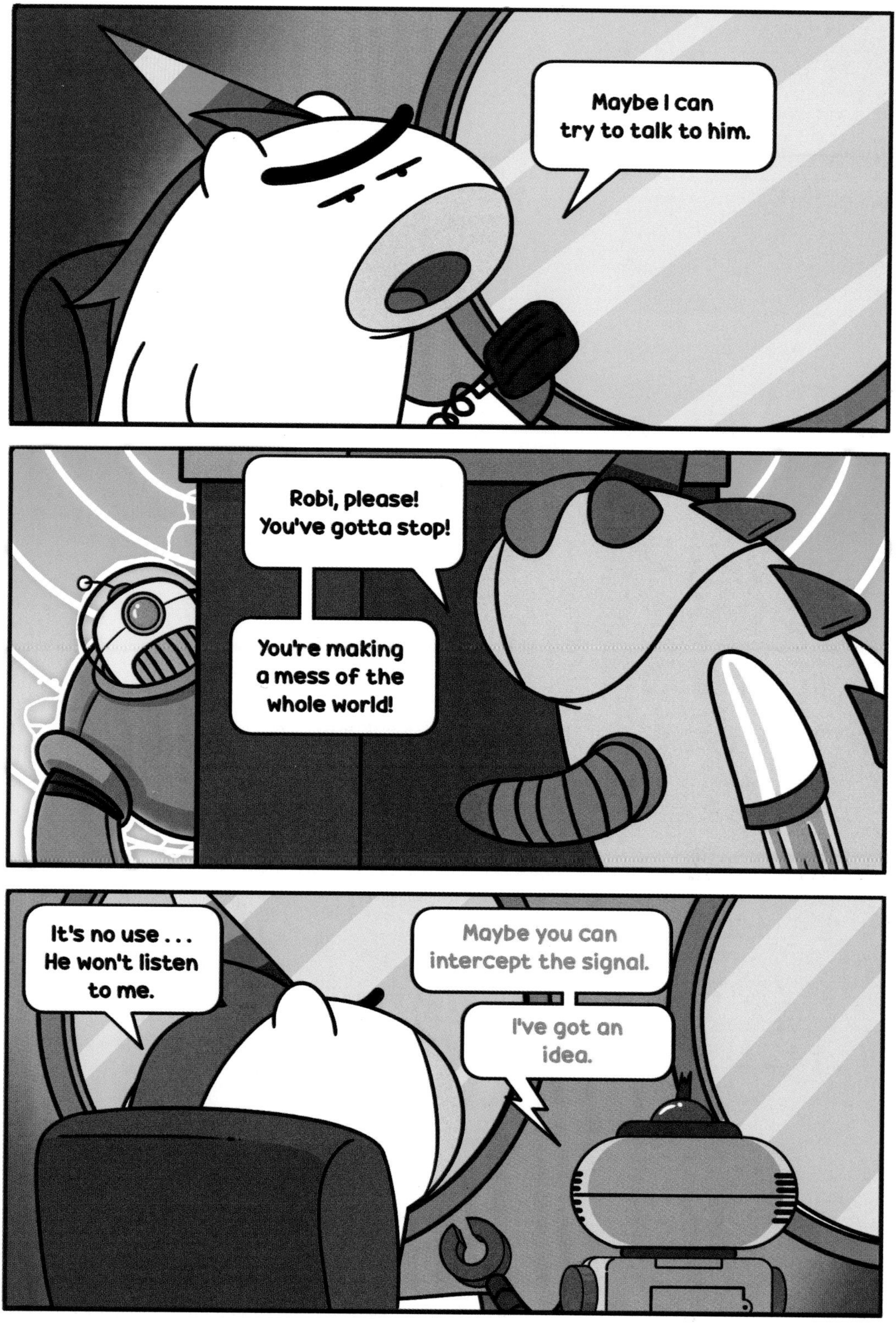
Maybe I can try to talk to him.
Robi, please! You've gotta stop!
You're making a mess of the whole world!
It's no use . . . He won't listen to me.
Maybe you can intercept the signal.
I've got an idea.

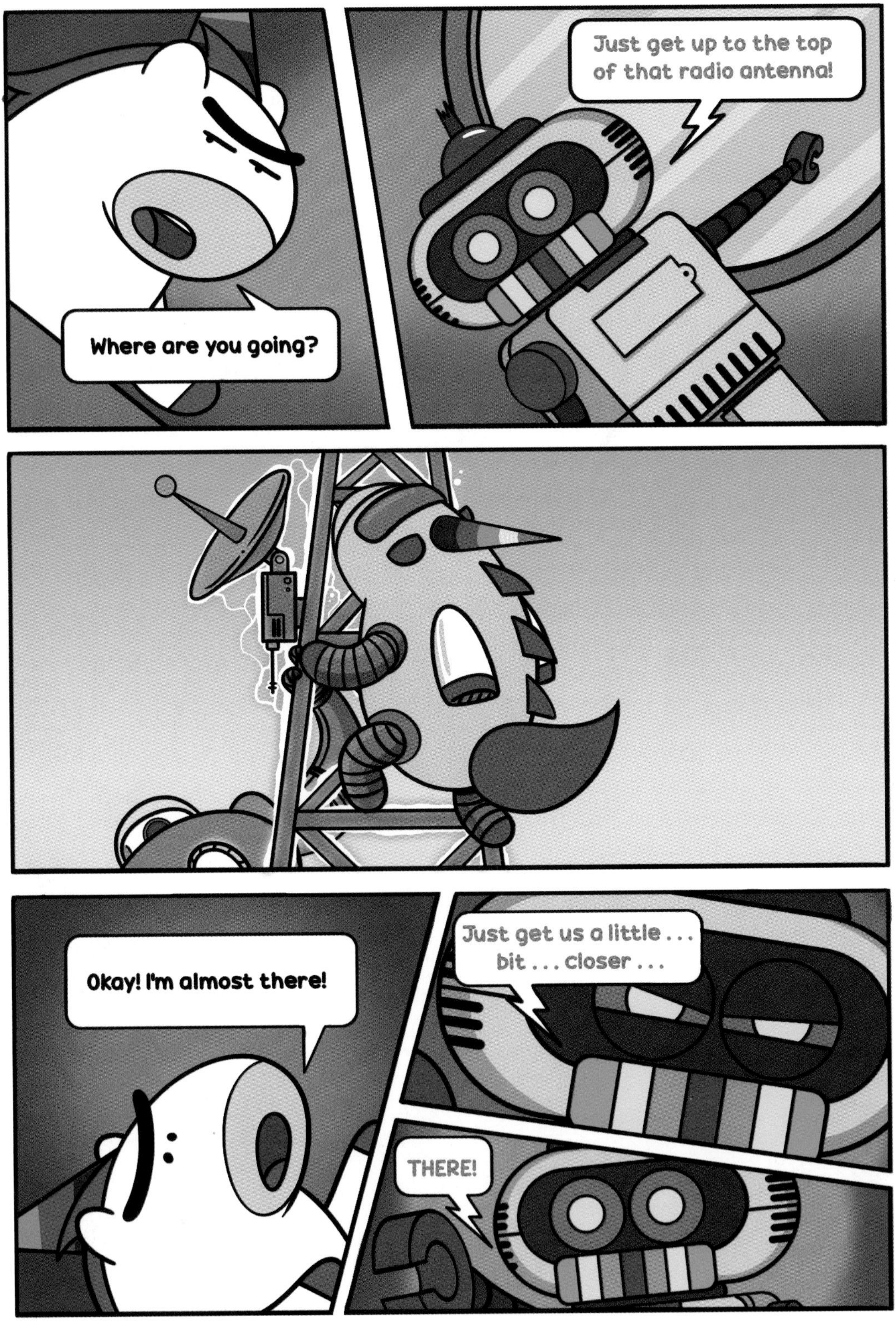
Where are you going?
Just get up to the top of that radio antenna!
Okay! I'm almost there!
Just get us a little . . . bit . . . closer . . .
THERE!

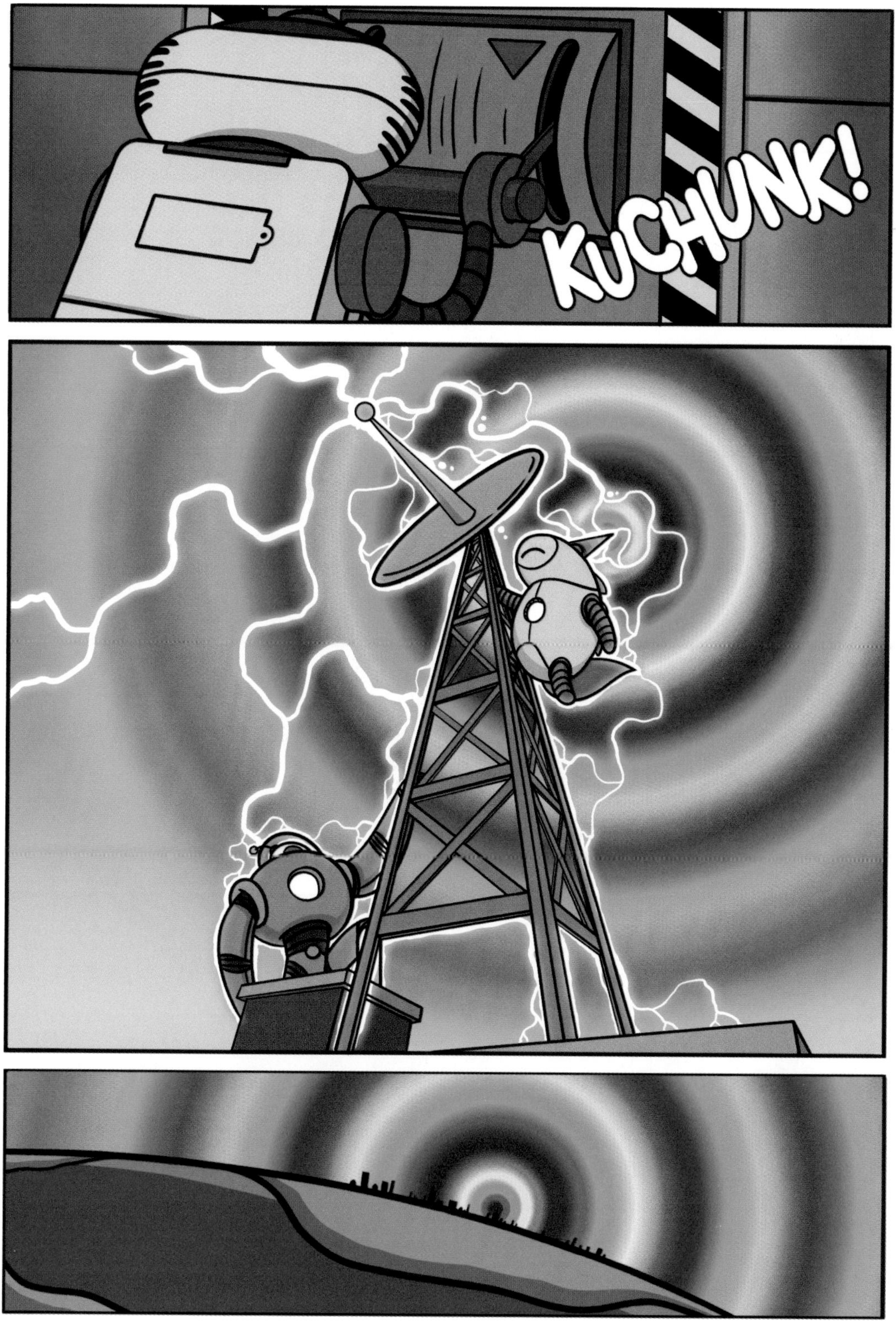
KUCHUNK!

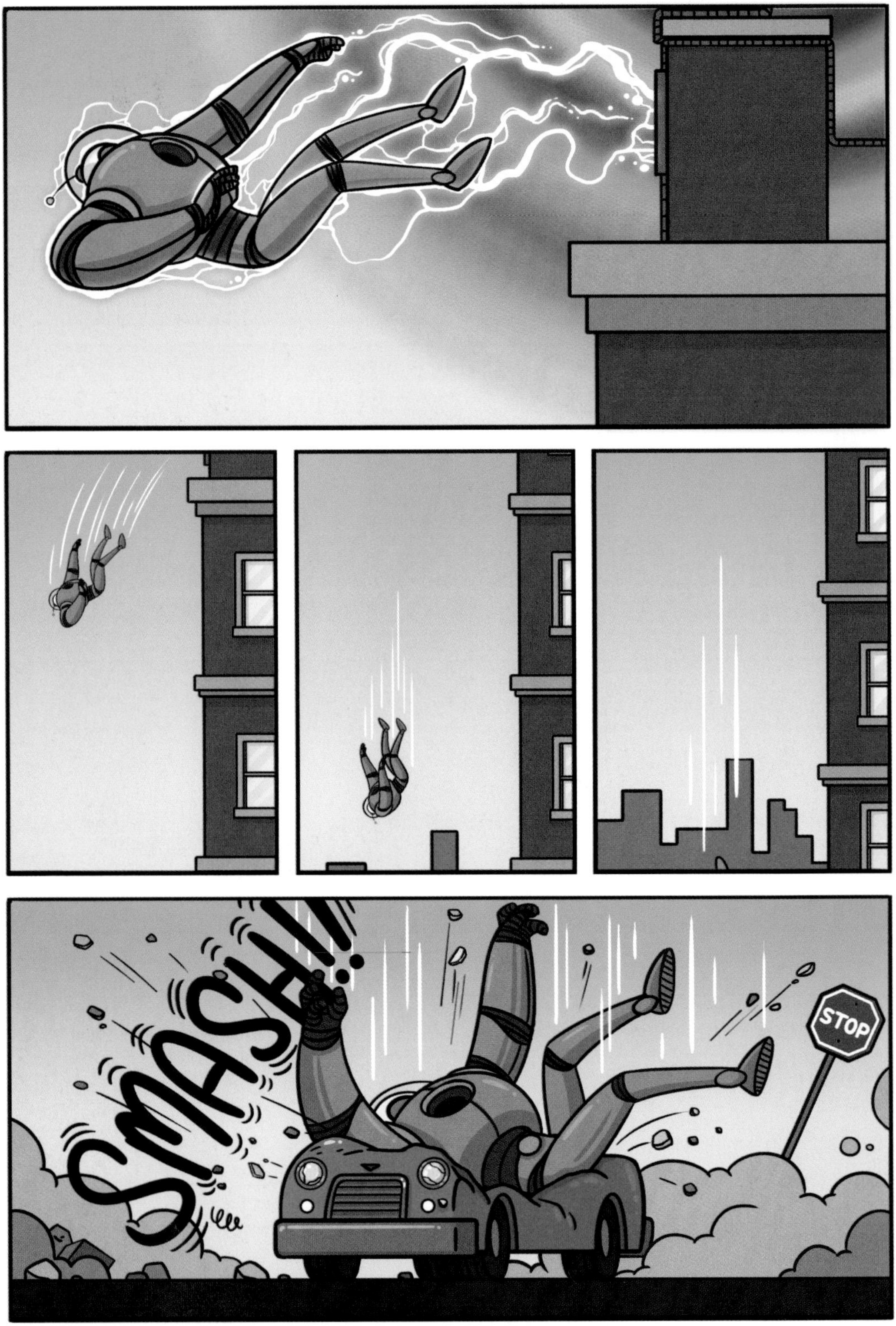
SMASH!!
STOP

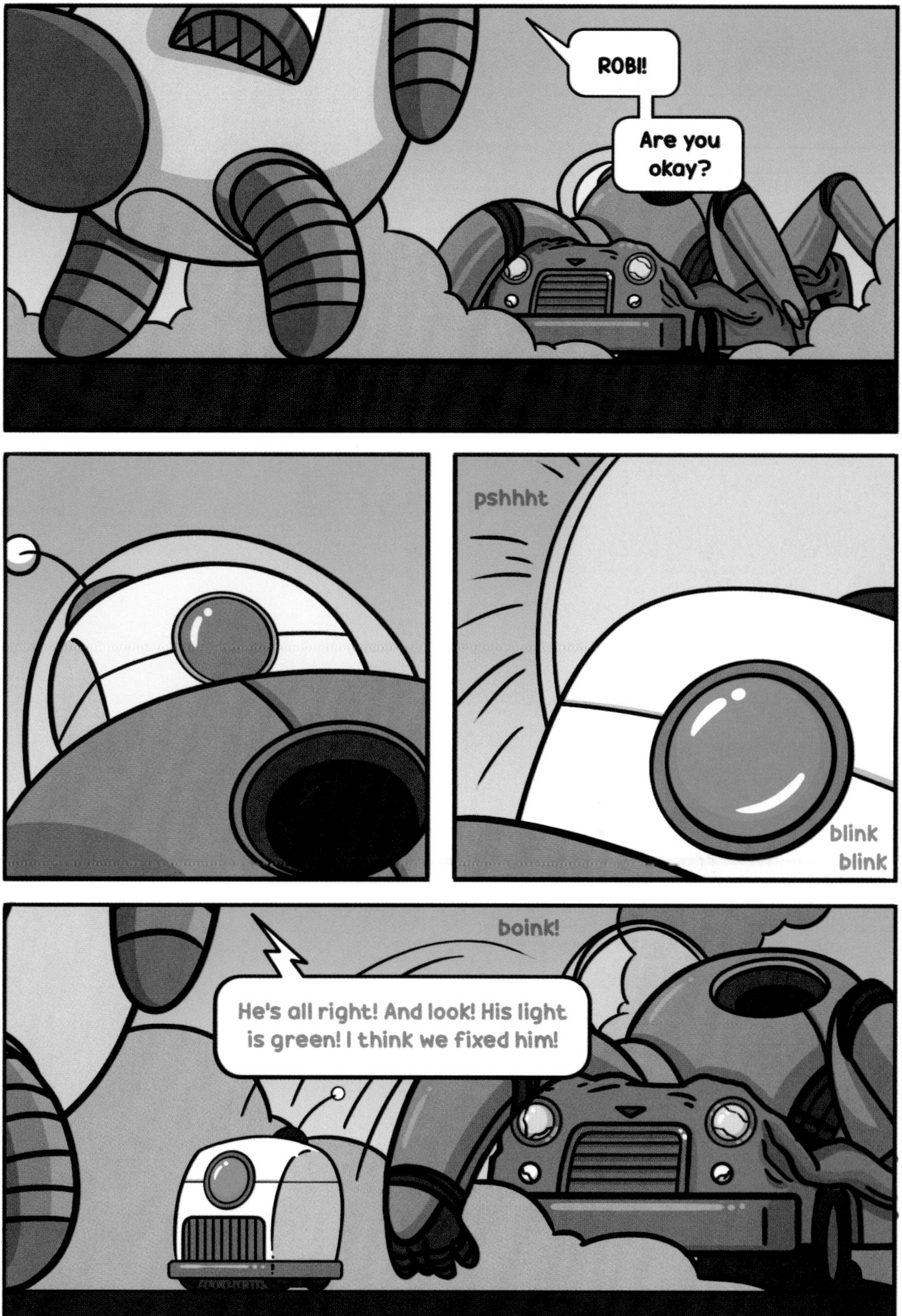
ROBI!
Are you okay?
pshhht
blink
blink
boink!
He's all right! And look! His light is green! I think we fixed him!

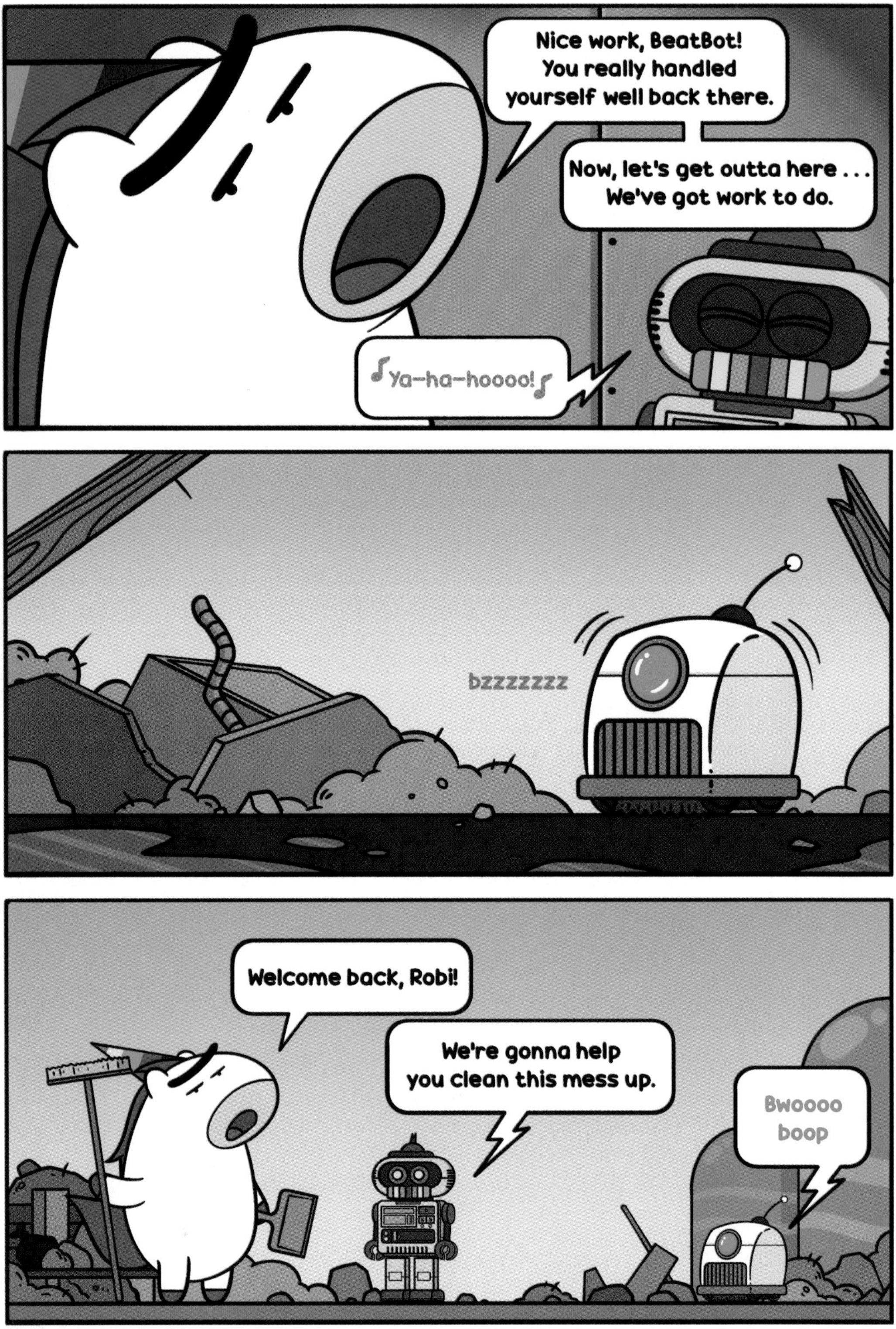
Nice work, BeatBot! You really handled yourself well back there.
Now, let's get outta here . . . We've got work to do.
Ya-ha-hoooo!
bzzzzzzz
Welcome back, Robi!
We're gonna help you clean this mess up.
Bwoooo boop

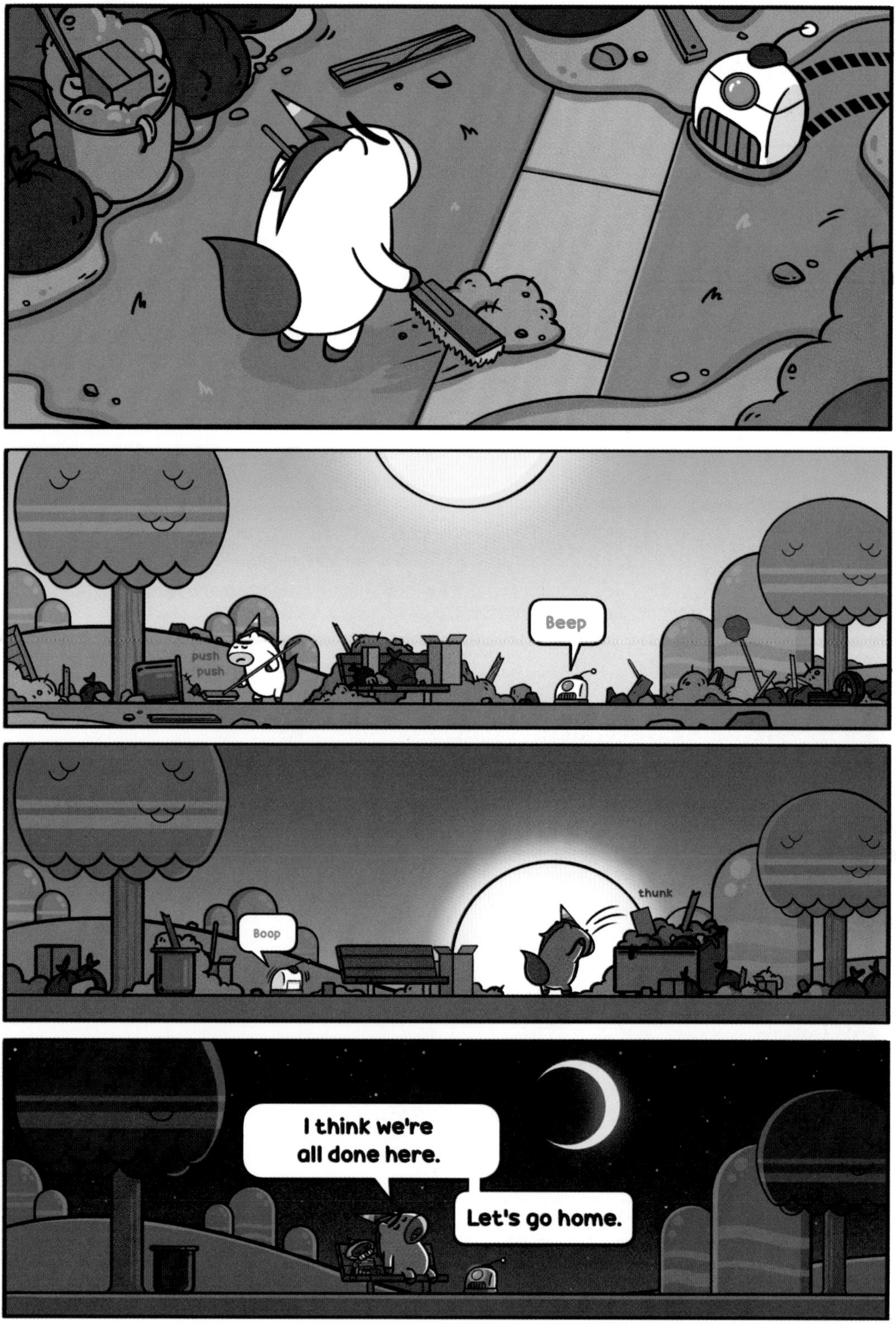
push
push
Beep
Boop
thunk
I think we're all done here.
Let's go home.

LATER THAT NIGHT

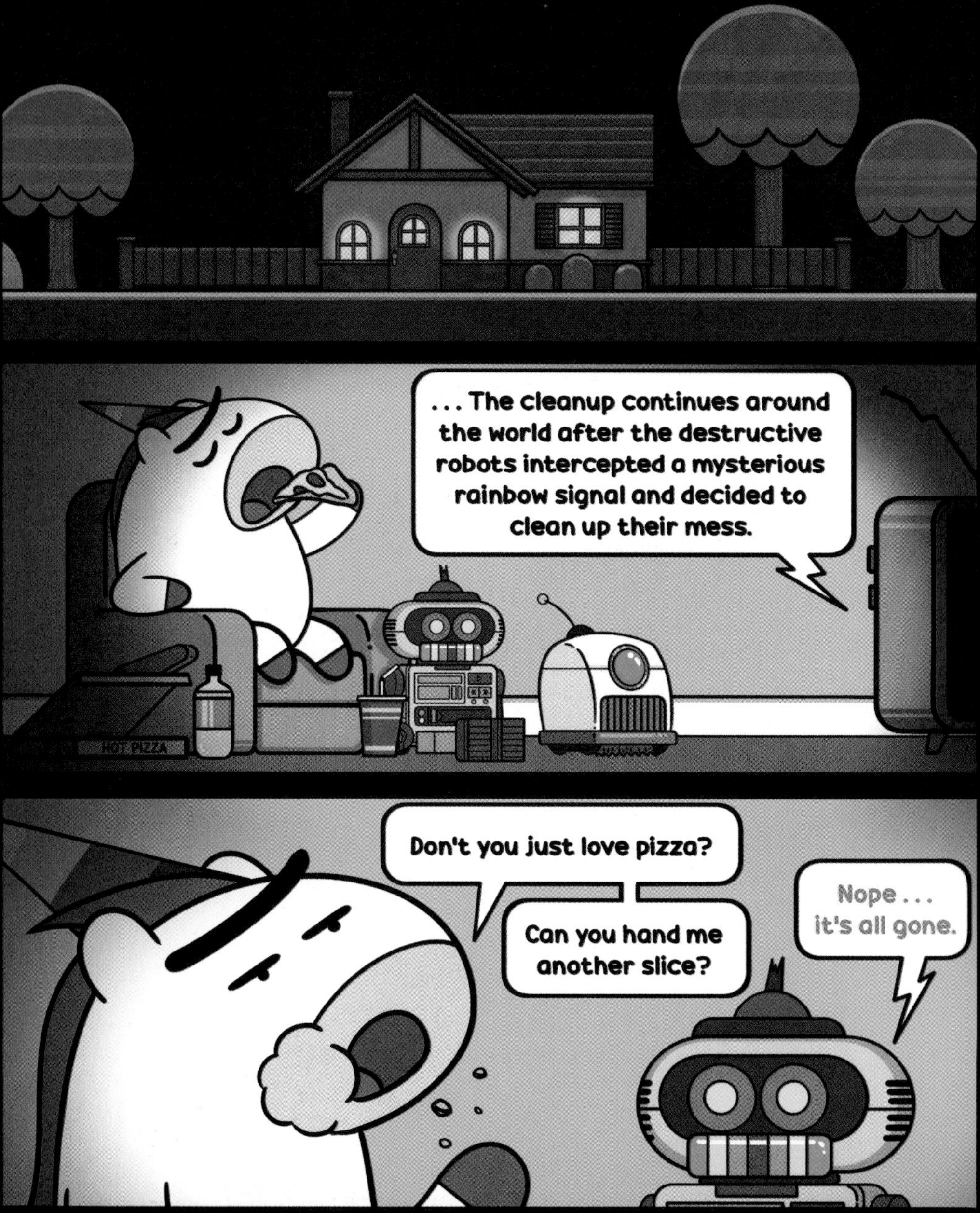
HOT PIZZA
. . . The cleanup continues around the world after the destructive robots intercepted a mysterious rainbow signal and decided to clean up their mess.
Don't you just love pizza?
Can you hand me another slice?
Nope . . . it's all gone.

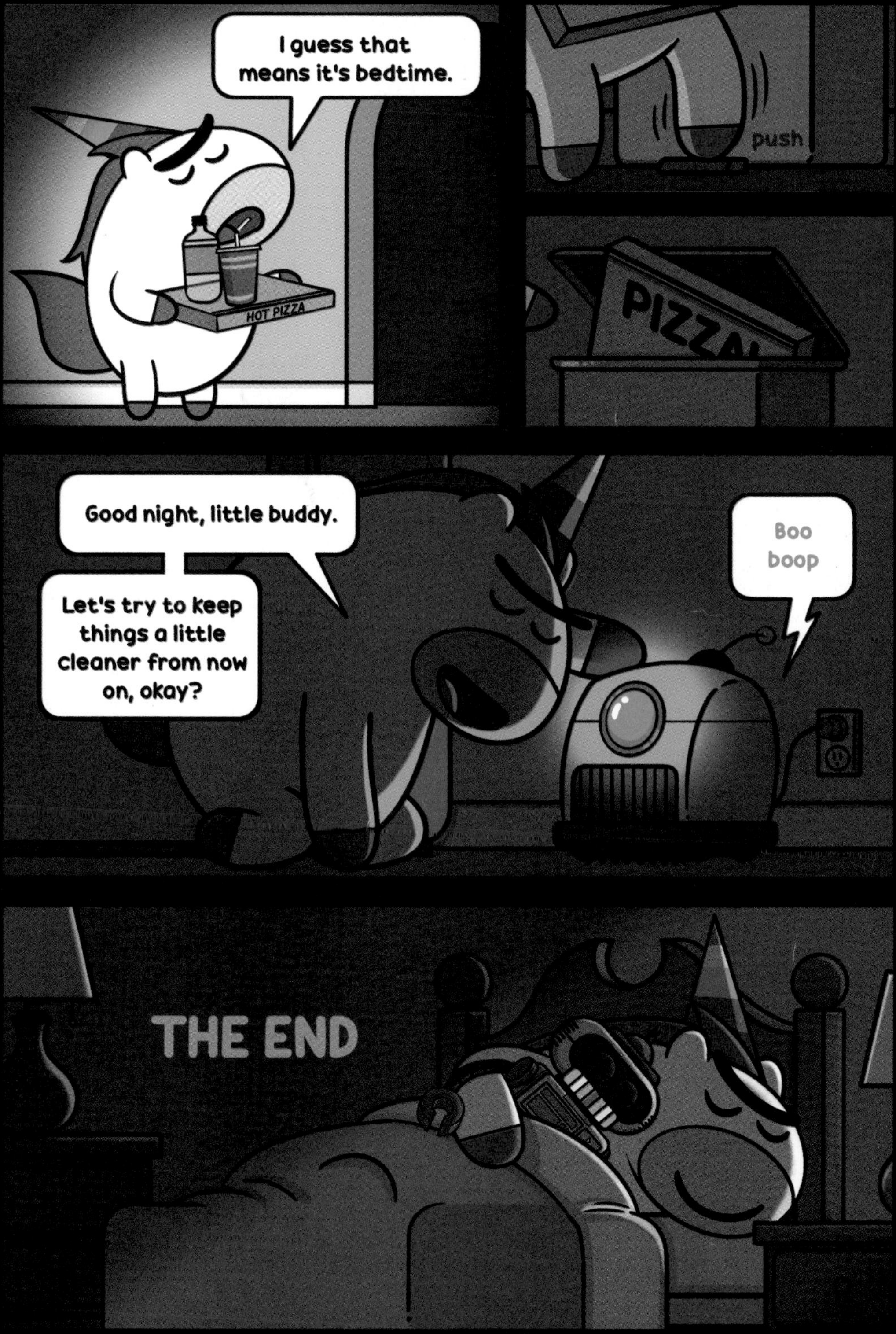
I guess that means it's bedtime.
HOT PIZZA
push
PIZZA!
Good night, little buddy.
Let's try to keep things a little cleaner from now on, okay?
Boo boop
THE END

ABOUT THE AUTHOR

Joey Spiotto is an author, illustrator, and creator behind *Alien Next Door*, *Firefly: Back From the Black*, and the print series Storytime. His artwork is regularly featured at the world-famous Gallery 1988 in Los Angeles, and he has previously worked on films, video games, clothing design, toys, and more. He lives just outside of Los Angeles with his wife and two boys, but you can visit him online at jo3bot.com.

ALSO AVAILABLE:

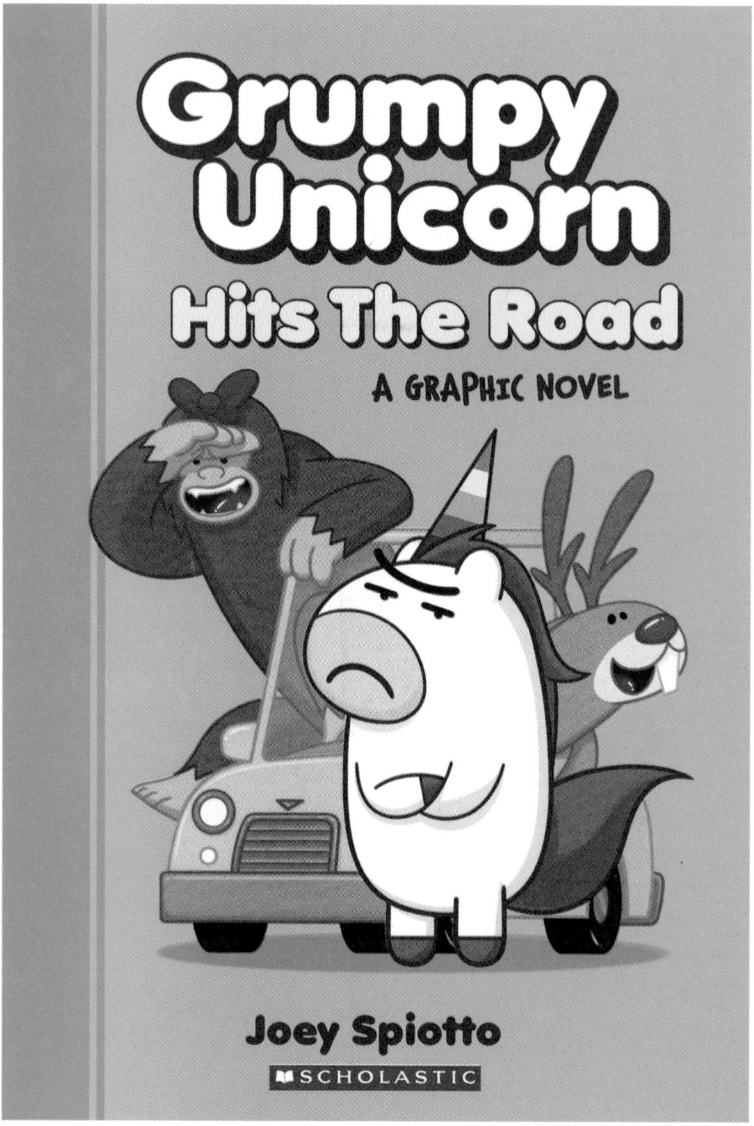
Grumpy Unicorn
Hits The Road
A GRAPHIC NOVEL
Joey Spiotto
SCHOLASTIC

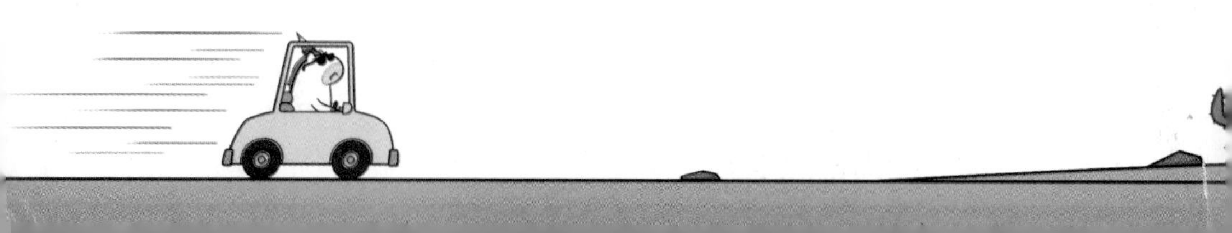